Maureen Child writes for the Mills & Boon Desire line and can't imagine a better job. A seven-time finalist for the prestigious Romance Writers of America RITA® Award, Maureen is the author of more than one hundred romance novels. Her books regularly appear on bestseller lists and have won several awards, including a Prism Award, a National Readers' Choice Award, a Colorado Romance Writers Award of Excellence and a Golden Quill Award. She is a native Californian but has recently moved to the mountains of Utah.

Karen Booth is a Midwestern girl transplanted in the South, raised on '80s music and repeated readings of *Forever* by Judy Blume. When she takes a break from the art of romance, she's listening to music with her college-aged kids or sweet-talking her husband into making her a cocktail. Learn more about Karen at karenbooth.net

Also by Maureen Child

Also by Karen Booth

Discover more at millsandboon.co.uk

TEMPTATION
AT CHRISTMAS

MAUREEN CHILD

HIGH SOCIETY
SECRETS

KAREN BOOTH

MILLS & BOON

First Published in Great Britain 2020
by Mills & Boon, an imprint of HarperCollinsPublishers,
1 London Bridge Street, London, SE1 9GF

Temptation at Christmas © 2020 Maureen Child
High Society Secrets © 2020 Karen Booth

ISBN: 978-0-263-28005-0

1020

MIX
Paper from
responsible sources
FSC® C007454

This book is produced from independently certified FSC™ paper to ensure responsible forest management.

For more information visit: www.harpercollins.co.uk/green

Printed and bound in Spain
by CPI, Barcelona

TEMPTATION AT CHRISTMAS

MAUREEN CHILD

To Patti Hambleton,
because since we first met at six years old,
she has been the friend I could always count on.
The sister of my heart. And the one person
I never have to explain the jokes to!
I love you.

One

Sam Buchanan hated Christmas.

Always had, but this year, he had more reason than ever to wish he could wipe the "holiday season" off the calendar for good.

"So go on a Christmas cruise," he muttered darkly. "Good call."

He'd known it would be hard, but he wasn't one to step back from duty just because it was difficult. Sam had a business to take care of and he wouldn't let the personal get in the way of that.

Didn't mean he had to like it, though.

From the owner's suite at the top of the Fantasy Cruise Line ship, *Fantasy Nights,* Sam looked out on the curved bow with its sky-blue deck and the sea beyond…because he didn't want to look at the dock. San Pedro, California, harbor was crowded with passengers excited to get their cruise to Hawaii going and damned if he'd look down on a bunch of happy, celebrating people. Once the cruise got underway, he could hole up here, in his suite, only venturing out to check on his employees.

Sam took four cruises a year—on different ships in the Buchanan line—to maintain good communication with both crew and passengers. He'd always believed experiencing the cruises in person was the best way to keep his fingers on the pulse of what his guests and employees needed. Not to mention it was the only certain way to make sure those employees were doing their jobs to his expectations.

Gripping his coffee cup, he narrowed his gaze on the expanse of ocean waiting just beyond the harbor. Once they were on the open sea, he'd slip out of his suite, check in with the ship's captain and then do a walk through the restaurants.

He wasn't looking forward to it.

Normally, the Fantasy Cruise Line didn't allow children onboard. Adult-only cruises were their mainstay. But at Christmas, the rules were relaxed so that families could enjoy sailing together on their smaller, more intimate ships.

So for this cruise, not only would he be faced with miles of Christmas garland, brightly lit trees and piped-in Christmas carols, but there would be dozens of kids, hyped up on Santa and candy, to deal with as well. And still, he told himself, it was better to be on this cruise than in his own home where the *lack* of Christmas would taunt him even more completely.

"Yeah," he assured himself solemnly, "no way to win this year."

The phone on the wet bar rang and Sam walked to it. "Yes?"

"Captain says we sail in an hour, Mr. Buchanan."

"Fine. Thanks." He hung up and listened to the silence in the owner's suite. There would be plenty of it for the next couple of weeks and he was looking forward to it even as he dreaded it.

A year ago, things had been different. He'd met a woman on another cruise and two months later, they'd had a Christmas-themed wedding. And they had taken this Christmas cruise for their honeymoon. Yes, for Mia's sake, Sam had even given Christmas a shot. He hadn't thrown himself into it or anything, but he also hadn't been quite the Scrooge he usually was.

Now the marriage was gone. She was gone. And Christmas was back, just to rub it in.

He set his coffee cup down on the bar top, shoved both hands into the pockets of his black slacks and stared around the beautifully appointed room. The owner's suite was twelve hundred square feet of luxury. Teak floors gleamed in the sunlight, paintings of the sea and several of Sam's cruise ships lined the walls. On the ocean side of the suite, the wall was one-way glass, affording an incomparable view of the ocean and the wide balcony that stretched the length of the suite.

Leather club chairs and sofas were gathered atop a rich, burgundy throw rug in the middle of the living room and there were tables with lamps bolted onto them, in case of rough seas. There was a flat-screen television on the wall and a dining room off to one side.

There were two bedrooms and three bathrooms along with the private balcony/terrace that added an extra two hundred square feet to the suite. The master bedroom and en suite bath boasted a view of the sea from behind one-way glass. He could see out, but no one could see in.

And in spite of his surroundings, Sam felt…on edge. He stalked out to the terrace and let the cold wind slap at him. Glancing down at the nearly empty deck of the bow, Sam noticed a woman with long, wavy red hair and it felt as though someone had punched him in the chest.

"It's not her. Why the hell would she be on this cruise?"

Still, he couldn't look away. She wore white slacks and a long-sleeved green shirt and her hair lifted and twisted in the wind. Then she turned sideways and Sam saw that she was very pregnant. Disappointment tangled with relief inside him, until the redhead stopped, looked up and seemed to stab his stare with her own.

Mia?

His heart jolted and his hands fisted on the cold, white iron railing. She's *pregnant?* Why wouldn't she tell him? Why didn't she say *something?* What the hell was she doing here? And why didn't she take off her sunglasses so he could see the green eyes that had been haunting him for months?

But she didn't comply with that wish. Instead, she shook her head, clearly in disgust, and then stalked away, disappearing from view in less than a moment.

Mia. Pregnant.

Here.

Sam went inside, rushed across the room and hit the front door at a dead run. Somebody had better tell him something fast. He didn't waste time with a phone call. Instead he went down to the main deck where passengers were still filing onboard. The purser was there, along with two of the entertainment crew, to welcome people onto *Fantasy Nights.* Ordinarily, Sam would have been impressed with how easily his employees handled the streaming crowds—all smiles and conversations. But today, he needed answers.

"Mr. Wilson," Sam said and the purser turned. Instantly, the older man straightened up as if going to attention.

"Mr. Buchanan," he said with a nod. "Is there something I can help you with?"

"Yeah. Has a woman named Mia—" he almost said *Buchanan,* but Sam remembered at the last minute that his ex-wife had returned to her maiden name after the divorce "—Harper, checked in?"

The man quickly checked through the list of names on the clipboard he held. Then he glanced at his boss and said, "Yes sir. She did. A half hour ago. She—"

That was Mia. A very pregnant Mia.

"Which suite is she in?"

He knew she had a suite because all of the staterooms on the *Fantasy Nights* were suites. Some more luxuriously appointed than others but every suite on this ship was roomy and inviting.

"It's the Poseidon, sir. Two decks down on the port side and—"

"Thanks. That's all I need." Sam threaded his way through the crowd already spilling into the atrium, the main welcome spot on any ship.

On *Fantasy Nights,* the atrium was two stories of glass-and-wood spiraling staircases, now draped in pine garland. There was a giant Christmas tree in the middle of the room boasting what looked to Sam like a thousand twinkling, colored lights, along with ornaments—that the passengers could also purchase in the gift shop. There was a group of carolers in one corner, and miles of more pine garland draped like bunting all around the room.

Hanging from the ceiling were hundreds of strands of blinking white lights, to simulate snowfall and on one wall, there were tables set up, laden with Christmas cookies and hot chocolate.

Sam barely noticed. He didn't have time to wait for the elevator. Instead, he headed for the closest staircase and took them two at a time. He knew every ship in his fleet like the back of his hand, so he didn't need to check the maps on the walls to know where he was headed.

The Poseidon suite was one of their larger ones and he wondered why Mia had bothered to book a two-bedroom suite. If she was pregnant, why the hell hadn't she come directly to him months ago? He had no answers to too many questions racing through his mind, so Sam pushed all of them aside, assuring himself he'd solve this mystery soon enough.

The excited chatter of conversations and bursts of laughter from children and their parents chased him down the first hallway on the port side. On most cruise ships, hallways dividing the staterooms were narrow and usually dark in spite of carefully placed lighting. Fantasy Cruise Line hallways were wider than usual and boasted overhead lighting and brass wall sconces alongside every stateroom.

Here, the floorboards were also teak and on each door was attached a plaque describing the name of the suite itself. For example, he thought as he stopped outside Mia's suite, her doorway held the image of Poseidon, riding a whale, holding his trident high, as if ready to attack an enemy. He wondered if that was an omen for what was to come.

He didn't have long to think about it. He knocked and a moment later, the door was yanked open. Long red hair. Sharp green eyes. Green shirt. White pants. Pregnant belly.

But not Mia.

Her twin, Maya.

Was he feeling relief? Disappointment? Both? Sam just stared at her. Damned if he could think of anything to say.

Maya didn't have that problem. She glared at him then and snapped, "Happy anniversary, you bastard."

Almost instantly, Mia appeared behind her twin. Rolling her eyes at her sister's drama, she said, "Maya. Stop."

Her sister stared at her for a second or two. "Seriously? You're going to defend him?"

"Defend me from what?" Sam asked.

"*What?*" Maya repeated, shifting a hard look to him before turning back to her twin. "Really? Even now you want me to play nice?"

"Really." Mia tugged on her sister's arm. "I love you. Go away."

"Fine," Maya said, throwing both hands into the air. She threw one last hard look at Sam. "But I'm not going far…"

"What the hell?" Sam muttered, keeping a wary eye on the woman as she walked away.

This was not the way Mia had wanted to handle this. But then, nothing about this trip was how she'd wanted it. She hadn't planned on bringing her entire family with her, for instance. But there was nothing she could do about that now, except maybe keep Maya away from Sam.

"Yeah, she's not your biggest fan," Mia admitted, then

stepped into the hallway, forcing him to move back to make room. She pulled the door closed behind her, leaned against it and lifted her gaze to the man of her dreams.

Well, she amended mentally, the *former* man of her dreams.

He was tall. She'd always liked that. Actually, it had been one of the first things she'd noticed about him the night they met. She was five feet nine inches tall, so meeting a man who was six foot four had been great. That night she'd been wearing three-inch heels and she'd still had to look up to meet his eyes.

And they were great eyes. Pale, pale blue that could turn from icy to heat in a blink of time. His black hair was a little too long for the CEO of a huge company, but it was thick and shiny and she'd once loved threading her fingers through it. In fact, even after everything that had happened between them, Mia's fingers itched to do it again.

He was wearing a suit, of course. Sam didn't do "relaxed." He wore his elegantly tailored suits as if he'd been born to wear them. And maybe he had been, Mia mused. All she was sure of was that beneath that dark blue, pinstriped suit, was a body that looked as if it had been sculpted by angels on a very good day.

Her heartbeat jumped skittishly and she wasn't surprised. She had met him and married him within a two-month, whirlwind span and though the marriage had lasted only nine months—technically—she knew it might take her years to get over Sam Buchanan.

Then he started talking.

"What are you doing here?"

Mia scowled. "Well, that's a very gracious welcome, Sam. Thank you. Good to see you, too."

He didn't look abashed, only irritated. "What's going on, Mia? Why is my ex-wife on this cruise?"

Hmm. More 'wife' than 'ex', she thought, but they'd get to that.

"This was the only way I could find to get you alone long enough to talk."

He snorted and pushed one hand through that great hair. "Really. You couldn't just pick up the phone?"

"Please." She waved that away. "Like I didn't try? Your assistant kept putting me off, telling me you were in a meeting or on the company jet heading off to Kat-mandu or something…"

"Katmandu?"

"Or somewhere else exotic, far away and out of reach apparently, of my phone."

Sam tucked his hands into his slacks pockets. "So you take a fifteen-day cruise?"

Mia shrugged. "Seemed like a good idea at the time."

"With Maya."

"And her family."

He glanced down the hallway and then to the closed door, as if expecting to see Joe and the kids pop out of hiding. "You're kidding."

"Why would I kid?"

The door flew open and Maya was there, glaring at him. Mia sighed, but gave up trying to rein in her twin.

"Why wouldn't she bring her family along as backup when she has to face you?" Maya asked.

"Backup?" He pulled his hands free, folded his arms across his chest and glared at the mirror image of Mia. "Why the hell would she need backup?"

"As if you didn't know," Maya snapped. "And another news flash for you, Mom and Dad are here too, and they're not real happy about it."

He looked at Mia. "Your parents are here?"

She lifted both hands helplessly. Mia hadn't actually *invited* any of her family along on this trip. She'd simply made the mistake of telling her twin what she was planning and Maya had taken it from there. Her family was circling the wagons to keep her from being hurt again. Hard to be angry with the people who loved you because they wanted to protect you.

Also hard to not be frustrated by them.

"Are Merry and her family here too?" Sam asked. "Cousins? Best friends?"

"Merry didn't trust herself to see you," Maya snapped.

Thank God, their older sister Merry had decided to stay home with her family or things would have been even wilder. It was comforting to realize that at least one member of her family was sane.

"Maya," Mia said on a sigh, "you're not helping. Close the door."

"Fine but I'll be listening anyway," she warned and slammed the door so that the sound echoed along the hallway.

And she would be, too, Mia knew. "Merry stayed home to keep the bakery running," she said. "Christmas is our busiest time of the year."

"Yeah, I remember."

"So busy," she continued as if he hadn't spoken, "Mom and Dad are cruising to Hawaii, but they're going to fly home from there to help Merry."

"I don't get it."

"Which part?"

"All of it." He shook his head, took her arm and steered

her further from the door, no doubt because he knew that Maya was indeed listening to everything they said. "I still don't know why you're here. Why you felt like you needed an army just to face me."

"Not an army. Just people who love me." Mia pulled her arm free of his grasp because the heat building up from his touch was way too distracting. How was she supposed to keep her mind on why she was there when he was capable of dissolving her brain so easily?

And that, she told herself, was exactly why the family had come along.

"We have to talk."

"Yeah, I guessed that much," he said, shooting a glance at the still closed door.

Just being this close to Sam was awakening everything inside her and Mia knew that she was really going to need her family as a buffer. Because her natural impulse was to move in closer, hook her arms around his neck and pull his head to hers for one of the kisses she had spent the last few months hungering for—and trying to forget.

But that wouldn't solve anything. They would still be two people connected only by a piece of paper. They had never been married in the same way her parents were. The Harpers were a unit. A team, in the best sense of the word.

While Mia and Sam had shared a bed but not much else. He was always working and when he wasn't, he was locked in his study, going over paperwork for the business or making calls or jetting off to meetings with clients and boat builders and—anyone who wasn't *her*.

Passion still simmered between them, but she'd learned the hard way that desire wasn't enough to build a life on. She needed a husband who was there to talk to, to laugh with—and they hadn't done that nearly enough. She wanted a man who could bend and not be constricted by his own inner rules and Sam didn't know how to bend. How to compromise. Mia had tried. Had fought for their marriage but when she realized that only she was trying, she gave up.

If he'd been willing to work on things with her, they'd still be together.

"Fine then. We'll talk," Sam said, still keeping a wary eye on the door of her suite as if expecting Maya to leap out again.

Mia would not have been surprised. Her twin was very protective.

"But not here where Maya's listening to everything we say…" He frowned thoughtfully. "Once we're underway, I need to meet with some of the crew, check on a few things…"

She sighed. "Of course you do."

One eyebrow lifted. "You know I take these cruises to get the information I need on how our ships are operating."

"I remember." In fact, she recalled the cruises they'd taken together after they were married. Two of them. One to the Bahamas. One to Panama. And on each of them, the only time she really saw her new husband was at night, in their bed. Otherwise, Sam the Workaholic was so busy, it had been as if she were traveling alone.

"That's why we're here. On this ship," Mia said. "I knew you'd be taking this cruise."

He laughed. "Even knowing I hate the Christmas cruises?"

"Yes. Because it helps you avoid having to be at home with a non-Christmas," she said.

His frown went a little deeper. Apparently, he didn't like the fact that she could read him so easily. But it hadn't been difficult. Sam hated Christmas and no matter how Mia had tried to drag him, kicking and screaming into the spirit of the holiday, he would not be moved. Her family had planned their wedding and he'd been surrounded by holly leaves, poinsettias and pine garlands. After the wedding, he'd given in to her need to have a tree and lights and garland, but he'd admitted to her that if she weren't there, Christmas would have been just another day at his house.

She'd thought then and still believed that it was just sad. In her family, Christmas season started the day after Thanksgiving. Lights went up, carols were played, gifts were bought and wrapped and her sisters' kids wrote and then revised letters to Santa at least once a week.

She'd tried to get him to tell her why he hated that holiday so much, but not surprisingly, he wouldn't talk about it. How could she reach a man if every time she tried to breach his walls, he built them higher?

So yes, she'd known that Sam would take a Christmas cruise to avoid being at home in what was probably a naked house, devoid of any holiday cheer. It hadn't made much sense to her until she realized that Christmas decorations meant nothing to him, but a house devoid of those very decorations only made him remember that he was different than most people. That he'd chosen to live in a gray world when others were celebrating.

"These cruises are booked months out," he said. "How did you manage to get suites for the whole family?"

"Mike arranged it."

Sam's eyes flashed and she wasn't surprised. His younger brother had always been on Mia's side and thought their separation was the worst thing to happen to Sam. So Mia had counted on his brother's help to "surprise" Sam on this cruise.

"Mike? My own brother?"

She might have enjoyed the complete shock stamped on Sam's features, if she wasn't worried that this situation could start an open war between the brothers.

"Don't fault him for it either," Mia warned. "He was helping me out, not betraying you,"

"What did you think I'd do to him?" he demanded and she heard the insult in his voice.

"Who knows?" She threw both hands up. "Fly to Florida and toss him in the ocean? Keelhaul him? Throw him in a dungeon somewhere? Chain him to a wall?"

His eyes went wide and he choked out a laugh. "I live in a penthouse condo, remember? Sadly, it doesn't come equipped with a dungeon."

Oh, she remembered the condo. Spectacular with an amazing view of the ocean through a wall of glass. And she remembered spending too much time alone in that luxurious, spacious place, because her husband had chosen to bury himself at work.

Okay, that worked to stiffen her spine.

"Fine," she said. "Then we're agreed. You don't give Mike grief."

"Or a Christmas bonus," he muttered.

"He's your partner, not your employee." Shaking her head, Mia snapped, "You're going to give him a hard time anyway, aren't you?"

"I was kidding."

"Were you?" she asked.

"Mostly. You know what? Forget about Mike." Sam

looked her square in the eye and asked, "Why are you here, Mia? And why'd you bring your family with you?"

She had needed the support because frankly, she didn't trust herself around Sam. One look at him and her body overrode her mind. She had to be strong and wasn't sure she could do it on her own. Still, she wasn't going to tell him that.

"They wanted to take a cruise and I needed to be here to talk to you, so we all went together."

"Sure. Happy coincidence. And why did you need to see me?"

"That's going to be a longer conversation."

"Does it include why you picked our anniversary to ambush me on a cruise ship?"

She could have kicked her twin. Maya wishing him a *Happy Anniversary* had been exactly the wrong thing to say. Mia loved that her family was so protective of her—and so really furious with Sam. But this was her life and she'd handle it her way. And reminding Sam about their anniversary, as if she were upset about it, wasn't her way. Of course, she *was* shaken by the fact that she was here to talk divorce with her husband on their first anniversary, but that didn't matter really, did it? Their marriage had ended months ago. What was happening now was just a formality.

And if he'd forgotten their anniversary, then Maya had just reminded him and that was infuriating, too. How could he forget? Was their all-too-brief marriage really that un-memorable? Was she? God knew, she'd forgotten *nothing* about her time with Sam.

Heck, just remembering the nights spent in his arms made her heart beat faster and her blood heat up until she felt like she had a fever. It was so hard to be this close to him and not lean in to kiss him. Touch his cheek. Smooth his hair back from his forehead. She muffled a sigh.

And all of this would have been much easier to handle if he didn't look so good.

From the first moment they'd met, on one of his cruise ships, Mia had been drawn to him. It had felt then like an electrical attraction and it seemed that nothing had changed there. His pale blue eyes still looked at her as if she were the only woman in the world. His mouth still made her want to nibble at his bottom lip. And she knew firsthand what it was like to have those strong, muscular arms wrapped around her and oh boy, she'd love to feel that again—even knowing it would be a huge mistake.

She could be in serious trouble.

"Are you okay?"

His question snapped her brain out of a really lovely fantasy and for that she was grateful. Sort of.

"Yeah, I'm fine." She looked up and down the corridor before turning her gaze back to his. "I didn't choose to find you on our anniversary. It just worked out that way. And like I said, we need to talk and I don't think this hallway is the place to do it."

"You're right." He glanced at the closed door behind which Maya was no doubt lurking. "But I'm not doing it with your sister around, either."

Mia laughed shortly. "No. Not a good plan. I'll come to you once I make sure Mom and Dad are settled in. And I want to help Maya with the kids…"

"Fine. Once we get into open water, give me an hour, then come to my suite."

She watched him walk away and her mouth went dry. Mia hated that her instinct was to chase him down and leap at him. She'd been doing so well, too. She was only dreaming about him three or four times a week now. Seeing him again, though, spending the next two weeks together on the same ship, was going to start up the fantasies and the desire all over again.

And there was zero way to avoid it.

Two

Mia being onboard this ship had already destroyed Sam's concentration. For an hour, he talked with the Captain, studied weather patterns with the First Officer charged with navigation, then finally had a meeting with the Chief Security Officer to get a report on any possible situations.

Through it all, he heard his employees but didn't listen with the same intensity he usually brought to his visits. How could he, when his mind kept drifting to his ex-wife?

Why did she have to look so damn good? And smell even better? He'd forgotten—or convinced himself—that he'd forgotten that subtle scent of summer that somehow clung to her. Her lotion? Shampoo? He'd never really investigated it because it hadn't mattered to him *how* that scent appeared—he had simply enjoyed it.

And now it was with him again.

Haunting him again.

"And it's Michael's fault," he muttered. Standing on the private deck of his suite, Sam gripped his cell phone, ordered it to "Call Michael," then waited impatiently for his brother to pick up.

"Hey, Sam! How's it going?"

Scowling at the sailboats skimming the water in the distance, Sam blurted out, "You know exactly how it's going."

Michael laughed. "Ah…so you've seen Mia."

"Yes, I've seen her. And her twin. And apparently the rest of the family is aboard, too. What the hell were you thinking?" Sam curled one fist around the thick rail. The Plexiglas wall for safety only rose as high as the handrail. He wanted the feel of the wind against his face and right now, he was hoping it would cool him off. "I can't believe you did this. I'm your *brother*. Where's the loyalty?"

"Why wouldn't I do it?" Michael argued. "I like Mia. I like who you were when you were with her."

"What's that supposed to mean?"

His brother sighed. "It means that she was good for you. You laughed more back then."

"Yeah, everything was great until it wasn't."

That time with Mia hadn't lasted. As he'd known going into the marriage that it wouldn't. And even knowing that it would probably end badly, Sam had married her because he hadn't been able to imagine life without her. He'd risked failure and failed. Now, not only did he not have Mia, he had memories that continued to choke him during long, empty nights.

"We're divorced, Michael. It's over. You setting this up isn't helping any."

"It was helping Mia," his brother countered, then asked, "and if it's over, why is this bugging you so much?"

Good question.

"Look, I don't know why she had to see you, but when she asked, of course I did what I could."

Naturally, Michael would offer to help. That was just who he was. Some of the anger drained away as Sam realized how different he and his younger brother were. When their parents divorced, the kids were split up. Michael went to Florida with their mother while Sam stayed in California with their father.

They'd stayed close because they'd worked at it, even though they were only together whenever court-mandated visits to the non-custodial parent kicked in. Their father had been a hard man with strict rules for how Sam lived his life. Their mother was a kindhearted woman who hadn't been able to live with that hard man.

So Sam grew up with the knowledge that marriage was a trap and never lasted—his father after all, had been married four times. As a father, he was disinterested, barely aware of Sam's existence. While Michael saw the other side of things with a mother who eventually remarried a man who had loved Michael as his own.

Now Sam was divorced and Michael was engaged and Sam sincerely hoped his little brother would have better luck in the marriage department than he himself had.

Mike was speaking, so Sam tuned in. "Why don't you just enjoy the situation?"

Sam was stunned speechless—but that didn't last. "*Enjoy* having my ex and her family—who all hate me, by the way—traveling with me for the next two weeks? Yeah, not gonna happen."

Michael laughed, damn it.

"Are you *scared* of the Harpers?"

"No."

Yes.

He hadn't known back then how to deal with a family who defended each other. Who listened. Who actually gave a damn. And he still didn't have a clue.

His brother knew him too well, that was the problem. Once they were grown the two of them had made time for each other. Building a relationship that might have been denied them because of the way they were raised. When their father died, and the business had come to the two of them, they'd carved out a workable solution that suited both men.

Michael took care of the east coast cruises, Sam had the west coast. They made major decisions for the company together and trusted each other to do what was best for the growth they both wanted to see happen.

"Okay, I admit that having her family there might be a little problematic."

"Yeah, you could say that."

"So fine. Ignore the family, enjoy Mia."

Oh, Sam would love to enjoy Mia. Every instinct he had was clamoring at him to go and find her. To pull her into his bed and never let her out again. But going there wasn't good for either of them. In their brief marriage it had become crystal clear that Sam and Mia weren't going to work out. She wanted more from him than he could give. Bottom line? They didn't belong together and they'd both acknowledged that in less than a year. Why stir the embers just to get burned again?

"For God's sake, Sam," Michael continued, "you haven't seen her in months."

He was aware.

"Yeah well, she'll be here soon to tell me why she's on this cruise in the first place."

And he couldn't wait to hear it. Had she planned to be here on their anniversary? Or was that just happenstance as she'd said? Did it matter? Either way their anniversary wasn't a celebration, but more a reminder of mistakes made.

He never should have married Mia, Sam knew that. But he'd done it anyway and so he'd only set Mia up for pain. That he hadn't intended, but it had, apparently, been unavoidable. Hell, maybe that was why she was here. Just to let him know that she was over him and moving on with her life.

Why tell him at all?

And even if she wanted him to know, why book a cruise for that?

Scowling at an ocean that didn't care what he was feeling or thinking, Sam heard Michael's voice as if from a distance.

"That's great. Talk to her about whatever it is she needs to tell you. And when you're done, keep talking."

"What am I supposed to say?"

"Wow. This is embarrassing. You're my big brother. And you can't figure out how to talk to a woman you were married to?" Michael took a breath and sighed it out. "Maybe you could tell her you miss her."

He straightened up. "What would be the point? She left me, remember?"

Sam remembered it well and didn't really want to revisit the memory.

"Yeah, I remember. Did you ever ask yourself why?"

"The reason doesn't matter. She left. I moved on. Done."

"Sure you did," Michael said. "Talk to her anyway. Maybe you'll surprise each other."

Sam snorted. "I don't like surprises."

"How arc wc related again?"

In spite of everything, Sam grinned and stared out at the ocean. "Beats the hell outta me."

"Me, too," Mike said, laughing. "Good luck on the cruise. I hope Mia drives you insane."

"Thanks."

"No problem—oh and Sam, Merry Christmas!"

"Not funny."

"Yeah it is," Mike said, still laughing as he hung up.

Then Sam was alone with the wind, the sea…and the faint sounds of Christmas carols drifting up from the lower deck. Just perfect.

The Buchanan cruise ships were much smaller than the mega ships most companies sailed these days.

Instead of thousands of people crowding a ship that offered sometimes very small cabins, there were only two hundred passengers total on a Buchanan ship and each cabin was a suite that didn't make one feel as if the walls were closing in.

But, Mia thought, it also meant that she felt the movement of the ocean more than she might on the bigger ships. Some people didn't care for that, but she loved it. She'd discovered her sea legs on the first cruise she'd taken—when she'd met Sam and her whole life had changed.

A year ago, she'd fallen in love and felt that the cruise was almost magical. Now, the magic was gone, but she was once again sailing on a cruise with the man she had believed was her future. She'd been foolish, believing that love at first sight was real and substantial and that the two of them together could do anything.

It hadn't taken long before Mia had realized that it *wasn't* the two of them. It was just her. Alone in a beautiful home with a man who seemed reluctant to do anything to save their marriage.

"Mrs. Buchanan."

Mia looked up to smile at one of the crew she knew from other cruises. About thirty, the man had blond-streaked brown hair, green eyes and wore the short-sleeved red polo shirt and white slacks that were the Fantasy Cruise Line uniform.

"Nice to have you aboard," he said.

"Thank you, Brandon," she answered, and didn't bother correcting him about the whole *Mrs. Buchanan* thing. Because honestly, until Sam signed those papers, she *was* Mrs. Buchanan, watching him as he hurried past intent on whatever he was doing.

Brandon walked away at top speed and she watched him go. She had to wonder how many of this crew she knew from her time with Sam. And she knew that even if Brandon was the *only* familiar face, by the time the cruise was over, she would know most of them.

Smaller ships meant a higher than usual crew to passenger ratio. At the end of the fourteen-day trip to Hawaii, the *Fantasy Nights* would feel like a small, insular village, where everyone knew everyone else.

"There's an upside and a downside to that though," she murmured and continued along the deck to the nearby staircase. Gossip would fly through the ship. And no doubt people would be talking about her and Sam, just as they had talked about them a year before on that first cruise.

Shaking her head, she ordered herself to stop thinking about Sam and try to enjoy being on the ship, seeing the ocean stretch out forever. Feeling the wind on her face and through her hair and listening to the distant shrieks and laughter of the kids onboard.

Christmas was stamped all over the sleek boat and she knew that had to be irritating to Sam. He didn't like the holiday at all and had only grudgingly accepted not only their Christmas themed wedding, but the Christmas tree she'd brought into their condo last year.

Since he was a kid, Christmas had been an exercise in emptiness. Sam's world was so wildly different from anyone else's that he never even tried to explain what it was about that holiday that left him feeling hollowed out. Who would understand?

Thinking back on it now, Mia wondered if the fact that he didn't like Christmas was part of the reason they just hadn't worked out. Well, maybe not the reason. But certainly a sign of things to come. She loved Christmas and everything it promised—hope, joy, love. And Sam tended toward the dark side.

Even as that thought registered, she shook her head. It wasn't as if he was some evil mastermind or something—but he was more cynical than she was. More likely to see the downside than the up. Which was strange, since he was a masterful businessman and didn't you have to be optimistic to run a multimillion-dollar company?

She caught herself as she started going down the all too familiar path of trying to figure out Sam. It was an exercise in futility because the man simply didn't let anyone in long enough to actually *know* him.

"You've already spent months trying to figure Sam

out, Mia," she lectured herself. "It's too late now, so just give it up already."

Taking a deep breath, Mia let go of the convoluted thoughts roiling through her mind and instead focused on where she was at the moment. Even though the reason for taking this cruise was a hard one, there was no reason she couldn't appreciate her surroundings.

There were brass pots displaying poinsettias bolted to the deck. Pine garlands were strung along the railings and the cushions on the chairs and lounges were a bright red and white. She smiled to herself as she realized that the whole ship felt like a Christmas snow globe, with the decorations and the happy people trapped inside the glass, just waiting for a giant hand to give it a shake.

The only way it could have been more perfect was if she didn't have to face her ex-husband and tell him they weren't as "ex" as they'd both believed. But she was only on this ship to confront Sam and get this whole thing settled, so the best thing she could do was to just get on with it.

Mia had plans, starting in January and she had to get this taken care of before she could move forward. She was tired of standing still. She wanted a future and the only way she was going to get it was to build it herself.

And still, as she made her way along the deck, Mia looked out at the sea, and paused briefly to watch the waves froth. She heard the slap of the water against the keel and took a deep breath of the cold, salty air. She smiled, in spite of the turmoil grumbling inside her.

Her family was upstairs in the atrium, no doubt huddled around the cookies and hot chocolate. She knew Maya's kids, Charlie and Chris, were already planning to explore the Snow Room that had been set up for children's play. Artificial snow, made just for the holiday cruise, was going to be very popular, especially with California kids who didn't get many chances to throw a snowball.

She kept walking, taking the stairs up, because it was faster than going inside and waiting for an elevator. Besides, she thought, as she looked out at the ocean, you didn't get a view from an elevator.

But no matter what she tried to tell herself about the view, the truth was, she was stalling. The thought of talking to Sam again had her unsettled. Off-balance. He'd always made her feel that way, though. It looked to her like nothing had changed.

On the top deck, Mia walked toward the owner's suite. She knew exactly where it was, because that suite was positioned in exactly the same spot on every Buchanan ship. The closer she came to that wide, closed door though, the more her stomach jittered and the faster her heart raced.

"Damn it."

This should be easier. She'd cried Sam out of her system months ago. Their marriage was over. So why the hell could the very thought of him make her want to go all gooey?

"Because apparently, I have a masochistic streak," she muttered, then knocked before she could talk herself out of it.

When Sam opened the door, her gaze went straight to his. That cool, pale blue was fixed on her as if she were the only thing in the universe. Mia sighed. Sam was the one man who had ever looked at her like that. As if nothing else, in that moment, mattered. The only man who could make her knees weak with a glance. The only man who made her want to crawl into his bed and never leave it.

Which is exactly why you're in this mess, her mind whispered.

A year ago, she'd followed her heart—and her hormones—and had married the man of her dreams. Only to watch those dreams crumble into dust.

She kept that thought at the forefront of her mind as she said, "Hello, Sam."

Nodding sharply, Mia walked past him into the well-appointed suite. Her gaze swept the room in spite of the reason she was there. How could she not admire the space? The view of the sea, provided by the French doors and the wall of glass, was immense. It reminded her of the view from his condo at the beach, only here, she was much closer to that ocean, almost a part of it.

Breathtaking. And so was the rest of the room. Hardwood floors, jewel-toned rugs scattered across the honey-colored planks. A couple of sofas, that looked soft enough to sink into and easy chairs drawn together, facing the view that demanded attention.

"Well please," Sam muttered from behind her. "Come in."

She whirled around to face him, mindful of keeping a few feet of space between them. "Sam. We've got a problem."

"I don't think *we* have anything anymore."

He folded his arms over his broad, muscular chest and dipped his head down to stare at her. It was a technique he used. That professor-to-stupid-student glare. And as often as he might have used it on everyone else, that look had never worked on her before and it didn't now, either.

"You're wrong," she said shortly.

One eyebrow lifted.

She still didn't know how he did that.

"Okay," she said, "here it is. You know how *we* signed the divorce papers?"

"I recall," he said flatly.

"And *we* overnighted them in?"

"How about *we* get to the point?" His arms dropped to his sides. "What's this about, Mia?"

"Well, it seems we aren't as divorced as we thought we were."

Sam's brain short-circuited.

That was the only explanation for him being unable to think of a damn thing to say in response. Of course, it might have been being so close to Mia that was shutting his brain down, but that didn't make him feel any better about the situation.

The whole idea of what she was saying was preposterous. Ridiculous. He'd accepted his failure. Forced himself to acknowledge that he'd hurt the one woman in the world he valued. He'd lived through it, put it behind him.

Of course they were divorced.

But if they weren't…something that might have been hope rose up in him briefly, but Sam squashed it in an instant. No. Screw that, he wasn't going down that road. They were divorced. It was over.

"How is that possible?" He shook his head and held up one hand. "No. Never mind. It's not possible," he finally blurted.

"Apparently, it is." Mia tucked both hands into the pockets of her white slacks, then pulled them free again.

Sam wasn't surprised. She'd always used her hands when she talked. And she did now.

Waving her left hand, he noticed the absence of her wedding rings and felt a twinge—of what, he didn't know. He wondered what she'd done with the gold, diamond-crusted band and the matching engagement ring he'd given her. Wasn't his business, of course, and simple curiosity would have to wait for another time. But it surprised him to note that it bothered him to see her not wearing the damn things.

Besides, he had to hear what she was saying rather than concentrating on her hands or the way that emerald-green silk shirt made her eyes an even richer, deeper green than usual. Her golden-red hair was long and loose laying across her shoulders, sliding against her neck and it was all Sam could do to keep from reaching out and touching her.

"So it turns out the overnight driver who was supposed to deliver our divorce papers to the court…"

"What?"

"He didn't." She shrugged helplessly. "He had a heart attack at work and when they went in to clean out his apartment, they found *mountains* of undelivered mail. The poor guy was a hoarder, I guess, and kept most of the packages he was supposed to deliver."

Sam couldn't believe this.

"Apparently, they even found forty-year-old Cabbage Patch dolls!" She shook her head and sighed. "Poor little kids never got the dolls they wanted."

"Seriously?" he asked. "You're worried about kids who are now in their fifties or sixties?"

"Well, yes." She frowned at him and lifted both hands in a helpless shrug. "People are slowly being notified about this mess and I got word just last week."

"Last week?" She'd known they were still married for a week? "Why the hell didn't they notify me?"

"Probably because it was my name on the return address on the priority envelope."

Sam took a few long strides, taking him further away from the woman watching him so closely, then he turned around to face his *wife*. Not ex. Wife.

Scrubbing both hands across his face, he then let his hands fall to his sides. "So we're still married."

"I know what you're feeling. I couldn't believe it either. So now you see the problem."

He slowly walked toward her. "I see a problem, yeah. What I don't see is the big emergency that caused Michael to dump passengers off this cruise to make room for you and your family." Staring down into her eyes, he watched her closely as he asked, "Why the hell was it so important you get on this cruise to tell me something you could have handled back home with a damn phone call?"

She tipped her head back to look up at him. "This really isn't something I wanted to do over the phone and you were in Germany last week. This cruise was the first chance I had to talk to you in person."

"Okay. I get that." He hadn't exactly been easy to get a hold of lately. Since he and Mia had split up, Sam had kept even busier than he had been before and he wouldn't have thought that possible. Traveling, working, staying away from home as much as possible because the emptiness of his condo echoed with memories he'd rather not think about.

Mia kept her gaze on his as she dipped one hand into her black leather purse and drew out an envelope. Holding it out to him, she said, "My attorney drew up a new set of papers—same as the others. All you have to do is sign them and when we get home, I'll take them to the courthouse myself."

He looked at the envelope but didn't make a move to take it. They were still married. He didn't know how he felt about that. Michael had been right, Sam *had* missed Mia. More than he had expected. More than he wanted to admit. And now she was back. But nothing had changed. This delay in ending their marriage only meant the pain of failure would be drawn out.

"Why can't they just use the first set of papers?" he asked suddenly. "Why the need for new ones?"

"I don't know…" She waved her left hand again. "My lawyer thought it would be best this way and really? After I heard all about this, I didn't ask a lot of questions. I just want to get this done and over."

Looking into those forest-green eyes of hers, Sam felt a punch of heat and regret slam into him. Didn't matter that she'd left him. He thought that he would probably *always* want her. For the last few months, he'd tried to push her out of his mind. He'd traveled the world and still the memory of her had chased him. And now she was here, standing in front of him and it was all he could do to keep from reaching for her. Hell, they were still married. They had a fourteen day cruise stretching out in front of them. Why shouldn't they spend that time together? Call it one last hurrah? She wanted divorce papers signed. So, maybe they could make a deal, he thought suddenly. That all depended on just how important this divorce was to her.

"You seem pretty eager," he said.

Her gaze narrowed on his. "Sam, we were done months ago. This is just the final step—one we thought we'd already taken. Why wouldn't I want it all finished?"

"No reason," he muttered, wondering if a deal was a bad idea. Of course it was a bad idea—but that didn't mean he wouldn't suggest it. He had to silently admit that it stung to see how impatient she was to cut him loose. He could remember a time when all they wanted was to be together. Hell, he still wanted that. And he could see from the heat in her eyes that she felt the same.

They were still married.

He was here, with his *wife,* and suddenly, divorce seemed light-years away. Moving in closer, he saw her take a deep breath and hold it and knew she was feeling the same pull he was. Her eyes were flashing, her lips parted as her breath came in short puffs.

"What're you doing?" Her voice came out in a strained whisper.

"I'm saying hello to my wife," he countered and gave her a half smile.

She slapped one hand to his chest. "The fact that we're still married is a technicality."

"Always liked technicalities."

Especially this one. Hell, even knowing their marriage was over didn't get rid of the desire pulsing inside him. The ache he'd carried around in the center of his chest was easing now because she was here. Because her scent had wrapped itself around him. And one look into her eyes told him she felt the same, though knowing Mia, she'd never admit to that.

"Sam, we've already said goodbye to each other," she reminded him. "Why make this harder than it has to be?"

He laid his hands on her shoulders and the heat of her body rose up to slide into his. "Hello isn't hard, Mia. Unless you're doing it right."

"Sam…"

He bent his head to hers and stopped when his mouth was just a breath away from her lips. Waiting for acceptance. For her to let him know that she shared what he was thinking, feeling.

"This could be a big mistake," she said, with a slow shake of her head.

"Probably," he agreed, knowing it wouldn't change anything.

Seconds passed and still he waited. Damned if he'd take what he wanted if she wasn't willing. Finally though, she dropped her purse to the floor, reached up to cup his face between her palms and said, "What's one more mistake?"

"That's the spirit."

He kissed her, pulling her up against him, wrapping his arms around her and holding her tightly.

Three

Sam's mouth covered hers, his tongue parted her lips and she opened for him eagerly, willingly. Then he was lost in the heat of her. Her taste, her scent, filled him and he wondered vaguely how he'd managed to breathe without her these last months.

Their tongues met in a tangle of desire that pulsed between them like a shared heartbeat. Her breath brushed against his cheek, her sigh sounded in the stillness and Sam lost himself in her. For this one moment, he was going to simply revel in having her back in his arms.

However briefly.

When he dropped his hand to that sweet butt of hers though, she gasped and pulled back. Breathing deeply, she held up one hand and shook her head.

"Oh no you don't," she said. "A kiss hello is one thing, but we're not going to do what you think we're going to do."

"And what do I think?" he asked, grinning at her.

"The same thing I'm thinking," she said and when he took a step toward her again, she skipped backward. "Seriously, Sam, I'm not going to bed with you."

"Why not? We're married."

"For now," she said.

"I'm only talking about now." Sam moved in another step or two.

"That's the problem," she snapped. "Right there. You never thought about anything beyond the *now.*"

Okay, that stopped him. "What the hell is that supposed to mean? I married you, didn't I?"

"Please." Shaking her head firmly, she bent to snatch her purse off the floor. Her fingers curled into the leather until her knuckles went white. "You know exactly what I mean. Yes, you married me, but then…nothing. You never wanted to talk about a future. About making a family. Buying a house instead of that condo."

"What the hell was wrong with the condo?"

"Kids need a yard to play in."

"We don't have kids."

"Exactly!" And she'd wanted children. Her own family was so close. Her sisters both had families of their own and Mia's heart had ached to be a mother. But Sam wasn't interested in being a father. He never said so outright, but whenever she'd brought the subject up he'd closed down. She couldn't understand why, either. They'd have made beautiful children together and an amazing life—if only he'd cared enough to fight for their marriage.

"You're talking in circles, Mia." He couldn't look away from the fire in her eyes. Mia Harper was the only woman he'd ever known who could turn from desire to fury to ice and back again in thirty seconds. He'd always loved that about her. She was passionate and proud and so damn bullheaded that even their arguments had been sexy as hell. "Just say whatever it is that's clawing at you."

Shaking her head, she said, "You didn't want children, Sam. And you didn't bother to tell me that until *after* we were married."

True. Sam could admit that silently. Every time Mia had talked about raising a family, he had changed the subject. He'd wanted Mia more than his next breath, but he'd never wanted to be a father. How the hell could he? His own father had sucked at the job, so why would Sam think he would be any better at it? He had hoped that she would change her mind about children. Hoped that he and the life they could have together might be enough for her.

He was wrong.

"What's the point in talking about a future that might not happen?" He took a step closer to her again and he could have sworn he felt heat pumping off her body and this time it was anger, not desire, leading the charge.

"If you don't have a future all you ever have is a past and the present."

"The present can be enough if you're doing it right," he countered.

"Why settle for 'enough' when you can have more?" She stared at him and he saw disappointment in her eyes. He didn't like that but there was little he could do about it.

"How much is more, Mia?" His voice was low, tight. "When do you stop looking for the more and enjoy what you have? Why do you have to walk away from something great because it's missing something else?"

Her posture relaxed a bit and she took a long, deep breath before saying, "I'm tired of being the favorite aunt to Maya's and Merry's kids, Sam. I want children. That's the *more* I need."

He closed off at that because his brain drew up images of Mia, surrounded by nieces and nephews who adored her. Guilt poked at his insides. Sam knew he should have told her that he wasn't interested in having kids before they were married. But he'd wanted her too much to tell her the truth. He'd convinced himself that his lies wouldn't matter once it all ended.

Maybe he had been a bastard. And that was on him. He'd made a choice to have Mia for as long as he could, even knowing that they wouldn't be growing old together. Because he'd wanted her that much, despite knowing in his gut that he wasn't husband material. And how the hell could he be a good father when his father had been so damned bad at the job? Sam's only role model for fatherhood had convinced him to never try it.

"I should have told you," he admitted, though it cost his pride. He wasn't used to being wrong, so he hadn't had to become accustomed to apologies.

"I'm not mad at you about that anymore," she said softly. "We're divorced, Sam. It's over. We don't have to keep tearing at each other over the past."

He gave her a half smile. "But we're not divorced, are we?"

Instantly, she wagged a finger at him. "Oh, no. Don't do that. We may not be divorced, but we're not exactly married, either."

Sam smiled, one corner of his mouth lifting. "Until your new papers go through we are."

"And now you *like* the idea of the two of us married? Why do you care, Sam?" she demanded, pushing her hair back behind one ear to show off a long twist of gold dangling from her lobe. Her eyes shone with a light that was either passion or fury—or maybe a combination of both. "You didn't care when it actually would have mattered."

That slapped at him. Of course he'd cared. It was the only reason he'd tried marriage in the first place. He'd wanted her. Cared for her. Didn't want to lose her, so marriage had been his only option.

"I did care." He said it simply because if she honestly believed what she was saying, he wanted to convince her she was wrong.

"Really?" She tipped her head to one side and her hair slid off her shoulders to follow the movement. Then she shrugged. "Okay, maybe you did and I just didn't *see* you often enough to notice."

She might have a point, but damned if he'd admit it. He hadn't made a secret of the fact that he *liked* working. That his company was growing and needed close attention paid to it. "You knew when we got married that I run a big company and I work a lot."

Anger drained away and she sighed. "I suppose I did. I just thought that—"

"What?"

"Doesn't matter. Not anymore." Shaking her head, she set the papers down on the nearest tabletop and said, "I'll leave these here. Just call me when you sign them— or even better, have one of your minions bring them to my suite."

He might have smiled at the *minion* remark, but one look into her bruised eyes made that impossible. Whatever had erupted between them only moments before, was gone now. That kiss still burned inside him, but if Mia was feeling the same thing, she was better at hiding emotions than she used to be.

Hell, one of the first things he'd admired about her was her openness. The way her eyes lit up with pleasure over things most people wouldn't notice at all.

On the cruise when they'd met, she'd tried paddle boarding for the first time when they were in port and immediately fell off into the ocean. Sam had helped her up, thinking she'd be scared or want to stop and go back to the beach. Instead, she'd come up from the water laughing, eyes dancing. She'd climbed back on that board and no matter how many times she'd fallen off—dozens—she hadn't given up. Not until she'd found her balance and conquered that board.

Sam had never had patience for quitters. So watching this gorgeous woman's stubborn refusal to give up had appealed to him. Not to mention her eyes, her laugh, her body, her interest in *everything*.

He'd had an awakening on that cruise a year ago. Meeting Mia had opened his eyes to a lot of things he'd stopped noticing years ago. Sunsets. Sunrises. Pods of whales sailing past the ship. How good it had felt to sit beside her on the deck and watch the world drift by.

That's what had drawn him and what had eventually pulled him away. Sam had realized that he and Mia were too different. Too much opposites to last, and hanging around longer than he should was only making it harder on *her*. He wasn't built for cozy. For *intimate*. Sam Buchanan had been raised to be a hit-and-run lover. Don't stick around. Don't get close and for God's sake don't let anyone in.

And nothing had changed, he reminded himself. So he looked into her eyes and nodded. "Fine."

She almost looked disappointed at his response, but he thought he'd imagined that because a heartbeat later, her features were cool and still. Polite and distant. Not something he was accustomed to seeing from Mia. But she was right. The more distance between them the better.

When she left, he didn't watch her go.

"What did he do?" Maya was waiting for Mia on the top deck at a table beneath a red-and-white umbrella.

Mia ignored the question and looked around for her nephews. There were a dozen other passengers gathered on the deck, talking and laughing, and from the deck below came spurts of laughter from excited children. No sign of Charlie and Chris, though. She looked back at her twin. "Where are the kids?"

"You're stalling because you don't want to talk about Sam."

Mia tapped one finger to the end of her nose. "Bingo. So, where are the kids?"

Maya scowled at her. "Joe has them. I think they're throwing snowballs already. And you know I won't quit asking, so just answer already. What did your miserable, no-good ex do?"

Mia groaned. "God, Maya, just stop, okay? You're not making this easier."

"Sorry, sorry." She waved one hand in the air as if she could erase her words. "Honestly, I'm not trying to make things harder for you. It's just that Sam makes me so furious."

"No. Really?"

Maya's lips twitched and Mia grinned. One thing she never had to doubt was her twin's loyalty. When her marriage had fallen apart, leaving Mia in a soggy, weepy, emotional heap, Maya had been there for her. She and their older sister Merry had plied her with bottles of wine and sympathy until Mia had found her feet again.

Her parents had offered support, but had tried to maintain neutrality and though that might seem like a betrayal of sorts to someone else, Mia had appreciated it. Sam wasn't an evil person. Not the Darth Vader of Seal Beach. He just hadn't wanted to be married.

"Okay." Maya picked up her virgin mimosa and signaled to a nearby waiter to bring another for Mia. "Let's rephrase. How did your most wonderful ex take the news?"

Mia gave her a wry smile, then thanked the waiter who handed her a beautiful crystal flute. "Let's not go too far the other way." She paused, thought about it, then said, "He was...surprised."

"Well, yeah. Who wasn't?" Shaking her head, Maya sat back in her chair. "I still can't believe people weren't complaining about not getting their packages delivered. How does a delivery driver become a hoarder with other people's stuff?"

"I don't know. And it doesn't matter now anyway," Mia said. "All I need is for Sam to sign the papers so I can get the divorce filed before January 15th."

"So he didn't sign them." Maya nodded sagely.

"Not yet," Mia agreed. "But he will."

"And you know this how?"

"Because he didn't fight the divorce, remember?" That still stung whether Mia wanted to admit it or not. When she'd first broached the subject of divorce it had taken everything she'd had. She'd prepared herself for his arguments. For his request for a second chance. But she needn't have bothered. He didn't argue. Didn't really say much at all.

She could still see his face in her memory. Standing opposite her in the living room of the condo they shared, he'd simply stared at her, his features blank and hard—as if he'd been carved out of stone. When he finally spoke, all he'd said was, "If that's what you want, I won't stop you."

Well, she'd *wanted* him to stop her. Wanted him to admit that he hadn't given their marriage a real shot. That he'd been wrong to shut himself off from her.

Instead, she'd gotten an uncontested divorce.

"Damn it," Maya blurted, snapping Mia out of her depressing thoughts. "I hate this. I hate seeing shadows back in your eyes. You were finally okay. Moving on without him. Planning a life and a future and now you're right back where you started a few months ago."

"Stop being so dramatic," Mia said and took a sip of her drink. "I'm not going to throw myself off the ship. This is just a bump in my formerly tidy world."

Maya narrowed her eyes on Mia and studied her until Mia shifted uncomfortably beneath that knowing stare.

"Why are you looking at me like that?"

"Because you're right. You *are* fine. And I want to know why." Leaning forward, she kept their gazes locked. "You weren't there long enough to have sex with him."

"Maya!" Mia glanced around to make sure no one else had overheard her sister.

"Well, come on. Even distracted by kids, a house payment and his job, Joe can last longer than twenty minutes."

"Too much information, thanks. Now I'll have that in my head when I see Joe next."

"I know envy when I hear it," Maya said with a grin.

Mia snorted a laugh and took another sip.

"But there's something different about you. Something..." Suddenly Maya's eyes snapped. "You kissed him. Didn't you?"

No point in denying it. Maya had always had X-ray vision when it came to things like this. For a moment, Mia pitied her nephews when they became teenagers. They'd never put one over on their mother.

"He kissed me," Mia finally said. "There's a difference."

"And you fought him off, of course," Maya supplied wryly.

"Desperately," Mia assured her, then set her glass down with a click on the glass table. "Fine. I kissed him back."

Maya huffed a breath in disgust. "I knew this would happen."

The sun shone out of a sky so blue it hurt to look at it. A sharp, cold wind brushed past them, setting the fringe on the red-and-white umbrellas snapping and dancing.

"Wow, you're wasting time working at the family bakery. You should be on the Psychic Network or something."

Maya smirked at her. "Please. Like I have to be a fortune teller to know that you'd fall back into his arms."

"Okay," Mia said, defending herself, "I didn't do that. It was a kiss. And I ended it."

"Before or after he got your shirt off?"

"Maya!" Mia goggled at her sister. As twins, they were close. As best friends, they knew each other way too well, so she wasn't surprised at Maya, so much as disappointed in herself. She had pretty much given in to the urge to kiss Sam again. But why wouldn't she? Just because they were divorced didn't mean she'd stopped loving him.

Just because Mia knew she could gain ten pounds just by *looking* at chocolate cake didn't mean she'd stop eating it.

"I managed to keep my clothes on, thanks for your support."

"Oh, you have my support, honey. But trust me, I know what's going on between you two." She patted her baby bump. "Remember. I'm on number three child. Every time Joe walks into the room, I want to jump him. Heck, at this rate, I'm going to have ten kids. So believe me when I say I understand."

Mia sighed a little and quashed that twinge of envy she felt for her sister's life. Maya's husband was a firefighter and their two boys, Charlie and Chris, were funny, ferocious and all around adorable. Now Maya was pregnant with another boy and Mia knew that in a year or two, her twin would be trying for a girl again.

Maya had everything that Mia most wanted. She had love. Family. Children of her own. It's what Mia had hoped for when she'd married Sam. Building a life together. Raising some kids together.

But Sam hadn't really wanted children. Naturally, she hadn't believed him when he told her on their honeymoon. She'd wrongly assumed that he had simply never been around kids, so didn't know how much fun—okay yes, and trouble—they could be. And maybe he would have changed his mind at some point—if their marriage had lasted. But now she'd never know.

"But jumping Sam won't change anything," Maya said and thankfully her voice was low, soft.

"Yeah, I know that." Didn't stop her from *wanting* to jump him, but she was stronger than her hormones. She hoped.

"Honey, once he signs those damn papers, you can pick up your life again."

"I know that too, Maya," she said tightly.

Her twin must have caught the fine edge of tension in Mia's voice because she said, "Fine, fine. I'll stop."

"Hallelujah."

"Funny. Let's see if you're still laughing after you spend the day with my kids."

"Your kids are great," Mia argued.

"Yeah, they are," Maya said. "But don't tell them I said that." She scooted her chair back and held one hand out. "Now, help your prego twin out of this stupid chair, will you? I've got to figure out where I'm going to put that Christmas elf in our suite."

Mia laughed and pulled her twin out of the chair. "You brought Buddy the Elf with you?"

"Of course I did." Maya threw her hands up. "Both boys look for him the instant they wake up in the morning. And they know that Buddy reports to Santa so..." She shrugged. "It seemed like a good way to keep the boys in line while we're on this cruise."

"Uh-huh."

Maya gave her a hard look. "Just wait until it's your turn to hide that elf and you have to find a new spot every day!"

Mia could hardly wait.

For the next couple of hours, Sam buried himself in work. It was the best way. Always his answer to avoiding emotional issues, he'd been doing it since he was a kid.

Back then, his father had made it clear that a man's duty was to take care of his business and his employees. Emotions were something to be *avoided*. He would point out that marrying Sam and Mike's mother had been the biggest mistake of his life, since he'd had to settle an enormous sum on her when they divorced. He considered his sons to be his only compensation for his relationship with their mother.

His father had always demanded that Sam *think*. That he never allow his feelings, whatever they might be, to rule any decisions made. Well, Sam had broken that decree when he'd married Mia. He'd allowed emotion to swamp his judgment and now he was paying for it. He'd taken the risk—and lost.

"You're not getting any work done," he muttered and tossed his pen onto the desk in front of him.

Avoiding Mia wasn't going to do him any good if he couldn't get her out of his mind. He stared out at the ocean, letting his brain wander, hoping it would come up with a strategy for how to deal with this.

Deal.

At the thought of that word, Sam's brain leaped back to the idea that had occurred to him earlier. He'd dismissed it at first of course, because he might be a bastard, but was he low enough to actually blackmail Mia?

Slowly, his gaze slid to the envelope Mia had left behind when she walked out of the suite.

Divorce papers.

He hadn't signed them yet.

And he wasn't sure why.

He wasn't holding onto the past. He'd already come to grips with the end of their marriage. But she was here now, he reminded himself. She wanted those papers signed and he had to wonder what she'd be willing to do to see that happen.

A knock on the door had Sam's head snapping up.

Mia? Come back to...what? Was she looking to expand on that kiss that was still sending sparks sizzling through him? His body responded to that thought with a rush of heat that staggered him.

He walked to the door, yanked it open and the heat instantly drained away.

"Hi, Uncle Sam!" Charlie Rossi, Maya's five-year-old son, raced past him into the suite and on his heels was his three-year-old brother, Chris. Chris didn't say much, but he waved in passing.

"Hey you guys, don't run!" Joe Rossi, their father and Sam's brother-in-law shouted, then turned to Sam and held out one hand. "Good to see you."

"Yeah," he said, shaking the man's hand. "You too. And surprising."

He'd expected that Mia's family was onboard just to throw stones at him and protect Mia from him. He hadn't been prepared to see a friendly face in the bunch.

"I'll bet." Joe walked past him, looked for his sons and relaxed a little when he saw them jumping onto the couch. "Stop jumping, that's not your trampoline."

Chris stopped instantly. Charlie was a harder sell. "Uncle Sam, Dad says we can have a snowball war if we're good and don't bug you so do you have cookies?"

"What?" Sam looked at the boy, whose sun-streaked brown hair was dipping into green eyes much like his mother's. "Uh, no. I don't have cookies."

"Juice box?" Chris asked.

"No, sorry." He hadn't expected to be entertaining kids. And his features must have said so, because Joe came to his rescue.

"Relax you guys, you just ate lunch." Joe walked to the couch, picked up a TV remote and said, "Here. Watch that cartoon movie you like so much while I talk to Uncle Sam."

"Okay," Charlie agreed happily enough, dropping onto the couch hard enough to make his little brother bounce and fall over. "Then snowball war?"

"Yeah," Joe said. "If you're good."

"Be good, Chris," Charlie warned.

"Right," Joe muttered, with a laugh, "because he's the problem." Glancing at Sam, he added, "Should feel bad about that," he confessed. "Using the TV for a babysitter, I mean."

Sam watched Joe with his sons and thought how differently the Rossi kids were being raised than Sam had been. Hell, if he'd jumped up and down on a sofa, his father would have hit the roof.

Shaking his head, he pushed all of that aside and asked, "Want some coffee?" Sam asked. "And I've got water and probably sodas in the wet bar if the kids—"

"I'll take the caffeine," Joe said quickly, "and pass on it for the kids, but thanks. They're fine."

"Okay." Sam led the way to the coffee station along one wall and poured each of them a cup. "So, I saw Maya…"

Joe winced. "She's not real happy with you."

"Yeah, that was pretty clear." He could still see Mia's sister glaring at him like he was Jack the Ripper or something.

"The thing is," Joe said cautiously, "most of us aren't."

Sam didn't like hearing that and it surprised him. But Sam had always liked Joe, and Merry's husband Alan and Mia's parents, too. Of course, he'd known going into the marriage that it probably wasn't going to work out, so he hadn't gotten close to any of them. But still, they were good people.

"I can understand that," he admitted, and took a sip of coffee. "What I don't get is why you're all here on this cruise."

"Seriously?" Joe snorted a laugh, drank his coffee then shot a look at his sons, completely wrapped up in some movie apparently starring some weird-looking snowman. Turning his gaze back to Sam, he said, "You should know the Harper family well enough to know that when one of them's in trouble, they circle the wagons."

"Against me."

"Pretty much."

Nodding, Sam said, "Fine. But this is still between Mia and me."

"You'd think so, but no." Shaking his head, Joe continued, "Whatever happens between you two affects everything else. It's family, Sam."

On an intellectual level, Sam got it. But otherwise, no. He hadn't grown up with anything like the Harper family. He was taught to stand on his own—*don't let anyone close and if they do get past your walls, shut down so they can't affect you.*

He'd learned those lessons well. Sam had taken a risk, gone against everything he'd believed and married Mia even knowing it would all come crashing down. If he had regrets, they were his own. And he wasn't going to bare his soul for the Harper family, either.

"If you're here to push me into signing those papers, you didn't have to bother," Sam said.

"Yeah, that's not why I'm here." He broke off, glared at his son and said, "Charlie, I said no bouncing on the furniture." Looking at Sam again, he said, "My wife is pretty pissed at you."

"Yeah. I know."

"What you don't know is I don't agree with her." He held up one hand and added, "And if you tell her I said that, I'll claim you're a liar."

"Okay…" This was as unexpected as the surprise visit.

"You screwed up."

"Thanks." Sam lifted his coffee cup in a silent toast.

"No problem," Joe said amiably. "But the thing is, one screw-up doesn't have to end everything. You and Mia were good together. And hell, I like you."

Sam laughed shortly. "Thanks."

"So I'm thinking you shouldn't sign the papers. At least not right away." Joe shrugged, shot his bouncing son another warning look, then continued, "What the hell, Sam. You've got a two-week cruise. Use it. Talk to Mia. Figure out what the hell went wrong and maybe you can fix it."

Sam already knew what had gone wrong. And talking about it wouldn't change a damn thing. He just wasn't husband material. Probably never would be. How could he be? His own father had sucked at all four of his brief marriages and then had spent the next thirty years bouncing from one temporary woman to the next. Not exactly a sterling role model.

There were lots of things Sam wanted to do with Mia, but talking wasn't one of them.

"I appreciate the moral support, Joe. Seriously. But I don't think this is salvageable."

"Huh." Joe looked at him. "Never pegged you as a quitter."

Insulted, he said, "Yeah, I'm not."

"Could have fooled me."

Sam laughed again. "First a pep talk, then insults?"

Joe shrugged again. "Whatever works, man." He set his coffee cup down. "Look. Up to you, but you're both on this boat anyway. Might as well make the most of it, don't you think?"

Sam frowned thoughtfully, and realized that what Joe was saying almost lined up with his idea about making a deal with Mia. Probably not what the other man had had in mind, but it did slide right in there.

Joe wasn't waiting for an answer. He'd already turned to his kids. "All right you two! Snow time!"

"Yay!" Charlie jumped off the couch and his shadow, Chris, was right behind him. "Bye, Uncle Sam!" he shouted as he headed for the door.

"Bye!" Chris echoed, following his big brother.

"See you around, Sam…" Joe lifted one hand, then led his kids out the door. Before he closed it behind him though, he said, "Think about it. Talk to Mia. What've you got to lose?"

The TV was still on and some silly song was rolling through the suite. Sam didn't hear it. Instead, he was thinking about what Joe had said and wondering if he should give in to what he wanted—or just let Mia have the ending she was asking for.

Four

Make the most of it.

Sam snorted as he told himself that Joe probably hadn't meant his advice in the same way Sam was taking it. But for the next two weeks, Sam and Mia would be stranded on this ship. And the *Fantasy Nights* wasn't big enough for them to be able to ignore each other for long.

"And why should we?" Frowning, he stared down at the deck below, watching his employees working with the passengers, laughing, talking, making everyone at home.

But while he studied the small crowd, his mind was on Mia. Not married. Not divorced. So didn't that clear the way for them to be whatever the hell they wanted to be?

And that begged the question—what exactly *did* Sam want?

That was easy. He wanted Mia. Always had. Since the first time he'd seen her, all he'd been able to think of was getting her alone. Getting her into the nearest bed and keeping her there. That hadn't changed.

Their marriage had been a mistake, no doubt. But that failure hadn't killed his desire for her. He didn't think that was possible.

They could have two weeks together. Sam wouldn't promise her forever. Not again. But he could give her now.

Of course the moment that thought registered, he remembered that Mia had accused him of only considering the "now." But hell, that's all any of them were promised, right? There was no guarantee of tomorrow and yesterday was already gone. So why not focus on *now*?

All he had to do was bring her around to that same realization. He scowled as he acknowledged that wasn't going to be easy. But maybe, if she couldn't be convinced, he could try a little friendly blackmail.

She could move into his suite for the duration of the cruise—and he'd sign her divorce papers.

No. Though everything in him wanted to, damned if he wanted Mia back in his bed because she thought she had no choice. Scowling he was forced to admit that there were some lines he wasn't prepared to cross.

"Why did you bring the elf with you?" Mia shook her head as she watched her twin stalk around their suite.

"My choice was…what? Admit he's not real?" Maya gave her a hard look. "Want me to tell the boys Santa's not real, too?"

"Of course not." Mia loved those kids like her own and seeing their excitement for Christmas and Santa was wonderful. She couldn't wait to experience it all for herself with her own children.

"Well then, Buddy has to be here." Maya frowned to herself. "You know, he reports to Santa every night on the boys' behavior. Using that as extortion is the one chance I have to make sure they don't destroy this boat while we're on it."

Mia laughed. "They're not monsters, Maya."

Her twin smiled. "No. But they are little kids with too much Christmas excitement rattling around inside them and it's bound to erupt at some point. Buddy the Elf is my only hope to keep it contained."

"And you have to do this right now?" Mia leaned back into the navy blue couch, propped her feet on the coffee table in front of her and said, "We've only been onboard ship for a couple of hours. What's the rush?"

Maya sighed and laid her forearm on the crest of her sizable baby bump. "Because Joe's got the boys out exploring, so I want to take the opportunity to look for elf places while I can."

"Fine. I'll help."

"It needs to be easy enough for the kids to find him in the morning. And I'll need a few of them, to last over the whole trip." Maya frowned and shook her head. "I can reuse the spots of course, the kids are so little, they won't really pay attention. But I'm going to need at least three or four." She turned that frown on her twin. "When you said you'd help, did you mean today?"

Mia laughed. "Jeez, you're crabby when you're pregnant."

"You try having a tiny human jumping up and down on your bladder like it's a trampoline and see what kind of mood you're in." A moment later, Maya groaned. "I'm sorry honey."

"It's okay."

"No," Maya said, "it's really not. I'm not really mad. Just…tense. I guess I'm still worried about Joe. He was so tired when he got back from that Idaho wildfire."

"He looks good now," Mia said and knew her sister would worry anyway. Joe and several others had flown from their fire station in Seal Beach to Idaho to help fight a fast-spreading wildfire. And for the five days he was gone, Maya had hardly slept. So it wasn't just Joe who needed this trip to relax and catch up on some sleep.

"He does." Maya nodded firmly. "And I'm probably overreacting—hormonal and all."

"And you love Joe."

"I do."

"So…" Mia stood up and forced a smile. "Let's find some hiding spots for Buddy and then go sit on the deck so you can relax a little."

"That sounds great."

Mia looked around the suite. There were two bedrooms. Joe, Maya and the boys had one and Mia had the other. And the living area was a good size, so they could surely find someplace to hide an elf.

"Oh," Maya said, "you should know that Dad says he's going to talk to Sam."

"Great," Mia said on a sigh. "That'll go well."

"Oh come on. Dad won't hurt him," Maya said. "Much."

Mia sat down again. "Maybe it was a bad idea bringing all of you guys along on this cruise."

"Thanks a bunch," Maya said, opening a cabinet door and shutting it again. "I feel so special now."

"You know what I mean. Backup is one thing," Mia said, "but I didn't want you all to be an attack squad."

"God, drama queen." Maya laughed. "Nobody's attacking Sam. Yet," she added with a grin. "We just sort of want him to know what he lost."

"Well, if you have to *tell* him what he lost, what's the point?"

"To irritate him, of course." Maya walked across the room and dropped carefully onto the closest chair. Her smile faded and she looked at her twin with sympathy. "Sweetie, we're on your side. We won't do anything you don't want us to. We just want to be here so Sam can't crush you again."

Her head snapped back and she winced at the description. "I wasn't crushed."

"Please." Maya's eyes rolled.

"Fine." She had been destroyed when her marriage ended. But she'd mourned what might have been more than what *had* been. Because if she were honest with herself, the marriage itself hadn't been worth her tears. She'd been alone for the most part and even when Sam was home, she felt as if she were the only one in the room.

He'd managed to be close to her and as distant as the moon all at the same time. It was as if the moment they got married, Sam had turned inward, shutting her out. The worst part was, she didn't know *why*. And probably never would.

"You're right. It was bad at first. The difference is, now I won't be crushed."

"And how're you going to prevent it?" Maya watched her and Mia thought that sometimes she really hated how her sister knew her so well.

"Because I won't let myself. I learned my lesson. I'm not going to believe in Sam again."

Maya continued to study her silently for several long

seconds, then finally nodded. "Okay then. I'm going to hold you to that."

"Go ahead. In fact," Mia said suddenly, "I'll bet you twenty bucks that I'll leave this cruise Sam-free and my heart in one glorious piece."

That wasn't entirely true and Mia knew it. Just thinking about Sam brought up images of them together in her mind. She felt the heat of the flames licking at her blood and the ache inside her only grew. The next two weeks, being so close to Sam was going to be the hardest thing she'd ever done.

But any pain she felt…this time she would hide it from the family and instead bury it so deep within that she'd never really have to face it herself.

Quickly, her twin said, "I'll take that bet."

"Thanks for your support," Mia said wryly.

"Hey, twenty bucks is twenty bucks." Maya sighed a little. "And the truth is, Sam is your Kryptonite."

"He used to be," Mia corrected, ignoring the memory of the blast of heat that had seared her during that kiss she'd shared with him. She wouldn't allow him to be that important to her again.

Mia had plans for her life. And to make sure those plans came to reality, she had to get Sam to sign those divorce papers. Keeping that thought firmly in mind would see her survive this cruise without letting her heart drop into Sam's lap.

"Well," Maya said, "now that we have that settled, do you think it would send the wrong message if Buddy was hidden in the liquor cabinet?"

Laughing, Mia pushed thoughts of Sam out of her mind and concentrated on the magical elf instead. At least for the moment.

* * *

The next day, Sam met with Kira Anderson, the navigation officer, on the prow of the ship. Out there, with only the wind and the sound of the sea slapping against the hull, Sam fought to concentrate as she walked him through the latest weather reports.

"It looks as though we might catch a break," she was saying as she pointed to the graphic she'd printed out. "The storm isn't a big one, and it's moving at a pretty good clip. About a half hour ago, it shifted position here, heading further out of our path." She pointed to one of the red lines on the paper. "There's still a chance it will swing around and be waiting for us. But right now, it looks as though we'll miss it."

Sam studied the paper she handed him. Only their second day at sea and already a storm was brewing. Both on and off the ship, he thought wryly. Hell, with Mia here, everything had shifted and Sam was still trying to find his sea legs. He hadn't slept the night before, because every time he closed his eyes, he saw Mia. That kiss was still lingering on his lips and the burn she engendered in him had him feeling as though he was on fire.

Shaking his head, he pushed those thoughts aside and looked at Kira. "And what if we don't miss it? How big a storm are we talking about?"

She considered that for a moment and looked out at the ocean as if looking for confirmation before turning back to him. "Nothing that could endanger the ship or passengers, sir. But it could make the ship's doctor really busy doling out seasick pills."

His lips twitched. Didn't matter what time of year they were sailing, there was always going to be at least one night when the waves were high, and the winds strong enough to turn even the most practiced sailor into a whimpering shadow of himself, praying for death.

"All right," he finally said, handing back the papers. "Monitor closely and keep me in the loop about what you're expecting."

"Yes, sir." She practically saluted before turning to head back to the bridge.

"And Kira," he called out and waited for her to stop and turn to him before adding, "I want to know your best prediction by seven. Let's give our guests time to prepare. I don't want anyone unnecessarily scared over this."

"Understood." She nodded and hurried away.

Alone again, Sam thought about the possible storm and scowled to himself. He wasn't worried about what might happen. Sam had been sailing all of his life and faced the worst storm he'd seen before or since when he was fourteen.

He'd taken his skiff out alone, wanting to escape a house that had felt like a prison. Sam had been sailing for two hours when the clouds rolled in. Lightning punched the sky, rain fell as if it'd been poured from an upturned bucket. Fear was a living thing inside him.

Visibility was so bad he didn't know which way the shore was and he knew that one wrong decision and his boat would be pushed out into the open ocean with chances of a rescue slim. But he couldn't do nothing, either. The waves had battered his small boat until he was sure it would fall apart.

So he made a decision and headed toward what he hoped was the shore. He was out there, in the storm, alone, for what felt like years, though it was only an hour before he landed on the beach, exhausted, wet and cold.

By the time he'd walked home, it was late and his father was waiting. The old man didn't want to hear about the storm. He said Sam was irresponsible. He didn't deserve a damn boat and he wouldn't be getting another one. And if he didn't know enough to stay out of the ocean during a storm, he'd send Sam to a private school in the desert. Dear old dad had made it clear that night, just how low Sam was on his list of priorities.

But if one good thing had happened that night—besides surviving that storm—Sam had finally accepted that his father didn't give a damn about him. He was on his own and the sooner he stopped waiting for someone to care, the easier it would be. The memory faded away and Sam realized his hands were fisted around the iron railing. Deliberately, he relaxed his grip.

"Yeah," he muttered now. "Hell of a role model, Dad."

Shutting off the ancient images in his mind, he looked down at the pool deck. There were kids everywhere of course, with the ship lifeguards on red alert. Adults strolled the deck, huddled by the pool bar or tried to lounge in the water in spite of the splashing and shrieking coming from the kids.

The sky was blue and dense with heavy white clouds. Waves crested and fell across the surface of the water and made Sam wonder if they were closing in on that storm faster than Kira had thought.

Then Sam spotted Mia's parents. He took a breath and let it out again as he studied the couple. They were at a rail, staring out over the ocean. At five foot ten, Henry Harper was a good six inches taller than his wife, Emma. He had his right arm draped across his wife's shoulders and she was leaning into his embrace. A unit. That's how Sam had seen them from the beginning. They could have been alone in the world instead of on a cruise ship filled with Christmas-hyped kids.

And a part of Sam envied them their unity. The Harpers had welcomed him into their family when he married Mia. But he seriously doubted whether that welcome was still alive and well. Actually, he knew it wasn't. Knew that when he left Mia, the Harper family had left *him*.

Yet they were here, on his boat and trying to avoid them for the next couple of weeks would be ridiculous.

"Besides," he muttered as he headed for the closest staircase that would take him to the pool deck, "they should be thanking me." Staying married to Mia would have been a disaster. By leaving, he'd spared her a hell of a lot of pain further down the road.

"Sure. They're going to believe that," he said to himself. Hell, even he had a hard time with it.

Sam walked a wide berth around the pool area, then headed for the Harpers. As if sensing his approach, Henry turned his head and pinned Sam with a cold stare.

Sam kept walking, though it felt as though he was making his way through a minefield. When he was close enough, he said, "Hello Henry, Emma."

Henry nodded. Emma didn't so much as twitch. It was as if Sam was invisible to her.

The sun was bright, the wind was cold and the air was filled with the kind of noise only twenty or thirty kids could make.

"Sam," Henry said, giving him a brief nod. The man's reddish-brown hair whipped in the wind and the green eyes he'd passed on to his daughters focused on Sam. "Didn't expect to see you."

"Really? I thought that was why you'd come on this trip with Mia. To see me."

"No." Henry shook his head. "We're here to make sure you don't hurt our girl again. That's all."

Sam gritted his teeth against that verbal slap because he respected Henry. He wouldn't argue with the older man, and how could he? He *had* hurt Mia. But he'd hurt her far less than he might have if they'd been married longer.

He glanced at Emma, who hadn't once shifted her gaze from the ocean to him. Sighing, he turned his gaze back to Henry. "Okay then. I won't keep you. I only wanted to let you know, we may be heading into a storm later."

Henry took a brief look at the sunny sky and the water, choppy, but hardly threatening, before saying, "Is your boat up to it?"

Sam laughed shortly and tucked both hands into his pockets. "Every one of the Buchanan boats are built for stability as well as comfort."

"Stability," Emma repeated.

Sam's gaze switched to her, but she wasn't looking at him. Frowning a bit, he said to Henry, "We'll be safe, but it could be a rough night."

Henry looked around at the people enjoying the day, then said, "You're not telling the other passengers?"

"We will, later. If it looks as though we can't avoid the storm." Sam winced when a wet beach ball smacked the middle of his back. Looking over his shoulder, he saw a young boy hurry after the ball before heading back to the pool. Focusing on Henry again, he said, "I didn't see the point in worrying everyone until we knew for sure."

"But you didn't mind worrying us?"

"That's not what I meant." Of course, that's how Henry would see it. But the truth was, Henry was a coolheaded person and wasn't inclined toward panic. "I knew you weren't the kind of man to overreact."

"Uh-huh." Henry watched him. "Think you know me, do you?"

Confused and a little wary, Sam said, "Yes. I do."

"Well," Henry told him, "I once thought I knew you. But I was wrong. So you might be as well."

"Henry—" Sam didn't know what he could say. Hell, what he wanted to say. But it felt as though he should be trying, somehow.

"No," the older man said, dropping his arm from Emma's shoulders. "I didn't get my say when all this blew up. You just walked out on my daughter and acted like the rest of us didn't exist."

"I figured you wouldn't want to see me."

"You weren't wrong."

Sam really didn't want this confrontation, but there was no way to avoid it now. Thankfully, with the crowd around the pool, the noise level was high enough that it would keep anyone else from listening in. Pulling his hands free of his pockets, Sam folded his arms across his chest and met Henry's gaze straight on. "Mia asked me for a divorce. I gave her one."

"And why'd she need that divorce, Sam?" Henry tipped his head to one side and stared at him. "Could it be because you didn't mind having a wedding, but you really didn't want to be married?"

That skimmed a little too close to home. "I'm not getting into any of it, Henry. That's between me and Mia."

"You making my girl cry over you?" Henry countered. "That makes it my business, too."

She'd cried. Of course she had. Sam hadn't let himself think about that because he just couldn't take the image of a teary Mia. Especially knowing it was his fault. If he'd never married her, none of this would be happening.

But he'd been so blinded by desire—by feelings he'd never known before, he hadn't been able to stop himself even when he knew he was risking disaster for both of them. Sam had known that Mia wasn't a 'temporary' kind of woman and so he'd tried. He'd taken that risk because he'd wanted her so badly. Hell, he still wanted Mia more than his next breath. She was the only woman who had ever tempted him to try marriage. And look where it had gotten them both.

Still, it was over and done now. Everybody should be moving the hell on. Sounded great, he thought. But he wasn't thinking about moving on. He was focused on finding Mia and kissing her senseless. Letting himself feel the burn of her touch and the rushing slide into a heat he'd only found with her. Shaking his head, he let go of those thoughts and looked at his in-laws.

"Look, Henry," he said, done trying to apologize for doing the right thing. As a husband, he was a failure. Should he have stuck around long enough that Mia was begging him to leave? "I can't change your opinion of me and frankly, I'm not going to try. I only wanted to give you and your family a heads-up about the possible storm. Now that I have, I'll leave you to enjoy yourselves."

It looked as though Henry had more to say, but instead, he smashed his lips together as if locking the words inside. But before he could go, Sam heard Emma speaking.

"You know something Henry," she said, still watching the water as if she were mesmerized, "if Sam were here, I'd tell him what a disappointment he is to me."

Sam felt that sting down to his bones. Emma had always been good to him. He'd seen her relationship with her daughters and it had been a revelation to him. He'd never known a *real* family dynamic and he'd liked it. Enjoyed it. He was accepted as a son—much like Joe and Merry's husband, Alan. He hadn't even known how much that had meant to him until it was gone.

Now, Emma wouldn't look at him.

"Emma—" he started.

"And," she continued, "I'd tell him if he hurts my baby again, the storm won't be his only problem."

There was nothing he could say to turn things around, so Sam just kept quiet.

Emma looked up at Henry and said, "Let's take a walk, shall we?"

Henry gave him a brief look, then nodded at his wife. "Sure. Let's go check on the kids in the snow room."

"That'll be fun," Emma said and walked past Sam as if he were a ghost.

And to her, he told himself, that's exactly what he was. The ghost of a man who'd made promises he didn't keep.

Sam watched them go, then stabbed one hand through his hair. When his marriage to Mia had ended, so had everything else. He'd tried to be nice to Henry and Emma. They weren't interested. So why should he keep trying to be Mr. Nice Guy? This was his ship. His world. They were only passing through.

Being here with Mia was a gift from the universe. The fires between them were still burning. He still ached to have her with him and now he had his chance. Once, he'd married her because the desperate need inside him had demanded it—and he'd let her go because she'd needed him to. Now he needed and damned if he'd waste this opportunity. And once this cruise was over, they'd go back to reality and never have to see each other again.

So maybe it was time to rethink that "deal" he'd considered earlier. A nice guy wouldn't do it. But apparently, that wasn't who he was.

And that opened up a world of possibilities.

Mia spent most of the day in the ship's kitchen. She knew several of the chefs from her time with Sam and it was good to see them all. But she acknowledged, at least to herself, that the real reason she was in the kitchen, was that it was literally the last place on earth she had to worry about running into Sam.

The Buchanan ships were small enough that it wasn't easy to hide—it would have been much easier to disappear into a crowd of thousands on the bigger cruise ships.

Chefs were moving about the kitchen as if they were in a well-rehearsed dance. Miles of stainless steel countertops were stacked with dishes being readied for the dining room and a dozen conversations were happening at once.

"This is great, Mia." Holly Chambers, pastry chef on the *Fantasy Nights*, was barely five feet tall and wore her black hair cut close to her head. Her blue eyes were always bright and smiling and a pair of gold studs were in her ears. When Mia and Holly had met a year ago, they'd bonded over baking.

The Harper family bakery, Your Daily Bread, specialized in…naturally, bread. But as Mia and her sisters took over more of the bakery, they were growing the menu, too. Now they offered Italian cookies, English scones, cannoli, sticky toffee pudding and a tiramisu that could bring tears of joy to your eyes.

But today, Mia was showing Holly how to make her mother's amazing rosemary bread. As she kneaded the fragrant dough on the stainless steel counter, Mia said, "This is one of the best sellers at the bakery."

"I'm loving it already and it hasn't been baked yet," Holly said, checking her notes to make sure she'd written the recipe down perfectly.

Mia smiled to herself. This was therapeutic to her. Kneading dough, creating something amazing out of flour and herbs.

"Oh, and it smells like heaven when it's baking," Mia said. If there was one thing the Harper kids knew, it was baking. All three of her parents' daughters had started working at the bakery when they were kids. They'd grown up around the ovens, the proving room where yeast breads rose, and the front of the shop where customers lined up every morning to buy the day's special.

Mia's mom's family was Italian and English, which explained why their dessert menu was so eclectic. The Harper sisters had grown up making those treats and experimenting with new dishes.

Now, the sisters had serious plans for growth. Not only to open another bakery, but they wanted to start a traditional British tea shop as well.

But that was still down the road, Mia thought. She had her life to straighten out first and she couldn't move forward with any of those plans until she'd put her marriage—and Sam—behind her.

And *that* thought brought up an instant wave of heat.

Ridiculous, that a simple turn of phrase "put Sam behind her" could remind her of all those times she'd *had* Sam behind her. Her breathing quickened and she told herself to stop it. Already, she was working on very little sleep because her dreams had been filled with Sam.

Memories crowded into her mind, forcing her to remember not just the pain, but the joy, the passion, the—

Okay, cut it out.

She punched the dough down a little more vigorously than required, and automatically began patting it into a domed circle.

Lost in her thoughts, Mia jumped when beside her, Holly called out, "Oh, hi, Mr. Buchanan."

"Oh, God," Mia murmured.

Five

He was watching her, his gaze fixed, his expression unreadable.

Mia took a breath, but it didn't stop her heart from jumping in her chest, or her blood from turning into steam in her veins. He wore a suit, of course. Navy blue, tailored to perfection, with a white dress shirt and a red tie. Cruise to Hawaii or not, Sam Buchanan was the picture of business elegance, with a touch of pirate, since his hair was a little too long.

Had she conjured Sam simply by thinking about him? No, that couldn't be true, or he would have been appearing in her apartment constantly over the last few months. He'd been the center of her thoughts since the day they'd met and even going through a divorce hadn't ended that.

Mia looked up and saw him, standing just inside the kitchen, watching her. Second day of the cruise and already she was seeing him way too often for her own good. How was she going to make it through two whole weeks?

"Hello Holly," he said, then added, "Mia."

The rest of the kitchen staff simply went about their business. They were busy prepping for dinner, so no one had time to talk—well, except for Holly. Her pastries wouldn't be part of the amazing onboard menu until morning and the breakfast buffet.

Mia said, "Hello, Sam," then turned back to the rosemary dough. "You can bake it in a simple round, like this," she told Holly, "or, you can actually divide it into three, braid it and then draw the ends into a circle. Not only is it delicious, but it makes for a gorgeous presentation."

"I'm convinced," Holly said with a grin.

"Once it's risen," Mia said, "bake it for about a half hour at 375 until it's nice and golden."

"Got it." Holly tossed a glance at Sam again and Mia could see she was a little tense with her boss standing there watching.

Mia knew just how she felt.

"Let me know how it turns out," Mia said and patted Holly's arm. Then she walked toward Sam and his gaze narrowed on her as she got closer. It was as if the hundreds of kitchen workers didn't exist. She and Sam saw only each other. She wished she was wearing something more impressive than a simple pair of white shorts and a bright yellow, scoop-necked T-shirt. Her hair was pulled into a ponytail and she wore a pair of black sneakers that were now dusted with flour. Damn it. He looked like an ad in *GQ* and she looked...well, like *her*.

She could have sworn she actually felt her skin sizzle

under that stare of his. But she wouldn't let him know it. She stopped right in front of him and keeping her voice low, said, "You're making Holly and probably everyone else in here a little nervous."

One eyebrow winged up and he shot a quick look around the room as if to see for himself that she was right. Shrugging, he said, "I didn't come here for them. I came to talk to you."

"How'd you know I was here?" And she'd thought her hiding place would see her through this cruise.

"It's my ship, Mia," he said, his gaze boring into hers. "I know everything that happens on it."

"Right." Someone had tipped him off. How nice to be a god in your own little world. She sighed. "Okay, you found me. Let's take this somewhere else, all right?"

Mia headed out the door and into the main dining hall. Scores of tables were set up, each of them covered in pristine white cloths. Waiters were already hustling around the room, setting up carafes of ice water while others placed water and wineglasses at every setting.

She didn't have to look behind her to know he was hot on her heels. Mia *sensed* his presence. The man was a force of nature. At least that's how it had always seemed to Mia. Her very own, personal Category 5 hurricane.

He had swept into her life and turned everything upside down. And even when he had left her, there was rubble in his wake.

Through another door and they were outside on Deck Two and the wind slapped at her. Mia turned her face into the cold, salty sting of it, hoping it would clear her mind. She walked to the railing, looked out at the choppy sea, then turned to Sam as he moved up beside her.

"Why were you looking for me?"

"Just wanted to talk to you."

"The papers?" she asked. "Did you sign them?"

"No."

She sighed again. Why was he making this so much harder than it had to be? "Fine. What is it, then?"

"Wanted to tell you that I spoke to your parents."

She laughed shortly, imagining just how that conversation had gone. Her parents were still furious with Sam and nothing Mia had said so far had done a thing to cool them down. She knew why, too. Her folks had welcomed Sam into their family. He'd been one of them. Then he'd walked away. From her. From the whole family. And the hurt was as real as the anger.

Maybe she hadn't been able to cool them down because *she* hadn't cooled off, either.

"Well," she said wryly, "I bet that was fun."

He rolled his shoulders, as if he were shrugging off a heavy weight. "Yeah, it was a party." He scowled, then said, "Look, I talked to them because I wanted to give them a heads-up about the storm we might run into tonight."

She blinked at him. Mia had been through storms at sea before and it was never fun. And having a storm so early on the cruise was harder still, because the passengers weren't even accustomed to being on the ship yet— let alone having to deal with high waves and seasickness. "Really? Second night at sea and a storm?"

"Yeah, I know." The wind ruffled his hair and he pushed it off his forehead impatiently, only to have it tossed there again. "We might miss it, but the way this day's going, I think we'll hit it dead-on."

He stared into the distance as if searching for its arrival on the horizon.

"Are you worried?" Mia knew that was a pointless question. Even if he were worried, he'd never admit it. Sam was a man who always projected an aura of calm command.

"No," he said, quickly. "And if it looks like a sure thing, we'll give the other passengers fair warning. But I wanted to tell you and your folks first."

"I appreciate that." She looked up into his eyes and told herself that the coolness reflected there didn't bother her a bit. That was a lie, of course. But then, she was lying to herself about Sam a lot these days. "Now, I'm going to go talk to Maya and Joe, tell them about the storm, so they're prepared just in case."

"That's fine. Just don't tell anyone else," Sam said. "Not yet."

"I won't," she said. "After I talk to my sister, I'm taking Charlie and Chris to the pool. I told them I'd swim with them this afternoon, so their mom and dad can have some time alone."

"Right." He nodded. "They probably need the break from the kids."

Mia cocked her head to one side. "You know, they actually like their children. Most people do."

"Not all," he muttered darkly. His eyes instantly shuttered and Mia recognized the look. Sam was shutting her out of his past, out of whatever it was that had made him so determined to go through his life alone.

She had tried for nearly a year to get past the walls he'd built around himself and hadn't succeeded. Maybe if she had, none of this would be happening. Regret and hurt rose up inside her and Mia had to choke it down.

He stepped aside so she could move past him, then he caught her upper arm and held her in place. "Mia..."

One touch and she was on fire. Mia really resented that he had that power over her. She looked from his hand to his eyes and when he immediately released her, she was sorry for that too. The silky burn of his fingers on her skin remained though, as if to taunt her.

"Was there something else, Sam?"

He looked as though he wanted to say more, but a moment later, he clamped his lips together and shook his head. "No. It's nothing."

Mia's breath caught in her throat and her heartbeat hammered. Standing this close to him was unnerving. She wondered idly if it would always be that way. Would she, in thirty years, run into Sam somewhere, shake his hand and instantly dissolve into a needy puddle?

That thought brought a sting of tears she didn't want to shed. Thirty years without Sam? When she'd been without him for only a few months and already his loss was tearing her apart? How would she ever go the rest of her life without seeing him? Being with him?

By building the kind of life you want, she reminded herself.

And that started in January. All she had to do was get him to sign the papers, survive the rest of this cruise and then she'd be free and clear to begin the journey she'd mapped out for herself.

"Well then. Like I said," Mia whispered, "thanks for the warning about the storm." She left quickly, because if she didn't, she might not leave his side at all.

And where would that get her?

Of course they hit the storm.

Alone, Sam told himself he should have proposed his 'deal' to Mia when he'd talked to her last. He'd thought about it, but the timing had felt…off. And now, that deal had to be put on the backburner.

"Have to give Kira a raise," Sam muttered. "She called it right down to the hour."

At seven, the first of the heavy waves began to push at the ship, as if trying to turn it around. But the Captain was experienced and one of the best in the world—Sam knew this because he and his brother Michael only hired the best. The ship pushed on and the sea fought them for every mile.

The sky shattered with crashes of thunder and splinters of lightning, illuminating the waves and the empty decks of the ship. The crew were hustling, checking on the passengers, and helping to keep everyone calm, by singing Christmas carols in the dining hall. The youth counselors were keeping the kids busy with games and crafts. For those passengers who'd elected to stay in their suites, their bedroom stewards were doing all they could to help.

Sam spent most of the early evening up on the bridge, where he could watch his employees defy the storm as the ship punched right through the middle of it. By midnight, the waves were a little higher, the decks a little emptier and Sam was tired of being shut up on the computerized bridge that looked futuristic enough to be a spaceship.

Braving the howling wind and the cold sea spray jetting up when wave met hull, Sam stalked the decks, doing his own wellness check. Walking wasn't easy and more than once, he had to make a grab for the railing. But he'd grown up around ships, so he was more than prepared to deal. He didn't run into another soul until he came around the corner on Deck Two, where ordinarily, lines of chaise lounges were set out, tempting passengers to stretch out and enjoy being waited on while they took in a spectacular view.

Now though, the lounges had been folded up and stowed away for safety. It was like a ghost ship—there was only the storm and Sam.

Then he saw her.

His heart leaped. His body burned and he knew that the backburner thing was done. Just one look at her and Sam was in a tangle of need and emotions that both confused and aroused him.

Mia was at the rail. Her hair was a twisted tangle in the wind and she wore jeans, sneakers and a windbreaker that probably wasn't doing much good.

Irritated that she was out by herself in a storm, all he could think was, she might be swept overboard and no one would know it until it was far too late to save her. That thought and the resulting images that appeared in his mind made his blood run cold. With the thought of losing her at the forefront of his mind, Sam stalked to her side and grabbed her arm.

Mia jumped, startled. "Damn it, Sam! You scared the crap out of me!"

"Good," he retorted. "Then we're even. Hell, when I saw you standing out here it damn near stopped my heart. What are you doing out here in this storm?"

"I like it," she said, then pulled her arm from his grasp and turned her back on him as if expecting him to turn around and leave her there alone.

Not going to happen.

He grabbed her again. Hell, the wind was strong enough to pick her up and toss her over the railing. "If you went overboard in this storm, no one would even notice until it was too late to save you."

"I'm not a complete idiot, Sam," she said, not bothering to turn her head to look at him. "I'm not going to fall overboard."

"Yeah, nobody *plans* to fall."

"Honestly," she snapped, finally looking up at him and tugging her arm free again. "I'm not your responsibility. Don't you have something more important to do?"

"Not at the moment," he said, glancing around the empty deck. Close to midnight, the night was quiet but for the thunderous slap of waves against the hull and the now distant growl of thunder. Deck lights threw puddles of lamplight into the darkness, illuminating the deck enough that any late-night wanderer would be safe. When they weren't in a storm.

"I couldn't stay in our suite any longer." She raised her voice to be heard over the cacophony going on around them. "You know I love a storm. At least you should know it."

"I do," he said. And memories crowded his mind. Any time a storm blew in off the ocean, Mia would head out to the balcony off the condo living room to watch it. Most women he'd known worried about their hair, their makeup, but Mia walked into the rain and the wind and never cared what she looked like. Which only made her more beautiful.

And he remembered a night like this one when they were on a cruise to Bermuda. They'd stayed on their private deck and let the storm howl around them like a living thing. They'd laughed like fools as the sea spray and rain soaked them and then the laughter had ended when they made love right there on the rain-slicked private deck.

His body twisted tight and hard and he nearly groaned

at the ache that settled on him. That night, Mia had said that the storm was magic—but Sam had always believed that *she* was the magic. Letting her go had been the hardest thing he'd ever done. But if he'd known, even then, that staying with her would have dimmed that magic and he couldn't take the thought of that. He didn't know how to be what she wanted him to be. So for her sake, he'd let her go.

"It's still dangerous, Mia."

"I'll risk it, Sam."

Hardheaded woman. Why did he like that so much? "You should head back to your suite."

"Are you?"

"No, but it's my ship. I want to check a few things."

"Isn't that your crew's job?"

There was an old argument. She'd always believed that he should delegate more. "They're busy. Why are you out here, anyway?"

"I told you, I like storms." When he only stared at her, she blew out a breath, curled her fingers around the top rail and said, "Well, the boys got seasick—though I think it had more to do with the gallons of hot chocolate they had after dinner than the rocking of the ship. That was an ugly hour or so." She grimaced. "Anyway, Maya was cleaning up and then she got sick. Between the ship rocking and the boys—well, another ugly hour. Joe put the boys in my bedroom so Maya could rest and I moved out to the couch to sleep."

"You're going to sleep on the couch?" The sofas were nice, top grade, but sleeping on one wasn't the best idea.

She shrugged. "It's not that bad. So far. Ask me at the end of the cruise. Anyway, I couldn't sleep with all the moaning going on, so I came out here to be *alone*."

He ignored that not-too-subtle hint, because Sam wasn't about to leave her alone on deck in a storm. "I can have maintenance go to their suite and clean things up."

She tipped her head to one side and looked at him. "Thanks. But not necessary. Our Bed Steward, Robert, helped Joe and I clean things up and most of the misery was over before I left…"

Sam made a mental note to give Robert a bonus. It sounded like he'd earned it. "You don't have to sleep on the couch, Mia."

"Well, it's better than the floor," she said on a half laugh. "And it's not the first time I've slept on a couch."

"No." He took her arm and turned her to face him. The wind buffeted them and sea spray soaked the air from the incessant crashing of the waves against the hull. Her long red hair was tangled and wet. Droplets of water clung to her cheeks and her green eyes were like a forest at twilight in the shadows.

Sam didn't want to feel this need for Mia clawing at his insides. But he didn't know how to make it stop— and even if he could, Sam knew deep in his soul, that he would miss it if it ever ended. What he felt for Mia was unlike anything he'd ever known before and maybe, he thought, that's part of why he'd had to walk away.

It seemed though, that desire for Mia was simply inevitable. She'd had this effect on him from the first moment he'd met her. Nothing had changed. Leaving her hadn't done it. A divorce wouldn't do it. Mia was his wife. Mia was the woman he wanted.

The one he couldn't have once this cruise was over.

His 'plan' rolled through his mind and he smiled to himself. The situation Mia found herself in right now, could feed directly into that plan of his. Now, his idea didn't only benefit him—but her, too.

"You don't have to sleep on a couch, Mia—"

"Well," she said, "I'm not staying in my parents' suite. What if they get frisky? I can't hear that."

"Yeah, I don't want to think about that either," he said. "And I have a solution. You can stay in my suite."

The ship rose up on a wave, then slapped down, making her stagger forward. She slapped both palms on his chest to steady herself. Sam's heartbeat jumped into overdrive.

As if she knew what he was feeling, she shook her head and said, "Oh, no. That is so not a good idea."

"What's the matter?" he asked, a smile curving his mouth. "Don't trust yourself around me?"

"Hah!" She grinned and shook her head. "You would think that, but no."

He didn't believe her. Even over the roar of the storm, he could hear her short, sharp breaths. "Then what's the problem?"

"We're divorced, Sam."

"Not yet."

"Not officially," she amended, shaking her head. "But still."

"It's a two-bedroom suite," Sam reminded her, his voice compelling. "You'd have your own room." *However briefly.*

As if she'd heard his thoughts, she snorted. "And how long would that last?"

"As long as we need it to."

"So," she said, "ten seconds?"

He grinned. "I think it's a great idea."

"Of course you do," she countered, shoving her wet hair off her face.

"Think about it." Sam kept his gaze fixed on hers and he could see, even in the dim light, that in spite of her arguments, she was tempted.

Damn, he'd missed this. Just talking to her. Standing so close to her that he could see her pulse pounding. Looking into green eyes that danced with magic or flashed with fire. He hated that he still missed her. Hated knowing that he probably always would.

He leaned one hip against the railing. Below him, the ocean churned, crashing against the boat. "If you were staying in my suite, Maya and Joe would have a room to themselves..."

"Yes, but—"

"Maya could probably use the break..."

She laughed. "Now you want to do Maya a favor?"

He shrugged. "I'm a great human being."

"Sure." Shaking her head, she looked out to the sea again, so Sam couldn't read her eyes. But he heard the indecision in her voice when she said, "Us sharing a suite would just create more problems, Sam."

"How? Like you said, we're already divorced. What else could go wrong?"

She looked at him. "You know exactly what."

"So again. Don't trust yourself?"

"It's not me I don't trust."

He slapped one hand to his chest and feigned innocence. "Hey, I'm a boy scout."

"Not how I remember it," she muttered.

Sam grinned. He knew how to manage a negotiation and the first step was always, don't show how much you want something. So he'd back off. For now. Let her think about his offer for a couple of days. Always allow the target to think they were in charge. Even when in reality it was Sam's game.

"Think about it, Mia. A room to yourself. Gotta be better than the couch in Maya's suite..."

Shaking her head, she stepped back and looked up at him. "You're doing this on purpose."

"Damn straight."

"Well, that's honest at least."

"It's a new thing I'm trying." He ran his fingertips down the length of her arm.

She shivered and said, "You're staring at me."

"Yeah," he said, moving in closer.

"You're going to kiss me." Her tongue swept her bottom lip and sent a shot of fire racing through him.

"Yeah," Sam said. "You have a problem with that?"

"No." She shook her head slowly for confirmation and added, "I should, but I really don't."

"Good to know." He took her face between his palms, let his gaze slide over her features, painting new memories in his mind. The curve of her cheek, the sigh of her breath, the dip in her top lip that made him want to bite it.

Slowly, so slowly it ached inside him, Sam lowered his head and slanted his mouth over hers. That first taste of her filled his head, his body. She swayed against him and Sam held onto her as if it meant his life. And maybe it did. Because kissing her, feeling her kiss him back, made his heart jolt in his chest as if he were being electrocuted. Every cell in his body sparked into life and hunger for her grew.

Mia wrapped her arms around his waist and he threaded his fingers through her hair, holding her head still. His tongue danced with hers, their breaths mingled, becoming one, then sliding apart again, separate but joined, apart but together.

Seconds ticked into minutes that flew past and at the same time seemed to last forever. And when he finally lifted his head to look down at her, the wind died, the thunder stopped and it felt as if the world was holding its breath while a different storm raged between them.

"This is crazy, Sam," she whispered.

"I don't care," he admitted.

Six

Mia didn't care, either.

Crazy or not, she wanted Sam so badly, it was all she could think about. All she could see. Her hand in his, she held on as he practically ran to the stairs leading up to his suite.

The ship rose and fell with the still roiling waves and Mia hardly noticed.

At the top of the stairs, Sam stopped and took the card key from his shirt pocket. Mia shifted from foot to foot—edgy, needy and well beyond trying to hide what she was feeling.

"Hurry, hurry…"

He shot her a fast look, grinned and quickly slid the key card in and out. The door clicked open and he stepped inside, pulling her in behind him. The room was dark, with only the palest of light streaming through the wall of windows, displaying the stormy ocean beyond the safety of the ship.

She didn't care. She didn't need light. She needed *him*.

"Now, Sam," she whispered, "*now.*"

"You got that right," he muttered and yanked her into his arms. Burying his face in the curve of her neck, he kissed her throat, tasted the pounding pulse point there and Mia let her head fall back on a sigh of pleasure.

It had been so long. Too long since she'd felt his hands and mouth on her.

He lifted his head long enough to claim her mouth with his and when their tongues tangled together, Mia was lost. She met him, stroke for stroke, as he walked her backward until her back slammed against the closed door. He broke their kiss as his hands moved up and down her body, cupping her breasts, sliding down to cover her core until Mia writhed against him, arching into his touch.

It wasn't enough.

"Damn it," she whispered, "we weren't supposed to do this."

"Baby," he countered with a half smile, "we were *born* to do this."

Hard to argue.

She unbuttoned his shirt and slid her palms across the broad chest she remembered so well. He hissed in a breath and she smiled to herself, loving that he was as affected as she was. He was beautiful. Muscled, tanned, and so strong, he took her breath away.

"That's it," he muttered, lifting his head to look into her eyes. "Clothes off."

"Oh yeah." She pushed at his shirt, dragging it off his shoulders and he did the same for her, tearing off her windbreaker and then the shirt she wore beneath it.

Then his clever hands unhooked the front closure of her bra and a heartbeat later, his palms were covering her breasts. She hissed in a breath and let it slide from her lungs. "Sam…"

His thumbs and forefingers tweaked and pulled at her nipples until Mia whimpered and bit down on her bottom lip to keep from moaning. "That feels so good," she said brokenly.

"Tastes even better," he assured her and bent his head to pull one erect nipple into his mouth. His lips and tongue and teeth pulled at that sensitive bud and Mia was helpless against the onslaught of sensation.

She held his head to her with one hand when he suckled her and she felt that pull deep into her center. Mia licked her lips, watched him sucking her nipple and whispered, "You're killing me."

"No," he murmured against her skin, then lifted his head again to look at her. "I want you alive and screaming my name."

"Good chance of that," she admitted and swallowed hard as one of his hands dropped to the unbuttoned waistband of her jeans and shoved them and her black panties down. Instantly, she stepped out of them, kicked her jeans and panties aside and gave him free rein over her body. His palm covered her heat, his thumb rubbing, rubbing over that tiny bud of coiled need until she groaned aloud and swiveled her hips against his hand.

While he stroked her into mindlessness, she quickly undid Sam's pants, then freed him, curling her fingers around the hard, thick length of him. Sam growled and she smiled to herself, loving the power she had over this strong man. She stroked him, rubbed the tip of him and listened to the harsh, fast breaths that shot from his lungs.

Mia trembled from the need coursing through her. Hearing his response to her, seeing it reflected in his eyes, fed the desire consuming her. And every time he touched her, that pounding drive inside hammered harder, faster.

He dropped both hands to her butt and lifted her off her feet. A rush of fresh excitement slammed through her as she wrapped her legs around his hips and felt his erection brush against her core.

"We're not going to make it to the bedroom this time," Sam murmured.

"Not even close," she agreed and gasped when he pushed himself inside her.

This was what she'd needed. What she'd missed so desperately for the last few months. The way Sam filled her. The way their bodies fit together—as if they were each the missing part of the other.

Mia took a breath and held it, savoring the feel of Sam buried so deeply within her. It was, as it always had been, *magic.* Then he moved and she moaned, letting him hear what he was doing to her. The amazing friction of bodies sliding together. His fingers curled into her butt hard enough to leave imprints on her skin. His breath filling her lungs as he kissed her again, driving his tongue into her mouth, claiming everything she was, silently demanding she hold nothing back. And she didn't. Mouths fused, they tormented each other with the tangle of tongues, the rasping breaths that slid from one to the other of them.

Her hands moved over his back, her nails dragging across his skin and he shuddered as a groan rolled from his throat. His hips rocked hard against her, pushing his erection deep inside. She wiggled against him, wanting more of him. "Harder, Sam. Harder."

"Hold on, honey," he said and quickly set a rhythm that she fought to match.

Desperation fueled his moves and her reaction. There was so much here, so much she'd missed. This was the danger with Sam. That she'd never felt like this with any other man. He was the only one who could make her experience the physical and emotional at the same time.

Again and again, he rocked in and out of her body, pushing her higher than she'd ever been before. Her heels were locked at the small of his back and she pulled him closer, silently demanding more of him.

The low tingle of expectation erupted at her core and Mia chased it, knowing what was waiting for her. She wanted it. Wanted him. He kept her racing toward completion, not giving her a chance to think, hardly allowing her time to breathe. And she didn't care. Who needed to breathe when there was so much more?

His fingers dug into her butt and she squirmed against him. "Sam… Sam…"

"Come on baby, go over," he whispered, staring into her eyes as he claimed her over and over. "Let me watch you. Let me see your eyes."

She wanted him to see what he did to her. Wanted him to know what she was feeling. Mia met his gaze, and held nothing from him. For this moment, all that mattered was Sam and what he was doing to her. She read her own need in his eyes and that was all she needed to finally rush toward the cliff's edge and eagerly jump over.

Mia screamed his name and held onto him tightly as her body exploded from the inside out. Wave after wave of pleasure rocked her, taking her beyond what she thought she could stand, forcing her to feel more and more.

She clung to him, the only stable point in a suddenly upside-down universe. Mia had missed him so much. Missed these moments. The touch of his hand, the warmth of his mouth and the incredible explosions of sheer pleasure that they shared.

Moments, hours, *years* later, Sam finally let go, gave himself up to the same release she'd just experienced, and Mia tightened her grip on him. Holding him to her, loving the way his body bucked and how his eyes went dark, nothing there but the glint of passion.

He called out her name as she held him and locked together, they slid down the other side of need.

When his head cleared, Sam looked into Mia's eyes and gave her a smile. Their bodies were still joined together, and the hum of release was still swimming through his veins. Being with Mia again smoothed out every jagged edge inside him. Sam felt as if after months of being stranded in the icy cold, he'd somehow found his way to a fire that warmed every inch of his body and soul.

And need erupted inside him again. He knew he'd never have enough of her. Be close enough to her.

His hands cupped her behind and his dick jumped to life inside her. "That was…"

Mia took a deep breath. "Yeah, it really was."

"But I'm not done," he admitted, leaning toward her to kiss her once, twice. He wanted more of that fire. The welcoming heat.

When he pulled his head back, she licked her lips, as if savoring the taste of him. And again, his dick reacted.

"I should go," Mia said softly and he felt a sharp stab of disappointment. That lasted only a moment though, before she said, "But I'm not going to. Because I'm not done, either."

"Thank God," Sam murmured and tightened his grip on her, easing her away from the wall.

She laughed and the shuddering of her body sent jolts of new pleasure through his. "I can walk, Sam."

"Yeah, but I like you just where you are."

"Hard to argue," she said as he headed across the darkened room to the master suite. Wiggling against him, she moaned softly at the resulting buzz of sensation.

"You keep that up, we're not going to make it to the bedroom this time, either," he warned.

"Right." She nodded solemnly, then grinned. "So hurry up."

"Yes, ma'am."

Sam had always liked that about Mia. She had no problem letting him know how much she enjoyed sex. How willing she was to try anything.

Instantly, his memories filled with images of her in his bed, against a wall, on the floor, on his kitchen's granite countertops, laid out like a goddess waiting to be adored. And he'd done his best. That night stood out in his mind and had haunted him ever since they'd split up.

It hadn't lasted. He'd lost her. Lost everything because as amazing as the sex was between them, it hadn't been enough to keep them together. But this time with her was something different. Impermanent. Perfect. And he wasn't about to question it.

Now he had her to himself again and he didn't want to

waste a second of it. Sam pushed through the open door to his bedroom, stalked across the floor and then laid her down on the king-sized mattress. They were still joined and he didn't want to break that bond, but he did anyway. It almost killed him to pull free of her body and hearing her groan of disappointment didn't help any.

"Don't," she whispered, lifting her hips, letting him see her need. "Be inside me, Sam. I need you inside me."

"I need that too, Mia," he assured her, then went up on his knees and leaned over her.

He dropped his head to her breasts and took first one then the other of her hard, dark pink nipples into his mouth. He loved the taste of her. Always had. And her scent filled his head, fogging his brain as he inhaled her deeper, making that scent a part of him.

Mia held his head to her breast and arched her back, moving into him and when he suckled her, she gasped. His dick aching, his blood pumping, he forced himself to slow down. To appreciate everything about her that he'd missed.

Her skin was so soft, her body so curvy and lean at the same time. And so willing. So eager.

He trailed his mouth down her rib cage, across that flat abdomen of hers and down to her center.

"Sam?"

"I'm hungry for you, Mia," he said, catching her gaze with his. He paused briefly to watch her eyes flash and then he knelt between her legs, held her open for him and covered her with his mouth.

"Sam!" Her shout echoed in the room and reverberated in his mind, his soul.

He ran his tongue over her center, licking, nibbling. Her legs trembled in his hands, but she lifted her hips blindly, helplessly, trying to feel more. He sucked at the nub of sensation crowning her core and he felt her body shake. Her breath quickened with every stroke of his tongue.

Sam listened to her whimpers, moans, pleas for release and those soft sounds fed the fires inside him. He pushed two fingers into her depths while his mouth worked that tiny nub of passion until she was a breath away from completion.

Then he stopped.

"What? What?" Her eyes sprang open and she stared at him. "You can't stop now. What are you doing to me, Sam?"

"Enjoying you, Mia," he said, then took hold of her hips and with one quick move, flipped her over onto her stomach.

"Oh." She threw her hair back out of her eyes and looked at him over her left shoulder. A tiny smile tugged at one corner of her mouth and then she licked her lips again. Slowly, slowly, she went up on her knees and Sam smoothed his palms over her behind.

"That's my girl," he murmured and edged off the mattress, pulling her along with him. When he was standing behind her, he held onto her hips and drove himself inside her.

Mia tipped her head back, pushed hard against him and moved in time with the rhythm he set. Back in her heat, Sam gave himself over to the moment. Rocking into her body again and again, he took them both as high as they'd ever been and then went further.

"Sam! Sam!" Mia's body shattered quickly, because she had been so close when he'd changed things up. She

trembled and cried out again and now, when he was so
close to joining her, he changed again.

He pulled free of her, flipped her onto her back and
lay down on top of her. Sliding into her once more, he
stared into her eyes, shadowed, passion-glazed, and let
himself take that long, last leap into the kind of passion
pool he'd only found with Mia.

Exhausted, energized, Mia lay on Sam's big bed and
looked over at the wall of windows. She knew the glass
had been treated, so that no one could see *into* the suite.
Which made it easy to feel decadent, naked with her
lover—her husband—and displayed to a world who
couldn't know what was going on behind the glass.

She hadn't meant for this to happen, but maybe it was
always going to end here. In bed. She and Sam had always had an extremely physical relationship. When everything else in their marriage had begun to dissolve,
the sex had never lost its magic.

Turning her head on the pillow to look at the man
sprawled beside her, Mia had to smile. Even in sleep,
he was contained, pulled into himself. There was no leg
tossed over hers. No arm reaching out for her. And that
broke her heart a little, as it always had. She wished she
knew why Sam spent most of his time trying to keep her
at a distance. But his brother Michael had refused to talk,
insisting it was Sam's story to tell.

She agreed. The only problem was, Sam wouldn't tell
it. And until she knew what she was fighting against, how
could she win? She couldn't. Which was why Mia had
finally admitted defeat and accepted that their marriage
was over. Outside, the storm had passed and moonlight
was fading into the first hint of the coming sunrise. That

thought propelled her off the mattress, which instantly brought Sam awake.

"Where you going?"

She stood up and scooped her hair back from her face. "I have to get back to the couch in Maya's suite."

He went up on one elbow. "Why? Just stay here."

Mia laughed and shook her head. "I don't think so. Maya doesn't need to know what happened here."

That was all she needed. Wasn't this exactly what her twin had been warning against? She really didn't want to hear Maya on the subject because Mia was already giving herself a stern, internal talking-to.

"Ashamed?" he asked.

"No."

The one-word answer encompassed everything she was feeling. She wasn't embarrassed or ashamed or whatever else he might accuse her of being. Heck, she couldn't even regret this because she hadn't felt this good in months. Her body was loose and limber and her mind was filled with new memories that would have to last her a lifetime. Because this time with him hadn't changed anything.

"Great," he said. "Then stay."

The man was almost impossible to argue with because generally, he could *not* be budged from his point of view. That's the way it had been throughout their marriage. Sam did what he wanted when he wanted. He'd never learned to bend. To give a little.

And she needed more than that.

"I can't." She turned then and walked naked out of the bedroom.

Outside the sky was lightening and she knew that soon, the boys would be awake and Maya only moments later. Mia really had to hurry.

Of course, Sam followed her into the living room, as naked as she and so tempting, she couldn't trust herself to look at him for long.

She passed the dining table and noticed the envelope containing their divorce papers. "Did you sign the papers?"

"Not yet," he said from right behind her.

Mia grabbed her jeans and panties from the floor. Stuffing her torn underwear into one of the pockets, she pulled the still damp denim on and shivered with the cold. "What's the problem?"

"What's the rush?" he countered.

Sighing, Mia bent over to pick up her bra and shirt. Thankfully, Sam hadn't ripped her bra as casually as he had her panties. She pulled on the black lace bra and hooked it. "I have plans," she said. "Starting in January. I need you to sign those papers."

"What plans?" he asked, crossing his arms over his chest. His feet were braced apart and he stood there staring at her like an ancient god.

Her mouth went dry, but still, she managed to say, "None of your business."

"It is if you want me to sign."

Mia paused to slip on her cold, damp blouse. "Blackmail? Really?"

"Oh, I haven't given you the blackmail offer yet."

Staring at him, she said, "You're serious."

"Damn serious." He walked toward her and Mia backed up. A naked Sam was far too dangerous. "You want those papers signed. I want more time with you in my bed. And I want to know your big secret plans."

"Sam."

Shaking his head, he said, "Think about it. You move

into my suite for the duration of the cruise. When we're back in Long Beach, I sign the papers and we're done."

Her heart was pounding and her mind whirling. She should have expected this. Hadn't he been trying to get her into his suite all along? Of course the businessman in him would use whatever leverage he had to get the outcome he wanted.

"So you're blackmailing me into having sex with you to get what I want."

"To get what we *both* want," he corrected.

She could fight him on this, but what would be the point? She'd proven only moments ago how much she wanted him, too. They had a little less than two weeks on this cruise together. Was she going to pretend that sex wouldn't happen between them again? Would she pretend she wasn't going to spend her nights slipping out of Maya's suite to come up here and be with Sam, then sneak back to that couch in the morning?

Sam walked closer and Mia knew she should move back, but she didn't. It was a little late to be circumspect. Barn door open. Horse gone.

He stepped up to her and slid his hands beneath the open edges of her shirt, skimming his fingertips across her skin until she sighed with resignation. There was simply no denying this. She wanted Sam. Always would.

So if the next two weeks was all she'd have of him, then she could be called the world's first willing blackmail victim.

"What do you say, Mia?" Sam bent his head to the column of her throat and kissed his way up to her mouth. By the time he got there, she was weak-kneed and helpless to say anything but what he wanted to hear.

"I say it's a deal." When he lifted his head, she met

his gaze and tried to read everything written in those depths she had once thought she knew so well. But he was a master at negotiations and all he allowed her to see was his satisfaction.

"So you'll move in here tonight."

It wasn't a question. "Yes," she said, and batted his hands away so she could button up her shirt. Looking around, she spotted her shoes where she'd kicked them off a lifetime ago.

She walked over, stepped into the slip-on sneakers then looked at Sam. He was exactly what Maya had always called him. *Mia's Kryptonite.* Even now, all she wanted to do was step into his arms and let him carry her back to the bedroom.

"And you'll sign the divorce papers." Also not a question.

His eyes flashed, but he nodded. "I will."

"Okay then. I'll see you later." While she still could, she opened the door, slipped outside and hurried back to Maya's suite. And on the way, she tried to come up with the words she would use to tell her family about what she was doing.

By the following afternoon, it was as if the storm had never happened.

Passengers were out enjoying the pool area, the spas and the shopping pavilions on the Sun Deck. At one end of the Sun Deck, the pool, hot tubs and the swim-up bar were busy. But at the opposite end, passengers were crowded around the five food stations, offering everything from sushi to sandwiches to stuffed Belgian waffles. And the shops were just as crowded. It looked to Sam as though everyone on board ship was determined to celebrate the end of the storm and the return of smooth sailing.

He walked the perimeters of the crowd, because he'd learned long ago that the best way to learn what people thought of your business was to interact with them. Watch them with the employees, and make mental notes of where to improve.

It was a party atmosphere, and even Sam couldn't help smiling at the small group of children playing by one of the Christmas trees set up on the promenade. When he realized what he was doing, his smile slipped away. Kids? Really? What the hell was that?

Were Mia and her family getting to him?

He shook his head and kept walking, skirting the edges of the crowd, making more mental notes on the waiters, the stewards, the chefs working the food stalls. Nothing escaped Sam's attention. Not the smallest detail. Though the traffic flow through this section seemed to be working well enough, Sam realized that putting more distance between the food stalls themselves would allow the passengers to get a better idea of what was being offered.

Waiters worked the crowd, delivering meals and drinks and the shops on this level were packed with customers. He appreciated how well the Christmas-themed cruise seemed to be working. The passenger list was mostly families and he told himself that it might be time to consider adding a few family cruises to their yearly lineup.

By banning kids from most of their voyages, they were cheating themselves out of hundreds of thousands of potential passengers. His brother Michael had made that same argument many times, but Sam had never been interested. Their father had started the adults-only cruises and Sam had never seen the point in changing something that was clearly working.

But now, he had to admit that family cruises could be very successful for the Buchanans. He'd have to talk to Mike about it. And even as he told himself that, Sam realized that he never would have considered making the change before this trip and a part of him wondered why he was doing it now.

He remembered the looks on the faces of his nephews—the excitement. The...well, the *joy* and multiplied it by the number of kids onboard. Maybe it was because this was a Christmas cruise and the kids would be excited by the holiday no matter where they were, but Sam had the feeling that being onboard a ship sparked the same kind of excitement in most of them.

"Sam!" He stopped, looked around until he spotted Joe Rossi, sitting at a table with their father-in-law.

Joe waved one hand and said, "Come sit down for a minute."

Sam hesitated, trying, he could admit to himself, to find a way out. But there wasn't one. And damned if he'd go into hiding on his own damn ship. He could handle a quick conversation for God's sake. He threaded his way past the crowded tables and stopped beside Joe and Henry's. Each man had a beer in front of him and in the center of the table was a huge bowl of nachos, corn chips smothered in cheese, onions, peppers and shredded beef.

"You make it through the storm all right?" he asked, looking from one man to the other.

"It was rough for a while," Joe admitted with a laugh. "But things are looking up now." He pulled out a chair. "Sit down, Sam."

He glanced at Henry and the older man nodded. With

no way out of spending a little time with his in-laws, Sam took a seat and signaled a passing waiter for a beer. He had the feeling he was going to need one.

"Mia told me the kids and then Maya were sick last night."

Joe's eyebrows arched. "She did, huh? Well, she wasn't lying. But everyone's better today. My A plus mother-in-law has the kids in the craft room making Christmas presents and Maya's relaxing with Mia at the spa."

That explained why he hadn't spotted Mia anywhere on the ship during his walkabout.

"When did you see Mia last night?" Joe asked.

Sam shifted a look to Henry. The older man was pretty cagey and always seemed to know more than he let on. So that led to the question—*what did he know about what had happened last night?*

"During the storm, late last night. I found her at the railing by the pool." Of course, that wasn't where he'd left her, but they didn't need to know that.

Joe winced. "That's probably our fault. Between the kids and then Maya getting sick…"

Henry nodded, never taking his gaze from Sam's. "No, Mia's always loved a good storm. And living in California meant she didn't get to see many."

"She does love the wind and rain," Sam said. He remembered again how Mia would stand out on the balcony of their condo to watch anytime there was a storm. Be a part of it.

Henry leaned forward, picked up his beer and sat back again. "I wanted to talk to you, Sam. Without the women around."

The waiter delivered Sam's beer, then disappeared into the crowd again. Sam lifted it, took a sip, then held onto the icy bottle as he waited for whatever it was his father-in-law was going to say next. He didn't have to wait long.

"I'm listening," Sam said tightly, waiting for the man to come down on him for breaking up with Mia. Or for hooking up with her last night. Or for not signing the damn divorce papers. Whatever it was though, Sam would take it. Out of respect for Mia's father.

He just hoped that Henry didn't somehow know what had happened between him and Mia last night during the storm. And what was going to happen the minute he got her alone again.

"You made a big mistake, Sam."

Well, that caught his attention. Sam didn't make mistakes often, but when he did, he surely didn't need someone else to tell him about them. "I don't think so, Henry."

The older man laughed shortly and shook his head. "That's because you can't see far enough ahead of you yet."

"Henry…" Sam paused, took a sip of beer and used that moment to think of something to say. But Henry beat him to it when he continued.

"Yeah, this is my talk, Sam," he said. "So you just sit there and listen, all right? I want you to know, Emma's still pretty pissed at you."

"Yeah, I caught onto that yesterday," Sam said wryly, remembering how his mother-in-law had talked *about* him as if he didn't really exist.

Henry smirked and shrugged. "She protects our girls with everything she's got. And when one of them gets hurt, then God help whoever caused that pain."

"Yeah," Joe put in. "We've been married eight years and Emma still hasn't forgiven me for standing Maya up one time when we first started dating."

"You're kidding." Sam just stared at him.

"I wish."

"The point is," Henry said, getting both of their attention again, "I want you to know that I get it."

All right, that he hadn't expected to hear. "You do?"

"You're not the first man to have the crap scared out of him by marriage."

Well, that was insulting. If he'd been scared of marriage he wouldn't have married Mia in the first place. He was scared of dropping his own issues onto Mia and corrupting her with them. He'd wanted her—loved her—enough to try, though in spite of the niggling doubts inside him. Hell, a part of him had hoped that she would be his cure. But he hadn't been able to let her get close enough to try. "I don't get scared, Henry. And I sure as hell wasn't scared of Mia."

"Didn't say you were. Said you were scared of marriage."

"And you're wrong again. I just wasn't any good at it." It cost him to admit that.

"Hardly gave yourself long enough to find that out, did you?"

"It was long enough, Henry." Sam set his beer down and looked at the older man. He had never liked explaining himself and didn't want to do it now. But maybe he owed Henry something. "I thought it was better that I leave when I did than wait until we were farther down the road."

"Uh-huh."

There was a smirk on Henry's face that irritated Sam so that he spoke up again quickly. "Better I left when I did. Yeah, she was hurt. But if I'd stayed, it would only have gotten worse."

Joe gave a long, low whistle and Sam frowned at him. What the hell did that mean?

"So you're the hero, is that it?"

His head snapped around to Henry again. "I didn't say that, either."

"Son, I'll tell you right now, you've cheated yourself and Mia out of what you might have made together. I don't believe you've got the first clue about what you're doing here."

Sam had had the same thought many times, but he knew himself. Knew that if he'd stayed with Mia, it would have become a misery and he wanted to save her—and himself—from that kind of pain.

"Maybe not, but it's my decision. Mine and Mia's."

"No, just yours. If it was her call to make, you wouldn't have split up."

"Mia's the one who asked for the divorce, Henry."

"That's true, but I'm guessing she didn't expect you to agree."

"You should ask her how she feels about it now," Sam muttered and took another drink of his beer.

Sex didn't count.

The sex between him and Mia had always been amazing. He'd never been with a woman he could laugh with during sex. Never had a woman touch him the way she did. But that wasn't enough to build a marriage on. It wasn't enough to make up for the fact that Sam had no damn idea how to be in a relationship for the long haul.

"All I'm saying is you should use this cruise to take a hard look at what you gave up," Henry said. "And ask yourself—was it worth it?"

Sam had been asking himself that question for months. And he still didn't have an answer.

"One more thing," Henry said, his voice low and tight. "If, when the cruise is over, you can't see what a treasure my daughter is—then you sign those papers and you let her go."

Seven

While Joe and Maya's dad were having a beer, the kids participated in a Christmas-themed scavenger hunt. Under the supervision of what appeared to be a battalion of crew members, children raced around the boat trying to find all of the objects on their lists.

When that was over, Emma Harper took her grandsons to the Christmas craft room to make presents for their family. Which gave Maya and Mia time to enjoy a spa day. After facials and a mani/pedi, the twins lay stretched out on plush, luxurious chaises waiting for their nails to dry.

"You don't have to stay on the couch," Maya said for what had to be the tenth time that morning. "The boys are feeling better so you can have your room back."

Mia had made it back to the couch before everyone got up and she was grateful for that. But the truth was, Maya and Joe both looked rested after getting a good night's sleep and the boys had a ball in their adjoining room. Sam had been right about that. Joe hadn't complained about anything, but she knew that part of the reason for this trip had been to give him a chance to rest up, too.

Joe and several other firemen from his company had just returned from fighting a fire in Idaho and he could use all the rest he could get.

"Yeah, about that," Mia said. "It's better with you and Joe having your own room. The boys get to laugh and talk to each other half the night."

"Sure," Maya said, pausing for a sip of her pomegranate fizz, "but you deserve more than a couch."

"I agree." She took a breath and added, "So, I've found a room and I'm moving into it when we're finished here." Of course, she knew her twin and was absolutely sure that Maya wouldn't accept that statement at face value. Mia had been dreading this conversation all morning. But the time had come, whether she liked it or not. Besides, this wasn't about Maya or what she thought. Mia was moving in with Sam because she wanted this time with him. It wasn't forever. Heck it wouldn't last longer than this cruise. But God, she needed him so badly, she was willing to put up with the inevitable pain to come just to have him now.

Maya pushed herself up on her elbows and looked at her. "How'd you find a room? The ship is sold out. Did you toss someone overboard?"

"No."

"What's going on with you? You keep getting really quiet, like you used to in school when you were figuring out how to do something without me."

Mia forced a laugh. "You're paranoid."

"No, just hugely pregnant and out of patience. So why don't we cut through everything else and you just tell me what's going on?"

"Okay, fine." Mia swung her legs over the side of the chaise and faced her sister. "I met Sam last night…"

"When?"

"Right after the hot chocolate plague."

Her features screwed up. "Ew. Don't blame you for leaving, even if it was in a storm. And you saw Sam where?"

"Out on the Sun Deck and…"

"*And?*" Maya's eyes narrowed on her and Mia wondered why she was feeling guilty. For heaven's sake, until they were divorced, she and Sam were married. Why was it bad that she'd had sex with her husband? And why was she leery about telling Maya?

"And we went back to his suite."

"God. You had sex, didn't you?" Maya struggled to sit up and lost. The mound of her belly kept getting in the way. She held out one hand to her sister and Mia stood up, grabbed that hand and hauled her twin into a sitting position. "My God, I forget what it's like to just sit up whenever the hell you want to," Maya grumbled.

Then louder, she said, "I knew you had a *just had sex* glow and I told myself I had to be wrong because my twin wouldn't be so stupid as to waltz right back into Sam's bed."

"Not stupid."

"Just horny?"

"Maya." Exasperated, Mia sighed heavily. "He's still my husband."

Maya waved that off. "A technicality."

"A fairly important one." Mia sipped at her drink and paced the small, private room. The spa treatment rooms were, of course, luxurious and soothing, with their cream-colored walls dotted with pastoral paintings and thick, pale blue carpet. The furnishings were designed to calm, relax. But, she told herself, it was going to take more than that to cool Maya down.

"Mia, you're supposed to be over him, remember?" Maya stared at her. "We're here so he'll sign the divorce papers and let you start the life you want to have. And you're sleeping with him?"

"Not sleeping," she mused and couldn't quite keep a half smile from curving her mouth.

"No need to brag," her twin snapped. "Has he signed the papers yet?"

"Not yet, but he will."

"And you know this how?"

"He told me he would." She took a sip of her fizz to ease a dry throat. "When we get back to Long Beach, he'll sign."

Maya studied her through narrowed eyes. "Why are you so sure all of a sudden?"

"I just am, Maya. Leave it at that." She really didn't want to confess that she'd been blackmailed into this deal, because even though it had given her the excuse she'd needed to do what she wanted all along, the truth was just too humiliating to admit that she was a willing victim.

"I don't think so."

"How about looking at it like this—if I'm right there with him, I can make sure he signs those papers."

"Sure. You sharing a suite with Sam and you're going to be thinking about business."

"He'll be a captive audience, won't he?"

She wanted her sister on her side because it would make things much easier. But the bottom line was, she'd already made her decision. She didn't like sleeping on the couch. Sharing a suite with her sister and the family was harder than she might have thought. Just the bathroom situation alone was enough to make her go for it.

And she almost laughed at her own ridiculous explanations for what she was doing. The simple truth was, she wanted to be with Sam. They had this cruise together and then they were finished.

She wanted this time with him.

Still…when they were married, Sam was rarely around. He didn't spend time with her—except at night in their bedroom. So wouldn't he find ways to stay busy somewhere on the ship? Probably. But the ship was a lot smaller than the city of Long Beach. He'd have a much harder time avoiding her, especially if she was sharing his room.

"Oh man…" Maya shook her head. "This is what I'm worried about."

"What?"

"You *want* him captive. You still *want* him."

"I didn't say that."

"You didn't have to."

"You're wrong," Mia lied and silently congratulated herself on sounding so convincing. "What I want is the future I'm planning. To get that, I have to deal with Sam."

And that's all she would do. She'd already made arrangements to move her life forward. That began in January and Mia wouldn't let anything stop it.

"Look, this will work out for all of us. You guys get your own room. I don't have to stay on a couch…" She threw up one hand. "Why shouldn't I stay with him? He's got the room. We're still married."

"And Sam's doing this just to be nice?"

"You have a suspicious mind."

"I know. I like it." Maya sighed. "What I don't like is that you're getting drawn back in when you were fighting your way out. I don't want to see you crying for him again, Mia."

She didn't want that either, but she had a feeling there was no way to avoid it. So if she had to pay later for what she wanted today, then she'd pay. She'd missed him too much to deny herself this chance to be with him again, however briefly. He was worth the coming pain. He was worth everything to Mia.

"I love you for that sweetie, I really do. But this is my decision."

Maya nodded grimly. "And your plans for January? Is that still a go?"

"Yes," she said quickly. "This doesn't change that. I still want children. I'm still going to keep my appointment at the sperm bank. But I need Sam's signature on those papers so there's no legal confusion when I do get pregnant."

She didn't want to risk still being married when she was pregnant through a donor. It might bring up custody issues and who knew how many other problems. No, she would stay with Sam until he signed the papers and then she would be free to build the family she'd always wanted. If she had to do that alone, she was ready. She had her extended family to stand with her and though her baby wouldn't have a father, Mia would make sure her child would never doubt how much it was loved.

"Okay, I won't say anything else about it…"

"Thank you."

"But—"

"I knew it," Mia muttered.

"If Sam makes you cry again, I make no promises."

She'd just make sure Maya never saw her cry. "That's so reasonable, I'm not sure who you are now."

Maya laughed, drained her pomegranate fizz, then set the glass down. "Okay, I'm done. Let's go pack your stuff so you can get started on your hormonal journey."

"Maya…"

After that "talk" with Mia's father, Sam had had enough of people. He went back to his suite and busied himself with the blueprints for their new ship. Sipping at coffee he really didn't taste and staring at the intricate details of what would be the Buchanan line's first Clipper ship, he tried to concentrate, but how the hell could he?

Ridiculous. When he and Mia were together, he hadn't had any trouble focusing on his company. All he'd had to do was remind himself that their marriage was doomed and that was enough to keep himself laser focused on business. He'd known that Mia wouldn't be satisfied with a husband who couldn't give her what she needed—real intimacy. And he couldn't bring himself to tear down the walls he'd built around himself. Not even for her. They were too strong. Too implacable. But he hadn't been scared.

"Scared?" He snorted, picked up his coffee cup and took a swallow, only to gag when he discovered it had gone icy cold.

He set the cup down, pushed away from the dining table and the detailed plans he'd been trying to study.

Instead he walked to the French doors and stepped out onto his private balcony.

The ocean wind rushed at him as if welcoming a long-lost friend. The scent of the sea and the distant sounds of people having a good time reached him and Sam wondered why the hell he felt so alien on his own damn boat.

He didn't fit in with the passengers. Or with Mia's family. Or hell, even with Mia. And yet she was all he could think about. He didn't much like that and hated admitting it, even to himself. But the truth was there and couldn't be avoided.

Mia's eyes, her smile, her laugh, plagued his memory. The way she moved, the way she sipped at a glass of wine then licked her bottom lip in a slow swipe. The sounds she made when they had sex. The way her hair fell around her shoulders as if it were caressing her.

The last few months without her hadn't been easy, but at least not seeing her had allowed him to tell himself that his memories were cloudy. That he was remembering everything surrounded by some stupid rosy glow.

But being with her again forced him to acknowledge that there was no rosy glow. It was all true. Every memory. Every haunted dream. And now she was moving in here with him just so he could what? Torture himself further?

"What's the damn point?"

Sex, his brain shouted at him.

And yeah, true. But also true was that being around her now wouldn't change anything. He'd still be a bad bet for marriage and that's what Mia wanted. What she deserved. A family. Husband. Kids. And as bad as he was as a husband, Sam felt sure he'd fail even more spectacularly as a father. Since he didn't allow himself to fail, he wouldn't put himself in a position to do just that…again. Marrying Mia the first time, when he'd known going in that it wouldn't last, had been the exception. He shouldn't have done it. He knew now he couldn't give her what she wanted so why was he going to take this time with her only to cut ties and leave again?

Because he wanted her.

More than his next breath, Sam wanted Mia.

Whatever it cost him.

Whatever it cost them both.

The knock on the door brought him up from his thoughts. He stalked across the living room, threw the door open and stared at Mia. She wore a pale yellow, short-sleeved shirt with a deep neckline and a string of tiny buttons down the front. The shirt was tucked into a pair of cream-colored slacks and her heeled brown sandals displayed toes painted a dark purple.

Her long, reddish-gold hair was a tumble of waves around her face and draped across her shoulders. Her green eyes watched him and, in the sunlight, he noticed the spray of golden freckles across her nose and cheeks.

In her three-inch heels, they were nearly eye to eye and all Sam could think was that he'd always liked that she was tall. Made it so much easier to kiss her.

"Are you just going to look at me?" she asked, tipping her head to one side. "Or are you going to help me carry my stuff inside?"

"I can do both," he assured her and still bent down to grab her suitcase. He stepped back and waved her inside, then followed and closed the door behind them.

Glancing at him, she said, "I thought I'd put my things in the second bedroom."

He'd wondered if she would try to back away from their deal. "You did? Why?"

"Because we're not here to play house, are we?" she asked. "It's sex we're both after, not *real* intimacy, right?"

He set her bag down. "I think we were pretty intimate yesterday." And he couldn't wait to be *intimate* with her again.

"Our bodies, sure," she said, dropping her brown leather bag onto the nearest table. "But that's all."

"Not enough for you?" he asked, even knowing the answer. Of course it wasn't enough. The sex they'd shared when they were together had been amazing, and it hadn't been enough. She'd still wanted out. Just as he'd known she would.

"It shouldn't be enough for anyone," she countered.

"Fine. Stay where you want," he said tightly. Damned if he'd *ask* her to stay in his bedroom. "But no matter where you sleep, our deal stands."

"I won't back out. And you won't back out of signing those papers, either."

"I won't."

"Good, then it's settled."

If it was, it sure as hell didn't feel like it.

She walked to the second bedroom and stepped inside. Sam followed after her, carrying the hot-pink suitcase. He set it down on the queen-sized bed, then folded his arms across his chest and watched her as she moved about the room.

It was smaller than his suite and the bathroom wasn't nearly as impressive, but he guessed she didn't care about any of that. "It suit you?"

She turned toward him, swinging her hair back from her face. "It's fine."

Nodding, he asked, "What did you tell Maya about where you were going?"

"The truth."

Perfect. "Bet she was happy to hear that."

Mia smiled briefly. "Believe it or not, she used to like you. A lot."

Wryly he said, "She hid it well." Why were they so stiff and polite all of a sudden? What had happened to the woman who'd been completely free and open with him yesterday? Was she rethinking their deal? And if she was, why was she here at all?

"Why are you here?" he asked aloud.

"You know why," she answered. "I need you to sign the divorce papers."

"And…"

She took a deep breath and let it out again slowly. "And, because I want you. I never stopped wanting you."

"I feel the same," he admitted. Then felt as though he should say more. Should make sure she knew that whatever they shared for the next ten days or so, nothing would change the reality between them. "You need to know, Mia, and to remember, that when we get back to Long Beach, everything between us ends. Again."

Mia laughed shortly and shook her head. "Do you think I'm daydreaming about white picket fences, Sam? No. I learned my lesson. You're a very good teacher."

The expression on her face tore at him. Hurt. Anger. Disappointment, before she buried it all beneath a small smile and cool green eyes. He pushed one hand through his hair, then scrubbed the back of his neck as he searched for the words he wanted.

"I didn't set out to hurt you, Mia."

"Imagine if you'd put some effort into it," she quipped and the sting of the words stabbed at him.

"Right. Hell, I knew before we got married that it wouldn't work out. I knew it was pointless."

Pointing her finger at him, Mia said, "And that's the attitude that killed it."

"What's that supposed to mean?" He hadn't killed anything. He'd married her, hadn't he? Even when he knew it would fall apart.

"Oh Sam." She sighed. "That's so pitiful. You knew it wouldn't work out. Don't you get it? That was a self-fulfilling prophecy."

"Seriously?"

"Yes. If you were so sure our marriage would fail, then you didn't have to try to make it work. So when it ended, you could pat yourself on the back and say *See? I was right.*"

While she opened her suitcase and unpacked, Sam stood in the doorway, considering. He'd never thought of it like that before and he didn't much care for the idea now, either. Besides, did it matter why their marriage had come apart? The point was that it had and the only thing Sam was interested in was *now.*

Then he scowled again when he realized that not long ago, she'd accused him of thinking only of the now. Her being right about that was more irritating than he wanted to admit. How the hell had they gotten onto this anyway? He didn't need therapy and if he did, he wouldn't go looking for it from his almost ex-wife.

"So why did you ask me to marry you in the first place?" she asked.

"Now you want the answer to that?"

"Better late than never," she quipped. "You said you knew it would fail, but you did it anyway. Why?"

"Because I wanted you."

"Not good enough."

He pushed one hand through his hair. "I wanted..."

"What, Sam? What did you want?"

"To belong, I guess." Sam's mouth snapped shut but it was too late, a bit of the truth had slipped out.

"Oh Sam, you did belong. With me." She shook her head. "And you let me go."

Yeah he had and she had no idea how much that had cost him. Losing Mia had been like ripping his own heart out. And still he'd done it because he'd believed it was better for both of them.

"So the plan is to give me a hard time?"

Her mouth worked and her eyebrows arched. "I don't think I'm in charge of the hard time."

"Funny. But the question stands."

"Oh relax, Sam. I'm not going to torture you or anything. It looks like you're doing a good enough job of that on your own." She carried a toiletry kit into the bathroom and glanced around. "Hmm. Tiny."

"You can use mine," he said.

"Thanks. I might." She came back into the room and looked up at him. "Anyway, you barely listened to me when we were married, so why would you listen now?"

"I listened."

She rolled her eyes and he gritted his teeth. Maybe having her stay with him hadn't been such a great idea after all.

"I thought we'd have dinner on our balcony tonight," he said, changing the subject. "I'll have the chef send up his specialties."

"Oh." She bit her bottom lip.

"Problem?"

Shrugging, she said, "I already ordered an early dinner to be sent up. It should be here any minute, actually."

"Really?" He smiled, feeling better about this whole thing. An intimate dinner, just the two of them, then to bed. Worked for him. "That's great. I'm glad you're comfortable here."

"Oh, absolutely." A knock on the door sounded and Mia patted his arm. "That's dinner."

It was only five, but if she wanted dinner now, Sam would find a way to be hungry. Besides, the earlier they ate, the earlier he could get her into bed, where he most wanted her. He followed her out and saw her open the door to two crew members carrying trays. Whatever she'd ordered, there was plenty of it.

"Oh, thanks, Brian," she said. "Can you guys just put it on the dining room table?"

"Sure thing, Mrs. Buchanan."

Sam moved fast, getting to the table first and sweeping up the ship blueprints he'd been studying earlier. Two covered trays were set down on the polished teak table and then the first steward asked, "Is there anything else we can get you?"

"No," she said, "that's great. Thanks again. Oh, is Steven on his way?"

"Yes, ma'am. And Devon's bringing the rest of the stuff you asked for."

She beamed at him and Sam couldn't blame the kid for flushing bright red. "Terrific."

"What stuff?" Sam asked and Brian slipped out the door to avoid having to answer the boss.

"You'll see," Mia told him.

"Fine." Sam looked at the trays a little warily. "So what's for dinner?"

"That's a surprise, too," Mia said with a grin, then turned to the door at the sound of a kid shouting.

Sam frowned but couldn't look away. As the stewards left, a young woman in a crew uniform approached, holding two kids by the hand. Maya's kids. Sam just barely muffled a groan.

"Aunt Mia, hi!" Charlie pulled free and raced to her.

Mia bent down to hug him, then grabbed Chris close too, as soon as the young woman got him up the stairs. "Hi you guys! Are you ready for your party?"

"Christmas tree?" Chris asked, looking past her into the barren, if luxurious suite.

"Soon, sweetie," she assured him. "Now why don't we go have dinner? It's your favorite. Hot dogs!"

"Yay!" Charlie raced to the table, shouting "Hi Uncle Sam," as he passed.

Both kids raced across the elegant carpet, leaving a trail of sweaters and what looked like bits of snow in their wake.

"Hot dogs?" Sam looked at her as she led Chris to the table, too.

"I thought it would be nice for us to give Maya and Joe and my folks an evening off. We can spend some time with the kids and the adults can go have dinner together." She shrugged and gave him a wide-eyed, innocent smile.

"Uh-huh." He glanced to where Charlie was standing on a hand carved chair, trying to lift one of the tray covers. Sam moved fast. He lifted the heavy cover, then told Charlie to sit down.

"I like ketchup," Chris said, scrambling for a seat himself.

"Mine's mustard, right Aunt Mia?"

"Right, sweetie." Mia moved up to the table and set out plates for both boys and fixed hot dogs for each of them. "Here's some mac and cheese, too. Don't use your fingers, Charlie. Chris, do you want some? And we've got juice boxes here somewhere too." She lifted the other lid, found juice and glasses and ice, along with a plate of chocolate chip cookies for dessert.

Chris reached for a juice and tipped the glass over. A river of what looked like cherry juice ran across the table and over the edge to land on the hand woven rug.

Sam muffled a groan and dropped a stack of napkins on the puddle. He was not set up for small children.

"I need more juice," Chris whined.

"Sure sweetie," Mia cooed and took care of that.

Sam was watching it all as if from a distance. His personal space had been invaded by a horde of barbarians and all he could do was watch.

"Yay! Can we watch a movie about Christmas because we get to decorate a Christmas tree and where is your tree, Uncle Sam?"

Sam's ears were ringing, but he stared at Mia as if he'd never seen her before. He should have suspected something when she'd arrived. She had been too smiley. Too accepting of the whole situation. Of course she'd had something planned.

"Christmas tree?" he asked.

She shrugged and smiled again. "If I'm going to stay here with you, we need to get into the spirit."

"Mia…" He didn't do Christmas and she damn well knew it. What was she up to? Trying to drag him, kicking and screaming, into the holiday? And using the kids to guilt him into agreeing?

"Steve, the cruise host is bringing in one of the trees that wasn't set up." She paused and said, "You had way more trees than you needed, so at least someone who works for you likes Christmas. Anyway, Steve said the extra trees were stored in the hold."

"Movie!" Chris shouted and took a bite of his hot dog.

"Small bites, Chris, and chew it really well," Mia warned. Sam looked at the kid like he was a live bomb. He really did not need one of the boys choking on a hot dog.

Mia picked up a remote, and turned the wide screened TV on. She hit the right channel and played *Home Alone* for the boys who started laughing the minute they saw their favorite classic.

Then she got back to her subject as she tossed a few silk pillows to the boys so they could lay on them. "So anyway, Steve's bringing the tree and Devon, the Assistant Cruise Director, said he'd find the decorations that were set aside in case they were needed and I thought we could have a decorating party with the boys."

"I'm *good* at decorating," Charlie told him. "Can we get snow from the snow room to put on it?"

"No," Sam said and ignored the kid's crestfallen expression. Looking at Mia, he said, "You got my employees in on this?"

"Yep, and they were really great. Everyone was so anxious to help out the boss's wife."

Yeah, he bet they were. "You set me up."

"I really did." Mia grinned, patted his arm, then leaned over to pick up a hot dog. Layering it with mustard, she added, "Now all you have to do is enjoy it."

Enjoy Christmas trees and decorations and kid movies and two kids laughing and talking at pitches only dogs should be able to hear? Yeah. He'd get right on that.

"I don't—"

"Like Christmas. I know. But it's just a tree, Sam." She pushed her hair back from her face and held her hot dog out to him. "Want a bite?"

He shook his head and she grinned at him. "So the question is, are you going to disappoint the boys— and me—or are you going to pretend to be a Christmas elf?"

"Our elf went swimming in the toilet today," Charlie said around a bite of hot dog. "Chris said Buddy wanted to swim so Chris put him in the toilet cuz it's like a little pool for elfs."

"Elves," Mia corrected.

"Mommy used her hair dryer on him, but he was still wet, so he's going to get a tan out in the sun tomorrow."

"A tan," Sam repeated.

Chris piped up and added, "Mommy says elfs can't swim good so I shouldn't put him in the pool again."

"Good plan," Sam said, then took a breath and blew it out.

Elves in toilets. Christmas trees. Hot dogs. He looked at Mia and he was lost. Her green eyes were sparkling with suppressed laughter. She was really enjoying all of this. The shouts, the kids kicking their heels against the chairs, the movie turned up to a deafening level and his consternation at what had happened to his nice, orderly world and his seduction plans.

What the hell was a man supposed to do with a woman like that?

A knock on the door sounded again before he could figure it out, and both boys shouted "Christmas tree!"

Mia just looked at him. Waiting.

He could leave. Do some work. Make some calls. But he wasn't going to. He may have blackmailed Mia into moving in, but it seemed, she was getting him to do things he wouldn't normally do, too. And, he thought, they both knew it. Shaking his head, Sam said, "I'll let them in. And I want mustard on my hot dog."

Eight

Three hours later, the boys were exhausted, the Christmas tree was beautifully decorated from the middle down and the scent of hot dogs was clinging to the air.

Mia smiled to herself. The evening had gone better than she'd hoped. Even though he'd been coerced into taking part in their festivities, Sam had come around. He'd put the lights on the tree, watched the kids hanging ornaments as high as they could reach and joined them for some chocolate chip cookies during the *Rudolph the Red-Nosed Reindeer* movie.

But the best part, she told herself, was seeing little Chris climb up on the couch to cuddle with his uncle and Sam automatically wrapping his arm around the boy. He probably hadn't even noticed when it had happened, but she had and Mia was still smiling to herself over it.

When Maya and Joe showed up to collect their kids,

Joe scooped Chris into his arms and Maya took Charlie's hand in hers. Looking around at the detritus left behind by her children in what was usually a tidy, elegant space, Maya grinned.

"Seems like everyone had a good time," she said, looking directly at Sam.

"It was fun," Mia told her and bent to kiss Charlie goodbye.

"Thanks for watching them," Joe said. "It was nice having dinner and only cutting up my own meat."

Sam laughed and Mia beamed at him. Really, he'd been great with the kids and her heart was feeling so full, she might burst. This was what she'd hoped for in her marriage. What she wanted most in her life. And this, she told herself had been what she and everyone else had worried about. Being around Sam, spending time with him, had her falling in love with him all over again.

Yes, he was a little stern and so dedicated to his business he barely noticed life around him most of the time. But oh my when she did have his attention, when he was relaxed, he made her feel so much. Made her think about possibilities.

Made her remember how much she loved him.

Her heart did a tumble and roll in her chest and she knew she was in trouble. She was supposed to be here to get the man she loved to sign divorce papers when all she really wanted was for him to stop her. For him to say he didn't want to split up. That he loved her and wanted to be with her always.

That he wanted this life they could have together.

And what were the chances of that happening?

Slim, she told herself firmly. So what she had to do, was remember *why* she'd wanted the divorce. It hadn't been because she didn't love him. But because she was tired of being married all alone.

Maya's expression was wary, as if she couldn't really believe that any of this was happening and Mia couldn't blame her twin. She'd hoped of course, that Sam would go along with her plan to watch the kids and have a Christmas evening, but a part of her had been sure he'd find a way to disappear. After all, when they were together, disappearing had been his superpower.

He'd surprised her tonight and clearly her sister was a little stunned, too.

"Thanks again," Maya said, holding onto her oldest son while cradling her baby bump with her free hand. "We're taking these two off to bathe and go to bed."

"Good idea," Sam said, tucking both hands into his pockets. "We've all got mustard, ketchup and mac and cheese on us."

Maya laughed and winked at her sister. "So, a typical dinner. Good to know."

Joe headed for the door and Maya was right behind him. But when she got to the door, she paused as Charlie broke free of her grip and ran to Sam to hug him around the legs.

"Thanks Uncle Sam. That was great!"

Clearly a bit embarrassed, Sam gave the boy an awkward pat and said, "You're welcome."

Charlie grinned up at him, then darted back to his mother. "Is Buddy the Elf dry yet, Mom?"

"Let's go check," she said and gave Sam a nod and a slow smile before they left.

Mia closed the door behind them and leaned against the heavy panel. Amazing how two little kids could completely exhaust you in a matter of hours. As much as she loved her nephews, she was grateful for the sudden silence that dropped on the suite. Looking at Sam, she asked, "Should we call the kitchen, have someone come and take away the trays?"

"What?" He shook his head, then reached up to push both hands tiredly through his hair. "No. Let's not. They can come for them tomorrow. I've had enough of people for tonight."

"Me too," she said and moved away from the door to walk to him. He had mustard on his shirt, dried ketchup on his chin and a stray macaroni noodle stuck to his collar. Smiling, she reached up and plucked it off, then showed it to him. "A different look from those tailored suits of yours. I like it."

"How the hell—"

"No one knows," she said. "Get too close to children and you'll come away covered with all kinds of interesting things."

"How do they have so much energy?"

"Another mystery." Mia moved into him, wrapping her arms around his waist, laying her head on his chest.

His arms came around her and he rested his chin on top of her head. "Did you enjoy all of that?"

She leaned back to look up at him. "I really did. How about you? Were you completely miserable the whole time?"

Sam frowned at her. "You know I wasn't."

"Yeah, I know. I just wanted to hear you admit it."

"Fine. Here it is then." Taking a breath, he looked into her eyes and said, "I admit it. It was fun. Watching the kids put the ornaments on the tree—" he glanced across the room to where the brightly lit, artificial tree almost seemed to be leaning to one side because the kids had clumped everything together. Looking back into her eyes, he continued. "Hot dogs for dinner. The mac and cheese was good..."

She held up the one dried-up noodle. "So I noticed."

Sam snorted. "I even liked that movie—*Home Alone*?"

Stunned, she asked, "You've never seen that before?"

"Why would I?" He shrugged. "I don't do Christmas, remember?"

"Sometimes you amaze me."

"Thanks." One corner of his mouth quirked up. "Anyway, it wasn't as terrible as I thought it would be."

"High praise indeed," she said, then went up on her bare toes to plant a quick kiss on his lips. "And now... I think I need a shower as badly as the boys need their baths."

"Right there with you."

"That's what I was hoping," she murmured, staring into his eyes.

"What?"

"I said," Mia trailed her fingers down his shirtfront. "I was hoping you'd be right there with me, in the shower— unless you're too wiped out."

Slowly, a wide grin curved his mouth. "Yeah, I think I'm getting my second wind."

"Good to know," she countered and headed for his bedroom and the massive adjoining bath. "We'll use your bathroom. I think we're going to need the space."

In minutes, they had stripped and were walking into the enormous, connected bathroom. The wall of glass lining one side allowed for a really astonishing view of the moonlight-kissed ocean and the cloud-tossed, starry sky above it.

The tiled floor was heated and felt delicious as she

walked unerringly toward the impressive, if a little scary, shower. It was completely made of glass and cantilevered to jut out from the side of the ship, so that she could literally look down at the ocean below while she showered. Naturally, the glass was treated so that the view was definitely only one-way. No one could see in. No one would know anyone was in that shower.

She turned to face Sam as he approached and her stomach jittered with expectation. There were no nerves between them. Only exploration. Mutual desire. Need.

Sam joined her in the middle of the shower, and said aloud, "Shower on."

Instantly, water, heated to the perfect temperature, erupted from six different showerheads placed at all different angles and heights. Surprised, Mia laughed and swiped wet hair from her face. "A voice-activated shower?"

He grinned at her. "Hands-free, so I can keep busy in other ways."

There were two dispensers attached to one wall and Sam reached for one of them, squirting body wash into his palm. The hot water pummeled them both as he lathered the soap then ran his hands all over Mia's body.

Slick. Slick and strong, each stroke of his hands drove her along the path she was so ready for. She rubbed her own palms over her soapy breasts then transferred that soap to Sam's chest, and smiled to herself when he sucked in a breath. Mia instantly reached for the dispenser herself and when her hands were soapy, she did to him exactly what he was doing to her.

She defined every muscle, every line of his amazing body and felt her eager response to him climb. Her right hand curled around his hard length and began to slide rhythmically. She watched his eyes, heard his tightly controlled groan and smiled to herself again.

The hot water continued to cascade across their skin and as they moved together, bodies skimming against each other, the heat in the shower intensified.

Yet it wasn't enough.

Sam called out, "Shower off," and the spray of water instantly stopped.

He picked her up and Mia sighed into his neck before running her lips and tongue along his throat. Her heartbeat thundered and her blood was racing. Sam's long legs carried them into the bedroom quickly and when he laid her down on the mattress, she reached her arms up for him.

"Just a minute," he murmured and reached for the bedside drawer. He grabbed a condom and in a second or two had sheathed himself before coming back to her. "We forgot last time," he whispered, "no sense pushing our luck."

"Right." A small curl of disappointment unwound in the pit of her stomach, but when Sam took one of her nipples into his mouth, that feeling was pushed to the back of her mind.

He joined her on the big bed and knelt down before sitting back on his haunches. Mia looked up at him and smiled as he reached for her. Lifting her easily, he settled her on his lap and Mia braced herself on her knees. She ran her hands through his still wet, silky black hair and leaned in to kiss him long and hard, letting her own need guide her.

Why was it that she never seemed to get enough of him? She wanted to keep touching him, to hold him, to have his mouth on hers and his body locked deep within.

And on that thought, she rose up on her knees and then slowly lowered herself onto his erection. Inch by tantalizing inch, Mia tortured them both by moving as slowly as she could.

Until finally, Sam muttered thickly, "Enough!" His hands at her hips, he pulled her down hard, pushing himself high inside her.

Mia groaned, let her head fall back and then deliberately swiveled her hips, creating a delicious friction that reverberated all through her. And when she lifted her head to meet his gaze again, she saw fire in Sam's eyes.

"You recovered from being tired really well."

"Just what I was thinking about you," he said and leaned close enough to taste the pulse point at her throat.

Mia shivered and moved on him again. He hissed in a breath and dug his fingers harder into her hips. Guiding her movements, he set the rhythm they danced to and she raced to keep up. Her arms around his neck, she locked her gaze with his and when the first ripples of completion gathered in her like a storm, she welcomed them.

"Let go, Mia," he crooned. "Just let go."

"No," she insisted, her voice broken, halting. "Together. This time we go together."

"Stubborn woman," he muttered and made a fast move, flipping her onto the bed and covering her body with his.

He lifted her legs and hooked them on his hips, then leaning over her, he drove into her heat with such a quickness Mia's breath was lost. Her head tipped back onto the mattress and she stared blindly at the ceiling as he rocked his hips against hers in a frantic rhythm.

Mia felt his body tighten, his muscles flex and she knew that he was as close to shattering as she was. She fixed her gaze on his again and he stared back, just as determinedly.

"Together," he whispered, through gritted teeth.

"Now," she countered. "Please, *now*."

"Now," he agreed and stiffened against her as her body splintered around his. They clung to each other like survivors of a shipwreck and when the tremors finally stopped, they collapsed together to ride out the storm.

Sam threw one arm across his eyes and waited for his heart rate to slow down to less than a gallop. Every time with Mia was like the first time. Every time with her only fed his hunger for *more* with her.

He dropped his arm away and turned his head to look at her. The satisfied smile on her face made him smile in return, though she couldn't see him. The woman was a mystery to him in so many ways. Whenever he felt as though he had her completely figured out, she threw another curveball that knocked him off kilter.

Most women he'd known would use those moments after sex to ply him with questions, or prod him to make promises he wasn't interested in keeping. But not Mia. From the first time they'd been together, she'd simply enjoyed that afterglow and had accepted what they had for what it was.

He was the one who'd proposed, though he knew she wasn't expecting it. *He* was the one who had taken that step though he'd known it wouldn't work out in the end. And now, here she was, forgetting about how he'd blackmailed her to get her into his bed and instead, enjoying this time together for however long it lasted.

"You're staring," she murmured.

"Guess I am," Sam admitted and she finally turned her

head to look at him. Her mouth curved and her eyes shone as her red hair spilled across the white pillowcase. His heart fisted as he watched her. "You're beautiful, Mia."

She blinked and he could see she was surprised at the comment. Had he not told her before? Had he kept that to himself even when she took his breath away? Was it so hard for him to give a compliment?

"Okay, now you're scowling. What's going on, Sam?"

"Good question." He wasn't sure and he didn't like the feeling at all. Indecision was a foreign concept to him. And it made him uncomfortable enough that he shifted the conversation to her rather than him. Staring into her eyes, he blurted out, "I'm curious. Why'd you want the divorce in the first place?"

"What?"

"You heard me." He went up on one elbow. "I didn't get it then—oh, I wasn't surprised by it, but I didn't understand your reasoning for it and I still don't. We almost never argued. The sex was great. So what was the problem?"

Shaking her head, she turned on her side and propped herself up. "Let me answer that with a question. Do you remember my grandparents' sixtieth anniversary party?"

Thinking about that, he had to frown. "No, I don't."

"Yeah, that's because you didn't go." She pushed her hair back from her face. "You promised me that you'd be there, but at the last minute, you 'had' to fly to Florida for a meeting with Michael."

Sam's frown deepened. He remembered that now. The truth was, even after they'd gotten married, he'd focused on the company because he'd known even then that the business was all he could really count on. His marriage would end, eventually. But Buchanan Cruises would be there forever—as long as he was a good custodian. "Sometimes business has to come first."

"Uh-huh," she said. "But the party's only one example of you disappearing without thinking about how it affected me." She shrugged, but Sam could see she wasn't taking this conversation as lightly as she was pretending to.

Then she was talking again. "You could have taken a later flight, but that didn't occur to you."

"Mia, I have a company to take care of."

"You had a marriage to take care of, too," she reminded him. "You were always so busy, Sam. If we had dinner plans, it was because you had decided that we could be together. When I decided I wanted to buy myself a car—suddenly one was in the driveway."

He remembered that. Sam had bought her a fire-engine red SUV because it was the safest car on the market. "That was a good car."

"It was the car *you* thought I should have. Even though you knew that I'd already decided to get myself a VW."

"The SUV was safer."

"And not what I wanted," she countered, shaking her head. "You never listened. You simply pushed your way down my throat, expecting me to roll along."

Sam decided he really didn't care for this conversation.

"My fault too," she added quickly, "because I *did* roll along. For a while. But being in love with you didn't mean I stopped having a mind of my own. Honestly, I think the real problem was that you never learned to bend. To give a little. Basically, Sam, I got tired of being all alone in our marriage. It's hard to be the one always giving and getting nothing in return."

He could see that and he didn't like having to admit that she was right.

"And I wanted kids, Sam," she said softly, her gaze locked on his. "I wanted a family with you—and you didn't."

It wasn't so much what she said as her expression when she said it. Sam could see the shadows of old pain in her eyes and knew that it hadn't been any easier for her to say all of this than it had been for him to hear it. He wanted to defend himself, damn it. He wanted to say that he'd known that he would be a lousy husband. That marriage to him was a losing bet right from the start. But that he'd married her anyway because he'd loved her.

He didn't say any of it though, because it felt to Sam as if he were trying to make excuses and he didn't do that. Ever. He took responsibility for his actions. Which was why he'd agreed to the divorce when she'd first broached the subject.

He'd failed. Not something he did often. Not something he really ever admitted to. Not something he was proud of. But his mistake—his duty to fix it.

"I'm not saying any of this to make you feel bad, Sam," she said and reached out to lay her hand on his forearm.

He felt that soft, warm touch right down to his bones.

"I accepted that our marriage was over months ago and started making plans for my future." She smiled. "I'm not broken anymore."

Broken.

He hated the sound of that. She was so strong, so confident, he'd never even considered that he might have the power to break Mia Harper. Knowing he had was like a knife to the heart.

The darkness of the bedroom was only relieved by the moonlight beyond the glass wall. And in that pale wash of light, her eyes were shadowed and almost impossible to read. Maybe, he told himself, that was a good thing.

When they returned to Long Beach, he'd be signing those papers, as promised. The two of them would no longer be linked, in any way. She had plans, as she'd said many times, for her future, plans that didn't include *him*.

Suddenly, he wanted to know what they were.

"You keep talking about your plans," he said, initiating an abrupt change of subject. "What are they?"

"Why do you want to know?" she asked, honestly curious.

"So, when I *do* take an interest and ask a question, you're not happy?"

"Fair point," she said and he saw the quick flash of a smile. "Okay. If you really want to know. I need you to sign those divorce papers soon because I have an appointment to keep on January twenty-fifth."

Now he was more curious than ever. "What kind of appointment?"

"At a sperm bank. I'm going to be a mother just as soon as I can arrange it."

Whatever he'd been expecting, that wasn't it. He was stunned. Okay, yes, he knew she wanted kids, but to do it on her own? Be impregnated by a stranger?

"*Why*?" he asked and sat up, drawing up one knee and resting his forearm on it. "Why would you do that?"

"Why wouldn't I?" she countered and sat up to face him. Both of them naked and not caring, they glared at each other for a long minute before Mia started talking again. "I wanted kids with you, but you shot that down."

All right, there was still some guilt left there. He lifted one hand and nodded. "I know. I should have told you where I stood before we married. It's not that I don't like kids. Your sister's boys are great. It's just that I'd be no better at being a father than I was at being a husband."

"That's crazy. You were great with the kids tonight."

"For three hours," he pointed out. "They weren't my kids."

"No, they weren't," she said. "And as much as I love them, they're not mine, either. And I want my own children, Sam. Why should I wait to try to find someone else to love?"

He didn't like the sound of that, either. "What's the big rush?"

"I'm thirty years old and I don't want to wait until I'm forty to get started. That's okay for some women, but not for me." Shaking her head, she lifted her chin, took a deep breath and said, "That's why I'm taking my future into my own hands."

"To get pregnant by a nameless guy who left a sample in a cup." He couldn't believe this. "Doing this alone, Mia? Not exactly easy."

"Nothing worthwhile is easy," she said and shrugged. "And I won't be completely alone. I'll have my family. They're all behind me on this."

He knew she was right there. The Harper family would circle the wagons to protect and help one of their own and just briefly, he wondered what that must feel like. To be able to count on people.

"Yeah. You said *children*. You're going to do this more than once?"

"Hopefully. I've always wanted three kids."

Stunned, he asked, "Have you always wanted to do it alone?"

"Of course not. I wanted to do it with my husband."

He gritted his teeth to keep from saying the wrong thing.

"But the fact that I am alone isn't going to stop me."

His brain was buzzing with too many thoughts at once. He didn't even know what to say to all of this. Imagining Mia pregnant with another man's child hit him hard, leaving behind an ache in his heart and a knot in his gut. But surely insemination was easier to consider than picturing Mia naked in some other man's bed.

He shouldn't care, either way. He knew that. They weren't a couple anymore and really—they never had been. They were married, but they weren't a unit. They lived together but led separate lives. So why the hell was this bugging him so much?

Sam climbed off the bed and stalked across the room to the balcony doors. Tossing them open, he let the cold wind rush into the room. Instantly, Mia yelped and he glanced over his shoulder to see her grab the quilt off the bed and wrap it around her. She clutched it to her chest as she walked toward him. The wind lifted her hair and drifted her scent to him and that did nothing to ease his mind.

"Why is this bothering you so much?"

He pushed one hand through his hair, then scrubbed that hand across his face. "I don't know."

"Geez. Good answer."

"What do you want from me, Mia?"

"Just what I've always wanted from you, Sam. Honesty."

"You want honest? Okay, how's this?" This idea had

just occurred to him a moment ago and now he found himself blurting it out.

"When we had sex the night of the storm, we didn't use a condom. Were you hoping you'd get pregnant then?" He kept his gaze fixed on hers and waited for the answer.

"Of course not." Her eyes went wide and in the moonlight, the insult stamped on her features was easy to read. "I wasn't thinking about protection any more than you were."

She had him there. That first night with her after months apart, a condom was the last thing on his mind. He'd been desperate to have her and he hadn't been capable of rational thought at all.

Still… "Okay, I grant you that. But you wouldn't have minded if you did get pregnant."

"You say that like it's some great shock to you. I've already taken steps to start my own family and that's why you signing those papers is so important. I don't want any custody questions later. But if I had gotten pregnant that night—no. I wouldn't have minded. Why would I mind getting pregnant by my *husband*?"

"And yet you keep saying we're not married."

"Oh for heaven's sake, Sam. I want kids. You know that. If I got pregnant the other night, of course I wouldn't care. But I also wouldn't have expected anything from *you*."

"Meaning…"

"Meaning," she said, "I would sign whatever you wanted, releasing you from child support or any other connection to my baby."

Hearing that he'd have been tossed aside once his usefulness was done wasn't easy to hear. "Just like that."

"You don't want children," she said. "I do."

He wouldn't be used. He wouldn't be discarded. He would, though, let her know where he stood on this.

Sam tipped her chin up with his fingertips. When her gaze locked with his, he said, "If you are pregnant because of that night…you might find that I'm not so easy to dismiss."

Nine

"Tell me something, Sam," Mia said, ignoring that last statement as she stared up into his eyes. "Why don't you want children? Why do you hate Christmas? You never would tell me before, but tell me now."

"Why would I do that?"

"Consider it part of our bargain," she said. "Once this ship docks we'll never see each other again. Don't you think I'm owed an explanation finally?"

"Maybe." He stared out at the darkness and she studied the tightness in his jaw as she waited. Finally, after what seemed forever, he started talking, his voice low and dark.

"Christmas doesn't mean anything to me because it never did," he muttered thickly. "Decorations…just empty gestures. Like putting a mask over the ordinary to pretend it's special even though it's not."

"I don't understand," Mia said softly, though her heart was already breaking a little.

He glanced at her. "My father was busy with his wives, then his girlfriends." He snorted as if choking out a laugh at his own pitiful memories. "There was no Christmas at my house. No Santa. For sure, no elves. The housekeeper put up a tree and some garland and crap, but it was still an empty house."

It was so hard for Mia to hear this. To imagine the boy he'd once been, alone and forgotten, watching the world celebrate without him.

"It sounds like the housekeeper tried," she offered, though she knew it was a lame attempt.

"Maybe," he said with a shrug. "But all it accomplished was defining the emptiness." He turned to look at her and her breath caught at the glint of old pain in his eyes. "Garlands and trees and all the other holiday crap doesn't mean anything to me because it was never special. Never a true celebration, so I don't have them. But not having decorations up, only reminds me of their lack. So yeah, no winning at Christmas time for me."

"It doesn't have to be that way." Mia reached for him, but let her hand fall without touching him. "We could have made new memories together, Sam."

"Empty is all I know," he muttered and looked back out at the ocean. Moonlight peeked out from behind the clouds and painted the foam on the waves a pale silver. "And trust me. You don't want a man who was raised by my father, being a parent to your kids."

"You're wrong. About all of it, Sam."

He didn't look at her and maybe that was best for both of them. At the moment, her heart ached for him but she was sure he wouldn't appreciate any semblance of pity or sorrow. And at the same time she wanted to shriek because he'd given up on them because of things that had happened to him before they'd ever known each other.

"I'm sorry Sam," she said.

"Don't want your sympathy."

"That's too bad." Mia reached up and touched his cheek gently. "Because I do feel sorry for that little boy. But now, I'm furious with the grown man."

"What? Why?"

"Because you let that lonely child decide your whole life. You wrapped yourself in the past so tightly that you can't even see a future, let alone build one."

Shaking her head, Mia said, "You should have trusted me, Sam. Together we might have found a way."

"This is crazy, Mia."

The following day, Mia's mind was still whirling with everything she and Sam had talked about the night before. And dealing with the family at the moment was dancing on her last nerve.

"No, it's not," she argued, meeting her twin's worried gaze. "And it's really not worth an *intervention*." She glanced from her mother to her father to Maya, then sat back and folded her arms over her chest.

Mia loved her family, but sometimes they didn't make it easy. Maya had invited her to come over for coffee and doughnuts—something everyone knew Mia wouldn't refuse. But when she walked into the suite, Maya and her parents were at the table, Joe had taken the kids to the snow room and Merry was on the computer via FaceTime.

They all had something to say about her relationship with Sam. But gathering everyone together to form a united wall was a little much, even for them. And all because she'd moved into Sam's suite.

"Don't think of it like that, honey," her mother said and reached over to pat her hand.

"That's exactly what it is, Mom." Mia looked at her father. In a houseful of women, Henry Harper had always been the voice of reason. "Dad, you can't really be okay with this."

He glanced at his wife, then said, "I don't want to see you get hurt again, Mia. But it's your life and you should run it your way. Your mother and sisters just want to talk to you. They're worried, is all."

"I'm not." Merry's voice came from the laptop open on the table.

Mia looked at her. "Thank you for your sanity."

"You're not helping, Merry," Maya said, then looked at her twin. "She's in love. Again. And not thinking about what that means."

Mia glanced at her twin. "I'm not an idiot, Maya. I love him, but I'm not expecting anything from him anymore." Especially after last night.

Once Sam had told her his secrets, he'd kept his distance from her—just like old times. The walls were down and now he was more defensive than ever.

"That's where you're making your mistake," Merry said and everyone looked at the computer screen.

"What do you mean?"

Sighing a little, Merry said, "Honey, you love Sam. But instead of fighting for what you wanted, you walked away."

"Um, he's the one who walked away, Mer."

"No, honey. You're the one who asked for the divorce. He just agreed."

Huh. That was true.

She hadn't considered it like that before, but Merry was right.

"If you want Sam, tell him," Merry said.

"And have him say no thanks? Yeah, that doesn't really sound like a good time."

"Mia, you don't know that's what he'll say unless you try it. If you love him, say so. See what happens. If he's not interested, you'll be no worse off than you are right now."

Maybe she had a point, but it was a step that Mia hadn't considered taking. Being Sam's lover again was supposed to be a short-time thing. She'd gone into it knowing that no matter how good it was, there wouldn't be a future for them. But what if there could be?

Maya leaned in closer to the screen. "What kind of feminist are you anyway?"

"Oh, stop it," Merry said, waving that off. "This is love, Maya, and all bets are off."

"Really? Why would you want a man who didn't want *you*?"

Merry laughed. "Since you guys called home to tell me that Sam and Mia are shacking up—I think we can reasonably assume that he *does* want her."

Maya grimaced, but said, "Okay, fine. But I don't trust him."

"Not up to you."

"It's not up to either of you," their mother said and caught everyone's attention.

Emma smiled at her husband then looked from one to the other of her daughters. "Your father made me see that as much as I want to protect Mia from being hurt again, it's not my decision to make. And it's not yours, either, girls. This is all up to Mia." She looked at her. "You know your own mind, Mia. You'll do what's best for you. And *we*," she glanced at everyone else in turn, "will support you no matter what you decide."

Quite a concession from her mother, Mia thought, then wished she actually knew what to do. That got Merry speaking again.

"Sweetie, stop thinking so hard and start feeling. Yes, you were unhappy in your marriage and I'm sorry about that. But maybe now, you're ready to fight for what you want."

"Why should I have to fight?" Mia asked. "He either loves me or he doesn't."

Her mother spoke up then. "Honey, sooner or later, you realize that everything worth having is worth fighting for."

Mia grabbed a doughnut, took a bite and only half listened as her family continued to argue and talk about her life, without *her*.

It didn't matter though, because her older sister's words were echoing inside her mind. Mia hadn't really fought for her marriage. Stood up for herself. Demanded that he pay attention. She'd simply given up on ever reaching Sam and had asked for a divorce. Sam hadn't fought either, but now, she knew enough about how he was raised to know that he wasn't used to being loved. And maybe she'd done exactly what he'd been expecting her to do all along.

Well, that was irritating. There was just nothing worse than being predictable.

"We're docking in Hawaii today, Merry," their mother said. "So we'll have a few days here and then fly home."

The trip was moving on. Soon her parents would be

gone and not long after that, the ship would be back in Long Beach and this whole interlude would be over.

Mia could either go back to her life not knowing what might have happened if she'd only spoken up. Or, she could take a chance, tell Sam she loved him and maybe get everything she ever wanted.

When his cell phone rang, Sam looked at the screen, rolled his eyes and answered. "Michael. Everything all right?"

"That's what I was calling to ask you," his brother said. "How're things going with Mia?"

There was a loaded question, he thought. Sam had been up and out of the suite before Mia woke up because last night's conversation was still running through his mind and he wasn't in the mood to continue it.

His sleep had been haunted with the kind of images that would probably keep him from sleeping for the rest of his life. Mia. Pregnant with a baby that wasn't his. Raising kids on her own—unless of course, she married some other guy and then she'd be having *his* babies and Sam would go on as he had been.

Alone. Wasn't that better, though, he asked himself. He'd already proven that he couldn't be the kind of husband Mia wanted and deserved.

"That doesn't sound good," Michael said and snapped his brother's attention back to the conversation.

"Let it go, Michael."

"Damn it, Sam," the other man said, clearly exasperated. "This was the perfect opportunity for you to get past what our dear father did to your brain and have a real life."

Sam scowled at the phone. What he did not need was a pitying lecture from his younger brother. "I have a life, thanks. And it runs just the way I want it to."

"Alone. Forever."

"I'm only alone when I want to be," Sam argued.

"Great," Michael said. "So you're going to be a man just like our father. A long string of temporary women coming and going out of your life and not one of them meaning a damn."

He didn't like the sound of it, but the truth was, that was what he'd been raised to be.

"Is there a reason you called besides a chance to hammer at me?" Sam demanded.

"Yeah. I wanted to let you know the new Clipper ship is taking shape. They've got most of it built out and it looks like they'll beat their own deadline."

"Finally," Sam muttered. "Good news."

"Even better news? They're thinking she'll be ready to take her first passengers in another six months."

"Good timing. Ready for the summer sailing crowd."

"That's what I thought. If this one works as well as we think it will, we should put the next Clipper ship on the routes leaving Long Beach."

"I think so too. Lots of people would want to take that kind of ship to Hawaii or Panama…"

"And since we agree on that, I'm going to push my luck," Michael said. "Don't blow this second shot with Mia, Sam. You don't want to be Dad, the sequel."

When his brother hung up, Sam stared out at the sea and told himself that his brother just didn't get it. But as he stood there at the bow of the ship, watching the waves slash at the boat, an idea began to form in his mind.

It was a damn good idea, too. He hoped to hell it would work out better this time—and he thought that maybe it could.

All he had to do was convince Mia.

Once they were in port and docked in Honolulu, the passengers fled the luxurious ship to explore the island. Mia's family was no exception. She watched her sister's family, along with their parents, take off for a day on land. She hadn't gone with them, because she needed to see Sam. To decide if she should try Merry's advice or not.

The notion of risking her heart again wasn't easy. Living through losing Sam once had nearly killed her. If she allowed herself to hope and lost again…the pain would be so much worse.

Still, it wasn't in Mia's nature to give up, so it had cost her to admit that her marriage was not what she had hoped it would be. But she'd finally come to terms with it and now, she was supposed to take a chance again? She didn't know if she was willing to or not.

"You look deep in thought."

That voice reverberated throughout her body. Mia's heartbeat jumped as she slowly turned around to look at Sam. Surprising to see him in khakis, a dark green, short-sleeved shirt and casual brown shoes. She was so accustomed to seeing him in a suit, she hardly knew what to make of casual Sam.

"No business meetings today?"

"No," he said and moved to stand beside her at the railing. In port, they could watch surfers and day sailors on their little skiffs with jewel-toned sails. The view, complete with huge white clouds and a heartbreakingly blue sky, was like a living painting.

"Where's the family?" he asked, and glanced around, as if expecting Maya to come growling around a corner.

Mia laughed a little. "They all went ashore. Mom and Dad for shopping, Maya, Joe and the kids to hit the beach."

"But you didn't go with them." His gaze was fixed on hers now and Mia thought that his eyes were an even nicer view than the one she had just admired.

"No, I wanted to stay here. Maybe…" she paused. "Talk to you again."

Nodding, he leaned his forearms on the railing and glanced at her. "Don't you think we said enough last night?"

"I don't know," she admitted. And that was part of the problem. Last night, he'd let down some of the walls surrounding him and maybe she was hoping he'd open up some more. Really let her in. If he didn't, would she push? Sex with Sam was wonderful, but it didn't clear up the situation either, it only confused things further.

"Well." He straightened up and laid both hands on her shoulders.

Heat swept through her and Mia felt powerless against it.

"Why don't we go ashore, too?" Sam asked. "Do the tourist thing. We can talk while we go."

Like they had before on the cruise when they'd met.

"That sounds good," she said.

"Great." He smiled at her and took her hand. "Let's go."

Sam took her to every spot they'd visited the year before. From the beaches on the north shore to the shops and restaurants in the city. In the rental car, they were out for hours, and it seemed that once away from the ship, the tension between them slipped away. They laughed and talked as they had when first getting to know each other and when they stopped for lunch Mia smiled at him and said, "Thanks for this."

"You're welcome. But it was for me, too," Sam admitted. "Seeing you again made me remember a lot of things I forced myself to forget."

She picked up her iced tea and took a sip. "That's the difference between us. I didn't want to forget."

"Didn't say I wanted to," Sam countered. "I said I forced myself to."

"Why?"

He laughed at that. "Seriously. Why? Because we weren't together anymore, Mia. Remembering was pointless. Painful."

"Was it?" she asked. "Painful, I mean."

He gritted his teeth and chose his words carefully. "Did you really believe that breaking up meant nothing to me?"

"It didn't seem to bother you," she said quietly, so that others in the tiny restaurant wouldn't overhear.

The restaurant was very small and obviously designed to attract tourists as there were grass skirts tacked to the walls and tiki torches along the patio outside. But the servers were friendly, the views were beautiful and the food smelled delicious.

"What would have been the point of indulging pain? It was over," he said, remembering the look on her face when she'd asked him for a divorce. He'd taken the hit because he'd been prepared for it from the moment they'd taken their vows. Sam was expecting the marriage to end, so pain wasn't unexpected.

"If you're so okay with this, why didn't you just sign those divorce papers the first day I gave them to you?"

Yeah, he didn't have a ready answer for that question. He wasn't even sure *he* knew the reason he'd delayed. A little self-torture?

"Never mind," she said, waving one hand in the air as if to erase her question. "Let's just have lunch and enjoy the rest of the day."

A tiny smile tugged at one corner of his mouth. "You mean, we should enjoy 'the now'?"

Her gaze snapped up to his and she grinned briefly. "Okay, yes. Let's enjoy the now."

"Welcome to my world," he said and lifted his glass of beer in a toast.

She did the same. Then there was silence for a couple of long seconds while Sam watched her, indulging himself by looking into her green eyes and admiring the fall of that red hair. Finally, he heard himself say, "Come to dinner with me tonight."

She blinked at him and he could see the surprise in her eyes. "Dinner?"

He shrugged, to downplay what he was feeling. "Why not keep enjoying the now?"

Mia looked at him for what seemed forever and he knew she was trying to figure out what he was thinking. He wished her luck with that, because even he couldn't make sense of his jumbled thoughts at the moment. But finally, she nodded.

"Okay. Dinner."

And after that, he promised himself, they'd celebrate by doing what they did best.

* * *

"Have I told you yet, that you look beautiful?"

Mia smiled at Sam. "You mentioned it, but thank you. It's nice to hear."

She was wearing a sleeveless, sunshine-yellow dress with a short, full skirt and a pair of taupe, three-inch heels. She'd left her hair down and the humidity had zapped some dormant curls into life.

Sam of course, looked gorgeous in a black suit with a white dress shirt and a deep, magenta tie.

And the setting was both lovely and curious. The Sunset Cliffs restaurant was just what the name implied. It sat high on a cliff side with a breathtaking view of the ocean and the beach far below them. The stone patio was dotted with a dozen cloth-covered tables—empty now— that each boasted a hurricane lamp where candle flames danced in a soft, warm breeze.

And at sunset, she remembered, the view was staggering as the sun turned the ocean orange and gold, scarlet and purple. She remembered everything about the night she was last here, a year ago when Sam had brought her here to propose.

She could see it all in her memory as clearly as if it had happened the night before. But she didn't look at it. Instead, she watched Sam and wondered why he'd brought her to this particular restaurant. She wouldn't have called him a sentimental man, so why?

Sipping at her glass of crisp, white wine, Mia tilted her head to one side and studied him until he shifted under that steady stare.

"What?"

She shook her head. "It's just—I'm glad you brought me here for dinner."

"Best restaurant on the island."

"And is that why we're here?"

"No," he admitted, then shifted to look out at the horizon where the sun was beginning to dazzle. "We took that trip down memory lane today, I thought we should finish it up right."

That made her sad and happy, which was just ridiculous and a total sign of how messed up she was over this situation. Was the restaurant just a memory to him?

Or was it that he wanted to experience that night all over again? Was there more to his motivation in bringing her here than he was admitting? She'd like to think so, but how could she be sure?

"Well, if you wanted to really relive that night we were here," she said, with a knowing smile, "there should be other diners at the tables."

He glanced around, then looked back at her and shrugged. "Buying out the patio just for the two of us seemed like a good idea. This way we can talk and not have people listening in."

Huh. What was it he wanted to talk about? Was he going to suggest they stay together and have those babies she wanted so badly? Had he realized that life without her wasn't nearly as good as life *with* her? Oh, Mia really wanted to think so. And in spite of her efforts to keep it in check, her heartbeat sped up, racing with possibilities.

Maybe Merry was right. Maybe this was the time to tell him that she loved him. That she didn't really want the divorce. She wanted him. And a family.

"What did you want to talk about?" she asked instead.

He reached across the table for her hand and folded it into his. "I wanted to tell you that these last few days with you have been…"

"...I think so, too."

"Good," he said, nodding, keeping his gaze fixed on hers. "Because since last night, when we talked, I've been thinking about a lot of things."

"Okay..." There went her heartbeat again as hope rose within in spite of everything.

The waiter brought their meals and Sam released her hand and waited until the man had left again before he started speaking. "When you said you were going to a sperm bank," he admitted, "I didn't like it."

She hadn't expected *that*, so she said, "I'm sorry, but that's my choice."

"I understand that." Sam lifted one hand for peace. "I do. And I get why you've decided to do it. But hearing your plan started me thinking and kept me up most of the night. Today, something occurred to me and that's been racing through my brain until I can't think of anything else."

"What are you talking about, Sam?" She held her breath because hope was a dangerous thing. Not enough hope and life wasn't worth living. Too much and you were setting yourself up for constant disappointment.

Their dinners were ignored as they stared at each other, while the sky went lavender and the dancing candle flame reflected in their eyes.

"I'm talking about what happened the night of the storm."

Confused, she asked, "You mean when we had sex?"

"Unprotected sex," he corrected.

Now her stomach jittered in time with her galloping heartbeat. She didn't know where he was going with this, but she really hoped she would like where they ended up.

"You could be pregnant right now," he said tightly.

She hadn't allowed herself to think about the chances

of that happening. Because the truth was, she would love being pregnant with Sam's baby. True that hadn't been the plan. But if she were pregnant with Sam's child, she wouldn't be disappointed. Even if it meant she still wouldn't have Sam.

"I suppose so." Instinctively, Mia's right hand dropped to her belly as if to protect the child that might be there.

"When I realized that, I decided something else." He paused, reached for her hand again and held on. "You want kids," he said. "Have mine."

She gasped. Had she heard him right? Of course she had. She wasn't deaf. She was just…stunned. Had he brought her back to this special place to propose again? To renew what they'd promised each other a year ago?

"Are you serious?"

"Why not?" He held her hand tighter, as if half-afraid she'd pull away before he was finished. He didn't have to worry, Mia thought. Now that he'd started, she had to hear the rest of his plan.

"We're still married, Mia."

"Yes, but—"

"We're good together."

"Okay…" Still confused, still hopeful, Mia told herself to wait. To keep hoping.

"So have my children," Sam said. "Stay married to me."

"You want us to be together again? To have a family?"

"That's what I'm saying."

"And how will it be different this time?" she asked.

"You'll have the kids you want."

Slowly, the air in her balloon of hope began leaking out.

"I will," she mused. "Not *we*."

"Mia, I've told you already," he explained. "I don't

know how to be a father. All I do know, I learned from watching my father and believe me, that's not a role model you want to emulate.

"I told you some of it last night. Understand that my father was a bastard and his kind of parenting is all I know."

"You're not him, Sam."

"That's the thing," he admitted. "I don't know if I am or not and it doesn't seem fair to some innocent kid to take the chance. I'm just not good with kids."

She hated hearing him say that because it wasn't true. Mia had seen him with Maya's children. And the boys loved him. Kids were always good judges of people. If they loved Sam, then he was better with kids than he believed he was.

"Yes you are. Charlie and Chris love you. So do Merry's kids."

Sam released her hand and sat back. His gaze stayed on hers. "That's different. Being an uncle doesn't require the same amount of patience and—never mind, I'm not going to get into this again."

"Afraid I might convince you?"

He shook his head. "Don't make what I'm offering something it's not."

"Then what is it, Sam? Be specific."

"It's simple. We stay married. You get the kids you want. And we go on as we were before."

And with that, she thought, the balloon was flat and dead.

"No, Sam," she said and felt him loosen his grip on her hand. "I can't do that. What we had was an empty marriage and it almost cut my heart out."

Frowning, he argued, "Come on Mia, it wasn't that bad. We got along great. We had a good time."

"When you were there," she said softly. "But you

stayed away as much as you could. Now you want to go back to the same thing that hurt me so badly? And worse yet, you want to add children into the mix—kids who would have their hearts damaged because their father wasn't fully there for them."

A chill dropped across the surface of his eyes. "I would make sure they had everything they needed."

"Except love." Mia sighed and looked out at the sunset, sorry to see the glorious colors had already faded and the ocean was going dark. "We missed it."

"What? Missed what?"

"The sunset," she said, though her heart was breaking. "We were arguing and we missed the beautiful show."

"It was a sunset," he said. "There's another one tomorrow."

She looked at him and really hoped she didn't start crying. She did not want to do that until she was alone and could really give in to it.

"Don't you see, Sam? Missing that sunset is a metaphor for what our lives would be like if I agreed to your plan."

"What the hell are you talking about?"

"If we got back together, doing the same thing that didn't work before, we'd miss the beauty."

"What beauty?"

"Of family," she said. "Of love. Of really being together."

"Mia…"

"No, Sam, let me finish." She looked at him, staring into those blue eyes of his until she felt steady enough to say, "I love you, Sam. I always have. Probably always will."

"That's a good thing, Mia."

"It should be," she agreed. "But I can't set myself up

for more pain when I know that nothing has changed. You still believe that marriage is a nightmare and I still want a family."

He leaned in toward her. "I can give you that family, Mia."

Yes, he could, but he didn't see the whole picture. He would hold himself back from her, and from any kids they had. And that sounded like an empty life.

"It's tempting, Sam. So very tempting because I love you so much. But I can't do it. I deserve more," she said softly. "*We* deserve more. Don't you see, Sam? If you had children and never shared yourself with them, then you would be doing exactly what your dad did to you. You say you don't want to risk being him, but this ...offer, is exactly that."

He stiffened and she knew she'd struck a chord. "You don't want that, do you Sam?"

"Of course not."

"I'm sorry. But I can't go back to having to fight for any scrap of attention from you. And I will not put my children through that."

"And that's it." It wasn't a question.

"That's it," she said sadly, then she picked up her purse. "If you don't mind, I'm not really hungry anymore. You stay. I'll take a cab back to the ship."

"Don't be ridiculous." He stood up, called the waiter over, handed the man a couple hundred dollars and told him to keep the change.

They walked out together—but separate—and Mia knew that's how they would always be.

It broke her heart all over again.

Ten

Sam drove in silence. What the hell could he say? He slanted a sideways glance at Mia and told himself that he'd tried. He'd offered her a life, the children she wanted, but it hadn't been enough.

The silence stretched on until it became a huge presence. A third passenger in the car, impossible to ignore and just as impossible to address.

From the corner of his eye, he saw Mia clutching her brown leather purse on her lap as if it were a lifeline. She sat poker straight and kept her gaze fixed on the road in front of them.

Man, this day had gone to hell fast.

At a stop light, his fingers drummed on the steering wheel, but he stopped when she said, "I'll move back to Maya's suite tonight."

He cursed under his breath and wished—hell, he didn't

even know what he wished anymore. All he did know was that he wasn't going to send her back to sleeping on Maya's couch. They might not share a bed anymore, but there were two bedrooms in his suite. No matter how hard it would be, being around her and not touching her, damned if she would move out.

"No you won't." He turned to look at her and found her gaze locked on him.

"Sam—"

"Let me finish." The light changed and he stepped on the gas. Steering through the traffic, headed for the port, he said, "You can stay in the second bedroom. There's no reason for you to go back to Maya's couch."

"I'll be fine," she said, her voice determined.

"Yeah, but why should you have to just be fine?" He shook his head, but kept watching the road. "You can even lock the bedroom door if you feel like you need to."

"That's not it," she argued and he believed her. "I just don't want to make this harder on either of us than it has to be."

"Right. But do you really want to talk to Maya about why you're moving back?"

"No," she admitted and her body slumped, her head dropping to the head rest. "I really don't. Not tonight."

"So stay." He felt her gaze on him and sighed. "Damn it, Mia, we're adults. I can be in the same room with you without making a move. And I think you're capable of saying no, even if I did."

"I know that. I told you, it's not about that. It's just—" She shifted in her seat so she was facing him. "I don't want it to be awkward between us now, Sam. And stay-ing in your suite, seeing each other all the time, but not being together anymore—not even temporarily—will just make things that much harder to deal with."

"Relax, Mia. If you can handle it, so can I." He scowled at the thought, but said, "We go back to being what we were to each other when the cruise started. And when we get to the ship, I'll sign the damn papers for you. Sharing a suite doesn't have to be intimate. We'll avoid each other when we can and that should be good enough."

Though he was sure as hell going to miss being with her. Having the right to touch her. To hold her.

He already felt the loss of her as he would a limb and the real torture hadn't even begun yet.

"You'll sign the papers before we get back to Long Beach?"

He threw a quick glance at her. "Is there any point in waiting?"

"No," she said softly, "I suppose not."

"Okay then. This isn't anything new to us, Mia." Though it was. Because he had offered her family. Kids. Everything he'd thought—hoped—she'd wanted. And she'd turned him down. That truth sank like a stone in the pit of his stomach. "We'll get through it."

And the silence crept back, settling down between them and this time, each of them hid behind the silence and were grateful for it.

For two days, Sam was like a ghost, slipping in and out of the suite at all hours and somehow managing to avoid seeing Mia completely. Clearly, he was doing everything he could to make it easier on both of them.

She didn't know whether to be angry about that or to leave him a thank-you note.

It was hard not seeing him, but it would have been so

much harder to spend time with him and know that now, it was truly over. But God, she missed him so much.

"He asked you to stay married."

She looked at Maya. "Yes."

"And have kids."

"Yes."

"And you said no."

Mia took a deep breath, turned her head on the poolside chaise and said, "Yes. We've been over this a dozen times in the last two days already. For God's sake, Maya, why can't you let this go? Can't you see I really don't want to talk about it anymore?"

"Well, I'm still stunned. He stepped up, Mia. He agreed to kids."

"Yes, but he didn't agree to being part of that family he offered to build with me." And that still stung.

Ever since Mia had told her family that it was really over between her and Sam, Maya had been doing interrogations that the CIA would have been proud of.

"But you're still staying in his suite."

Mia groaned dramatically. "Maya, I beg you…"

"With no fun stuff."

"None." Mia sighed. Her twin was not getting past this anytime soon. But then, neither was Mia. And oh, how she missed the fun stuff with Sam. Every time she took a shower now, she remembered being with him, his hands sliding over her skin, caressing her breasts until she was mindless with need.

But strangely, even more than the sex, she missed having coffee with him in the morning. Missed laughing with him. Missed curling up next to him on the bed—until he stretched out his arms and legs in his sleep and nearly pushed her off the mattress. She missed laying out on their private deck holding hands and watching the stars. Missed…oh hell.

She just missed *him*.

"Did you know he took the boys up to the bridge yesterday?" Maya smiled and shook her head as if she still couldn't believe it herself.

Mia was stunned. Sam had spent time with the boys without her nudging him? "He did?"

Maya nodded and added, "He even got the Captain to let them take turns steering the ship. I've got to say, I'm glad I didn't know that the boys were in charge, even if it was only for a minute or two."

Mia's heart squeezed. "He didn't tell me."

"Well," Maya pointed out, "you did say you two aren't even talking now."

"No, we're not. In fact, I've hardly seen him in two days."

"Well, the boys were so excited after all of that, he and Joe took them for ice cream."

"What?" Mia shook her head as if she hadn't heard her sister right. That was so unlike Sam, she didn't know what to make of it. And in the end, it only made her feel worse, knowing that he was so good with kids—seeing that he was good with them—and he didn't realize it.

"I know," Maya agreed. "Shock time. That's one of the reasons I keep asking you about what happened. I mean, this sounds like a man who loves you."

The surprises just kept coming. "I can't believe you're defending Sam."

"Yeah, it's stunning to me, too." Maya tugged her hat brim a little lower onto her forehead. "You know how furious I was when you guys broke up?"

"Yeah," Mia said wryly. "I remember the fury and some mention of putting a curse on him."

Maya ignored that. "What I didn't tell you was the reason I was so mad? I *liked* Sam. And when he hurt you, I was furious at myself because I hadn't seen it coming."

Mia smiled at her twin, reached out and grabbed her hand for a quick squeeze. As irritating as family could be, Mia couldn't imagine her life without a twin who was so fiercely defensive of her.

But Maya wasn't finished. "And then we come on this ship and I watch him watching you and I'm pretty sure he loves you and then it all blows up again and he still loves you. And he's good to my kids. So I'm furious all over again."

They had all been on a roller coaster for far too long. The adrenaline rushes alone were exhausting. And Mia had cried herself out so that she woke every morning feeling dehydrated.

"You really need to dial it down, Maya. I know you're upset and I love you for it, but that baby you're carrying needs peace and quiet."

"Then he's coming to the wrong house," Maya said with a half laugh.

They sat beneath a red-and-white striped umbrella and watched everyone in the pool from the safety of shade. The breeze was lovely and the cruise would be short as the ship made its way to Kauai for two days. For the first time since boarding the ship, Mia was wishing the cruise was over. But there was still a week to go before they were home again. Would she make it through another week in that suite with Sam?

Mia was thankful that their parents had flown home

the night before, ready to get back to work at the bakery. At least, she only had Maya's sympathy and outrage to deal with.

"I know you don't want to move back to our suite," Maya was saying, "and I get it, since just sitting on that couch hurts my back. But if you really don't want to stay with Sam, maybe you could take over Mom and Dad's suite."

Mia shook her head. "No good. I already checked. The suite was booked a week ago. Someone taking the trip to L.A. and then back again on a different ship."

"Well then, maybe you should take that as a sign."

"A sign of what?"

Maya shrugged. "Maybe the universe *wants* you and Sam to work this out and that's why it's keeping you together."

"The universe can butt out. Besides, I'm sorry," Mia said, turning to face her twin. "Aren't you the one who was telling me to run fast, run far from Sam just a few days ago?"

"I was," Maya admitted with a gracious nod. "And I changed my mind."

"As historic as that is," Mia commented, "I don't think talking is going to change anything."

Maya sighed. "Fine. I'll stop now."

"Thank you."

"After I say—"

"Maya…"

"After I say that I'm on your side in this, Mia."

She sighed and smiled. No matter what, she could count on her sister. Her whole family, for that matter. So she would keep doing her crying in private so she wouldn't worry them. And then on the twenty-fifth, Mia would begin her journey toward a family of her own and Sam would be only a memory.

A wonderful, haunting, memory.

"Mrs. Buchanan?"

She turned to face the waiter standing beside her chaise. "Yes?"

"Mr. Buchanan asked that this be delivered to you at noon." He held out an envelope and when Mia took it, he turned and went back to work.

"Wow," Maya said. "He *really* doesn't want to talk."

Mia ignored her, opened the envelope and pulled out the single sheet of paper. Sam's bold, handwriting sprawled across the page.

Mia—I took an early flight out this morning. I'm headed to Bermuda on business. The suite is yours, so enjoy it.

It was good to be with you again. However briefly.

Be happy.

Sam.

"He's gone," Mia whispered.

Maya snatched the paper from her suddenly nerveless fingers. "He left? Without a word?"

"He sent word, Maya. You're holding it."

"Yeah, but come *on*. He couldn't look you in the eye to tell you he's leaving?"

"It's over," Mia whispered, finally accepting that Sam didn't want what she did. Sam didn't feel what she did.

"Well, look out," her sister grumbled. "I'm changing my mind about him again."

"Don't," Mia said, looking at her twin. "Just accept it for what it is. Sam and I just weren't meant to be, I guess."

And saying that out loud ripped at Mia's heart. She'd let herself hope and even though that particular balloon was now flat and empty, it was hard to let go of it completely. But then, she had years ahead of her to face the emptiness that was waiting for her.

So she'd build her own family, love her own children and dream about what might have been if Sam had only trusted himself as much as she'd trusted him.

Sam stayed in Bermuda for two weeks. He spent most of his time at the shipyard, consulting with the builders, going over every detail of the new build.

He buried himself in work so that he didn't have time to think about Mia and how silent his life felt without her in it.

He stood at the window of the house the Buchanans kept on the island. Sam's grandfather had built the house, saying that he spent so much time there with ship builders, he needed his own place rather than a hotel. And then Sam's father had used it—as a place to bring the long string of women he'd been involved with.

But for one week every year, Sam and Michael had been together at this house. Every summer, the boys had a week to explore, to play, to be the brothers their parents had kept them from being. So there were good memories here for Sam. And he tried to focus on them, to keep the thoughts of Mia at a distance.

It didn't really work.

He hadn't expected to miss her so much. But he did. Waking up next to her, talking over coffee, listening to her laugh. Hell, he even missed how she shoved him over in the middle of the night and fought him for blankets.

And he remembered that night with the boys, decorating a Christmas tree, and how Mia had shone brighter than the twinkling white lights. For the first time in his life, Christmas decorations had been…beautiful.

Though he kept her out of his mind during the day, at night in his sleep, she was there. Always. Her sighs. Her smiles. The way she touched him and the way she came apart when he touched her. He woke up every morning, dragging, his mind cloudy, his chest tight as if he'd been holding his breath all night. And maybe he had been.

All he knew for sure was that getting over Mia was going to take years.

"You look lost in thought."

Sam turned and saw his younger brother standing in the doorway. He'd never been so glad to see anyone.

"I am—or was. Now that you're here, maybe that'll stop."

Michael moved into the main room, walked to the wet bar on the far wall and grabbed two beers from the under-the-counter fridge. He carried one to Sam, then opened his own.

"So what thoughts are you trying to get rid of?" He looked at the ceiling, tipped his head and said, "Hmmm. Let's think. Could it be, Mia?"

"Knock it off," Sam said, opened his beer and took a sip. "Didn't I just say I was glad I could stop thinking?"

"Okay, I'll think for you," Michael said and dropped into a chair. "I think you miss Mia. I think you had a great time on the ship and I think you didn't want to leave."

"I think you should mind your own business."

"You're my brother. You are my business."

"Fine. Mind a different business." Sam took a sip of beer and looked away from Michael so the other man wouldn't notice that he'd really struck a chord with Sam. "Don't you have a fiancée you could be bugging?"

"Alice is nuts about me," Michael said with a grin that slowly faded. "So tell me about you."

"Nothing to tell," Sam lied easily. He wasn't going to dump everything on Michael. There was no reason for it. He'd made his decision and like his father, once his mind was made up, there was no shaking him from it.

"Right." Michael looked around the room. "Hey. When did you paint in here?"

"When I first got here," Sam said. He'd hired a crew to come in and redo his father's office. Hell, he'd been meaning to do it for years but he'd never made the time. But during this trip, the dark maroon walls with their white crown molding had felt as if they were closing in on him.

His father had insisted on dark colors because he claimed they made him calm. Well, Sam didn't remember a time when his father was calm. Or relaxed. And maybe this place had fed into that.

But whether it had or not, Sam hated the darkness of the place, so he'd paid a premium to get a crew in and completely redo not only this damn office, but the whole blasted house. Now the walls were cream colored with pale blue molding and Sam had felt years of depression slide off his shoulders with every room completed.

"It looks better," Michael said. "Wish you looked better, too. But damn Sam…"

"Thanks." Sam sat down and kicked his legs out straight ahead of him. "Maybe I just need a fresh coat of paint."

"We both know what you need, Sam."

He sighed, stared down at the open neck of his beer bottle. "I got a call from my lawyer this morning. He says the divorce papers have *definitely* been filed this time. It'll be official in a couple of months."

"Good news, is it?"

Sam shot him a hard look. "Of course it is. Mia wants a family. Kids. I can't do that."

"Can't or won't?"

"There's no difference."

"Sure there is." Michael took a sip of his beer. "You choose to say no to something—someone—you want. That's won't. Not can't."

"I offered to give her the family she wants. She still said no." Hard to admit. Pain shook him, but he pushed it aside.

"Because she wants you, Sam. She wants you to be there. A part of it all."

"Damn it Michael, I was raised by our father. And you know damn well what a crap role model he was."

"And yet, you're letting *him* decide your life."

"Oh, that's bull." Sam snorted.

"Is it? You're walking away from a woman you love because you think you'll be like Dad."

"Won't I be?" Sam jumped up from the chair because he suddenly couldn't sit still. He walked out onto the stone patio at the rear of the house and looked out over the exquisitely trimmed lawn, the gardens and the ocean beyond.

It was paradise here and yet, for all he noticed, he might as well have been living in someone's garage with a view of a brick wall.

"I can give you one example right now of how you're not like Dad." Michael walked up beside him, sipped at his beer and stared out over the yard.

When his brother didn't continue, curiosity got the better of Sam. "What?"

"You married Mia. Did Dad ever once marry for love?"

"Well, there's our mother..." Though he'd never seen evidence of love in that relationship.

Michael snorted and as if reading Sam's mind, asked, "Did their marriage look like love to you?" He shook his head. "When I got engaged to Alice, Mom told me how happy she was. She said when they got divorced, Dad told her the only reason he'd married her was *his* father had ordered him to marry her and have at least two children. He wanted to assure the whole Buchanan legacy thing."

That hit Sam harder than it should have. He felt an instant stab of sympathy for his mother that made him even more glad that she'd finally found real love in Sam and Michael's stepfather.

"Yeah, Dad was a prince," Michael muttered. "But my point was, you married Mia because you loved her."

"It still ended."

"Because you let it."

Sam glared at him. "There was nothing I could do. She wanted the divorce, Michael."

"Because you weren't there for her." Michael took a step and stood in front of his brother, forcing Sam to meet his gaze. "I think you were so worried about screwing it up, you stayed away as much as you could. Which was stupid."

"Thanks." He had another sip, but even the beer tasted flat, flavorless. Like the rest of his life.

"No problem. But the solution here is to see what you did wrong and change it."

"She wants kids."

"You do, too," Michael said on a laugh. "You're just scared of screwing that up—and news flash, so's everyone else. So you work at it. You love your kid and you do your best. And I know you, Sam. When you do your best, you never fail."

Was he right? About all of it? Though Michael had been raised by their mother, he'd spent enough time with their dad to know what he was talking about.

Most of his life, Sam had been trying to avoid turning into his father. Yet he'd never noticed that he was nothing like the old man. Just this house was proof of that. The darkness that Sam's father had surrounded himself with had been banished for good. So couldn't he banish darkness from his life, too?

Thinking about Mia again, Sam saw her face in his mind, felt that hard jolt of his heartbeat and knew that whatever else he did in his life would never come close to being as important as his next move would be.

"She filed the papers, Mike," he muttered.

"You've got at least two months before it's final."

Was he right? Should Sam take a good hard look at who he really was? Was it too late?

He looked at his brother. "You gave me a lot to think about, Michael. Thanks."

Michael slapped him on the shoulder. "Any time. Oh. Did I mention that Mia's coming to my wedding?"

Sam looked at him as a slow smile curved his mouth. Suddenly, his breath came a little easier and the day looked a little brighter. "Is that right?"

Mia had to go to Michael's wedding.

She'd always liked Sam's brother and his fiancée was just as nice as he was. Besides, just because she and Sam were finished didn't mean she would give up her relationship with Sam's brother.

But seeing Sam. Being in the same small church

with him. Was so much harder than she'd prepared herself for.

The papers had been filed. The divorce would be final in a couple of short months and yet, love still flavored every breath she drew. She'd lived through Christmas with her family and managed to keep her pain from shadowing everyone else's good time.

But she'd gone home from the cruise once again inflating that hope balloon. This time hoping that she might be pregnant. But when that dream died, she had to accept that it was time she let go. Get ready for her appointment at the end of the month. Prepare to welcome her own child and start building the family she wanted so badly.

Sam wouldn't be a part of it and that would always hurt. But she would smile anyway and live the life she wanted.

During the ceremony, she tried to focus on the bride and groom, but her gaze kept straying as if on its own accord, to Sam. So tall, so handsome in his tailored tuxedo. He stood beside his brother and she wondered if he thought about *their* wedding, a little over a year ago. Mia did and the memories brought a pain so bright and sharp it was hard to breathe.

Of course, the two weddings couldn't have been more different. She and Sam had been married on a cliff in Laguna Beach during a bright December morning. Michael and Alice were having a black-tie, evening ceremony in a tiny church that was draped in flowers of white and yellow.

She slipped out of the church from the back row before the bride and groom had a chance to rush smiling down the aisle. She had to try at least to avoid Sam. Otherwise, she'd be a masochist.

Mia hurried out to one of the cars provided by the couple to transport everyone to the reception. The party was being held on one of the Buchanan ships and when she arrived, she saw balloons, streamers, flowers and yellow-and-white garland wrapped along the gangway.

Once aboard, waiters with silver trays holding flutes of champagne greeted the guests. Mia took one and immediately had a long sip. She was going to need it if she was to face Sam.

Flowers lined the route to the main reception, where a band was playing and every table was decorated with more flowers and candles in hurricane globes that sparkled and shone in the twilight.

She sipped her champagne and avoided the growing crowd in the room by stepping out onto the deck. Here in Florida, the weather was warm, even on a January evening, but the ocean breeze sighed past her in a cool embrace.

"This is good," she whispered to herself. "I'll have to see Sam, but maybe that will help me get over him." It didn't make sense even to her, but Mia hoped it was true.

"Don't get over me."

She took a deep, quick breath and steadied herself by laying one hand on the railing in front of her. Sam. Right there. Behind her.

"Mia—"

"God, Sam," she said, not turning to look at him. "Don't do this to me. Please. Just let me enjoy Michael and Alice's wedding and go home again."

"I can't do that," Sam said softly, then laid his hands on her shoulders and slowly turned her until she was facing him.

He was so handsome he took her breath away. And he

wasn't hers. Even the heat slipping into her body from his hands at her shoulders was only temporary. Not hers to keep.

"I'm sorry," he said and simply stunned Mia speechless.

She took a sip of champagne and let the icy bubbles wipe away her suddenly dry throat.

"You're sorry? For what?"

He released her, swept both hands through his hair and then shrugged. "For everything, Mia. I'm sorry I didn't show up for our marriage. Sorry I made you feel as if you weren't important to me when the truth is, you're the *most* important person in my life."

Cautiously, Mia watched him, tried to read his eyes, but too many emotions were dazzling them for her to identify them all. So she waited. To see where he was going with this.

He laughed shortly. "Before I say everything I need you to know, I have to tell you that you're so beautiful, it makes my chest tight."

She laughed too. Mia wasn't a fool. She knew she looked good. She'd made a point of it, since she'd known she'd be seeing Sam. She had wanted him to see her and to be filled with regret for letting her go.

She'd bought a dark red, off-the-shoulder dress with a sweetheart neckline, a cinched waist and a short skirt that stopped mid-thigh. Her black, three-inch heels brought her nearly eye to eye with him, so she could see that he meant what he was saying.

"Thanks. I bought this dress on purpose. To make you suffer."

He laughed again and some of the shadows left his eyes. "Well, mission accomplished."

"What is it you want, Sam?" she asked, bringing them back to the reason he was standing there in front of her.

"You, Mia. I want *you*."

Her heart clutched. "Sam…we've been over this."

"No, no we haven't. Not like we're about to."

She bit her lip and took a breath. "What's that mean?"

"It means," he said, with a rueful shake of his head, "that I finally understand that I'm not just my father's son, but my mother's as well. Mom got past her time with my father. She found love with her second husband and I saw it. They were happy. Hell, Michael grew up in Disneyland comparatively speaking."

"I know your dad was hard, Sam, and I'm sorry about it."

"This isn't about him anymore, Mia." He cupped her face with his hands and stroked his thumbs over her cheekbones. "I've let him go. At last. I finally get that it's my choices that will define my life. Not who my father was."

She stared up into his eyes and read only love shining back at her. Her heart started racing again and that silly balloon of hope was back.

"I want to believe, Sam. I really do."

But how could she? He'd chosen his work over her so many times, she didn't know if he even *could* change.

"Do it, Mia. Believe me. Take one more chance on me. I won't let you down this time. I'm tired of emptiness, Mia. I want the magic and the magic lives inside you. I want real Christmases. I want laughter. Joy. Passion. And that's all with you." His cell phone rang and grumbling, he took it out of his pocket and never checked the screen before he wound up and pitched it over the rail and into the ocean.

"What?" Shocked, she turned to look at the sea then back to him. "What did you just do? That could have been work calling."

"I hope it was," he said firmly and held her again, looking into her eyes, willing her to believe him. "I hate that you're surprised by me choosing you over a business call. You shouldn't have to be. You should have been able to expect that your husband—because we *are* still married—would choose you over business or anything else.

"I'm so sorry for that, Mia. Sorry for not realizing what I had while I had it."

"Oh Sam." Her heart was full and her hands were shaking so badly, champagne sloshed out of her glass onto her hand.

Sam took it and tossed it, too.

"Stop doing that!" Shaking her head, she said, "I never expected you to ignore your work. I love my job at the bakery. I only ever wanted to know that I was important to you, too."

Sam threaded his fingers into her hair and let his gaze move over her face. "You are more important than anything else in my life."

It was so hard to breathe with her heart pounding and the hope balloon swelling until it filled her chest.

"What does that mean for us, Sam?"

"It means I want to stay married. We can have the lawyers pull the divorce papers before they go through."

"Sam…"

"Stay with me, Mia." He kissed her fast. "Make babies with me."

"Really?" She blinked up at him and her eyes filled with tears. She had to blink faster just to clear them.

"I want a family with you. Maybe I always did but I

was too scared to even consider it." He bent down and kissed her again, harder, faster. "But I'm more scared of losing you than I am of trying to be a good father."

"You will be a good one," she said. "A great one."

He gave her a half-smile. "I can promise to do my absolute best. I love you, Mia. I will love our kids and we'll have as many as you want. A family with you—a future with you—is all I really want. Mia, you're all I can see of the future. Without you, I don't have one."

"Sam, you're making me cry."

"That's a good sign," he said with a grin. "I like it."

"Of course you do," she said on a laugh.

The first stars appeared overhead and the sounds of the party drifted to them as they stood alone on the deck.

"We'll buy a house anywhere you want," he said quickly as if trying to convince her before her tears dried. "Hell, we can live next door to Maya and Joe."

Now she laughed harder. "Next door might be a little *too* close."

"Okay. That's fine, too. Anything, Mia. Anything to make you happy. I swear I'm a different man."

"Not too different I hope. I always liked—loved—who you were, Sam. I just wanted more of you."

"You'll have it," he swore. "And if I ever do screw up again, you have to call me on it and I'll fix it. I never want to lose you again."

Smiling through her tears, Mia said, "I can't lose you again either, Sam."

"You won't. I swear it." He let her go long enough to dip into his pocket and come out with a ring. He took her right hand in his and slipped the emerald-and-diamond band onto her finger.

When he looked into her eyes this time, he said,

"We're already married, so I expect you to put your rings back on when we get home."

She laughed and nodded, looking from the ring to his eyes.

"But this one," he said softly, "I want you to have to mark my promise to you.

"I will love you forever, Mia Harper Buchanan. And I will love the children we make together and I will give you all everything I have."

Mia looked down at the glittering ring on her finger, then up into the most beautiful blue eyes she'd ever seen. "I love you, Sam. Always have. Always will. And I'm so glad you came home."

"You're my home, Mia. My home. My heart. My everything."

And when he kissed her, Mia felt her whole world come right again and she knew that the future stretching out in front of them was filled with all the love she'd ever dreamed of.

* * * * *

HIGH SOCIETY
SECRETS

KAREN BOOTH

This book is for all women who make a point
of supporting and lifting up other women.
You make the world a better place.

One

Clay Morgan was too much—a skyscraper of a man with stormy blue-gray eyes and a mop of nearly black hair that begged for Astrid Sterling's touch. She watched him from across the room at the bustling cocktail party as he stood apart from the crowd, observing. Taking it all in. An architect, he possessed a brilliant mind, a brain that could create something out of nothing. It was a marvel to see in action, a luxury Astrid had every workday. But Clay also had a stern heart, possibly chiseled out of ice. Or at least that was all Astrid could surmise, judging by the disposition he saved for her.

She'd done nothing to deserve it. Not a thing. And it was slowly driving her mad.

Grant Singleton was hosting this evening, at his showpiece of a home in La Jolla, California. Grant was CEO of the company Astrid worked for, Sterling Enterprises, a real estate development firm started by Astrid's now-deceased ex-husband. Astrid also owned seventeen percent of the company, so she wasn't your average employee. Although Clay, who worked with her on the Seaport Promenade team, treated her as though she was.

She plucked a glass of champagne from a tray when one of the party's servers offered. "Thank you," she said to the young man.

"Beautiful night," he answered, by way of small talk.

Astrid looked over her shoulder. Outside the wall of windows rimming Grant's modern home, tall palms bent in the swift ocean breeze. The fronds chaotically ruffled in the wind, set against an inky, moonlit sky. The scene was like Clay—shadowy and mysterious— but calling to her all the same. She wished she could be out there with him right now, so they could be alone, away from the office, and she could try to shake free some of what was pent up in his head. She was desperate for answers. Why was he so cold and closed off? Why did he treat her with such utter disdain?

"Absolutely gorgeous." The server's voice got her attention.

Astrid turned back, catching him as he stole an eyeful of her. She smiled and ignored the way it made her feel like an object. She was more than used to it by now, and had learned not to acknowledge it or question it or even care. It happened dozens of times a day. Funnily enough, when she'd been a gangly and awkward teen, she would have done anything for that sort of male attention. When she finally grew into her frame and her sharp edges began to round out, her whole world changed—a modeling career, a one-way ticket out of her home country of Norway, and ultimately, a boulder of a diamond from Johnathon Sterling. The marriage didn't last, but she'd had a few years of his love. She was grateful for what it had given her. She certainly wouldn't be standing in this room right now if it hadn't been for him.

"Thank you again," she said to the server, impatient to return her focus to Clay. This was one of the rare times she got to see him away from work, and she wanted to study his interactions with others, particularly his sister, Miranda, who had just arrived. Astrid's connection to Miranda was improbable—Miranda had been married to Astrid's ex-husband, Johnathon, when he died two months ago. Astrid also, quite unfortunately, had learned a terrible secret about the start of Miranda's marriage to Johnathon. Astrid was desperate to keep it buried forever, but it was eating at her nonetheless. Astrid liked Miranda quite a bit. Plus, she knew what it was like to have once been wed to a man who took whatever he wanted.

"Let me know if you need anything," the server said before departing.

What I really need is a map of Clay Morgan, or at the very least, a set of instructions.

On the other side of the room, Grant gently tapped a spoon against his champagne glass, begging for everyone's attention. Tara, the first of Johnathon Sterling's wives, joined him. Together, Tara, Miranda, and Astrid had controlling interest of Sterling Enterprises. The announcement Grant was about to make likely impacted them all, greatly.

"I first want to thank you all for coming this evening. I have several exciting announcements to make."

Grant's warm brown eyes lit up with anticipation. He loved his job and was an able company leader.

Clay, for his part, stuffed his hands into his pants pockets and leaned against a nearby column. Astrid couldn't help but admire the long plane of his body—the defined chest currently wrapped up in a well-made black dress shirt, the dip of his trim waist, and the legs that seemed to stretch on for eternity. She marveled at his ability to convey power and brilliance in the most casual of ways, all while he remained oblivious to the effect he had on her and quite possibly, other women.

"As many of you know," Grant continued, "About two weeks ago, on September 7, Sterling Enterprises passed the first round for the Seaport Promenade project with the city. We couldn't have done it without the dedication of the entire team, including Clay Morgan, Astrid Sterling, and of course, Tara." Grant reached for Tara's hand, and Astrid saw the moment when their fingers hooked and their connection became palpable. They'd fallen in love, despite the fact that Tara had sworn there was nothing going on between them. "Which leads me to my next announcement. Tara and I are not only planning to operate the company as co-CEOs from this day forward, we're engaged to be married."

There was a gasp from the throng of guests, followed quickly by a roar of applause and guests hurrying to offer their congratulations. Astrid hung back, and she couldn't ignore the fact that Clay was doing the same. Astrid had her own reasons for being reticent about the purported happy news. She, Tara, and Miranda had a deal. They were supposed to be a coalition within Sterling, and the whole thing had been Tara's idea, a plan hatched after Johnathon divided his majority interest in the company between his three wives. Tara's engagement to the current CEO would at best divide her loyalties, and at worst, tear them away for Miranda and Astrid.

Astrid wound her way through the crowd until she reached Miranda, who was standing not far from Tara and Grant, apparently waiting for the moment when she could congratulate them.

"Did you know about this?" Astrid asked.

Miranda shook her head. "I had my suspicions. It makes perfect sense, doesn't it? They've known each other for years, and the few times I've been around them both, I definitely sensed a spark."

"But co-CEOs?" Astrid asked the question as quietly as possible. "Between that and the engagement, it seems that Tara has fully aligned herself with Grant, when she was supposed to be doing that with us."

Miranda nodded, focusing on Astrid. She was one of the few people who took Astrid seriously. "Let's talk to her, then. See where we stand."

They approached Tara, who seemed totally swept up by the moment. "Can we talk with you?" Astrid was already leading them into a corner of the room for privacy.

"Yes. Of course. What's up?" Tara asked.

"First off, congratulations," Miranda said.

Astrid was more than a little annoyed that she had to be the one solely focused on business right now. "Yes, congratulations. I'm very happy for you both." She scanned Tara's face, which was relaxed and confident. "But I also have a question."

"Let me guess," Tara said. "You're concerned that I'm in too deep with Grant."

"You're getting married and you're co-CEOs. I don't think it's possible for you to be in any deeper," Astrid answered.

"Don't you have to consult with us before you assume the position of co-CEO?" Miranda asked.

"Technically, yes. And of course, you two are able to register your objections, if you have any. But this is good for the three of us. I'm no longer merely floating around the company with an ambiguous role. I have the title and all of the power that affords me. That's good for us. If anything, it protects our interest in the company."

Astrid wished she could be so sure. "As long as you're still dedicated to the Seaport Promenade project." As far as Astrid was concerned, this was the perfect time for her to be selfish and push her own agenda. That project, a large undertaking for the city that involved what would eventually be a vast public space, kept her working with Clay. She very much wanted the chance. If he truly didn't like her, she at least had to figure out why.

"Yes. I need some assurances that it will happen," Miranda added. She had her own reasons for caring deeply about the Seaport. It had been Johnathon's pet project before his untimely death more than two months ago. "Any progress on naming the park after Johnathon?"

"I'm still working on that," Tara said.

Just then, Grant waved Tara over. Clay had joined him, and the two were quickly deep in discussion.

"I hope you can excuse me for one minute," Tara said, not waiting for an answer and marching over to the two men.

"What are those three talking about?" Astrid asked.

"I have a feeling I know," Miranda said. "I think there's big news for my brother."

"One last announcement, everyone," Grant called out before Astrid had a chance to inquire more. "I want to congratulate the firm's star architect, Clay Morgan, on being a finalist for the state Architect of the Year."

Miranda began to furiously clap, and so did Astrid, but her heart was also breaking a little as she watched Clay's reaction. He offered the obligatory smile, but it was so glaringly obvious, at least to her, that he was not enjoying this moment in the spotlight. How sad was that? This was a big accomplishment. What was it about him that he seemed to take no joy in anything?

Astrid felt an urgent need to at least fix that look on his face, and she rushed over to him in Miranda's wake. She watched as Miranda and Clay embraced. There was an obvious warmth between them as brother and sister, a bond that seemed strong and loving. So he wasn't made of pure ice, or at least not when it came to family. Miranda stepped back and Clay's sights flew to Astrid. For a moment, it felt as though her heart was being squeezed like a stress ball as their gazes connected and she tried to decipher what must be going through his head. In that split-second, she reached no conclusion, other than that she wanted to hug him, too, but she was certain he would recoil.

Instead, she did the only thing she could think to do. She offered a handshake. "Congratulations, Clay. It's so exciting. I'm honored to be working with you on the Seaport project. I can't wait for us to start on the next phase together."

Clay looked down at her hand. "Thanks. But I'm going to ask to be taken off the project."

Astrid's heart dropped so low it was currently residing near her feet. "But why?"

"I'm not sure you and I work well together."

It hurt like hell to say that to Astrid, and the devastated look on her stunning face was making it that much more difficult. But it was the truth. They *didn't* work together well. He was endlessly distracted by her. He made mistakes when they worked together and he prided himself on not doing that. He'd made a gaffe on the Seaport Promenade several weeks ago and it could have cost them the entire project. Luckily, Tara had discovered his mistake before the first presentation. The Architect of the Year definitely did not suffer such lapses, and he wanted that award more than anything. Aside from his young daughter and his sister, Miranda, Clay had nothing else in the world to pin any happiness to. His job was a crucial part of his life. It helped to define him.

Astrid—with her willowy legs, sweet personality, and beguiling honey-gold hair—was standing between him and the very function of his brain. They'd been working together for well over a month and things weren't getting better. In fact, they might be getting worse. When she was around, he was all thumbs. He found himself searching for words, and he was a man with a large vocabulary—surely there had to be some verbiage that was easily accessible. But no. Not when Astrid was close.

He instead found himself concentrating on the curve of her full lips, enchanted by her wide cocoa-brown eyes. He couldn't afford to fall for another beautiful face. It had ruined his entire life the other time he'd shown such weakness, for the woman who became his wife, only to leave him and his precious daughter behind.

He would not take a single step toward that mistake again. His daughter and career were too important. But he wasn't about to throw Astrid under the bus. She was a capable partner in her work, leaving him with no choice but to remove himself from the equation. It was a sacrifice he had to make to save his own skin.

"You can't be serious," Astrid said in reply to his assertion that they didn't make a good team. "We work together so well. We made it through the first round on the Seaport project and don't forget, that was on a very tight timeline."

"What was that I heard about Seaport? Are you two talking shop?" Grant turned and stepped into the middle of their conversation.

Clay had planned on speaking to Grant about this in a private meeting on Monday morning, not launching into it in front of anyone else, especially not Astrid. "We were, actually. I'm wondering if I can be taken off the project, so I can shift to some of the more pressing jobs we have ahead."

A deep crease formed between Grant's eyes. "I thought you were enjoying it. And it's such a high profile assignment. I would think that with the Architect of the Year nomination, this is your time to step into the spotlight, not out of it."

Tara had apparently overheard and excused herself from the person she'd been chatting with. Clay wanted to disappear into himself. He never should have allowed this to be discussed in the middle of a cocktail party. It was stupid and foolish and entirely too public. Clay was a deeply private person. He'd always been that way.

"Everything okay over here?" Tara asked.

"Clay wants to be taken off the Seaport project." Grant slipped his arm around Tara's waist, but he still seemed deeply concerned.

"No. Absolutely not. You and Astrid are the dream team. Plus, now that I'm officially stepping into my role as co-CEO, I need you two to steer the ship on that project. I'm planning on handing Astrid all of the work I've been doing."

If only Tara knew that she was only making his argument that much stronger. She'd at least been a bit of a buffer between Astrid and him. Now she was leaving it to just the two of them? "The project right now is nothing more than adapting the existing plan to meet the city's needs. Those are small details that are best left to one of the more junior architects." Clay hoped this new line of thinking would convince them.

Tara shook her head and pinched her lower lip between her fingers. "I don't know." She turned to Grant. "I would just feel a whole lot better about things if Clay was still the principal. He's been working on it from the very beginning. It would make me very nervous to step away from it if he wasn't still there."

Clay could not catch a break here. He kept losing ground, despite having dug in his heels.

"It's my fault," Astrid interjected, surprising the hell out of Clay. "The truth is that Clay has a hard time working with me. But don't worry. I will do better. We will work out our difficulties and everyone can proceed with their plans. Don't worry about it."

Tara returned her sights to Astrid, then directed them at Clay. "Is that what this is really about? Office politics?"

"There's more to it than that," Clay answered.

"Do you want to tell me what, exactly?" Tara countered.

As for further explanation, Clay had none. It looked as though his bed had been made for him and he'd better learn to lie down in it, however much it bothered him. Perhaps he could start wearing blinders to the office or tell Astrid that they should only communicate via email. "Look, it's my fault. Not Astrid's. I'm too rigid in my ways." He didn't want to cast himself in a bad light, but he also didn't want Astrid to take the heat for this. He'd started it.

"Give us some time," Astrid said. "We'll work it out. And if we don't, I'll take myself off the project."

A frustrated grumble fought to leave Clay's throat. That wasn't what he wanted either. But he didn't really have a choice. He could live with the torment of Astrid for another week or two, then he'd figure out his next move. "Yes. Fine. We'll find a compromise."

"Okay, then," Grant said, seeming satisfied. He and Tara were quickly whisked back into the flow of the party, celebrating their many bits of good news.

Clay knew he was supposed to be happy tonight. He had the nomination he'd worked hard for. And if things were simpler for him, he could allow himself to feel at least a little jubilation. He might even flirt with Astrid, or at the very least, not let her get to him so much.

"I hope I didn't put you on the spot," Astrid said. "I just don't want things to be strained between us." She looked down at her feet, then back up, capturing him with the storm in her eyes. "I mean, any more than they are."

Good God, he was a jerk. Part of him wanted to explain what his problem really was, but even he failed to fully comprehend it. He only knew that there was a force deep inside him telling him to stay away. It was a reflex. He couldn't help it. "I'll see you at the office on Monday, okay?"

"I'd like to have a meeting first thing so we can talk about this some more."

He shook his head. "No need for a conversation. It's not you. It's me." He pulled his keys out of his pocket. He needed to get out of there, get back to his daughter, Delia, and sleep off the effects of this night. Perhaps he'd have a clearer head in the morning. He scanned the crowd for his sister, but she was nowhere to be seen. He'd text her when he got home. "Have a good weekend," he said to Astrid before starting for the door.

"There's no way it's just you." Astrid was right behind him, trotting along in her heels, the ones that made her legs look unbelievable.

"Trust me. It is." He pulled the door open, but out of habit, he stood aside for Astrid. Damn his gentlemanly ways.

Astrid turned back to him as soon as she was out on the flagstone landing. The night breeze blew her hair across her face, and she shook it free. He struggled to remain standing. How could any woman be so beautiful? "It's never just one person's fault. And I know there has to be a reason you treat me the way you do."

Clay had worried his cold shoulder had gotten to be too much. He closed the door behind him. "I'm sorry if I haven't been the most fun to work with. I'm under a lot of stress. It's not an excuse, but it might explain some of it."

"I know I can be overly enthusiastic. I'm just excited

to have a job where I feel like I have more of a purpose. I was a model for years and that didn't make me feel very valuable."

"I'm sure your employers were very happy with your work." How could they not be? She was so damn sexy, she could sell a brick to a man standing on a diving board. He resumed his trek to his car.

"Maybe. I don't really know. But I do know that I enjoy being at Sterling and I don't want that to change."

"You own a chunk of the company. You can write your own ticket, can't you?" He stopped and turned to her. "Honestly, do you even need to work?"

"Do you?" She artfully arched both eyebrows at him.

No, he didn't need to work, at least not for the money. He and Miranda had inherited the entire family fortune when their grandmother died. But he did need to work for his own sanity. It kept his mind occupied. It kept him from constantly rehashing his past. "How do you know that?"

"I ask questions."

Clay did not want anyone digging around for information about him. That didn't sit well with him at all. "Well, don't. You and I are coworkers. There's no reason for you to know anything about my personal life." Anger was bubbling up inside him. He just needed to get to his car.

"I'm sorry. I'm trying to understand."

"Understand what? Me?" He nearly started laughing. As far as he was concerned, he was an easy case. If he was left alone to live his life, he'd be fine.

"Yes, you." She gripped his elbow and her warmth traveled through his body at warp speed. "I want to be able to work with you. I want to learn from you, and collaborate, and try to soak up at least a little of your brilliance."

He stood paralyzed. He didn't know what he was supposed to say to that. She was so earnest, so unrelenting in her pursuit of a compromise. As far as he was concerned, that only made her more dangerous. Why couldn't she simply give up on him, go back inside, and forget about this whole thing?

"Why do you hate me, Clay? I'm struggling to understand what I did."

"I don't hate you." *It's that I can't stop thinking about you.*

"But it feels that way sometimes."

"I'm sorry. I don't know what else to say." He clicked the fob and strode double-time to his Audi, fumbling for the door handle like a fool. He wasn't going to let another woman get to him. Not like last time. Not ever again. He started the engine and the lights immediately came on. Straight ahead, Astrid stood there, shaking her head in disbelief. Even in the harshest light he could imagine, she was beautiful and alluring and the exact woman he wanted to take in his arms and kiss. She was also so difficult to understand. What could make someone so eager to trust in a virtual stranger?

He'd learned long ago to trust in virtually no one.

Two

A peace offering was in order for Monday morning. Astrid decided that hers would be simple—baked
goods. Clay displayed no weakness for anything, but
he did sometimes duck out of the office in the morning
for a doughnut from the bakery across the street from
Sterling Enterprises. Was satiating his sweet tooth the
way out of the dog house with Clay? Astrid wasn't sure,
but it couldn't hurt to try.

The line was always long. Sometimes it was out the
door, but this morning, Astrid must have been lucky,
because that wasn't the case. She took her place in the
bustling, lively space, where six or seven people worked
the counter, taking orders, ringing up customers, bag-
ging pastries and making lattes. Heavenly smells of cin-
namon, chocolate, coffee and steamed milk swirled in
the air. It was a warm and cozy spot, which did make

Astrid wonder about Clay. People got a sliver of happiness here—is that why he liked to come? Or did he feel out of place?

Astrid knew very well what it was like to feel that way, starting with her family. She was the youngest of six, and the only girl. One could argue that she'd been out of place from the word *go*. Her mother had apparently always wanted a girl, but her father had been opposed to the idea of more children. There were already plenty of mouths to feed and their four-bedroom house in Bergen, on the southwestern coast of Norway, was bursting at the seams.

Astrid's five brothers were all tall, strapping young men, who not only treated Astrid as though she were made of glass, but also acted as though she might be an alien. She'd had to fight for their attention, and most important, to be included. They all had their lives pretty well worked out when Astrid came along. She was the intruder, the one who disrupted the family equilibrium. It didn't help that her mother, who was loving and full of heart, was always nagging her brothers to take her along when they went places and let her be included in their activities. It wasn't until she had a growth spurt at age eleven and convinced her oldest brother to let her play football with them that she finally earned some respect. She'd gotten pretty roughed up that day, but she'd stood nearly shoulder to shoulder with them and she'd competed. She'd forced them to include her.

Astrid couldn't ignore the parallel here, with Clay not wanting her around and Tara taking the role of her mom, urging them to find a way. But Astrid was not a little girl, she was a grown woman, and she owned just as much of the company as Tara did. She would sort this out for herself. She didn't need anyone else's help. She just needed doughnuts.

When she finally reached the front of the line, she was pleased to see they still had several of Clay's favorite, the Diego, filled with dark chocolate custard and topped with caramelized sugar like crème brûlée. She ordered three, two for Clay and one for herself. She might as well see what all the fuss was about. As she was waiting for her coffee, a familiar face caught her eye—Sandy, a woman who'd worked at Sterling as a general assistant when Astrid first arrived. Sandy was a valuable member of the support staff, confident and capable. Sandy had also essentially disappeared.

As she approached the door, Astrid eyed her, unsure if she'd identified her correctly. When the woman caught sight of Astrid and quickly looked away, Astrid knew she had to say something. "Sandy? Is that you?"

She turned, confirming Astrid's suspicions. "Oh. Hello, Ms. Sterling. How are you?"

"Good. I'm on my way into the office." Astrid held up the bag of doughnuts. "I have to say that we miss you. We were all a bit puzzled about the way you left. You didn't say goodbye. You didn't even give any notice. It was quite a scramble before the first deadline on the Seaport project."

All color had drained from Sandy's face. Apparently she wasn't used to being called out on things, but Astrid had no reason to be anything less than up front about it. "I know. It wasn't my finest moment. I got pulled away by a second job. I didn't want to tell anyone, but I was moonlighting a bit at the time. San Diego can be so expensive."

"Yes, it can be. Weren't you being paid well at Sterling?"

"I was. I definitely was. It's just that my other employer and I have a long history." She shifted back and forth on her feet, seeming uncomfortable. "I owed my boss a favor, and he wanted me to work on a project and wouldn't take no for an answer. It's a long story."

Astrid nodded, realizing this might be as much as she'd ever learn about this. "I see. Well, I hope it all got straightened out."

Sandy shrugged. "I ended up getting let go, actually."

"So you left Sterling for nothing?"

Sandy nodded sheepishly. "It was so stupid."

Astrid drew a deep breath in through her nose. "We've filled your position, but do you have my number? Call me if you don't end up finding anything. Maybe there's something we can do."

"Thank you, Ms. Sterling. I'll do that."

"Sandy, do you mind me asking you what your other employer does?"

"Just more real estate development, but nothing in California. They're based in Seattle."

Seattle and real estate development made Astrid think of her ex-husband's estranged brother, but surely there were a lot of companies like that in Washington state. "Well, good luck with everything. And call me if you find yourself still looking for a job."

Astrid strode out of the bakery and made her away across the street, taking the elevator up to the Sterling offices. As was always the case, especially on a Monday morning, it was buzzing with activity. She bid her good mornings to coworkers as she filed through the maze of halls to Clay's office. His door was open, but her heart still flipped at the thought of looking inside. Just the idea of seeing him and offering a pastry made her nervous. It wasn't right. This was a professional setting. They were adults. She had to stop acting like a fool.

When she peeked inside, she realized that seeing him wasn't the problem. *Not* seeing him was. *Dammit. He's not here yet.* She stepped inside his office and flipped on the light. It wasn't like Clay to be late for work. Astrid really hoped he hadn't decided to resign over the weekend. He didn't like her much, but he didn't really hate her to that extent, did he?

She drew in a deep breath, weighing her options. She didn't want to wait too long and appear truly desperate. The only answer was to leave the doughnuts and a note. At least if he wasn't pleased by the gesture, she didn't have to witness his reaction. Grabbing a piece of paper from the credenza, she scribbled out a note.

I thought you might enjoy some of your favorite doughnuts.
—Astrid

She stared at what she'd written, realizing it was all wrong. Only someone who had been very carefully watching him would know what his favorite doughnut was. This was quite possibly the stupidest idea ever. She folded up the paper, stuffed it in her pants pocket and plucked the bakery bag from his desk. Just as Clay walked in.

"Uh. Good morning?" He looked as confused as could be.

If Astrid thought her heart was misbehaving earlier, it was now up to no good, thundering away in her chest.

"Good morning." God, he looked good in his charcoal-gray suit. It was well-cut for his broad shoulders and towering stature, but Astrid had always noticed that it was a little snug on his arms. That suit couldn't hide whatever glorious muscles were under there. It could only flaunt them.

Clay cleared his throat and walked behind Astrid to his desk. "Is there something I can help you with?"

Astrid realized that she had no choice but to come clean. "I brought you doughnuts. I know you like them." Dead silence followed her admission, which made her feel even more stupid.

"I forgot to eat this morning, so thank you." He set down his laptop case.

Astrid hadn't realized she'd been holding her breath, waiting for a blip of positivity from him. Finally, she could exhale. She presented the bag, then remembered that they weren't all for him. "Actually, one of those is mine."

The smallest of smiles crossed his lips, which sent zaps of electricity through her. She immediately began conspiring, wondering what she could do next to bring about another grin. "You don't seem like a person who would like sweets," he said.

She opened the paper sack and fished out one of the doughnuts, then handed the bag over to Clay. "Are you kidding? Anything sweet is fun. I'm fun." She peeled back the parchment partially wrapped around the pastry and took a big bite. Chocolate custard oozed out at the corners of her lips, but she was so overcome with how delicious it was, she didn't care. "Wow. That is so good."

"I know. Right?" He went in for his own taste, his eyes drifting shut for a moment.

Astrid had to steel herself as she watched the blissful

look cross his face. First a smile then this. She might start buying doughnuts every day. "Did you oversleep this morning?"

"Huh?" He licked a bit of custard from his thumb, making her light-headed.

"You said you didn't have time for breakfast."

"No. My daughter. She wanted her hair a certain way for school and she's not quite able to do it herself." He wiped his hands with a napkin, then held them up. "Obviously these things aren't good at braids or whatever it was that she wanted. I'm not sure I even know how to properly operate a barrette."

Astrid had admired Clay's hands from the moment she first met him in this office. They were big and strong, but deft when he showed his architectural brilliance and drafted by hand. Now that she had the wholly adorable image of Clay and his young daughter having a spat over her hair, his hands were now enticing in a whole new way. "You don't talk about your daughter very often. How old is she? What's her name?"

"I don't want to talk about her at work."

"You brought her up, not me."

"And now I'm asking you to not talk about her."

He was so infuriating. "Okay, but if you ever need help with her hair, I'm happy to come over. Braids are very traditional in Norway, so I know how to do them dozens of different ways."

"No, thanks." He cleared his throat and averted his eyes. "I can figure it out on my own."

And just like that, Astrid felt as though she were back at square one. Apparently, she could only offer Clay so much niceness at one time. Too much and he would cut her off. "Okay. Whatever you say."

* * *

Clay hadn't meant to shut down Astrid's offer to help with his daughter's hair so quickly. It was a reflex. He would do anything to protect Delia, and that meant keeping everyone he didn't fully trust away from her. What if Astrid came over and Delia became attached, and then Astrid flitted back to Norway or decided one day that she no longer had time for his daughter? Clay couldn't subject Delia to that kind of rejection. Delia had already suffered the ultimate rebuke when her own mother had left them. He would not let anyone come close to hurting her like that again.

"You're a smart guy. I'm sure you'll figure it out," Astrid said. "I guess I'll take my doughnut and head back to my office."

Clay felt like such an ass. Astrid hadn't done anything other than be her usual sweet self. Why did he have to be so wary of kindness? "Thank you for that. It was nice."

"I'm trying to make our working relationship a little better."

Now he felt even worse, but he also knew that she was missing the point. The more wonderful she tried to be, the more drawn he was to her. And the more tempted he felt by her, the more dangerous she became. He would not put his heart on the line again. He couldn't do it. "Don't feel like you need to do anything outside the normal course of our professional interactions. It's not necessary."

Astrid stopped at his doorway and turned back to him. She was wearing a simple black dress today, one that showed off her slender curves and made the deep brown of her eyes even more intense. He couldn't see n single flaw in her, and he'd spent plenty of time looking for one, hoping he could assign a reason to not be so attracted to her. He'd failed.

"What's not necessary?" Tara appeared at the entrance to Clay's office.

"I brought Clay a doughnut this morning. He was just telling me why I didn't need to do that." Astrid shot him a look that was born of pure annoyance. It was so ridiculously hot that everything in his body went tight.

"So I take it neither of you had a chance to cool off this weekend?" Tara stepped inside and sat on the small sofa in his office. Astrid joined her, perching on the arm and crossing her legs.

Cool off? Clay needed an ice bath after even five minutes with Astrid, especially right now when she was distracting him by letting her black pump dangle from her foot. "All I said was that she shouldn't go out of her way to be nice to me."

Tara shook her head slowly. Now he had two women displeased with him. "Grant and I talked about it and we think the only way for you two to get past your troubles is to spend more time together."

Clay's stomach sank. "Wait. What?"

Tara held up her hand. "Hold on a minute. Hear me out. We think some time together outside the office would be a good idea. You both work incredibly hard and we think that the stress of the Seaport project has likely been the main reason you got off to a rocky start."

"I think there's more to it than that…" Clay wished there wasn't such a distinct edge of panic in his voice. It wasn't a good look.

Astrid let out a frustrated grumble. "Did you have something specific in mind, Tara?"

Clay was consumed by a flurry of silent wishes. *Please no spa retreats or trust falls or anything involving a beach or Astrid in a bathing suit.*

"I was specifically thinking the Architect of the Year Award ceremony in LA. You should go together. It will give Astrid a chance to meet more people in our industry, and it will give you two a chance to connect outside the office."

"But that's next weekend," Astrid blurted.

Finally, someone else in the room was willing to help him put on the brakes. "Exactly," Clay said.

"What's your objection, Astrid?" Tara asked.

"I need to find a dress."

Tara eyed Astrid. "You and I both know you will have zero problem finding a dress in time for you two to leave for LA. I'll go shopping with you. We can invite Miranda and talk business at the same time."

Astrid lips curled into a smile. "That sounds great."

"This will be good for Sterling, too. Clay has an excellent chance of winning, and it would be nice if he wasn't standing there by himself if he does."

Clay drew in a resigned breath through his nose. He had planned on going alone, but that was only because he was filled with existential dread over the ceremony. He desperately wanted to win, but he didn't want anyone to feel as though they needed to assuage his disappointment if he didn't. It was simply easier to be there on his own. "I guess I see what you're saying."

"It's settled then," Tara said. "I'll get my assistant to book an extra room at the hotel for Astrid."

"Okay," Astrid said.

"And I take it you're all set with a babysitter for Delia?" Tara asked.

"Miranda is taking her for the night. Those two adore each other, so it won't be a problem."

"Perfect. I'll let Grant know this is all settled. Where are we at with Seaport?"

"We're digging into the more detailed changes the city requested and coordinating with the landscape designers for their side of the project," Astrid said. "I estimate we're ahead of schedule for the next presentation in mid-November."

"Good. That will allow for any mistakes," Tara said.

Clay suddenly found it hard to swallow. He had made the crucial gaffe on site orientation for the first proposal. It had almost cost them the project, and Clay was committed to never having another misstep like that one. "It won't happen again."

Tara got up from the couch and made her way for the door. "Still, it's nice to have a little wiggle room."

Clay dropped down into his office chair, and he and Astrid sat in silence for several moments after Tara left. They both seemed equally stunned and unsure, as if Clay needed another means of feeling more connected to Astrid.

"I wasn't expecting that," she finally said.

"Me neither."

"If you don't want me to go, I won't. Even if you want me to tell Tara at the last minute that I'm sick or something. It's your night and I don't want to ruin it."

Clay's shoulders dropped. Would this feeling of being torn in two ever go away? "I had envisioned being on my own, but it might be nice to have some company."

"Might?"

"I don't know, Astrid. I don't know how you are in a situation like that. I'm already plenty nervous about it.

This is a professional accolade I've worked very hard for. It means a lot to be recognized and I know I'm going to be pretty worked up about it that night. Maybe you don't like being around someone who's so on edge."

Astrid unleashed a light and musical titter that filled the room.

"What's so funny?"

"Clay, you are always on edge. Always. And I don't know you that well, but I suspect it's because you spend a little too much time in your own head."

She wasn't wrong, but he wasn't about to admit it. "What's your point?"

"My point is that I'm already used to handling you at your worst. And I've attended more award ceremonies than you can possibly imagine. I have no problem putting on a beautiful dress and walking the red carpet. I can do it in my sleep."

Of course she could. Her modeling career had put her in untold glamorous settings. Surely dozens of men had made their overtures to Astrid, and she'd had her pick of the lot. It was one more reason to keep his brain on this very narrow path he'd carved out for them—the one where they were colleagues and nothing else, regardless of his attraction to her. Clay didn't know her romantic history, but he could imagine a long string of broken hearts in her wake. He wasn't about to be the next.

"And more than anything, I'm very good in a crisis," Astrid added. "So if you panic or get too nervous, I'm sure I can find something to distract you."

He already knew she'd have no problem doing that. But maybe this wasn't the worst idea. It was a work trip and nothing else. He could introduce her to some people, and it would be nice to not be alone after the winner was announced—good news or bad, he was sure he'd need a steady hand to hold on to. "Okay. As long as you're good with it."

Astrid rose from her spot on the couch. "Of course I am. I like the idea of being someone's insurance policy."

"What do you mean by that?"

Astrid smoothed the front of her dress. "I mean that even if you lose, I don't think anyone will be feeling sorry for you."

Clay swallowed hard as he watched her walk out of his office. This was going to be a test unlike any he'd experienced in quite some time. He picked up his phone and pulled up Miranda on speed dial.

"Hey. This is a surprise," she said when she answered.

"I was hoping you and I could talk one night this week."

"Sounds serious."

"I need some advice about how to ignore my attraction to a woman."

"No way. I'm not doing that. I want you to pay attention if you're attracted to someone."

Clay sat back in his chair and cradled his forehead in his hand. "Yeah. That's not going to happen."

Three

Clay arrived at Miranda's house Thursday night around six with his daughter, Delia, in tow.

"My two favorite people," Miranda announced as she threw open the door.

"Aunt Miranda!" Delia exclaimed, bounding inside and into his sister's waiting arms.

Clay smiled as he watched the pair embrace. They had quite a lot in common, both with long dark hair, big brown eyes and of course, him wrapped around their little fingers. There had been a time, when he and Miranda were young, that he never would have dared to imagine such a loving scene in his future. The day their mother dropped them off with their grandmother, never to return, was the start of their treacherous past. The details of that day would always be murky for Clay, who had only been five years old, but Miranda, who had been only two, didn't remember it at all. One thing Clay did clearly recall was the feeling of losing all hope, and the fierce need to protect Miranda at all costs. They'd stood there together, holding hands, looking at a stern and cold woman they hardly knew, who was suddenly about to rule their whole world.

He stepped inside the foyer and closed the door behind them. "Delia, do you want to go look at the aquarium?" Miranda had a large tropical tank in her home office, stocked full of live coral and dozens of colorful fish.

"Can I?" Delia asked.

"Of course," Miranda answered, laughing as Delia skittered off. "You want a drink? Somebody might as well enjoy a glass of wine since I can't." Miranda pressed her hand to her pregnant belly, which was only a slight protrusion. She was a little shy of four months along, so that would soon change. Single parenthood was another life detail Miranda and Clay shared now. Miranda had been about to announce the pregnancy to her husband, Johnathon, on the day he was killed by a line drive on the golf course.

"No, thank you. I'm fine." He wanted to keep a clear head when discussing Astrid, plus he needed to drive Delia home. "How are you feeling?"

"Good, but definitely like my stomach is starting to pooch out. I already have a little bump."

Clay slung his arm around his sister's shoulder. "I didn't want to say anything, but…"

Miranda gently elbowed him in the ribs. "You're welcome to keep your mouth shut, mister. Come on. Let's go sit in the living room." She led the way, taking the end of one of the comfortable sectional couches. "So, you wanted to talk? We should probably do it now while Delia is in the other room."

Clay found himself feeling uncertain about discussing the topic of Astrid with his sister, but he knew he could trust Miranda with his life, so if he had any chance of setting his mind straight about this, she was his best shot. "It's Astrid."

Miranda narrowed her eyes, seeming confused. "Okay. And we're not talking about your work relationship?"

"Yes and no. It's a mix of work and personal and I don't know how to deal with it."

"You're going to have to be a lot more specific or I can't help you at all." Miranda's eyes lit up as if she was putting it all together. "You two aren't involved, are you?" she whispered.

"No. We aren't. But if our situation was completely different and if I didn't have Delia to think about or have any worries about the past repeating itself, I might want to be." He felt foolish to make that admission, like he was a teenager. Why did Astrid make him so unsure of himself?

"Interesting." Miranda sat back, seeming satisfied with the leap she'd taken.

"What?"

"I've been wondering when you would finally want to get out there again. It's been four years since the divorce, so I guess the timing is about right."

"No. That's not what this is. I am not out anywhere. Not at all."

"Then why don't you tell me what it is?"

He sighed heavily and just came out with it. "I can't stop thinking about her." He went on to explain that he was hopelessly attracted to Astrid, and not just because she was beautiful, but because everything she did only seemed to confirm that she was too good to be true. Clay reminded Miranda that he had fallen prey to that very idea when he met his ex-wife, Delia's mom. Of course, Miranda had been there for the whole disaster. She'd helped him pick up the pieces. "I asked to be taken off the Seaport project, just in the hopes that distance would make it easier to stay away from her. But Tara and Grant disagreed, and now they want the two of us to attend the Architect of the Year awards together."

"I heard."

"You did?"

Miranda nodded. "Yep. She wants Tara and me to go dress shopping with her. I'd say your plan backfired."

"Spectacularly." He laughed quietly, trying not to take this situation too seriously. "You've spent more time with Astrid than I have. What do you think of her?"

"You do realize this is an odd situation for me to comment on, right? She was married to Johnathon before I was. I see why men would be attracted to her, but I don't like to think about it too much."

Clay could appreciate that he'd put his sister in an awkward spot. "Fair enough. I get it."

"I don't really know what you want me to say anyway. Are you asking for my blessing?"

"No. I was hoping you would tell me that I'm right to want to stay away from her. At least as far as anything outside our professional relationship."

"Well, I don't know her that well. I'd like to think that Johnathon would never have married a woman who was anything less than amazing and wonderful, but I don't know for sure, and no person is perfect. Everyone has faults. And we might have mutual interests in Sterling Enterprises, but I don't trust her unconditionally."

Somehow, these negatives weren't nearly the comfort Clay had hoped they might be. "Okay. That's good to know."

"But…"

Clay hadn't bargained on a *but*.

"I do trust her somewhat," Miranda continued. "There's something about her that makes you want to give her whatever she asks for."

It was as if his sister had pulled the words straight out of his mouth. "Yes. How does she do that?"

"I don't know. Although I will say that she has a good heart. She had every reason to be horribly jealous of my pregnancy. She and Johnathon suffered through years of infertility. That's what drove them apart."

"It did?" This was the first he'd heard about the conditions under which Johnathon and Astrid had split up.

"Yes. She wanted a baby with Johnathon and I'm the one who got what she didn't." Miranda's sights fell to her belly.

"I had no idea."

"She doesn't exactly go around chatting about that part of her life. She might be very open, but some things are too painful to share." Miranda sat a little straighter and reached for Clay's hand. "She's been very sweet to me about the baby. She didn't even hesitate to congratulate me when she found out. That takes a big heart. And I'd like to think that anyone with such a generous nature would be a good person to fall in love with."

Clay nearly laughed. "That's a pretty big leap. I'm

not going to fall in love with Astrid. I'm just not. That's not in the cards for me."

"Why not? Why do you keep clinging to this idea that you'll never find love again? It makes me so sad."

"Daddy," Delia called from the other room. "Come watch the fish with me and do the thing where you make the funny voices."

Clay gestured over his shoulder with a nod. "That's why. Delia is my life. I can't let a woman come into our lives and get close to her and then leave again. It wouldn't just kill me, it would hurt her. I need to worry about her, too."

"I still think you have to take that risk at some point. If you're going to have a full life, you might need to take the leap."

"You, Delia, and my job are my life. That's enough for me. There's no reason to get my heart squashed again." He got up from the couch, but Miranda stuck out her leg to stop him.

"Hold on a second."

"What?"

"I just want you to promise me one thing."

Clay dropped his head to one side, knowing that whatever she was about to say would likely make his life more difficult. "What's that?"

"Promise me that you will at least be open to the idea that love might find you again. It doesn't have to be with Astrid and it doesn't have to be right now. You don't even have to be open all the way. Just a little bit. I hate the idea that one person hurt you and you aren't willing to try again."

"I'm not sure that advice helps me for my trip to LA with Astrid."

"For that, I want you to have fun. You've worked too hard for too long not to simply enjoy the ride."

Miranda had officially not helped him get anywhere with his thinking, but she wasn't responsible for his inability to see clearly on this matter. "I'll try to keep that in mind."

"Daddy!" Delia ran back into the room with a look of pure concern. "I'm waiting."

Clay couldn't help but smile at Delia. "I know. I'm coming."

"Clay? One more question," Miranda said.

"What's that?"

"Any thoughts on which direction I should point Astrid in when I go dress shopping with her?" Miranda got up from the couch and rounded it to face him.

Clay couldn't begin to formulate an answer to this question. "I have no earthly idea. Surprise me."

Miranda snickered. "I'd be careful what you wish for."

Most people probably assumed that a former model would live to shop for clothes. The truth was that Astrid saw it as a necessary evil, especially with her job, where she needed to look the part of capable businesswoman. Attending the awards ceremony with Clay would require a far different look than was appropriate for the office. She was relieved she was going to have Tara and Miranda on hand to be her sounding board.

She met them downtown at Ruby, an exclusive high-end boutique, early Friday evening. The store manager, Cherise, had a bottle of champagne on ice for Tara and Astrid, and for Miranda, she'd brought in a smoothie from a juice bar nearby and sparkling water. Cherise had also taken much of the deliberation out of this process by pulling two dozen dresses from their extensive selection, after speaking with Astrid on the phone and finding out the nature of the event and what Astrid wanted.

Tara and Miranda set their purses on a brilliant fuchsia velvet settee. Above them, chandeliers dripped with crystals and provided soft lighting, while a plush white carpet beneath their feet made every step feel luxurious. The three of them began the process of perusing the gowns the manager had selected.

"What sort of look are you going for?" Tara asked.

Astrid glanced at Cherise. This had been a difficult thing for Astrid to put into words during their phone conversation. "Classic. Beautiful. Tasteful. But still sexy." Astrid pinched her thumb and index finger together. "A little sexy. Nothing too over the top."

"Smart. You'll be in a room full of nerdy architects. You don't need anyone fainting or going into cardiac arrest," Tara said.

Astrid laughed. "That wasn't my worry. I was thinking more about professionalism."

"You don't want to play it too safe and look like you walked straight out of the office." Miranda chose a slinky black gown from the rack. "How about this?"

Astrid considered the dress, which had a very low neckline and an especially slim silhouette. If she'd been going for full-on seduction, it would have been a no-brainer. But this was a work trip and Astrid intended to dress accordingly. "I think that might be too sexy." Plus, she didn't want to be the center of attention that night. It was Clay's accomplishment. She was his support system. But still, she could imagine the silky fabric draping her bare skin, and what it might feel like to stand next to him while wearing it. Every nerve ending in her body would come to life, a torment she wasn't sure she could endure. To feel that sexy while with the man she couldn't get out of her head, when she knew that it was in everyone's best interests to keep things professional? That would be a waste of a perfectly beautiful dress.

"What about this?" Tara offered another choice, a simple off-white strapless gown.

"Elegant, but don't you think that's a little bridal?"

That turned Miranda's head. "If anything is going to terrify my brother, it's a wedding dress."

Astrid had wondered about the fate of Clay's marriage to his daughter's mother but had been understandably terrified to ask him. She only knew that he was divorced. "Was it that bad?"

"Yes. She ripped my brother's heart out and walked all over it with the wardrobe of Louboutin and Jimmy Choo shoes she bought after cleaning out one of his investment accounts and subsequently moving to the Maldives." Miranda rolled her eyes. "Like she needs all those heels in a place where there's nothing but beaches."

Astrid was floored. She had no idea it had been so dreadful. Was that part of the reason Clay was so closed off? "How could a woman do that? And leave behind her child?"

Miranda shook her head in disbelief. "I have no idea. I mean, I'm sure my brother is not easy to be married to, but he was devoted to her and he would do anything for Delia. I don't know what else she could have possibly wanted from him."

Astrid felt as though her heart was being tugged

from her chest to her throat. The thought of what Clay had been through was so sad. "That's so awful. I feel terrible for him."

"Me too," Tara added. "Every time I hear that story, it sounds more and more unbelievable."

"Oh, it happened," Miranda said. "I was there for the aftermath and trust me, it was not pretty."

"Hence the fear of wedding gowns," Tara said.

"Precisely." Miranda returned her attention to the rack of dresses. "Let's get back to a topic that's a bit more fun. Like finding you the perfect gown."

A few more minutes of browsing and they decided on three options, then Astrid went into the fitting room to try them on. The first two were instantly rejected by Tara and Miranda. One was deemed too drab and the other too ill-fitting. With less than a week until they left for the ceremony, there was no time for major alterations. Astrid tried on the final option, an off-the-shoulder navy blue gown with a fitted bodice and full skirt. It was absolutely gorgeous and struck the perfect balance between professional and sexy.

"I think this is the one." Astrid zipped open the curtain and emerged from the fitting room.

Tara and Miranda looked at Astrid, then at each other. "Yes. That's it," they said in unison.

"It's perfect," Miranda added. "My brother is a lucky guy to have you as his date that night."

"It's not a date," Astrid quickly followed.

Miranda cleared her throat. "Right. Of course."

Astrid took one more look at herself in the full-length mirror. When she swished the skirt, she realized there was a high slit hidden in the folds. "Do you think this is okay?" she asked, kicking it open.

"With your legs?" Tara asked. "Yes."

Astrid smiled and shook her head, then retreated into the dressing room, relieved this much was decided. She didn't want to think about it anymore. She changed back into her regular clothes and asked Cherise to ring up the dress. Then she took a seat with Tara and Miranda.

"I wanted to ask you both about something. Johnathon's brother, Andrew, has a development firm up in Seattle, right?"

"He does," Miranda answered. "Why?"

Astrid pressed her lips together, wondering if she was pulling at seemingly random threads. "Tara, do you remember Sandy? She was already working at Sterling when I started."

"Of course I do," Tara answered. "She was on staff when I started as well. In fact, Grant gave her the job of being my assistant on my first day. She'd been working with Johnathon and knew about his interest in the Seaport project. She was able to help us deal with the city."

"And then she disappeared. At the most inconvenient time as I remember."

Tara downed the last of her champagne and got up to pour herself another glass. "It was a total nightmare. She vanished on the Friday before the presentation. Grant and I spent all weekend trying to fix the mistake Clay made."

Astrid was still putting all of this together, but she was certainly suspicious that something wasn't quite right. "That's what always bothered me. The idea that Clay would miss a detail like the site orientation. I've worked with him for nearly two months now and he simply doesn't make errors like that."

"Anyone can mess up," Miranda said. "Even my brother, the control freak."

Astrid sighed. "Okay, well, here's the thing. I ran into Sandy the other day at the bakery across from the Sterling offices."

Tara's eyes grew impossibly large. "You did? Did you talk to her?"

"Of course I did. I wasn't going to leave without trying to find out what happened. She said that she'd been moonlighting while at Sterling. Then something about her other boss pulling her away. Something about owing him a favor. When I asked what the other company did, she said it was a development firm in Seattle." To Astrid's great surprise, the theory that had been tumbling around in her head didn't sound nearly as half-baked now that she'd had the guts to say it out loud. "That got me thinking about Andrew. He's in Seattle. He has a real estate development firm. He and Johnathon had been estranged for years. Andrew didn't even come to Johnathon's funeral."

"Right," Tara interjected. "And Grant and I ran into him in San Diego two weeks later, which seemed really odd to me. He could come to town for a baseball game, but he couldn't show up to pay his respects?"

Miranda shook her head. "I don't know where you two are going with this, but remember that Andrew reached out to me when he was here right after you and Grant saw him? He came over to the house. We had a very nice conversation. He was contrite and apologetic. He felt bad that he hadn't come to the funeral."

"So you don't think he's capable of interfering with Sterling?" Astrid asked.

"I think it's cute that you want to explain away my

brother's mistake, but I really don't see how Andrew could possibly do anything like that," Miranda said. "What would Andrew get out of it, anyway? Silently tampering with a job? It seems like if he was trying to get even with Johnathon, he would have done something considerably more public. Now that Johnathon is gone, it seems even more unlikely."

"Maybe," Astrid said, gnawing on her finger. "You're probably right."

"How did you leave things with Sandy?" Tara asked.

"I told her that if she needed a job, she should call me. She was a great employee, even though she quit with no notice. And something told me not to burn that bridge."

Tara pursed her lips. "Let me know if she calls you."

"Oh, I will." Astrid's mind was swirling with the details. None of it seemed to add up. And maybe that was Miranda's point. Astrid's theory went nowhere and she needed to leave it alone.

Four

Clay wanted to believe that he saw things others couldn't. Possibilities. Potential. His sister Miranda, a gifted interior designer, was the same way. It was a talent they'd both seemingly been blessed with at birth, and according to their grandmother, they got it from their mom. Not that either Clay or Miranda was ever able to confirm this for themselves. She'd left them behind when they were still young.

This talent made Clay quite good at predicting how a situation would go. As much as he'd been thinking about the trip to LA for the Architect of the Year award, he had not seen it happening like this—Astrid in the passenger seat of his Bentley SUV, distracting him in every way imaginable. It was more than just her beauty and beguiling smell, a most intriguing mix of spring rain and vanilla. He'd trained himself to ignore a few of her more alluring qualities. But Astrid was a fidgeter. She couldn't sit still. She was constantly shifting her weight in her seat, adjusting the direction of the air vents in front of her, and straightening her clothes.

"Everything okay?" he asked, hoping there was some way to make it stop. He needed to keep his eyes trained on the road and she was drawing his attention every few seconds. If there was a problem, he desperately wanted to fix it. He was already on edge knowing the awards show was awaiting him that evening.

"It's not like you to ask how I'm doing," she quipped.

"And it's not like you to not offer a long-winded answer that somehow manages to weave in your entire life story."

A breathy burst of indignation left her lips, and she smacked his leg with the back of her hand. "You're so mean."

He couldn't help it, but the strike and her accusatory tone made him run about five degrees hotter. "I'm just being honest. You do like to tell people everything about everything."

"That's better than being so closed off. You don't tell anyone anything." She leaned forward and shot him a sideways glance with narrowed eyes. She had the most expressive face he'd ever seen, and of course, the most beautiful. "It's one of your most annoying qualities."

A corner of his mouth betrayed him by twitching with the beginnings of a smile. Astrid was normally so painfully kind that it felt as though he was dying a slow death. He liked it when she was being spirited and calling him out. He felt as though they were on a more even playing field. "If you want me to talk, I'll gladly share the things you do that drive me nuts." *Your chest heaves before you sigh, which is often. And you are constantly gathering your hair in your hands, twisting it, and pulling it over one shoulder, when all it does is fall back into place in a pleasing cascade of waves. And I see you laugh when you talk to other people, and your face lights up like the brightest sunrise. You never laugh when you're around me.*

"Just tell me. You can't hurt my feelings."

Oh, but he sensed that he could. She'd tried to play things off the night he attempted to quit the Seaport project, all under the guise of wanting to work through their problems, but he'd sensed that he was getting under her skin. It was the only thing that had made him back off. He knew she could hurt him, but he didn't have it in him to do the same to her. That was part of what made her such a dangerous, unknown quantity. "You ask a lot of questions. Personal questions."

"I'm trying to understand you. You are a puzzle."

"Do you think you can solve me?"

"I know I can. It might take some time, in part because you're hiding so many of the pieces."

He knew very well what she was getting at—she'd asked about Delia that day in the office when she'd brought him doughnuts and was trying to mend things between them. It had been an admirable attempt and he'd swatted it away, but she had no idea how deep his instinct was to protect Delia. "You asked about my daughter the other day. What do you want to know?"

"Is this a trick?" The thicker part of her Norwegian accent came out when she was particularly skeptical of something.

"No. I'm not saying I'll tell you everything, but you are free to ask."

"I don't know a thing. What's her name? How old is she?"

"Her name is Delia and she's five years old. She's in kindergarten."

"What is she like? Is she like you?"

"Are you asking if she's grumpy and no fun at parties? Because those would be odd qualities for a five-year-old."

She unleashed a quiet laugh, and it did something to him. It propped up his ego and made him want to try for more. "I meant is she brilliant? Is she very smart?"

He hadn't been prepared for that question at all, but he wasn't surprised that Astrid would pick up on everything, even the things he tried to downplay. "She is exceptionally smart. I'm certain she'll eventually outpace me in that department."

"What does she like to do?"

"She loves books and playing outside. She's crazy about anything with a rainbow on it or that sparkles. She's very observant, so she likes to take it all in."

"Just like her dad."

"It's true. I do like rainbows."

Astrid burst into even more laughter, the musical tones filling the entire car. "That's not what I meant. I was talking about being observant. You love to sit back and watch. You study everything and then decide what to do."

"You aren't wrong." Her insight was uncanny, which was remarkable considering they'd only known each other for two months. He did do that, but it was simply his personality. He was far less likely to make a mistake if he took in all available information first before formulating a plan or making a decision. Being precise and measured always paid off. And the times when he hadn't done that, the times when he'd followed his heart without thinking too much, he'd ultimately paid a steep price.

"What about Delia's mother? Miranda told me a little bit about her. I'm so sorry."

Just like that, whatever happiness he was feeling about having this effortless back-and-forth with Astrid went up in thin air. He had to wonder what his sister had been thinking when she'd shared details of his personal life with Astrid. "Next topic." He didn't want to be cruel and cut her off, but he also didn't want to explain what had happened. How does a man go about illustrating the greatest rejection of his life? That would only lead to more questions. His marriage was contained in Pandora's box, and he wanted it kept closed.

"I knew I'd hit a dead end with you, eventually."

He had to turn this around—he couldn't take any more tension between them. Not with the nervousness of the awards show ahead. "What about you? Why don't you tell me more about you? I don't know much other than that you and my sister both married the same man."

"I thought I talked too much about me. That's basically what you said ten minutes ago."

"But what about your childhood? Your upbringing? You don't talk much about that at all. What were you like as a child?" He could imagine Astrid as the ingenue, sweet and girly, wearing pink dresses and dreaming up fantastical ideas in her head.

"I don't really like to talk about myself as a little girl. I did not have an easy childhood."

This was not something he'd anticipated. Astrid's generosity had made him assume that she'd had an easy upbringing and a nurturing home life. Where else could that have come from? And to think he'd always assumed they had little to nothing in common. "You don't have to talk about it if you don't want to."

She turned to him and he stole a quick glance, then returned his eyes to the road. Even in that split second, he saw an ocean of vulnerability in her eyes. It only made him want to save her from whatever hurt was bottled up inside her. "No. I will tell you. It's only fair, since you told me about Delia." She cleared her throat and wrapped her arms around her waist. "I am the youngest of six kids and the only girl in the family. I spent my entire childhood trying to get the attention of my father and brothers, but all they wanted to do was to push me aside to keep me safe."

"That doesn't sound so bad. It's natural for anyone to want to protect the most vulnerable member of the family. As the youngest and the only girl, I'm sure they saw you that way."

"I didn't want to spend my life on a high shelf, like a china teacup. All I ever wanted was to be included." She went on to explain that she used to dress like her brothers, in jeans and sweatshirts, and she begged them to let her play football with them. Her mother, who had wanted a sixth child only so they could try for a girl, had been hoping she could finally have a heavy dose of feminine trappings in the household after years of being the only woman, but Astrid wanted nothing to do with it. It caused friction with all members of the family.

"A lot of times, I felt like an intruder in my own home. I never belonged," she said, again shifting in her seat. "And that extended to school. The boys thought I was ugly and only a few of the girls wanted to be my friend."

"Ugly? You have got to be kidding." There wasn't an un-beautiful bone in Astrid's body. She was nothing less than pure grace and refinement, like she'd walked out of a portrait in a museum. "You must have just gone through an awkward phase. That happens to everyone."

"Until I was eighteen? That's a long time."

"What happened when you turned eighteen?"

"I went to university and figured out that if I stopped hiding under bulky sweaters, boys would pay attention to me."

Clay swallowed, finding it hard to get past the tightness in his throat. The thought of her revealing herself in the interest of drawing the male gaze did something to him. "But you became a model. You walked runways and were on the covers of magazines, right? That must have felt like a triumph. You showed them all that they were wrong."

She sucked in a deep breath and cast her sights out the window. "Maybe. But it didn't change who I was for all of the years before that happened. I still feel like that awkward girl a lot of the time."

"Even now?" If only she could see the way he saw her—flawless and composed. A woman to be admired, and quite possibly reckoned with.

"Even now." Astrid shifted in her seat again. "Honestly, your sister made me feel like that at first. It was hard to be around her and know that she was ultimately what my ex-husband wanted, all because I had fallen short of his expectations."

"Miranda was also robbed of her future with Johnathon, so I don't know how much there is in her situation to envy."

"She has his baby. That's no small thing." Astrid's voice cracked, and Clay felt as though the earth had shifted beneath him. The heartache Miranda had told him about was very real. And against his better judgment, there was a big part of him that wanted nothing more than to take all of it away.

Astrid swallowed back the emotion of her admission. Being vulnerable with Clay was far more difficult than it was with any other person she'd ever known. His tough outer shell was not only familiar, it was impenetrable. She knew the way he dismissed weakness and feelings as nothing more than a nuisance. She hoped he didn't think any less of her because she'd been willing to open up. The desire to keep him thinking the best of her was a strong one, with a fiercely beating heart and a need to survive. "We don't need to talk about me anymore. I want to know how you're feeling about tonight."

He noticeably tightened his grip on the steering wheel. It was another chance to admire his hands, just like she often found herself doing when they were in the office together. She especially loved to watch them in motion when he sketched up ideas before working them out on the computer. He openly admitted to being old-school and preferring paper and pencil to a mouse and a monitor. Just the thought of him employing some of that artistry and brilliance when putting his hands on her body was enough to make Astrid shudder. She couldn't imagine him ever wanting her like that.

"I'd be lying if I said I wasn't at least a little bit nervous. But I already told you that I would be."

"You must feel some certainty that you're going to win."

"I know nothing of the sort. The field of nominees is exceptionally talented. Men and women I deeply admire."

"I still think you'll win. And I think you know that, too." She didn't believe for a moment that he didn't know his own excellence.

"I don't."

"You're so confident. Everything you do at work is exact and deliberate. I often wonder how you can spend your whole day being so sure of yourself." It was the absolute truth and it amazed her that he might not actually see it. Astrid would have done anything to have one-tenth of the confidence he did.

"I am sure of my work. But that doesn't make it the best. It's only *my* best." He shrugged and exited the highway. Soon they were on Hollywood Boulevard, and then in the thick of Beverly Hills, with its wide boulevards and endless stream of luxury cars. This was a familiar landscape for Astrid. She had moved to Los Angeles after the grind of living in New York got to her. She'd yearned for wide open spaces and sunshine. Little had she known that she should have gone to San Diego for that. In LA, she'd mostly gotten bad traffic and fewer modeling jobs. But it was also where she met Johnathon, so she couldn't regret the move she'd made. It not only led her to the romance she'd never thought she would have, he opened up her whole world. Johnathon was fantastic at showing her the possibilities in life.

Clay pulled up in front of the Essex Beverly Hills Hotel. The bellman rushed to open Astrid's door as the valet rounded to Clay's side of the car. Astrid waited while he handed over the keys, then joined him as they walked inside. Astrid had stayed at five-star hotels all over the world, but it didn't make the lobby any less glamorous or beautiful, with a true old Hollywood feel. She loved being here with Clay, although what she really wanted to know was what it might be like to arrive with him, holding hands, as his partner. Instead, she was the tagalong, the woman who had been instructed by the company to attend.

They were greeted at the check-in desk by a female clerk who was, in Astrid's estimation, exceptionally pretty. Astrid couldn't help but notice that this didn't seem to register on Clay's radar. The realization made her feel a bit better about her own failure to capture his attention. Perhaps he was so focused on everything else in his life that women weren't even a passing thought. Was that because of his daughter's mother? Despite not knowing the full story of Clay's past, she thought there seemed to be considerable pain in that part of his life.

She wanted to know more. She longed to know it all, to at least have all of the pieces of the puzzle that was Clay Morgan so she could try to assemble them. The next twenty-four hours might be the only true chance she had to crack open his hard exterior and get to the root of what made him tick. She knew what he was like in the office—all business. And at most social events, at least back in San Diego, he was as distant from her as she could imagine. This was her window. If only he would let her in.

The clerk clacked away at her keyboard, then cocked her head to one side. "Mr. Morgan, I see you have a two-bedroom suite on your reservation. Is that correct?"

"No. It should be two rooms. Separate rooms."

The clerk returned to her computer, shaking her head from side to side. "I'm sorry, but I only see one room on your reservation, sir. It's a beautiful suite with two separate bedrooms and bathrooms. Will that be suitable? I'm afraid the rest of the hotel is booked for the state architecture commission's annual awards."

"Yes, I know that. That's why I'm here." He blew out an exasperated breath.

He was frustrated and Astrid saw no reason for it, other than his regular requests to be far away from Astrid. "It's fine, Clay. Really. It's fine. I'll stay on my side of the suite. You won't have to worry about me."

He turned to her with a pained expression on his face. "That's not what I'm saying. This just isn't what I expected."

"I'm very sorry, sir. The hotel will send up a bottle of champagne as a way of apologizing," the clerk said, offering two key cards.

"I don't think we need champagne."

"We do need the champagne. Thank you very much." Astrid took the cards from the woman. "Can you point us to the elevators?"

"Opposite side of the lobby."

"Thank you."

Astrid wasn't about to wait for Clay so he could further tell her why he was so disappointed to learn they'd been booked in the same room. He caught up with her at the elevator bank.

"I'm sorry," he said. "I just don't do well with surprises. And I guess the stress of the award show feels more real now that we're here."

Astrid slowly drew a breath through her nose, silently

begging the universe for strength. "I understand. It'll all be fine." The elevator dinged and she stepped on board.

Clay and Astrid rode up to the top floor of the hotel. They wound their way around to their room, which was tucked away at the far end of the hall. Clay waved the key in front of the electronic lock and the light shined green. He opened the door, but held it for Astrid to enter first. She gladly accepted the chivalrous act from him. It felt like one of the few times he'd admitted that she was a woman and he was a man.

The room was just as elegant as the lobby downstairs, with a generous living area decorated in a color scheme of warm gold and cool gray with accents of black and white. "They've done a lovely job with the Hollywood Regency decor," she said. "It's all quite accurate to the period, as near as I can tell. Of course, I'm no expert. What do you think?"

"Do you know about Regency from when you lived in Los Angeles?"

Astrid set down her purse and padded over to the window to take in the view of the pool area below, ringed by palm trees, the water a pure blue. Now that it was fall, there were only a few guests sunning themselves in the slightly cooler temperatures. "I've been studying at night. I want to understand the art and architecture side of what we do at Sterling."

"Really?"

"Why? Does that surprise you?"

"To be honest, it does."

Astrid shot him a pointed glance. He looked so perfect, standing there with his hands stuffed into his pockets. All she wanted to do was to kiss him, if only to gather a few more pieces of the Clay Morgan puzzle.

What would it be like? Would he want the same things she did? The questions sometimes kept her up at night. "I can't always get to sleep. So I spend time researching these things. And I am truly interested. I know that you do more than design buildings to make money. I know you put a lot of attention into the process. I just want to understand how much."

He nodded, and Astrid scanned his face for some sign that she was softening him, but there was no real indication things were moving in that direction. "Well, good. I'm glad you're taking things at work so seriously."

"Does that make you feel like we might be better suited to work together than you previously thought?"

He pressed his lips together tightly. "The jury is still out on that. We're very different people."

Astrid felt as though everything with Clay was two steps forward, two steps back—the world's most frustrating cha-cha. "Sometimes different is good. It helps to see more than one point of view."

There was a knock at the door, giving Clay his excuse to take a break from their conversation. It was one bellman with their bags, and another wheeling a room service cart with champagne on ice, two glasses, and a plate of strawberries. If only she and Clay were there for romantic reasons...the mood would have been perfectly set.

Clay tipped the bellmen, then went to take their two hanging bags.

"Let me hang these for you," the bellman said. "The longer one is quite heavy."

"Heavy?" Clay asked.

Astrid waved the man in her direction, deciding she would take the bedroom on the farthest side of the suite. "Gowns are not light."

"I hope you didn't bring anything too extravagant," Clay called after her.

As if she needed more confirmation that he wanted her to stay buttoned up, professional, and platonic. "Trust me," she answered. "It's the exact right amount of extravagant."

The bellman snickered as he hung the garment bag in the closet for her. "Anything else I can do for you, ma'am?"

"Not unless you can figure out how to get my room-mate to loosen up."

"The champagne?"

"Not a bad idea." Astrid led the way back into the living room and the bellmen departed, leaving Astrid and Clay all alone in their exquisite surroundings. She beelined for the bubbly. "A drink to take the edge off before we get dressed and head downstairs?"

Clay nearly lunged for the bottle, grasping her hand to stop her from peeling back the foil. "No. It's not a good idea."

"Why not?" She peered up at his handsome face, try-ing not to fixate on the tempting slack in his lower lip as he tried to stop her or the way the warmth from his hand was sending shockwaves through her.

"Champagne is for celebrating. I'd rather save it for later."

Astrid waited for a heartbeat or two, then plunged the bottle back into the ice bucket. "Fine." She would not let this development ruin her evening. *Later* sounded vaguely promising. She'd cling to whatever hope she could.

Five

Clay didn't like to worry. It was a waste of time and energy, especially when he found himself doing it over things he couldn't control, like the Architect of the Year awards. "You can't do a thing about it. Relax," he said to himself in the mirror as he straightened his bowtie.

But I care about this. Thus he was stuck in what felt like an endless cycle of unease. As much as he didn't care about other people's opinions, and was confident in his work, there was this part of him that needed the validation of the award. With little to no parental guidance as a kid, he'd spent his entire life without a stamp of approval from anyone, except perhaps Miranda. Their grandmother certainly hadn't provided it. If anything, she'd treated the two of them as a burden. He wanted this accolade. He'd worked so hard to get it.

He took a cleansing breath, determined to shake off

his unsettled feelings. He just needed to get through the next few hours until they announced the winner. Then he'd deal with whatever had happened. And for now, perhaps it was best to focus on his next challenge: facing Astrid and whatever maddening dress she'd chosen for tonight.

He opened the door to his room and strode out into the central living area of their suite. He wasn't the type to pace, but he found himself doing exactly that, thinking about Astrid in her room…wondering what state of dress, or undress, she might be in. He swallowed hard, realizing what an additional test this would be, spending the evening with Astrid when he was admittedly already weak. It was creating a whole new layer of trepidation within him, one that he felt physically. Yes, she was there for moral support. Nothing else. But if he was being honest, he wanted more.

For the time being, he needed a drink to soothe his ragged edges. He should have taken Astrid's suggestion that they open the champagne an hour ago, but he hadn't. He'd made the excuse that it was for celebrating, when in reality he saw it as too romantic. Now, he could easily imagine the repercussions of opening it without her. She'd be mad. So instead, he went for a bottle of good bourbon from the well-stocked bar. Clay unscrewed the top and poured a healthy dose into a cut crystal glass. It was nearly to his lips when he heard Astrid's door open behind him. He turned, and the instant he saw her, the only logical reaction was to toss back his drink. The whole thing. One gulp.

"Thirsty?" Astrid asked.

He nodded eagerly, unable to peel his eyes from the vision of her. She was nothing short of pure elegance in a deep blue dress that showed off her beauty in a way that nothing she'd ever worn to work could possibly do. The gown clung to her upper arms, flaunting her sculpted shoulders and dewy skin. The neckline was understated, but dipped low enough to drive him crazy, accentuating the swell of her bust. It took too little effort for his mind to sketch in the hidden details of her breasts, the fullness and what they might feel like in his hands. Her long and graceful neck was adorned with a single gleaming gem in a square cut hanging from a chain.

"Is that a diamond?" he asked, fighting for his voice to reach full volume.

Her slender fingers found the stone. Something about seeing her touch herself made the tension in his hips grow even tighter. "It is. It was a gift from Johnathon. I couldn't bear to part with it, even after the divorce."

There was the reminder of just how intertwined Clay and Astrid were—she and his sister had been married to the same man. Astrid owned a chunk of the company he worked for. There were a million reasons to not feel the way he did about her, but there seemed to be just as many thinly veiled excuses to pick her up and take her back into the bedroom right now. His dream might be waiting downstairs in the hotel ballroom, but it also felt like it was standing right in front of him.

Get your head on straight.

"It's beautiful." He poured himself another drink and downed it just as fast. The burn was vicious, and he knew that he deserved it for the things that were going through his head right now. "Can I make you a drink? Or we could open the champagne if you really want to."

"I'll take one of whatever you're having." She floated

closer to him, bringing along his first real breath of her perfume. It was warm and sweet, just like her. "You were right. We should save the champagne for after the ceremony. To celebrate your achievement."

"Stop saying that."

She took one more step, closing the gap between them. She smoothed the lapel of his jacket, while all he could do was stare down at her hand on his chest and fight the wish that he wasn't wearing this suit and her dress was puddled on the floor. "I believe in the power of positive thinking. You're brilliant and talented. The rest will work itself out."

It was a mystery how she could have so much confidence in him when she'd only known him for a few months. He'd had to live with himself for thirty-five years and he wasn't convinced of anything she was saying. "But the decision has already been made. Somewhere downstairs in the hotel ballroom is an envelope with a name on it that might not be mine."

She peered up at him, her impossibly warm eyes flickering with optimism. "Positive thinking, Clay. Only good thoughts." She patted his chest, then looked away. "Now, where's my drink?"

"Oh. Right." Clay felt as though half of his brain had suddenly decided to take the night off. He grabbed a second glass and poured a splash of bourbon for her.

Meanwhile, Astrid traipsed over to the end table next to one of the sofas and picked up the house phone. "Yes. Hello. We have a bottle of champagne in our room that needs fresh ice." She grinned at him, her whole face lighting up with a hint of mischief. "We're going to be celebrating later this evening and it would be a shame if it had gone warm."

He was so drawn to her right now, it was comical. If only she knew she could ask him for anything and he would give it to her without reservation. "Thank you for doing that," he said as she ended the call. "I'm sorry I didn't want to open the bottle earlier."

"I understand you're feeling superstitious. It's okay."

Once again, Astrid saw right through him. "It sounds silly, though, doesn't it? Plus, you're the one who's talking about being positive. I'm not employing logic or optimism."

"You really are worked up about tonight, aren't you? All that talk about nerves was real."

"I'm sure it makes me seem like a fool, but yes. I don't enjoy crowds. I don't enjoy phony social situations, and I do not relish the thought of sitting in that room, hearing my name announced among the nominees, and not ultimately hearing that I won. I know it won't be the end of the world, but I'm still dreading that moment."

She approached him slowly, making him feel like he was a buck alone in a meadow, poised to run off into the woods at any time. Stopping mere inches from him, she reached up and reassuringly rubbed his arm, and his defenses wavered. It would be so simple to kiss her and take her in his arms.

"I think you need to give up control tonight," she said in a calm and measured tone.

"Excuse me?"

"You like to be in charge. You like to manage every little thing. But it's not going to work in this situation. You have no control."

"So what do I do? Radically change my personality and suddenly become laid back and relaxed?"

She shook her head. "No. You put me in the driver's seat. I am in charge. You do what I say. No exceptions."

He didn't mean to scoff at her suggestion, but the breathy grunt escaped his lips before he could even think about it. "That won't work."

"But it will. I just need you to trust me."

"I don't do that, either."

She fluttered her long, dark lashes at him—it felt deeply manipulative and yet it might have been the sexiest thing he'd seen in his lifetime. "Let me put it this way. If you don't give me control, I'm leaving. Do you want me to go?"

He tried not to look at the enticing contours of her bare collarbone or think about what it might be like to kiss her there, but he failed. The thought of Astrid abandoning him was unthinkable, even for the man who'd spent so much time pushing her away. "No. I don't want you to go."

Astrid wasn't about to gloat over her win in getting Clay to acquiesce to her plan. At least not outwardly. On the inside, she was doing a victory dance. Progress. Finally. If nothing else good happened in the next twenty-four hours, she would at least know that she'd convinced him of something.

She held his hand on the elevator as they rode down to the lobby. He shot her a questioning look when she first did it, and she returned the expression, but hers came with two arched eyebrows and the subliminal reminder that she was in charge and he'd better not question her methods. Luckily, the presence of several other guests kept him quiet. She knew that human contact would help him stay grounded. It would help him relax.

Even when he radiated so much tension she was worried he might snap in two.

Downstairs, they wound their way through the elegant lobby and back to the ballroom where the dinner and awards ceremony were being held. They waited in line to check in, and Astrid noticed that there was a photographer with professional lighting and a backdrop waiting for them after that step. She already anticipated that Clay wouldn't want his picture taken, and she armed herself with the appropriate argument.

"Yes. Hi. Astrid Sterling and Clay Morgan," he said when they reached the table. "We're both with Sterling Enterprises in San Diego."

Astrid hadn't realized how much pride she would take in her job and the fact that she worked with Clay until she heard him say that. It made her heart swell.

"Yes, Mr. Morgan. We have you at table two right in front of the stage. Good luck this evening."

"Just what I wanted," Clay muttered sarcastically to Astrid. "To be on full display, right in the very front of the room."

"Optimism. Think of it as a shorter walk if you win." She nodded at the photographer. "Ready to get your picture taken, guy who doesn't want to be in the spotlight?"

"Do we have to?"

"Yes. We do. You'll be fine. I've done this a million times."

"Am I supposed to stand a certain way?"

"One hand in your pants pocket, the other at your side. Don't square your shoulders to the camera." She tugged on his hand until they were standing before the backdrop. Astrid instinctively angled her body and placed her hand on her hip.

Clay took her directions perfectly. So much so that the photographer took note. "You two look like you've done this before."

Clay actually smiled. "It's all her. She's the pro."

"Well, you look amazing together. Enjoy your night."

Astrid could hardly contain her grin as they strolled into the room. She was certain that they *did* look good together. Very, very good. "Shall we get a drink before they have us sit for dinner?"

"Yes. Let's see if there's anyone you need to meet."

Astrid relinquished a bit of control as she allowed Clay to lead the way through the throng of people in the ballroom. A steady din of conversation fought with the jazz piped through the sound system, and Astrid couldn't help but notice that there weren't nearly enough women in the room. She worked in what was still a male-dominated industry, which only made her want to recommit herself to her role at Sterling. She, Tara, and Miranda were in a position of power and they couldn't squander the opportunity.

"What would you like to drink?" Clay asked.

Of course he didn't know her cocktail of choice— this was one of very few times they'd seen each other in a social setting. "White wine."

"Nothing stronger?"

"I need to keep my wits about me. I am in charge tonight." Again, he smiled, fueling Astrid's desire for him. *Focus on the awards. Focus on support.*

After Clay got their drinks from the bar, he spotted a few people he wanted her to meet, mostly architects from the firm in Santa Barbara where he'd once worked. "I want you all to meet Astrid Sterling. Astrid and I work together. She's the project manager for our bid on the Seaport Promenade project in San Diego."

"I hear good things," one of the men said. "The buzz is that Sterling is at the top of the heap for that one."

"We still have two more phases of the bid process to go through until it's final," Astrid said. "But thank you. I appreciate your kind words."

"Astrid is amazing," Clay said. "She's so good at keeping us on schedule that we're actually a bit ahead of the game."

Astrid could've been knocked over by a puff of air. Clay spent so much time saying they didn't work well together. It never occurred to her that he actually thought she did a good job. Of course, she wasn't about to let on while they were standing with a group of their peers, but she did tuck away the compliment in her memory. She'd keep it close for quite some time. "Clay's the real rock star of our team," Astrid said. "Without him, we wouldn't stand a chance."

"Exactly why he was nominated tonight," the man said, just as a chime was sounded, announcing that everyone should take their seats for dinner. "Wishing you the best of luck."

Astrid and Clay found their seats at table two, where it turned out they were seated with the other three finalists and their guests. After cursory introductions, Clay sat next to Astrid, his face drawn with stress. "This is all too real."

"Real is good," she whispered into his ear, letting her mouth linger near his neck so she could breathe in the warm scent of his cologne.

He reached under the table and took her hand, making her heart nearly stop beating. His mouth was right by her cheek, his breath soft against her skin. "Whatever happens tonight, I'm glad you're here."

"I wouldn't want to be anywhere else."

Dinner was soon served—a succulent red snapper with Thai flavors of coconut milk, lemongrass, and ginger, along with jasmine rice and sautéed spinach. Clay picked through his plate, not seeming interested in food.

"Don't you like it?" Astrid asked.

"It's delicious. I just don't have an appetite."

Astrid hated seeing him like this. She wished she could push fast-forward on the ceremony so he could get on with his life. "Does that mean I can have your dessert?"

Clay slung his arm over the back of Astrid's chair, which made her sit a little straighter in her seat. It made her dig deep for breaths. "If there's chocolate, probably not."

"Fair enough."

The dessert did indeed have chocolate—a flourless cake with a salted caramel drizzle. Everyone was enjoying it, even Clay, when a woman took the stage and began the presentation. Again, Clay set aside his fork, seeming disinterested. *It really must be bad if he isn't finishing that cake.* She was beginning to see that he had a weakness for sweets.

He shifted in his seat as the first slate of awards were given, all in the area of residential architecture, which was not Clay's area of expertise. The plates were cleared from the tables, glasses of champagne were delivered to all, and Clay continued to struggle to sit still. Astrid would have done anything to make his trepidation go away. As the awards shifted to commercial architecture, she leaned closer and raised her head to speak into his ear. "You're almost there. Just breathe."

He nodded, looking down at the table and a cocktail napkin that he was folding and unfolding with one hand, like he was creating the origami equivalent of worry beads. Astrid decided she would occupy his other hand, so she reached under the table and found it resting on his firm and muscular thigh. She pushed past her own desire to explore his long limbs and instead squeezed his hand. Every time he cleared his throat or shifted in his seat, she held it tight again.

"And finally, we come to the final award of the night. The Architect of the Year. As you all know, this award is open to both commercial and residential architects, so it really does represent the best of the best in our state. The nominees have demonstrated excellence with their vision, creativity, professionalism, and devotion to their craft."

The room was remarkably quiet and Astrid found herself now being as nervous as Clay was. Possibly more so. What was going to happen if he didn't win? Why had she been so stupid as to assure him that he would? She could easily imagine what their working relationship was going to become if he did end up losing. She would be an everyday reminder of the milestone he hadn't reached. It had her rethinking every optimistic thing she'd said over the last few hours. So much for her ridiculous attraction to him. She might have ruined any chance she ever had.

The show host announced the nominees, but the names came out muffled as Astrid's mind swirled with worry.

And then, just like that, it cleared.

"The winner is Clay Morgan, Sterling Enterprises."

Astrid and Clay looked at each other and froze. Then they both burst out laughing. Before she could think how to act, she found herself bolting up out of her seat and wrapping him up in the most enthusiastic hug she'd ever given anyone.

"Thank you," he said, loud and clear and right to her, as the audience rose to their feet and erupted in applause.

"Get up there," Astrid blurted. "You can thank me later."

Clay ascended the stairs up onto the stage and accepted his award. The way he admired the figurine told Astrid all she needed to know. The expression on his face was one of pure satisfaction and pride. "Wow," Clay said into the microphone. "Thank you for this honor. It means so much to me. I won't bore you with a long speech, but I want to thank everyone at Sterling Enterprises. Our team is incredible. I also want to thank my sister and my daughter, neither of whom could be here tonight, but to whom I owe everything. They are my life." He drew a deep breath and a pleased smile bloomed on his face. "Thank you."

Astrid was exactly the sort of woman to cry at happy moments, and the tears were streaming down her cheeks as she watched Clay leave the stage and accept congratulations from the people he passed on his way back to their table.

When he reached her, he was shaking his head. "I should have thanked you specifically from the stage. I'm so sorry. My mind was a blur up there."

"But you did thank me. I'm part of the team." She waved it off, not wanting to admit that she was slightly disappointed to not have her name mentioned. "Don't worry about it. I'm just happy for you."

"But you are an important part of my work life and I've been a jerk. I guess it took spending this time with you to see that we *can* work well together."

Astrid was flushed with warmth from head to toe. She was not only immensely proud of him for his award, she was glad they'd finally broken through a barrier together. Was this a taste of things to come? Could he ever let her in? "I'm so happy to hear that."

"Not half as happy as I am, knowing that you and I have a bottle of champagne waiting for us upstairs."

Six

"You're sure you don't want to go to the reception?" Astrid had been struggling to get a word in. A constant stream of friends, acquaintances, and even strangers kept stopping to congratulate Clay as they filed out of the ballroom. "I'm sure the other winners will all be there."

"Going to a party is the last thing I want to do." It wasn't the celebration of the award that he'd been seeking. It was the recognition. As far as he was concerned, that could have been a quiet exercise. It didn't have to be a big show. But there was more to his disinterest in the party than that. Here in a different town, away from the office, his family and outside influences, Astrid was the center of his orbit right now. She had made this night amazing. She'd forced him out of his own head and out of his comfort zone. If he'd been left to his own devices, he would have been his usual one-man island. And he didn't have to imagine the empty feeling he would've been stuck with if he'd been here all alone. He knew that feeling all too well.

"So we'll go upstairs and toast your big win?"

"As long as you're okay with it. I don't want you to miss out on any fun. You look so beautiful in that dress. I wouldn't blame you if you wanted to make the rounds at the party."

"Are you flirting with me, Clay?"

It was no longer an easy task to breathe. *One kiss. That's all I need.* But he would not kiss her. He wasn't even sure she was attracted to him. Still, he was prepared to be honest with her about his reasons for having struggled to work with her. She deserved the truth. She'd earned it. He was prepared to live with the consequences.

"It's not flirtation. It's the truth." The ballroom had largely emptied out. "You are easily the most beautiful woman I have ever seen. I'm sure hundreds of men have told you that."

Her eyes bore no judgment for what he'd admitted. Only curiosity. "You really think that?"

"Isn't it a bit obvious?"

"Hundreds of men have not told me that. Not the way you did just now, with sincerity."

"You must have left a long string of broken hearts behind you."

She shook her head slowly, never breaking eye contact with him. "No. I haven't. Men will admire me, but they don't have the nerve to be honest with me in any real way."

"That's important to you? Honesty?"

"Immensely."

This was as good a time as any to come clean. "If we're being honest, Astrid, I need to tell you that I have struggled with being very attracted to you." He watched as her eyes flickered with a mix of surprise and delight. He wasn't about to wait for her response. "But I want you to know that it's not just because you're stunning. You're so open and generous. You're so sweet. I don't really know what to make of it. I only know that I'm drawn to you."

She cracked half a smile and shied away for a split second. "You wouldn't say I'm so sweet if you knew what I was thinking about you in that suit."

Clay's sights narrowed on her, but he caught the corners of his mouth trying to twitch into a smile. "What?"

"You're not the only one who's struggled with attraction, Clay. My jaw dropped the first time I met you."

Ripples of heat began moving through him, like a tide that rolled in but never receded. "Wow. I was not expecting you to say that."

"Did I manage to surprise the unflappable Clay Morgan?" Her eyes glinted with flirtation, sending his brain off in a very specific direction, the one that led them upstairs.

"You did. And the only thing that will help me shake off my surprise is a glass of champagne. In our room."

"Exactly what I was thinking." Astrid hooked her arm in his and they beelined for the door.

Outside the ballroom, there were dozens of people still milling about and talking. Clay ducked through the crowd, pulling Astrid behind him in his wake. When they broke free, it was her turn to tug on him as she took extra long strides across the lobby—so long that

Clay noticed something he hadn't before. Her gown had a high slit. That flash of her bare skin spiked his body temperature so much he nearly broke out in a sweat.

Luckily, the elevator had just dropped off a handful of guests when they reached it. They hopped on board and Clay jabbed the button for the top floor of the hotel, then went for the one that would close the doors. They were both short of breath after rushing through the lobby, and Clay couldn't help but have his sights drawn to Astrid's décolletage as every inhalation filled out her curves. She was a feast for the senses, without so much as a single touch.

They were about to reach their floor when Astrid dropped her clutch handbag. Clay bent down to pick it up just as Astrid did the same, except she crouched, which caused her leg to poke out through the slit, all the way to her very upper thigh. The elevator dinged and the door slid open, but they were both frozen, staring at each other. It felt like a silent admission that something was going to happen between them. He hoped like hell neither of them lived to regret crossing that line.

They stepped out into the hall and the sense of urgency between them was even more pronounced than it had been downstairs. Clay pulled loose his bow tie as he strode ahead. He couldn't take it anymore. Something had started downstairs and continued in the elevator. Hell, it started the minute they met. But he'd had enough of resisting her appeal. Spending every minute with her in the office and all day on their trip together had been too great a test.

Every inch of Astrid was temptation. Next to her in the elevator, the view had been incredible, but looking was no longer enough. He needed to touch her, without that beautiful dress. He wanted her in his bed, so he could get lost in her, if only for one night. This was their chance and he sensed it. Back in San Diego, everything and everyone else would get in the way.

He flashed his key in front of the electronic sensor and the lock clicked open. Holding the door for her, he filled his lungs with the soft strains of her perfume. He didn't know what would happen next and he would follow her lead, but his heart was still thumping out a steadfast beat, like his own body was trying to remind him to take note of what might be about to happen.

He closed the door behind them as Astrid placed her bag on the table in the entry. She planted her hand against the wall and kicked off her shoes. "These things are killing me."

Clay laughed quietly. Her former career had been built on fashion, but she wasn't afraid to be real with him. He stooped down to pick them up for her and that was when she placed her hand on his shoulder. On bended knee, he gazed up at her. It was the perfect illustration of the way he viewed their dynamic—he was at her mercy and in perpetual awe. "I was trying to be a gentleman."

She nodded slowly, and it felt like seduction, the way her face was beckoning him. "I know you were. And I adore you for it." Her other hand went to the side of his face, her palm pressed against his cheek. "I like you, Clay. I like you a lot. Even when you don't always seem to like me…"

He placed his hand on his knee and pushed himself to standing. "No. Stop." He took one of her hands. "I have always liked you. I just haven't always liked the way I am around you. That's my fault. Not yours."

"I know you like control. Does it maybe feel like you lose it when you're around me?"

"That's probably part of it. I don't like knowing that I have any weaknesses at all."

"We all do. It's part of being human."

If only she understood that her reasoning brought him no comfort. "We need to stop talking about me. I want to know what you want." He rubbed the back of her hand with his thumb.

"Are we talking about right this minute, or long-term?" She cocked one of her perfectly groomed eyebrows at him.

Any discussion of the future would only circle back to his cache of reasons to avoid anything physical or romantic with Astrid. "I vote for right this minute."

She popped up onto her tiptoes and reached for his neck. "I want this." Before he could think twice about what she was doing, her lips were on his, just as soft and giving as everything else about Astrid. *Is this happening?* Her mouth was so lush, it took his breath away. Wanting to be closer to her, he lowered his head, and she responded by running her tongue along his lower lip and punctuating it with the gentlest of nips. *Wow.* He tightened his arms around her waist, tugging her closer as she bowed into him, doing everything he could to not rove too far with his hands. He wanted nothing more than to bunch the supple fabric of her dress in his hands, walk his fingers through it until he reached stretches of her skin. Just the thought of touching her like that made his body go tight. He wanted her in ways he couldn't begin to understand. These weeks of admiring her every day, wanting and resisting, had forced his mind and body into a war—this first glimmer of a truce was so heavenly he would have waved one hundred flags of surrender.

"I need to know that this is really what you want, Astrid," he said. His mouth wandered to her jaw and then her neck, his lips skimming the chain that held the diamond pendant at her throat. The kisses were meant to put this all on pause for a few seconds while she answered, but she let out a soft moan of appreciation that felt like her attempt to pour gasoline on the flame. "If even one inch of that dress comes off, if we have sex, our entire dynamic at work is going to change."

She reared back her head and narrowed her gaze. "Are you kidding me? I want to destroy the way we interact at work." She threaded her hands inside his jacket, rolling them over his shoulders until she could push the garment to the floor. "I want to set it on fire and let it burn until it's a pile of ashes."

He'd never heard such colorful consent. Damn, he was a lucky man. And not because he'd won a major award earlier that evening. "Okay, then. Let's melt it to the ground."

Astrid's mind was like a tornado in the heat of summer, a whorl of thoughts at conflict with each other, fueled by the electricity that sparked out of thin air. She wanted him so badly it hurt to think about it, but she had no earthly idea what was on the other side of making love to Clay. Would this change their working relationship for the better? Was she really lucky enough to have that happen?

She reminded herself that even if she had answers to her questions, there were no guarantees, especially with a man as hard to pin down as Clay. Better to give in to what she wanted and actually pin him down—to her bed. Now that his jacket was gone, she went for his shirt, untucking it, then letting her fingers race through the buttons. He kissed her neck again and she reached back to unlatch her necklace, placing it on the table. His mouth was unbelievable and that hit of wet heat against her skin made a real task of keeping her eyes open. She just wanted to let them drift shut, so she could give in to his ministrations. But now that his shirt was on the floor, she had to admire the firm plane of his chest.

She flattened her hands against his hard pecs and kissed her way across the broad expanse. His hands went to the zipper of her dress, drawing it down slowly, a hint of cooler air hitting her skin as he went. The sleeves slumped to her elbows, but the tight-fitting bodice still covered her breasts. She wanted nothing more than to be bare to him. Vulnerable. So she took a single step back and straightened her arms, letting the weight of the gown pull it down past her chest, waist, and legs, giving him full view of her in only a lacy black strapless bra and matching panties.

Clay's eyes went even darker as they raked over her body, his expression full of hunger. "I know I keep saying this, but you are unbelievably beautiful." He cradled her face with both hands, bringing her lips to his, then turned her around until her back was to him. He unhooked her bra, then pulled her shoulders back against his chest. He placed his hands flat against her lower belly, his fingertips brushing the top edge of her panties, then caressed his way up until the hands she had admired countless times were cupping her breasts. Her nipples went hard from his warm touch. Her spine tingled. He took full advantage, rolling the tight buds of sensitive skin between his thumbs and index fingers. It was as if he'd closed a circuit in her body, sending zaps of electricity down her stomach and between her legs. She needed his touch there. She craved it. The longing was so fierce that she whimpered.

She took his hands and pulled them down her stomach, hoping to convey her wants. He took the hint and nudged her panties down past her hips. Astrid wriggled out of them, feeling deliciously free. It wasn't an equitable situation, though, so she went straight for his pants, unbuttoning, unzipping, and tugging them and his boxers out of the way. She didn't want to stare, but he was magnificent now that she could see all of him… every last inch. She kissed him softly, reaching down and taking his erection in her hand. He groaned from that first touch, a sound that dipped lower as she took long, careful strokes. He got harder in her hand, further showing his approval by deepening their kiss. She could feel the old walls between them melting away. She couldn't have guessed how good it would feel.

Clay took her hand and led her to one of the plush upholstered chairs. He pressed lightly on her shoulder and she sat, not knowing what he was doing or what he wanted. The anticipation was killing her, but every tick of the clock brought another gleeful discovery, a glimpse into what Clay Morgan wanted. What he liked. Astrid took note of it all, hoping that she might get a chance to use this knowledge more than once.

He dropped to his knees, his eyes full of a fiery lust. It was such a turn-on to take in the visible evidence of his desire. He took one of her calves and draped it over his shoulder, spreading her legs wide and urging her to lean back in the chair. He kissed her belly, then the inside of her thigh, blazing a trail with his mouth straight to her center.

Astrid gasped when his mouth found her apex and he rolled his tongue in tight circles. Her eyes clamped shut, her hands raking deep into his thick hair and curling into his scalp. He slid a finger inside her, then two, satisfying yet another desire as he curled into her most sensitive spot. The pressure built quickly. Higher and higher, then another step closer again. Her breaths were hard and short as she teetered on the brink. Then he sent her sailing past her peak, right over the edge. She arched her back and gave in to the jolt of pleasure, and the waves that followed, all while he pressed his unbelievable lips to the sensitive inside of her thighs. As her mind slipped into the present, she knew one thing: she wanted him inside her.

She sat up and kissed him. "Do you have a condom? Please tell me you do."

He frowned. "Maybe in my toiletry kit. I'm not sure."

Astrid did not have one. She hadn't been intimately involved with a man in three years. There'd been no one since Johnathon. It all made sense, but now that she was thinking about it, she did wonder why she'd allowed herself to be so unprepared. She really had been reluctant to admit how much she wanted Clay. "We have to look. I need you."

They both hurried to their feet and rushed into his bedroom, then into his bathroom. Clay dug through the bag as Astrid stood behind him and kissed his back, her hands on his hips. "One," he announced. "I found one."

"Perfect. That's good enough." She plucked it from his hand, ready to take charge. She wanted to rock his world. She wanted to show him that they could work together perfectly. No, this wasn't the office, but there were other ways to demonstrate compatibility.

She grabbed his hand and walked backward into his bedroom, pulling him along as she went. He grinned like a man who knew he was in for something good. *You have no idea.* She stretched out on the silky bedding and he did the same, their bodies drawn together as lips met lips, arms coiled around the other, and Astrid hitched her leg around Clay's hip. His fingers dug into the fleshiest parts of her bottom, telling her how badly he wanted her. The feeling was mutual.

Astrid pushed him to his back and kneeled between his legs. She drew a finger up the center of his thigh, from his knee to the deep contour along his hip. He closed his eyes and rolled his head to one side as she repeated the trail on the other side.

"Do you want me to touch you?" she asked. The answer was obvious, but she still wanted to hear it.

"Yes. Please."

She lowered her head and huffed warm air against his length. "What about now?"

"Now you're just being mean," he groaned. "Although I like it. I like you being mean."

She planted her hands on either side of his chest and kissed his pecs softly, all while her thigh brushed against his erection. "I don't have it in me to be cruel. I just want to make you happy." She didn't want to make him beg. That wasn't her point. She only wanted it to be amazing. She reached down and took him in her hand, wrapping her fingers around him tightly.

"I'm happy as long as you're touching me."

She smiled to herself, caressing his length, up, rolling her palm over the tip, down to the base, tightening her grip as she went. Again, she made mental notes of his reactions, the things that made his mouth go slack with pleasure. She also loved having this small bit of control over him. Normally she felt as though she was at such a disadvantage.

He popped up to his elbows and opened his eyes. "I can't wait any more. I need to be inside you." He took one hand and pushed her hair from her face tenderly and kissed her—a slow, soft, wet kiss.

"I want you, too, Clay." Funny how there were no negotiations inside the bedroom. Only agreement. She took the condom from the bedside table and opened the pouch, rolling it onto him carefully.

He watched every move she made, not tearing his sights from her. The instant she was done, he pulled her down on top of him, then rolled her to her back. It was so forceful and strong, it nearly knocked the breath out of her. She hadn't felt that desired and wanted for so long. There at his mercy, she dropped her knees, opening herself to him. The wall was about to be gone.

He drove inside, and she waited for the moment when she would slip into the haze of pleasure and the world around her would recede. But that didn't happen with Clay. As much as she'd dreamed of this, he made it very, very real. He delivered the strokes so artfully that there was no choice but to pay attention. To meet every motion he made with a rock of her hips, and every kiss with one of her own.

He placed a hand on one side of her face, holding up his body weight with his other arm. "Talk to me, Astrid. Tell me what you need."

For that man of few words, this was a surprise indeed. "Now you want me to talk?" she kidded, raising her head and kissing his chest, then his neck.

"This is important. I don't want you to be anything less than satisfied."

The truth was that this had already far surpassed her hopes, but she shifted herself a tiny bit, then grasped his shoulder, pulling him down. "I need your body weight on me."

"I'll crush you."

"You won't."

She pulled her knees higher, enjoying every incredible inch of him as he rode inside and out. "That's it. Right there."

He sank down against her, adding to the pressure, kissing her deeply and with unending passion. She explored his back, found his incredible ass, giving him a good grab. All the while, each thrust brought her closer to the edge. Her insides were tightening, coiling and about to spring at any second.

"I'm close," she muttered. Her peak was toying with her, pushing closer, then pulling away.

"Me, too. You feel so amazing."

She smiled and nestled her face in his neck, letting his stubble rub against her cheeks. She closed her eyes, her muscles contracting faster. He matched her intensity and she clutched his body, grabbing him with everything inside her. She called out sharply as the pleasure drove through her. Then Clay followed, his torso going rigid for a moment, then relaxing as he gave in to it all. He collapsed at her side, but immediately pulled her close, into the safe and warm cocoon of his arms. She hadn't expected post-sex snuggling. Not from Clay. This was so much like an expression of affection.

He was a man of many surprises. No question about that. "That was incredible." She sighed, drinking in his smell and still not quite believing this had happened. She'd fantasized about it so many times, but to her great surprise, her mind hadn't managed to make it anywhere close to this good.

the warmth of it, and yet something didn't feel right about it. Her mind spun lazily. There was danger here somewhere, but she kept losing it in the softness of the moment, then, there, a tingle of warning. An admonition threaded through sleep, urging her to wake. Something...

Seven

Clay woke with a hum of satisfaction in his body and the pleasing warmth of Astrid's even breaths on his chest. Her head rested on his shoulder, silky hair draped on his arm, a delicate hand on his stomach, and long leg wrapped around his. He was blissfully aware of the press of her soft breasts against his rib cage, and of the velvety contours of her lower back as he settled his own hand there. It had been a long time since he'd experienced this much closeness with a woman, and he was a man divided against himself because of it. The sunnier parts of him could get used to this. But his more pragmatic side was fighting against that, telling him to run. It was an insidious loop to be stuck in. His past had worn a rut in his thinking, but there was certainty in remaining romantically unattached. There was safety there. For himself, but more importantly, for his daughter.

Still, Astrid was simply amazing. Last night had been electrifying, their physical connection intense. He wanted more of what they'd shared, but that was the irrational part of his brain whispering that it would be okay to wade back into these waters. The truth was that he couldn't put life on pause. They were about to drive back to San Diego in a few hours. He would spend his weekend with Delia. He and Astrid would return to work on Monday. And they had just managed to make their professional relationship even more complicated. He'd made a mistake, and now he had to fix it.

He was mulling over how to address this with Astrid when his phone rang. He glanced at the clock on the bedside table. It was nine a.m. This was likely Miranda and Delia.

"Astrid. I need to get this call." He uncoiled himself from her and scrambled across the room for his phone. To make matters worse, it was a video call. He pressed Accept, but left the phone facing up, so the only view Delia and Miranda would get would be of the ceiling. "Hey, guys. What's up?" He quickly put on his boxers, then grabbed the jeans he'd packed from his suitcase.

"Why are we looking at a ceiling?" Miranda asked.

Across the room, Astrid was sitting up in bed, pushing her messy hair back from her face. How was she so damn beautiful, even first thing in the morning?

"Sorry," Clay said. "I'm putting on a shirt. I just got out of bed." He held a finger to his lips to silently beg Astrid to be quiet.

"We called to say congratulations," Miranda said. "We were surprised you didn't call us last night, but Tara texted me to say she was excited that you won."

Guilt washed over him. He'd reached his pinnacle

and hadn't thought to call the two most important people in the world. Now that he was dressed, he picked up
his phone and looked at the screen. There were Delia
and Miranda, sitting on the sofa in her living room. "I'm
so sorry. There was a big party afterward and so many
people. I just didn't have a spare minute to myself." He
hated that little white lie. He had totally fallen down
on the job by not calling them last night. This was the
perfect illustration of how much he allowed himself to
be distracted by Astrid. He lost all coherent thought
when he was with her.

"Party?" Miranda asked, seeming incredulous. "You
hate parties."

"You do hate parties," Astrid whispered to him as
she climbed out of bed. "Don't lie about it."

Clay shushed her.

"Did you just shush me?" Miranda asked.

"I don't always hate them," Clay shot back as Astrid walked up to him, completely naked. Her body
was so incredible it made his head swim—her rounded
hips, her lovely breasts, and her lush bottom. She was
a feast for the senses. He was not sated. And he had to
get over it.

"Daddy, when are you coming home?" Delia asked.

Clay glanced at Astrid as she walked away from
him to the bathroom, wagging her hips with every step.
Never? Is that a valid answer? "Soon, honey. Soon. I
need to shower and pack up and grab some breakfast.
I should be back a little after lunchtime."

"So Aunt Miranda and I can go swimming?"

"Take your time," Miranda said with a quick arch of
her eyebrows. Was she on to him? He never should have
asked for advice about Astrid. He never should have put

the thought in his sister's head. He'd hoped she could help him straighten out his thinking, but she'd had to go and muddy the waters with that stuff about staying open to the idea of love. That was an easier prospect for Miranda. She'd lost the person she loved by a cruel twist of fate. He'd had to find out that he'd married and had a child with someone he'd read all wrong. That mistake would always hang over his head.

"Love you both," he said.

"Love you, too," Miranda and Delia said in response.

Clay ended the call, his heart and conscience heavy.

He looked up to see Astrid standing in the doorway to the bathroom, leaning against the frame, her glorious body on full display. "Did I hear something about a shower?" She punctuated the question with a subtle pout.

He knew that what he was about to say would come out badly, but he also didn't want to lead Astrid down a path where he wasn't clear about his intentions. She deserved better than that. He wasn't about to be the man who took what he wanted and then ended it all. It wouldn't be right to do so.

He rose from his chair and approached her. With every step closer, his stomach knotted tighter and he regretted his situation a little more. She was so tempting. She was quite possibly the perfect woman. But she was also an unknown quantity. They barely knew each other. That made her dangerous. It was one thing to put his heart on the line, but he wouldn't do that to Delia. "I do need to take a shower, but I wanted to talk first."

She wrapped her arms around his neck, digging her fingers into his nape. Her nakedness was so distracting—every part of her that he wanted to touch was mere inches away. "What do you want to talk about?" She popped up onto her tiptoes and kissed his neck.

His hands reflexively went to her hips, and the instant his skin touched hers, the battle inside his body was reborn. His need for her was fiery and intense, making every drop of blood race to the center of his body. He wanted her so badly he couldn't see straight. "Us. Last night."

"It was amazing," she whispered into his ear.

"It was. It absolutely was. But we didn't talk about our personal situations before clothes started to come off, and getting that call from Miranda and Delia just now only reminded me that I have other people to worry about other than myself."

"Oh. Okay." She dropped back down to her flat feet and stepped back from him. "I guess we could talk about it now."

"My situation is complicated. Which is why I fought my attraction to you. I can't get involved with someone. It's not that easy. I need to focus on Delia's happiness. She's been through so much."

Astrid walked over to the vanity and grabbed a towel, wrapping it around her body. "Of course. I understand."

But did she? Really? She didn't know the harsh truths of his past, and he intended it to stay that way. "And then there's work. You and I both know what the rumor mill is like in that office. If anyone gets wind of this, it'll be all anyone talks about. You have a financial stake in the company and so does my sister. Can you see how this isn't a great idea?"

Astrid's face fell, but she very quickly forced a smile on her face. "Don't take everything so seriously, Clay. This was just a little sex between friends. No big deal."

"Are you sure?" Nothing in her expression matched her words.

"Yes. You worry too much. I've told you that before." She patted him on the shoulder. "I'll take a shower in my own bathroom."

Clay swallowed hard, realizing what he had just passed up. *I'm either super smart or a complete idiot.* "Ready to go in an hour?"

"I can do that." She nodded and started for the door.

"Do you want me to call down to room service and order coffee? Maybe some pastries?" He was so pathetic, trying to ply her with sweets.

"It's okay. I'm not hungry." With that, she disappeared.

Clay sighed and walked into his bathroom, planting both hands on the vanity and staring at his own reflection. How had everything gone so upside down? Last night, he'd been on top of the world. And that wasn't merely because of the award. Astrid had made him feel alive in ways he hadn't experienced in a very long time.

But his needs and wants weren't what was most important. This was a question of priorities. He and Astrid had work to accomplish together. And Clay had a daughter and his heart to protect.

As soon as Astrid stepped out of Clay's bedroom, she was confronted by too many reminders of last night. The champagne in the bucket, still not consumed and probably room temperature by now. Her diamond pendant on the table, the one that Johnathon had given her so many years ago. And last, there was Clay's tux and her dress, intermingled on the floor. She might have had the time of her life last night, but now it was the next, very depressing day.

She gathered the necklace, her gown and her undies from the floor and carried them into her room, tossing them onto the still-made bed. She was angry, frustrated and confused, but she was not going to allow her hopes to be crushed by a man. She'd been through that routine hundreds of times during her marriage to Johnathon. It might be a well-worn path, but she was damned if she was going to get back on it. It didn't matter that the man putting her on notice was Clay, and that she'd wanted him from the moment she'd met him. She'd had her taste and now he was taking that away. It was his choice. Now she needed to think about her own choices. What did she want? And how was she going to get it?

In the bathroom, she waited for a moment to let the shower heat up, then stepped inside. With multiple spray heads, the hot water hit her from all angles. She tried to think of it as therapeutic, washing away the remnants of last night. It had been unbelievably gratifying, both emotionally and physically, but it was over now. There would be no breathless kisses, sexy glances, or flirtation from Astrid. Clay had shut the door and she planned to go out of her way to stay on the other side. Instead, she needed to focus on the one thing she'd done so little of in her first thirty-two years on the planet—figuring out what she truly wanted. Love, family, and career had always been atop the list, and she couldn't deny that those things made real sense in her heart and mind. It was simply time to redouble her efforts.

Clean and shampooed, Astrid shut off the water and climbed out of the shower, wrapping herself up in two of the hotel's fluffy white towels. She took the hair dryer and aimed it at the mirror full-blast to clear the fog. As it receded, she watched her own face come into view. This was what she needed to do—focus on herself and clear away everything that was clouding her judgment. That meant pushing past her desire for Clay.

The trouble was that for the moment, her career goal of establishing herself as an indispensable part of the Sterling team was impossible to reach without Clay. The Seaport project was her most important, and every step of the way was dependent on him. She reminded herself that this wasn't one a one-way proposition. There were two sides to this coin. He needed her, too—to stay on top of the hundreds of tiny details from the city and to keep to the schedule. She would do her job and he would do his. They would succeed together, but with professional distance. It was the only way.

She did not want to return to the dynamic of old, the one where she felt shut out by Clay and every day was a battle of wills. Yes, sex had probably made the next phase of their relationship even more complicated, but those were the cards they had to play with right now. Best to get on with it. Otherwise, she might need to consider other alternatives, like getting on a plane and returning to Norway. She wasn't ready to claim defeat yet.

Clay checked them out while Astrid waited at the valet stand for them to bring his Bentley around. She stood there with her Chloé sunglasses on, staring straight ahead as a parade of expensive cars buzzed by on Sunset Boulevard, wishing she could wiggle her nose and teleport back to San Diego. She was dreading the ride home with Clay.

She slid the valet a generous tip and climbed into the passenger seat while he held the door for her. Clay strode out of the hotel moments later, managing to suck the breath right out of her. He was way too hot, too formidable, tall, and broad. The sight was loudly sounding echoes of last night in her head…his magnificent naked body weighing her down, taking her to new heights, and lavishing her with far more passion than she'd ever dared to imagine. Clay may have given her only one night, but it would be impossible to shake the memory fully. Selfishly, she didn't want to. At least they'd managed to get on the same page for a few hours last night. They'd declared a truce in the most indelible way she could've imagined.

"All set?" Clay asked, fastening his seat belt.

"Yes." Astrid looked straight ahead, unwilling to grant him so much as a smile or even a pleasant glance. She was done with being kind to Clay. Or at least done with going out of her way to offer niceties.

"Would you like to choose some music?" He handed over his phone.

She was tempted to send a message with her selection. Perhaps something desperately sexy and romantic, just to needle him? Or something raw and loud, to mirror the hurt he'd inflicted on her this morning with his preemptive rejection. After all, Astrid hadn't asked for a single thing from him other than to shower together. He'd only assumed that she would want more than that.

She pressed Play on a pithy pop playlist she found in the app's menu. If nothing else, it might wear on him the way his presence wore on her. As he drove, Clay occasionally offered a question or a comment, but otherwise stayed quiet. The purely platonic tone of everything he said was annoying—comments about the weather or traffic or work, but Astrid wasn't about to change the subject. Clay had said his piece back at the hotel—they were colleagues and nothing else. The sooner she got used to this, the better.

As they approached San Diego, Clay seemed to get antsy, fidgeting in his seat.

"Need a bathroom break?" Astrid asked.

His shoulders dropped and he shot her a look. "No. I'm just eager to see my daughter. I'm about to drive past the exit for Miranda's on my way to your place."

"Go get her. Please don't wait on my account. Trust me, I have nowhere I need to be." *Absolutely nowhere.*

"Are you sure?"

"I would love to meet your daughter. And I always enjoy seeing Miranda." Astrid couldn't ignore what this all meant—it was only after he'd laid down the law that he'd actually considered letting her meet his daughter.

Clay immediately flipped his signal and zipped down the off-ramp to head to Miranda's house. Astrid didn't need yet another thing to admire about Clay. In fact, she was wishing for things to dislike about him, but his frantic desire to see his daughter was nothing short of endearing. Damn him.

Minutes later, they were pulling up in front of Miranda's house, the one she had once shared with Johnathon. Clay had hardly killed the engine before he climbed out of the car and let his long legs carry him to the front door. Astrid wasn't sure what her role was in all of this, and Clay's previous touchiness about Delia made her think it was best if she hung back. If a man was going to be protective of his child, Astrid was not about to stand in the way of that.

Miranda answered the door and caught sight of Astrid, waving to her and casting a smile. Then she disappeared back inside with Clay, leaving the door open. Astrid's stomach twisted with guilt at the secret she was still carrying around, the one about Astrid's tryst with Johnathon when she hadn't realized he had a new love in his life, a woman who just happened to be Miranda. Astrid told herself this was another reason to be glad Clay had set boundaries between them. If the secret came out and Clay learned what had happened, he would never forgive Astrid, even if she had her reasons for keeping it to herself.

Astrid took her time getting to the front door, wanting to afford Clay and his daughter the happy reunion he'd been so eager to have. But when she walked inside the house, she realized she wasn't quite prepared for what it would be like to see this strong man wrapped around the finger of a tiny girl. He had Delia in his arms, her long dark hair flowing in ribbons as he twirled her in a circle.

"Did you miss me?" he asked, using the same nearly unrecognizable tone he'd taken on the phone that morning.

Delia narrowed her eyes on her father's face in much the same way he did at work when he was annoyed by a question Astrid was stupid enough to ask. "Daddy, I told you I did on the phone. Remember?"

"Okay. Okay. I just like hearing it." He pushed her hair back from her face and kissed her cheek. Astrid, still keeping her distance, felt as though her heart was being squeezed tight. Clay was such a different man when he let down his guard. She'd seen it last night and she was witnessing it now that he was around Delia. It was hard to believe he was the same gruff guy she had battled with at work.

Miranda approached the pair and placed her hand on her brother's back. "She did miss you, but not as much as you probably hoped. We had way too much fun."

"We swam in Aunt Miranda's pool and we colored and watched movies and had popcorn."

Clay glanced at Miranda over his shoulder. "Let me guess. You watched *The Snow Princess*."

"Only three times," Miranda answered.

Delia wriggled her way out of her father's arms and pointed at Astrid. "Who are you?"

A look of horror crossed his face. "This is Astrid. She and I work together at Sterling Enterprises."

As if Astrid needed another reminder of the box Clay wanted her to stay in. Astrid stepped closer to Delia, crouching down to get on her level. "I already know who you are. You're the famous Delia. I've heard a lot about you."

A slight smile crossed the little girl's lips, but she seemed to be sizing up Astrid, trying to figure out what she was or where she fit into her life, if at all. "Hi."

Astrid planted her hands on her knees, still stooped down. "So, you like *The Snow Princess*?"

Delia nodded eagerly. "It's my favorite."

"Did you know it's based on a story from Norway?"

"It is? How do you know that?"

Astrid smiled, thinking back to her childhood and the folk tales her brothers used to tell her. They always chose the darkest stories in the hopes of scaring Astrid, but it never worked, and they were confounded. Astrid always wanted to believe the happier parts of those fables. "It's called *The Three Princesses*. The story is different in the movie. It's much more fun."

"Where does the snow come from?"

"There's a lot of snow in Norway and the winter can be very long. That's where I was born and where I grew up."

Delia's eyes went wide. "Really? I've never seen snow in real life. Sometimes you can see it on the mountains around San Diego, but that's not the same."

Clay was carefully watching over their exchange, not letting on as to what he thought of it. "Come on, Delia. Let's get your things packed up. Astrid needs to get home. I'm sure she has a lot she needs to do today."

"Okay." The pair started upstairs, hand in hand.

Astrid couldn't help but feel as though she would only be intruding during the drive home. Clay had made his priorities clear and she couldn't blame him for it. Delia was adorable. Anyone would want to protect her. If she were Astrid's daughter, she would have felt the same way. "Clay? Hold on a minute."

He came to a stop and looked down at her from the top of the stairs, his eyes dark and questioning. "Yes?"

"I'll call a car to take me downtown. You and Delia enjoy the rest of your day together."

Relief washed over his face. He nearly smiled. Nearly. "Thank you. That would be great. I'll see you at the office on Monday."

Astrid forced a grin. The thought of work soured her stomach. "Yes. Absolutely."

Clay and Delia disappeared up the stairs, leaving Miranda and Astrid downstairs alone.

"So?" Miranda started. "How was it? Do you think that spending that time with my brother will make things easier at work?"

Astrid wasn't quite sure how to answer that question. Nothing about her night with Clay was going to make anything "easier." "We'll see. Your brother is a tough nut to crack."

Miranda nodded. "He always has been. I'm sorry if it's difficult."

Astrid shrugged. "Thank you. I appreciate it." Astrid really had no choice but to soldier through all of this, but she was also starting to wonder if it would ever be worth it. "I wanted to ask if you're available for dinner one night this week. I'd like to have you and Tara over."

"Is this for fun or are we talking business?"

"A little of both. I've just been thinking about my future with Sterling."

Miranda reached for Astrid's arm. "I hope you aren't questioning it because of Clay. I promise he's far more bark than bite."

If only Astrid could tell Miranda what she was really thinking, that Clay had already taken a chunk of her heart and she wasn't sure she could stick around in the hopes of ever reclaiming it. "It's more than your brother. A lot of it's on me." The words echoed in her head. *It's on me.* If she wanted happiness and fulfillment, she had to find it for herself. Not that long ago, she'd thought she'd found a new purpose at Sterling, but the road ahead seemed bumpy at best. She was going to have to hold on tight if she wanted to get past it.

Eight

Astrid arrived at work on Monday morning to a surprise sitting on her desk—a photo of her and Clay from Friday night at the award ceremony. It came with a note from Tara: *You two look great! I hope you had fun.*

Astrid slumped down in her chair and sighed, picking up the photograph and trying to ignore how sad it made her feel. She and Clay looked better than amazing together. They looked like they belonged together. Why did he have to be so deeply opposed to that idea? Did his hurt from his ex-wife really make him that unwilling to ever pursue love? She understood wanting to protect Delia, but surely he realized that all romance involved risk. There was no such thing as a relationship where you didn't ultimately put your heart on the line. She wondered if she'd ever get the chance to tell him that much, or if he would even listen. His stubborn streak was a mile wide and just as deep.

Astrid got to work, deciding to stay in her office and take care of things like paperwork, research, and answering emails. On any other Monday morning, she would have gone in search of Clay so they could re-group on the Seaport project and set the agenda for the week ahead. That would have to happen eventually, but for now, she was going to put it off as long as possible.

A little after noon, she was about to head out to grab a salad for lunch when her cell phone rang with an un-familiar number on the caller ID.

"Hello?" she answered.

"Ms. Sterling? This is Sandy."

Astrid sat up straighter in her seat and fumbled around the desk for a pen. She wanted to take notes so she could report back to Tara and Miranda. "Oh, hi, Sandy. How are you?"

"I'm good. Really good. You said that morning we ran into each other at the bakery that I could call you."

"Right. Of course. Are you looking for a job? I haven't had a chance to make a formal inquiry into what might be available, but I can certainly do that and get back to you. I would suggest a meeting with Mr. Singleton so you can discuss your departure. I do think the air needs to be cleared about that."

"I actually don't need a job. I got a new one and it's great. I'm working with the city planner's office. That's why I'm calling."

Astrid had not expected this, and she had to wonder why Sandy would choose to let Astrid know about it. Maybe she was just being paranoid. "Oh. I see."

"I feel bad about the way I left you guys high and

dry last time. So I wanted to let you know that if you need anything at all from me, please feel free to ask. I'll be here to answer any questions or provide details about any aspect of the process as we move through the second bidding phase of the project."

"Fantastic." This truly was great news. Astrid's other contact at the city was terrible. She rarely returned Astrid's phone calls and if she did, it was always days later. This could be a real boon for Astrid. "Can I get your direct line?"

"Actually, just use my cell. I called you, so you can grab the number from that. Our phone system here is a nightmare, and that way, you can reach me any time you need me. Even on weekends." Sandy hesitated for a moment. "I did want to let you know that there's been a change to the date for the next pitches. It'll be Friday, November 13, rather than the sixth."

Astrid scribbled more notes. "Wow. So we have an extra week?"

"Yes. One person on the committee had to take some time off with a sick relative. We thought we should give everyone some extra time. There will be a longer wait after this round until we announce the firm that will actually get the project. It won't happen now until after Christmas."

That would be a long wait. The original schedule had it slated to be announced before the holidays. Apparently, Astrid would be staying in San Diego until at least January. Then she could decide if Sterling was a place where she had a real future or if it might be better to return home to Norway. "I see. Well, thank you so much for the update. I really appreciate it."

"My pleasure, Mrs. Sterling. I do have one more

bit of information though, and I'm afraid it isn't good news. I know that Sterling had inquired about naming the park that will be on site after Johnathon Sterling, but I'm afraid that just won't be possible. The city will be retaining naming rights."

That made perfect sense to Astrid. Things like stadiums and museums and concert halls all had some sort of corporate affiliation now. There was simply too much money to be made. "I understand. Better to know now rather than later. Thank you for letting me know."

"No problem. I'm going to get going, but I guess I'll talk to you soon."

"Bye." Astrid hung up and knew that she was going to have to relay this information to Clay. Best to do it now and get it over with. She strode down the hall to his office, poking her head inside. He was at his drafting table, with his back to the door, headphones on. He often listened to music when he was working. Jazz, mostly. He said it helped him concentrate and create at the same time.

Not wanting to surprise him, she knocked firmly on his door, but apparently the music was too loud. With no other option, she tapped him on the shoulder, then hopped back. Sure enough, he jumped. He grabbed the headphones and pulled them from his head, plopping them on the table. "Astrid. You surprised me."

"I'm sorry. I knocked, but you didn't hear me."

He drew in a deep breath through his nose, but avoided eye contact. Apparently things were going to be awkward for a while. "Can I help you with something?"

"I heard from Sandy. Tara's old assistant? You'll never guess where she's working. The city planner's office."

"Good for her." He walked over to his desk and sat, waking up his computer.

"Do you not understand what I'm saying? We now have a direct line of communication with them. Hopefully that will mean less red tape, which should make things easier on us both. In fact, she called to tell me the deadline has been pushed back a week because of some internal scheduling issues."

"I guess that's good."

Astrid was so frustrated she was about to scream, and she was tired of hiding these emotions. She planted both of her hands on his desk. "Are you going to look at me, Clay? Are you going to engage in actual conversation with me?"

His jaw tensed, but he finally looked up at her. "Astrid, I'm trying my best, okay? I just think that it's better for both of us if we keep some distance at work."

"That would be nice if we weren't working on the same crucial project, but we are. And again, just as I told you in LA, you don't need to take everything so seriously. If we're done, we're done. Let's move on." She was going to have to repeat those words to herself until she began to believe them. But that was a problem she would keep to herself.

Clay got up from his desk, looked out in the hall, then closed the door behind him. Astrid couldn't help it, but knowing that they were alone made her stomach do a somersault.

"Miranda knows." Clay crossed his arms over his chest, which was its own distraction—the way it made his upper arms strain was a little too alluring.

"Wait. What? How?" Astrid couldn't imagine how they possibly could have given themselves up when they'd gone to Miranda's house that afternoon. They'd been so careful. Clay had gone out of his way to keep his distance.

"I really don't want to talk about this right now. Not in the middle of the day in the office. There are too many loose lips."

He was right on the money about that. "Okay. Well, I'm guessing you don't want to tell me over a drink or dinner."

"That's probably not a great idea." He ran his hand through his hair. Astrid wished she could be doing that right now. She wished everything standing between them would just go away. "Let's talk at six, when most people are gone. I'll get the nanny to stay late with Delia."

"It's that serious? Why can't you just tell me how Miranda knows?"

"There's more to it than that. I feel like I need to explain myself."

Astrid wasn't sure what to think anymore. "Okay, then. I'll be back at six."

Clay was watching the clock. Astrid was always on time for everything, and he had a feeling tonight would be no exception. He didn't relish telling her the things he was about to. He didn't go about laying his soul bare. It was easier if her kept it all inside and hidden. That way, no one could use his feelings against him.

But after Miranda deduced what had happened in Los Angeles, and after she'd found out that he'd ended things with Astrid then and there, Miranda had insisted. She said that at the very least, Astrid deserved a full explanation of why he felt the way he did. Miranda had also tried to encourage him to give Astrid another chance. He wasn't sure he could do that. It didn't seem smart, especially after he'd already done the hard part and cut things off. Still, he did rely on his sister for guidance when it came to matters of the heart. She had a way of getting to the root of things, and most important, she understood him like no one else.

Astrid appeared in his doorway at 6:02, smiling wide and holding a recognizable bag from the bakery across the street. "They're all sold out of doughnuts this late in the day, but they just pulled some of those monster chocolate chip cookies out of the oven. If we're going to have a big talk, I figured sugar might lighten the mood."

For what felt like the one hundredth time, he felt as though he was stuck in the role of the beast while she was the kindhearted beauty. "Thank you so much. I could definitely use a pick-me-up." He went to his office door and closed it behind Astrid. The click of the latch made it all seem more real. He had to come clean. "Can I get you something to drink?" Clay had a fully stocked mini-fridge in his office. It had been his only request when they'd designed his office.

"Water is fine."

Clay retrieved two bottles and handed one to her. Drinking in the office might be a relic of the 1950s and '60s, but Clay could see the appeal right now. A finger or two of bourbon might make this easier.

He joined Astrid on the couch, sitting at the opposite end. She turned to face him, pulling her leg up onto the cushion between them. "I think we should start with how your sister found out what happened. I can't see where we could've possibly tipped our hand at her house." As if to soften the blow of the topic, she handed over the bakery bag after pulling out a cookie for herself.

"When I was video chatting with Miranda and Delia, I sat in the chair in the corner of the room and you got up to walk to the bathroom. There was a mirror behind me and she saw your naked reflection. It was only a split second, but she saw it." He'd been so distracted, he hadn't noticed it at all, but then again, he'd had the real thing right in his field of view.

"You don't think Delia saw me, do you? That would be horrible." She took an anxious bite of her cookie.

"I asked Miranda that same question, but she's pretty sure Delia would've said something."

"Okay, good." Astrid cracked open her water and took a long drink.

Clay tried hard not to fixate on the curve of her lips around the opening of the bottle, and instead focused on his cookie, which was impossibly good but still not as appealing as Astrid. "Miranda and I talked for a bit after you left, and after she told me she knew what had happened. Delia was occupied with saying goodbye to the fish in Miranda's aquarium."

Astrid stuck out her lower lip. "That's adorable."

"I know. It is." Astrid wasn't making this any easier. He brushed away a piece of lint on his trouser leg, searching for words. "Miranda didn't want to let it go because I told her before we went to Los Angeles that I was struggling with my attraction to you and I didn't want anything to happen."

Her eyes flashed as if she was trying to solve a mystery and she'd just had her "aha" moment. "Was that why you were angry when we ended up in the same room?"

"I wouldn't say I was angry."

"Annoyed. Miffed. Irked. Those are all emotions you direct at me."

He sat forward and rested his elbows on his thighs, running his hands up over his face and back through his hair. "I know. I'm sorry I do that. It's just that…"

"I don't need your apologies. I just want to know what's really going on here. This feels like so much more than the fact that we work together. It feels like so much more than you not wanting to get involved. So, please. Explain it to me so I can understand."

"I can't bring myself to trust a woman again, Astrid."

"That's it?"

"That's the essence of it, yes. My ex-wife destroyed any faith I ever had in love, which wasn't much to begin with. You know, Miranda and I have been on our own since we were young. Our mother left us with our grandmother, who was furious that her only daughter stuck her with such a huge responsibility."

"I didn't know about that." Her voice was so soft and understanding, it nearly broke his heart.

"But, somehow, I fell in love when I met my ex-wife. Or at least I thought it was love. Obviously it wasn't, because she left, too. And when she did, she took my trust and Delia's along with it." The emotion was welling up inside him, threatening to overflow. He wouldn't let it. He had to stay in control. But still, it was easier if he kept directing his stare down at the carpet. One look at Astrid and it would be all over. "Do you have any idea how confused Delia was? The number of times she woke up in the middle of the night and wanted her mom and all she had was me? As hard as my childhood was, that was harder, and that was all while I was trying to get over a broken heart."

Astrid scooted closer on the couch and placed her hand on his shoulder. "You really loved her, didn't you?"

"I did. She was everything. She was sweet and kind and beautiful. She was generous and giving." There it was. There was the essence of what was eating away at him from the inside. He turned his head and felt brave enough to look Astrid in the eye. "She was so much like you. Or at least she pretended to be. At first."

Astrid froze for a moment and dropped her head, then pinched the bridge of her nose as if she had the worst headache in the world. He knew he was doing that to her and the realization killed him. "I'm not your ex-wife, Clay. If I seem to have some of the same qualities, I'm not the same person. I could never, ever do the things that she did. Lying to my husband? Stealing his money? Leaving behind my child? Never."

"So you know the whole story. I don't even have to tell you." He sat back in his seat and shook his head. Here he'd thought he would need to come clean and she already knew.

"I didn't know about your mom. Miranda told me the rest. The night she helped me pick out my dress. It was only because she cares about you so deeply. I didn't say anything because you don't like it when I get too personal."

"And then I went and made things extra personal the other night." Should he be regretting his decision to sleep with Astrid? He didn't want to.

"No. We both did that. I wanted that. I needed it." She took his hand and pulled it into her lap, stroking his palm with her fingers. "I don't regret it. I won't. I refuse." She sucked in a breath so deep it made her shoulders rise up around her ears. "But it did mean something to me. It meant a lot. When I tried to act all nonchalant the next morning, that was a lie. That wasn't what I was really thinking." Her wide eyes scanned his face, as if she was looking for some sort of answer.

"If we can't be honest with each other, I don't see how we could ever be involved."

"I was protecting myself. You're doing the same thing. I don't see a difference. Would it have made it easier that morning if I had protested? Begged you to want more from me? I won't do that, Clay. I do have some self-respect." She got up from the sofa, dropped the second half of her cookie in the bakery bag and threw it in the trash. "Maybe this was all a mistake. Maybe we need to accept that and move on."

"I hate that word. *Mistake.*"

"And yet you use it all the time. I'm guessing it's gone through your head many times as pertains to me."

"If anyone made a mistake, it was me."

She shook her head in disbelief. There was also some disdain mixed in with her expression. This was what he deserved—her scorn. "Thanks. That makes me feel even worse." She reached for the doorknob and he bolted up from the couch.

"Astrid. Wait. Stop."

She turned her head so fast her hair whipped in the air. "What?"

"I'm sorry."

"Again, I don't want apologies."

"Then what do you want?"

Her eyes softened. "I've asked myself that question many times since Friday night. And I'm still not entirely sure of the full answer, but I do know a few things. I want a family. I want a career. And I want love. Real, passionate, unquestioning love. I want the sort of love that lasts. Forever. I know now how hurt you have been. And I appreciate that. But I've been hurt, too. And I'm not going to put my heart on the line for someone who simply isn't capable of returning my feelings. You aren't the only one with skin in the game."

Clay held his breath. She was right. So damn right. And he was a fool. "I know that. I do."

She let out another exasperated sigh. "I care about you, Clay. But I think this is another illustration of how infrequently you and I are on the same page. So perhaps we should focus on work, since that's the part of our relationship that impacts other people. Let's try to get along and get through the Seaport project. As near as I can see, that's our best case scenario."

It didn't sound like much of a best case to him, but he didn't have a retort. He'd stirred up the confusion, and he was the person always arguing for a sensible course of action. Astrid's idea was practical. Logical. Nobody would get hurt. "I agree. You're right."

"Bye, Clay. I'll see you tomorrow." Astrid opened the door and marched out of his office.

He leaned against the jamb and watched as she walked away. He'd hoped he might feel better after opening up. Instead, he felt as though he was right back where he was before he and Astrid ever went to Los Angeles.

Nine

It had been a hell of a week and it was only Thursday. Astrid couldn't stop thinking about her conversation with Clay and everything he had been through. She liked him—a lot—but did she really want that much trouble in her life? Her existence with Johnathon had been hard. Years of vying for his attention and affection, month after month of infertility treatments, and ultimately, the realization that the love between them turned into something far less warm and caring than she ever would have wanted. What if that happened again?

At work, she and Clay had returned to their old dynamic, but there was a layer of unease in the air that hadn't been there before. That was saying a lot—their interactions before LA had been plenty uncomfortable at times. Perhaps it was all in her head and Clay wasn't thinking about her at all, or about the things she'd lobbed back in his court. She hoped that wasn't the case and that he'd taken at least *some* of it to heart. Yes, he had been hurt, badly. But he wasn't the only one carrying around battle scars. At some point, he was going to have to admit that he might not be protecting his heart. He might be slowly smothering it to death.

For tonight, Astrid would have a distraction from her turmoil over Clay. Tara and Miranda were coming over for dinner. That was fraught with its own complications. Miranda had figured out what happened between Astrid and Clay. Astrid was legitimately surprised she hadn't received a phone call about it during the week, but she was certain that meant it was going to come up in conversation. With Tara there, Astrid wasn't sure how it would all shake out.

Tonight would mark the first time the wives had ever met at Astrid's penthouse apartment in downtown San Diego. All previous gatherings of the three wives had happened at Tara's or Miranda's, aside from the times they'd convened at places like Ruby's to shop for Astrid's dress, or on much sadder occasions like Johnathon's funeral or the lawyer's office for the reading of his will.

That day seemed as though it had happened a decade ago, but it had only been a few months. Astrid had never bargained on becoming business partners with either of them, let alone both, but that had been exactly what happened when Johnathon split his shares of Sterling Enterprises between them. For the most part, she liked Tara and Miranda very much, and she was grateful that he had managed to bring them together after his death. Was that what he had always wanted? For the three of them to be friends? She could see his ego trying to engineer that—three women he'd once loved, united because of him. In her mind, it was an awfully prideful pursuit, but that was Johnathon—he bent the world to suit his needs. Astrid needed to take a page out of Johnathon's book and start doing the same for herself.

Astrid's personal chef had come over yesterday to prepare tonight's meal, which she merely had to heat and serve. On the menu was honey-glazed salmon with roasted vegetables. For dessert, they had chocolate mousse. Astrid didn't believe in not satisfying her sweet tooth every chance she got. Life was too short.

Tara and Miranda arrived together, Tara with a bottle of wine. She was dressed in all black—silk blouse and tailored trousers, an elegant ensemble that made her look every bit the powerful and in-control woman. "I wasn't sure what you were serving, but I figured we couldn't go wrong with a nice chablis."

Astrid accepted the gift, instantly recognizing the label. "Oh, I love this wine. Johnny took me to the winery every time we went to France. He loved it there."

"It's so cute when you call him Johnny." Miranda looked radiant in a plum-colored dress that showed off her raven hair and her growing baby bump.

Astrid was embarrassed. "It's an old habit I need to get rid of. No one else called him that."

Miranda smiled and patted Astrid's shoulder. "I understand. We all have our special memories of Johnathon. For me, one was that winery in France." She gestured to the wine bottle. "Because he took me there, too."

"Same," Tara said. "And for the record, he found out about the winery from me. I was the wine aficionado in our marriage."

The three wives exchanged knowing glances. It did

feel as though they were learning new things about Johnathon all the time, simply from spending so much time together.

"Interesting. He always framed himself as the expert." Astrid led them into the heart of her apartment, with its open floor plan, high ceilings, and admittedly unpractical color scheme of nothing but white and cream. She had everything she could ever want here, a spacious living space, a formal dining room, and state-of-the-art gourmet kitchen. There was only one bedroom, but it was a generous size and so comfortably appointed with high thread-count bedding in shades of cream and pale gray that Astrid sometimes referred to as her cocoon. It had a spa-like bathroom with a separate shower and a two-person soaking tub, plus a walk-in closet even she had a difficult time filling. Still, as perfect as her home was, it was a solitary existence living alone perched atop a skyscraper. She sometimes felt like a princess shut away in a tower.

"Your place is stunning." Miranda was drawn to the windows at the far side of the apartment. On the twentieth floor, it had incredible views of the city and the bay, especially at night, when lights twinkled like diamonds against the backdrop of an night sky.

"Thank you. Johnathon bought it for me soon after we started dating. He wanted me in San Diego more often, but I wasn't about to move in with him when we'd only known each other for a month. Now that I look back on it, it seems a little crazy."

Miranda nodded and turned back to Astrid. "He did like to push things along quickly, didn't he? I felt like our courtship was so fast. We were dating, then we were engaged and married, all within six months."

Astrid's stomach soured, just thinking about that particular sequence of events. Somewhere in the midst of that, Johnathon flew to Norway and seduced Astrid, without saying a peep about his new love.

"I think he took things faster as he got older," Tara offered. "We dated for over a year before he popped the question. Now I know that some of that had to do with Grant."

"Really?" Miranda asked, taking a seat on the white linen sofa in Astrid's living room.

"I'll get the wineglasses while Tara tells us this story. I want to hear every last thing. Miranda, what can I get you to drink?"

"Sparkling water, if you have it."

"Coming right up." Astrid ventured to the wet bar on the opposite side of the room, first serving Miranda's drink before opening the wine and pouring herself and Tara each a glass. She joined Miranda on the couch while Tara sat in one of two high-backed upholstered chairs.

"You know, I met Grant and Johnathon the same night," Tara said.

"I guess I didn't know that," Miranda said.

"Grant and I had serious sparks, but Johnathon was the one who pursued me, so I figured that my connection with Grant was all in my imagination. I didn't know this until recently, but he and Johnathon butted heads about it several times. We're talking very heated arguments. That's part of why I got forced out of Sterling Enterprises at the beginning. Grant told Johnathon that he couldn't work with both of us, and of course, Johnathon wasn't about to get rid of his best friend. I was already his wife. I wasn't going anywhere."

"So guilt was the reason he gave you a third of his shares in the company?" Miranda said coolly. She'd made it clear from the beginning that she felt Johnathon had shortchanged her.

"I take it that still bothers you?" Tara asked.

"Well, of course it does, but my beef is with Johnathon, not with you two. I really appreciate that we've found a way to come together." She took a sip of her sparkling water and set the glass back down on the coffee table. "I don't have any family other than Clay and Delia. I don't have more than a handful of close friends. The interior design business is incredibly competitive. People will be nice to your face and then they'll stab you in the back. It might be counterintuitive, but I trust you two. I guess it's because Johnathon trusted you, too."

The guilt was bearing down on Astrid with unrelenting force. If Miranda trusted her now, it would be destroyed if Astrid's secret was ever revealed. Perhaps it would be better if she simply came out with it. But then again, it would cause so much pain. Miranda would feel betrayed by the man whose baby she was carrying and that could never be resolved. She'd never be able to speak to him and work it out, find out why he'd done what he'd done. It would forever change her image of the man she had loved so greatly. Astrid took a deep breath and a healthy gulp of her wine. No, she would live with the secret and keep it from hurting anyone else.

Her secret aside, Astrid had a different unpleasant topic she had to bring up. "Since we're discussing Johnathon, I'm afraid I have to let you both know that we can't name the Seaport park after him if we get the project. The city is retaining naming rights."

"That's not terribly surprising," Tara said.

"It's still disappointing." Miranda placed her hand on her belly. "I had visions of taking the baby to that park, and being able to tell them that it was named after their father."

Astrid could hear the heartbreak in Miranda's voice. They were all still grieving, but Miranda was the closest to the loss. "I'm sorry. I really am. If there was anything I could do about it, I would have."

Miranda sniffled, but nodded. "I know you would have. I don't blame you."

The timer went off in the kitchen. "That's dinner," Astrid said. "If you two want to take your seats at the dining table, I'll bring it out."

"I'm going to run to the ladies' room first," Miranda said.

"Down the hall on the left." Astrid got up from her seat and headed into the kitchen.

Tara trailed behind Astrid. "Let me help."

Astrid was putting on a pair of oven mitts. "The plates are right there." With a nod she gestured to the kitchen island. She pulled out a large sheet pan and set it on a trivet. "Tara, can we talk about something?"

"Of course." Tara watched as Astrid removed foil from their meal, steam billowing in the air. "That looks and smells amazing."

"Thanks. My chef made it for us."

"What did you want to talk to me about?" Tara leaned back against the counter.

"Remember the day you introduced me to Clay and I saw the picture from Miranda and Johnathon's wedding?"

Tara's eyes went wide. "And everything you told me afterward?"

Thank God Astrid didn't have to explain it further. "Yes. That."

"What about it?"

"I just want to be sure we will always keep it between us."

"Oh, of course." Tara stole a roasted carrot from the pan. "That needs to be forgotten. Someone will just get hurt."

"Who's getting hurt?" Miranda appeared in the kitchen doorway.

"Nobody," Tara and Astrid said, nearly in unison.

"Then what were you talking about?"

"There's a paper shredder in the office that has a mind of its own," Tara blurted, somewhat unconvincingly.

"Then throw it out." Miranda narrowed her sights on Tara.

"Smart. We'll do that."

Astrid could finally exhale. "Everyone hungry? I think this is going to be good."

"I'm starving," Miranda said.

"Good. Because we have tons of food." Astrid dished up each plate and they took them to the dining table. Astrid appreciated that she could keep things informal with Tara and Miranda.

Tara raised her wineglass for a toast. "To Johnathon Sterling's three wives. May we always get along."

Miranda laughed and shook her head. "That's not particularly optimistic."

Tara shrugged. "You never know what's going to happen."

Astrid knocked back the last of her first glass of wine and poured herself a refill. Tonight might be a big test of her nerves.

"So, Astrid. Any highlights from your trip to Los Angeles you care to share?" Miranda asked the question with a tone that said Astrid had better spill it.

Okay, then. That had happened lightning fast. "You're talking about me and Clay?"

"Yes." Miranda nodded then took a bite of her salmon. "Delicious."

"Did I miss something?" Tara asked.

"You could say that." Miranda jumped in with response before Astrid had a chance.

"You two weren't arguing on that trip, were you? I honestly don't understand it."

Astrid was desperate to take control of the conversation. This game was grating on her nerves. "Clay and I slept together." She shot a pointed look at Miranda, then Tara, before stabbing a sweet potato with her fork. Astrid kept herself composed, hoping to hell that neither of them would ask for details.

"What happened?" Tara asked.

Well, that didn't last for very long. "Part of it was because we ended up in the same hotel room. You said you were going to put us in separate rooms, but that's not what the hotel had for us when we arrived."

"That's your excuse?" Tara set down her napkin. "You're a shareholder in the company and you slept with one of your coworkers?"

Astrid shot her a pointed stare, doing her best to convey just how ridiculous Tara was being right now. "Are you kidding me? What about you and Grant? One could argue that was far worse. You two were both in positions of power, and you didn't do a very good job of hiding it, either. At least I didn't kiss someone on the Kiss Cam at a Major League baseball game."

"Grant and I have history. And we're engaged now."

"Astrid's right, Tara. You did the same thing," Miranda said. "And you put our mutual interest in the company at much greater risk."

Astrid didn't want to gang up on Tara, but she did appreciate that Miranda had her back. "I really don't think either of us is in a position to throw stones right now."

"Obviously I wasn't there, but I have a feeling it didn't happen simply because you two were in the same room. Judging by the conversation I had with Clay before you two went to LA, I'm guessing it would have happened even if you'd been at completely different hotels," Miranda said.

"So I heard," Astrid said.

Now it was Miranda's turn to be surprised. "He told you?"

"He did. And we had a long conversation about why he called things off the next morning."

"Wow," Miranda said. "He actually listened to what I said."

"I don't know exactly what you told him to do, but we did have a heart-to-heart. I think we understand each other better." She was still guessing at these things. There was nothing certain about Clay.

"Where did you leave things?" Tara asked.

"Are you asking me as a shareholder and co-CEO of Sterling Enterprises, or are you asking as a girlfriend?"

Tara waited a moment to answer, buying time with

two sips of her wine. "Since it's just the three of us and we're off the clock, I guess I'm asking as a friend."

"We agreed that it was a one-time thing. That was it. We're both single and we were caught up in the excitement of his big win. But it wasn't anything more than sex." Except that it had been, at least for Astrid. She needed to banish those thoughts from her mind, immediately. All they did was make her want Clay more. "And we also agreed that we would keep it quiet. Obviously that didn't work here, but I hope I can trust you both to keep it to yourselves."

"In my experience, the 'it was only sex' excuse doesn't hold water. Especially if you have to keep working together," Tara said. "Is this going to interfere with the Seaport project? Or anything else for that matter?"

"It won't. We're back to being strictly platonic. I swear. There isn't even a glimmer of flirtation between us."

"That's a little disappointing," Miranda said.

"It is?" Tara asked.

"Yes. I mean, come on. Sterling is going to be fine, whether or not two of its employees become romantically involved. The world isn't going to suddenly stop needing new office buildings or corporate campuses." Miranda sat back in her seat. "But I am worried about my brother and what kind of life he's living right now. He's lonely. I know he is. And he's a little lost, to be honest. I'd love it if he found a partner who could help steer him in the right direction. Someone who could make him happy."

"Are you attempting to play matchmaker here, Miranda?" Tara asked.

"I guess I am. Astrid is great and I love my brother, so I fail to see how that could be a bad thing."

Astrid felt stuck. She loved having Miranda's endorsement and she believed that Miranda was right about Clay. He *did* need love in his life. But this was also a lot of pressure to put on Astrid. She couldn't fix Clay. He had to do it himself. "I don't know if he believes that I could, in fact, make him happy. And to be honest, I'm not sure of my ability to do that, either. We don't know each other that well, and I don't know how to change that. We agreed to keep things strictly professional at work, and from the company's standpoint, that's the best course. I can't see him agreeing to see me socially, and I'm not about to ask, just so I can be rejected."

"Then let's make an opportunity. Surely we can think of something between the three of us?"

"A party to celebrate his award?" Tara offered. "We could invite the press. Turn it into some publicity for Sterling."

"I really don't think he would go for that," Astrid said. "He hates parties."

"I agree," Miranda echoed Astrid's assertion. "But I do have another idea."

"Let's hear it," Tara said.

"I found out the baby's gender this week. Well, I didn't find out. The doctor wrote it down and it's in a sealed envelope. Everyone's doing those gender reveal parties now, and with Johnathon gone, I don't want to find out on my own. I'd rather have people I care about with me."

"That sounds like fun," Astrid said. "I'd love to host." With so little social life, it would give her something to do. Plus, she wanted to let Clay into her world, and show him who she was.

"I read in a magazine about a couple who gave their

results to a baker who filled cupcakes with blue or pink frosting. The guests all took a bite at the same time to find out the gender," Miranda said.

"If baked goods are involved, you will have no problem convincing Clay to be here," Astrid said.

Miranda laughed. "That is so true."

"I love the whole idea," Tara added. "I'm sure Grant would love it, too."

"I do think we should at least toast to Clay's award," Astrid said. "He doesn't like to be in the spotlight, but he deserves it."

"So much. Let's make it an evening event, too. It's more romantic." Miranda punctuated her suggestion with a wink.

Astrid grinned, looking at Tara and Miranda, thankful for this unlikely sisterhood she'd found. "So are we doing this?"

"Yes. I think so. If you plan the whole thing, I'll be sure to get my brother here."

Ten

A small, intimate gathering should not be stressful. And yet, Astrid was a ball of nerves. It went beyond the fact that it had been a crazy busy week at work and she'd spent too little time arranging the small details of this party.

Honestly, this whole idea was a bit absurd, that she and Clay would somehow grow closer over the course of the next few hours. But it seemed as though it was worth trying, and she had wanted to celebrate the baby on the way in some public way for a while now. She simply didn't know how to bring up the topic. She and Miranda were still forging their bond.

Astrid read through the instructions her private chef had left for the food to be served. Just a few hot appetizers, along with a cheese board and veggies. The cupcakes, with the mystery filling, were already on site, sitting on the kitchen counter. Really, everything was set, and she only needed to shower, get dressed and take a deep breath.

The bell for her apartment door rang, but it was a little less than two hours until guests were to arrive. There was only one other apartment up on the top floor of her building, so it was rare to get unannounced visitors, but she had left her guest list with the doorman already. Perhaps it was Tara or Miranda stopping by to say hello. She opened the door, and there before her was Clay, looking good enough to eat in black trousers and a crisp gray shirt, with a bouquet of pink tulips in his hand. Astrid practically swooned.

He surveyed her from head to toe, his forehead wrinkling with confusion, probably because she was in jeans and a light sweater at the moment. "Am I early?"

"Yes, actually. By nearly two hours."

"Miranda told me it started at five."

So that was what this was—a ploy by Miranda to get them together. Astrid approved. And also felt the need to cover for her. "We talked about five at one point, but I moved it to seven. I'm so sorry she didn't tell you."

"Should I come back?"

Astrid shook her head and grasped his arm. "Don't be silly. You can keep me company."

"Oh. Okay." Clay walked inside and Astrid closed the door behind him. He was quick to thrust the flowers at her. "Here. These are for you. I thought about a bottle of wine, but the truth is that I'm really a bourbon guy, and that seemed like an odd hostess gift."

Astrid smiled. They might not be a romantic gesture, but she loved getting flowers from Clay. "Thank you so much. Tulips are my favorite."

"I noticed that you sometimes have them in your office."

Wow. "Careful, Clay. That's downright thoughtful of you."

He leaned against the kitchen counter. As perfect as they'd looked together in that photo from the night in Los Angeles, she thought he looked even more perfect in her apartment. "Actually, it's good that I got here early. I've been wanting to talk to you about our chat the other night at work."

She had no idea what he was about to say, but she was glad he'd been thinking about it. She'd been stuck with a nonstop loop of their conversation in her head. "Of course."

"I wanted to say thank you for being so understanding and listening to me. I also want to thank you for calling me out on a few things. I love my sister, and she does tell me when I'm wrong, but she also probably gives me a little too much latitude."

"Does that mean you've changed your mind about what you will allow to happen in your romantic life?" She might as well put it all on the line. Better to know now what he was thinking.

"Let's just say that my hard-lined approach might be softening." He had a sly glint in his eye that made Astrid's heart flutter.

She didn't want to take too much latitude right now and spook him, but this revelation did make her feel more optimistic about the way this night might go. "Any interest in helping me wrap a gift for your sister?"

"I didn't know we were doing gifts."

"We aren't, technically. But she mentioned this specific thing and I had to get it for her, but it's going to be impossible to wrap. It's a pretty big job, but since you're an architect, I'm thinking you're up to the task."

He seemed skeptical. "That hardly sounds like a job I'm qualified for."

"Come on." Astrid led Clay through her living room and back to her bedroom, where the gift was waiting. "There. I need to figure out how to wrap that."

Clay looked at her as if she had a screw loose. "You can't wrap a stroller."

"Why not?"

He walked over to it and gave it a push across the hardwood floor. How did he manage to make the role of dad so super sexy? "I don't know. Because it's ridiculous? Just put a bow on it."

"Don't you think it would be funny? If we bring it out to Miranda and it's obvious what it is, but it's still wrapped?"

He regarded the stroller and let out a quiet laugh. "I guess."

"Look, I want tonight to be special for your sister. Just help me, okay?" She stepped to the corner and grabbed the extra-large roll of heavy-duty wrapping paper she'd bought, then handed Clay the scissors and tape.

"Alright then, let's get to work." Together, on hands and knees, they wrapped every square inch of the thing—the handle, the frame and seat, and even the wheels. It required a lot of tape and a lot of one person holding the paper in place while the other made sure it all stuck together. At nearly every juncture there was a brush of hands. The bumping of shoulders. The exchange of smiles. Each time they made contact, the hunger inside her grew a little more, as Astrid was hit with a different memory of her night with Clay. The raw passion of the first time. His mouth on her body. Her hands all over his.

"I have to ask you," Clay said when they were nearly finished. "Why would you host a baby-related event for my sister? For that matter, why buy her an expensive gift? Doesn't it hurt, considering that you and Johnathon tried to have a baby and it didn't happen for you?"

Astrid sat back on her haunches. "You know about that?"

"I do. You hinted at it in the car on the way to LA, and my sister mentioned it as well."

"Ah, Miranda. She does enjoy sharing people's stories, doesn't she?"

His eyes, so warm and welcoming in the soft light of her bedroom, settled on her face. "She does when she cares about someone. Believe me, everything she said was only in the context of marveling at your generosity. She was genuinely surprised at how you took the news of her pregnancy. I think it means a great deal to her."

"And there's your answer. It doesn't hurt to help her celebrate. We're still welcoming a baby into the world, and this baby is special. He or she will be one half someone I loved very much. Plus, I can't help but be excited by the idea of all children. That's part of why I've always wanted to be a mom."

"That is the sweetest thing I have ever heard." His voice was low and soft, and she sensed now that there was an invisible tether between them. There was a reason she was so drawn to him. "How are you so amazing? Are you even real?"

She would have laughed if the question wasn't putting her on a pedestal she never asked for. "Of course I am. I'm flesh and blood like anyone else. I'm just as breakable as anyone." She didn't want to cry, but as her sights traveled between Clay and the stroller, all she could think about was what might have been, both in her distant past and the more recent. She and Clay could have been something. They could still be something, if he'd only let her in. A tear leaked from her eye and she quickly swiped it away.

"I didn't mean to upset you."

"I'm fine," she lied.

Clay spread his arms wide. "No, you're not. Come here."

"No. I'm not going to cry."

He tilted his head to one side, waving her closer with his hand. "Astrid. Come on. I'm not going to think any less of you."

"It's not that." She turned to confront him, frustrated that she wanted him so badly. "It's that I want happy things between you and me. We've both been hurt. We've both had pain. I want to focus on what's good between us. Just us. Nobody else."

"Okay. I can do that."

"Can you, Clay? Can you really?"

He nodded eagerly. "Of course I can."

"Then show me. Do something that will make us both happy."

"Don't you have guests coming in an hour and a half?"

Boundaries. Limitations. Rules. The man was so damn preoccupied with everything that wouldn't allow them to enjoy each other. "Stop telling me no, Clay. I just want to hear you say yes."

A knowing smile slowly rolled across Clay's tempting lips. "Let me figure out how many ways I can say it." He reached for her hair, gently combing through the strands about her ear. He trailed his fingers along her jaw, sending goose bumps racing over the surface of her skin. That right there was the reason she always wanted Clay to say yes to her—there was no match for the thrill of his touch. He caressed her lower lip with his thumb, lifting her chin. She smiled as she snaked his arm around her waist, tugged her hard against his firm body.

This was going to happen again and she hoped to hell this time wouldn't be the last.

Clay had wanted this moment since they'd left LA. He'd just been too conflicted to admit it. And now that it was hurtling at him, getting Astrid into bed wasn't happening fast enough. His pants were so tight he wasn't sure how he was still breathing, let alone still upright. He had to have her, body and soul, now. Heat raged inside him, his erection already fierce and insistent.

She walked backward to the bed, pulling him along with her. He grabbed the hem of her sweater and lifted it above her head. It felt as though he was revealing his reward, a prize he wanted all for himself. He kissed her and unhooked her bra, admiring her beautiful breasts before giving them a squeeze. Her eyes drifted shut halfway, and the pure ecstasy of her expression made him want to do that to her again and again. He unbuttoned her jeans and pulled them down her legs, stopping to kneel before her, gazing up at the beautiful length of her body.

He dotted her belly with soft, openmouthed kisses as he tugged her panties past her hips. "Lie down, Astrid." He stood as she climbed onto the bed and stretched out before him.

"What about you? You need to take your clothes off."

He did. He really did need to do that, but his mouth and hands were telling him to wait just one more minute. He placed one knee on the bed and gathered her wrists in one hand, raising her arms up above her head. "Are you alright?" he asked, stealing a kiss.

"Perfect," she replied.

He lowered his mouth to one of her breasts, her velvety skin nearly melting into his touch, conforming to his lips. Her nipples were tight and pert, and every time he touched them, her skin flooded with warmth.

He stood. "Don't move. Keep your hands where they are."

A gorgeous smile spread across her lips as she wriggled in place on the bed. He shucked his shirt, pants and boxers, watching her as she watched him.

"You're magnificent with no clothes on. You know that, right?" she asked.

"I'd say the exact same thing of you." He'd never craved a woman the way he did her, as if he could spend the rest of his life exploring her and he'd never stop learning and admiring. He stood with his knees pressed against the side of the bed and lifted her leg, holding her ankle, trailing the back of his other hand along the creamy skin of her inner thigh. He knew they were on a strict timetable here, but it was impossible to not want to take his time. "Can we call your doorman and tell him not to let anyone else up to your apartment?"

"You're terrible."

He bounced his eyebrows up and down. "I hope not." He again placed a knee on the mattress, and bracketed her hips with his legs, reaching up with one hand and holding her wrists in place above her head. His heart was in his throat, knowing he had her under his control. With every passing second, with every pump of blood through his body, she further occupied his heart. She could have had absolutely anything from him. Absolutely anything.

He shifted above her, lowering his head and kissing her deeply, then moving to her jaw, her slender throat, and then kissed the tender undersides of her breasts, coaxing breaths out of her. He traveled down her, milling with his lips, the kisses becoming deeper and longer. She sucked in a sharp breath when he palmed her thighs and spread her legs wide. Then he kissed her apex and he seized control again, exploring her most delicate places with his tongue and lips. He knew what he was doing, but he still loved hearing her reaction to it, the way her breaths stopped and started.

Her hips bucked off the bed as his tongue traveled in circles. She dug her hands into his hair. "That feels so amazing, but I need you. Right now. I need you to make love to me."

He took a few more passes, just enough to show her how dedicated he was to making sure she enjoyed this, then he pressed his lips against her lower stomach. "Do you have a condom?"

She nodded. "I do. In the drawer of the bedside table."

He found the box, which was unopened, and removed one of the foil packets.

"Let me do it," she said, scooting to the edge of the bed.

"Please. Be my guest." He handed it over, standing before her, the tension in his hips and groin almost impossible to take.

She wrapped her fingers around his length and stroked firmly, looking up at him, her gaze locked on his. Heat didn't merely plume in his belly, it roared, spreading to his hips and down his thighs. He couldn't imagine her doing anything more pleasing, but then she switched to a lighter touch, her delicate fingers slow and teasing, and that made his need for her even deeper. He wasn't sure how many more passes he could take, but she finally rolled on the condom and he gathered himself.

He lowered his head, cupped the side of her face, and drew her into a deep kiss. He wanted to drink in her very being, and it felt as if she was doing the same to him, relishing every heavenly sensation of the other's touch. She eased herself to her back and he positioned himself at her entrance, driving inside. The moment was intense. As his heart thundered in his chest, he struggled to comprehend her warmth, and the way her body held on to him so tightly.

He went deeper and their bodies were fully joined. He inhaled her sweet scent and nestled his face in her neck while she wrapped her legs around him and muscled him closer with the backs of her calves. She tilted her hips with every stroke, meeting him when he was deepest. She seemed to want a faster pace, and so he made small but powerful thrusts, keeping their bodies as close as possible.

He was teetering on the edge of release, his breaths

so shallow he couldn't fill his lungs. Hers were coming hard and fast, her lips parted and eyes closed as she seemed lost in the dreaminess of pleasure. He wanted those lips on his when she gave way. He wanted to feel every second of her vulnerability.

She gasped and clutched at the sheets. He realized just how close she was to release. "Kiss me," he said. He lowered his head and she raised hers, the kiss reckless and perfect. She bucked her hips against him and he thrust deeper, closing his eyes to feel just how tightly wound she was around him. He couldn't take much more, but he would do his damnedest to wait for her. With a sudden shock, she knocked back her head and arched her spine, and that was his cue to give in to the pleasure. He wasn't sure which way was up and which was down. His head spun fast and hard. Then he went into free fall, floating down to earth in a haze of deep satisfaction.

He collapsed next to her and she instantly curled into him. Their breaths slowed, falling into synchrony. She caressed the side of his face, sweetly rubbing her nose against his cheek and chin. Their lips connected, soft and warm, and he could feel the smile in her kiss. He couldn't think of another place he wanted to be. And he couldn't believe that it had taken him days to think about whether or not Astrid might be a good idea. She was better than that. She might be the miracle he hadn't known he was waiting for.

He dared to look at the clock. "We have twenty-five minutes before your guests arrive."

She groaned adorably and propped herself up on her elbow, dragging her fingers through his chest hair. "Whose idea was it to have a party anyway?"

He pressed a quick kiss to her lips. "I think it was yours." He didn't want to move a muscle, but he knew that the sooner he resigned himself to their social obligation for the evening, the better. "Come on. I think we'll live."

They both climbed off the bed and he padded into the bathroom to dispose of the condom. After washing his hands, he found his clothes and attempted to shake out the wrinkles that might be difficult to explain, especially to his sister, who did not miss many things. Not that he cared much at this point.

Astrid was in her closet as soon as he was dressed. She was working her way into a pair of heels, sexy, mussed hair cascading past her shoulders. He couldn't resist the chance to step behind her, grasp her shoulders and kiss her on the cheek.

"Does this look okay?" she asked, turning to face him.

"You would look good in a paper bag, but yes. You look amazing." He kissed her on the lips. "I wish I could stay over, but I stupidly told the babysitter that I would be home before midnight." As soon as the words had left his lips, he realized the presumption he was making. "I mean, not that you were inviting me or anything."

She laughed quietly and grabbed a pair of earrings from a large drawer of jewelry. "I would love for you to stay, but I understand. Plus, I think that you and I would do well to take things slowly." She gestured with a nod to her bedroom. "That was amazing, and I can see how it could quickly become addictive, but you and I will need to rebuild some trust."

"Trust is immensely important."

"Good. Now let's go get ready for everyone to arrive."

They started in the kitchen, Clay in charge of setting up the bar while Astrid preheated the oven to pop in some appetizers. It'd been a long time since he'd done something so domestic like this with a woman other than his sister, and he was pleased to realize that this wasn't putting him on edge. Astrid's comment about rebuilding trust had done so much to reassure him that opening himself up to her might be the best decision he'd made in a long time.

Promptly at six thirty, Tara, and Grant arrived, followed shortly by Miranda's best friends from her office, Brittney and Shay. Clay was busy serving drinks when Miranda showed up. He dropped his party duty to help her with her coat.

"You told me this started at five," he muttered, kissing her on the cheek.

"Did I? That's weird. I guess it's just pregnancy brain. That's a thing, you know." Miranda was an expert at covering her tracks, but Clay could see through it by now. Apparently she really did want him to give Astrid a chance.

"Come on," he said. "Astrid bought all sorts of pregnancy-approved drinks."

Everyone congregated in the living room of Astrid's apartment while she and Clay shuttled out food. This was the exact right size for a party as far as Clay was concerned, and he also liked that everyone was so focused on discussing the baby. He knew very well that Miranda would have a big hill to climb as a single parent. A support system would be a big help. He hadn't allowed himself anyone's help with Delia, aside from Miranda's. He knew his sister wouldn't be so foolish.

"Any wagers on whether it's going to be a boy or a girl?" Grant asked, holding hands with Tara on the couch.

"I think girl," Tara answered.

Grant shook his head. "No way. It's a boy."

"We will find out soon enough," Astrid said. "But first, I have a gift for Miranda."

"Astrid," Miranda pled. "We said no gifts tonight."

Astrid shrugged it off playfully. "I'm not good at following the rules. We'll be right back." She waved Clay in the direction of her bedroom. Together, they picked up the stroller and carried it into the living room. Of course, the instant everyone saw it, there was an roar of laughter. The wrapping job had done its job.

"I wonder what this could be," Miranda joked, getting up from her seat.

Astrid was positively beaming. She took such joy in pleasing others. He wanted to kick himself for ever trying to shut that out. "Open it."

Miranda tore back some of the paper. "I can't believe you bought me the exact model of stroller I wanted. I mentioned it one time, totally in passing. How did you remember?"

Astrid tapped her temple with her finger. "It's all locked away up here."

Clay and everyone else watched as Astrid and Miranda embraced. It was a very sweet moment. Johnathon Sterling had certainly had magnificent taste in women. "Does this mean we get cupcakes?" he asked.

"Yes," Miranda said. "I'm dying to find out."

Clay brought out the platter of bakery treats topped with white icing and a mix of pink and blue sprinkles. Astrid handed out dessert plates and napkins while everyone took a cupcake. "We'll count to three and everyone take a bite," Astrid said. "The frosting inside will give us our answer."

"Everyone ready?" Miranda asked. "One, two, three."

On cue, they followed the directive, which was quickly followed by a chorus of exclamations. *It's a girl.*

Miranda instantly burst into happy tears, as did Astrid. Clay found his eyes getting misty, but more than anything he was just so glad for his sister. She'd been through so much. These glimmers of joy were well-deserved. He quickly pulled her into a big embrace, rocking her back and forth in his arms.

"Just what you needed," Miranda said. "Another woman in your life."

"Are you kidding me? I'm the luckiest guy in the world." It was then that he caught sight of Astrid and she returned his gaze. Her smile lit up her entire face, especially her mesmerizing eyes. It was the truth. He was lucky. And this time, he was going to do his damnedest not to ruin it.

Eleven

The party at Astrid's ushered in two blissful weeks for Clay and Astrid—stolen kisses at work, lunch hours where they raced to Astrid's to be alone, sexy glances and flirtation in the stressful throes of finishing the second Seaport Promenade proposal. Every day was full of promise. Clay had a spring in his step he hadn't had in so long. He had optimism he wasn't sure he'd ever had. Astrid was amazing.

But he knew he had to make a change. They were also sneaking around. He might not be ready for full-blown commitment, and Astrid was clear about taking things slow, but it still didn't sit right with him. She'd been waiting for her happy ending for her whole life. He knew she deserved better.

For now, he had more pressing matters, namely Delia and her Halloween costume. Despite his best efforts over the months, Clay was not getting better at braids.

"Daddy, that looks bad." Delia frowned at him via her reflection in the mirror. "It doesn't look like the picture." She pointed at the cover of her *Snow Princess* DVD.

Indeed, he had failed to create six equal-sized braids circling her head, as well as the spirals that were supposed to be secured to her head with bobby pins. This hairstyle was like Princess Leia ran headlong into a Rubik's Cube, and he had zero confidence in his ability to solve the puzzle in time for trick-or-treating. As if the universe was conspiring against him, one of the elastics popped off its braid and it began to unravel. A single tear rolled down Delia's cheek, her lower lip quivered, and her chin dimpled.

"Please don't cry. I'm begging you. Don't cry."

"Then fix it," she pleaded.

That was it. He had to call in the big guns. "What if I call Astrid?"

"Yes, Daddy. Do it now."

He grabbed his cell phone from the bathroom counter and found Astrid on his favorites list.

"Hi," Astrid answered with a purr. One word and his stomach flipped. Memories of being with her over the last few weeks inundated his mind—blinding passion, unbelievable heat, and tender moments he never expected.

"I need help with Delia's hair for her Halloween costume. I have no idea what I'm doing and it'll be dark in an hour."

"I'm on my way. Fifteen minutes if I hit the lights right."

"Thank you."

"Of course. Anything for you."

Again he was struck by his luck. He couldn't mess this up. "Astrid will be here very soon, okay?" he asked Delia. "She'll fix everything."

Delia sat straighter, the tears a distant thought. "I'm excited to see her."

Clay felt a distinct tug in the vicinity of his heart. Every fiber of his being wanted Delia to like Astrid. There was so much riding on it, but he also knew that he couldn't force it. He had to let this happen naturally. "Good, honey. I'm glad."

Delia read a book while they waited for Astrid to arrive. Clay kept looking out the window, anxiously waiting. When her little silver convertible pulled into the driveway, he opened the door. "Thank you so much," he called as he thundered down the front stairs.

"Of course. I would never leave Delia in the lurch." Astrid climbed out of her car, looking amazing in a simple white blouse and curve-hugging blue jeans.

He pulled her into his arms and kissed her softly, but kept it quick. He wasn't ready for Delia to see that. "I'm glad you're here."

"So am I." She smiled wide. "Now let's fix Delia's hair."

Clay led her upstairs, through his master bedroom and into his bath, where Delia was still perched on a barstool, patiently waiting. "Astrid's here," he said.

Delia's eyes immediately lit up. "Thank you thank you thank you." It came out so fast, it was nearly a single word.

"I heard Daddy was having a hard time." Astrid set down her handbag on the marble counter and took one of Delia's hands.

"He was trying his hardest."

"I'm sure he was."

Astrid grinned. Then her gaze connected with Clay's. It felt like a lightning bolt straight through his heart. Witnessing this sweet exchange between her and Delia was making the effect even more powerful.

Clay stood and observed while Astrid went to work, sectioning Delia's hair and braiding thin strands, and picking up more hair as she went. He'd watched a few tutorial videos, but she made it look so effortless. By the time she had two of the six done, Clay felt like he could breathe again. It was going to look beautiful and Delia would be happy.

"How did you ever practice this?" he asked. "I thought you only had brothers."

Astrid wound a rubber band on the end of another braid. "I had a neighbor who watched me after school. She let me practice on her hair. My brothers were always busy with sports and both of my parents worked."

"I wish I had a brother," Delia said. "Or a sister. It's just me and Daddy and it gets very boring sometimes."

Astrid cleared her throat and shot Clay a look. "Well, brothers can be a big pain in the butt, too. So they're both good and bad." She juggled the strands of hair between her fingers. "You must have lots of friends at school to play with. Friends can be even better than siblings."

"I guess," Delia said.

Astrid finished the last braid. "I'll coil the ends and pin them, then lock them down with hairspray." She slid Clay a questioning look. "You do have hairspray, don't you?"

"I didn't realize it was that important."

Astrid dug through her purse. "Don't worry. I don't go anywhere without it." She returned to Delia's hair, making quick work of the final steps. "Well? Good?"

Delia picked up the DVD case and consulted it, then admired herself in the mirror. "It looks just like the picture." She hopped off the barstool and flung her arms around Astrid's waist. "Thank you so much."

This was a sight Clay hadn't been fully prepared for. Seeing Delia and Astrid forge a bond made his chest swell with pride and happiness.

"Can I put my costume on now?" Delia asked him.

"Yes. Do you need help?"

Delia shook her head. "I can do it."

"Just yell if you change your mind." Delia left and Clay turned his sights to Astrid, who was leaning against the bathroom counter. Dammit, he wanted to kiss her more than almost anything. "You really bailed me out. It kills me when she's not happy."

"Of course it does. You're a great dad." She straightened and looked around the room, then walked off through the bathroom door and into his room. "So this is your bedroom. It's beautiful. Not overly masculine. Just the right amount."

Clay swallowed hard as he watched her walk over to the bed and swish her hand across the comforter. "Miranda designed it for me."

"Did you and your wife live here?"

"No. I was worried it would traumatize Delia to stay. I lucked out with this house, actually. I designed it for a client, but the whole time I was working on it, I was falling in love with it. The client ended up taking a job in Dubai and sold it to me."

"You did luck out."

"And we're so much closer to Miranda here. I knew I was going to need her help as much as possible."

"But you didn't call her about the braids?"

That was when it hit him—his first thought had been to seek Astrid's help. He was so conditioned to go to Miranda. Apparently that had changed. "You offered. And I figured I needed an expert."

Astrid nodded in agreement, but something in the look on her face said that she was on to him. If she hadn't known that he was falling for her, perhaps she knew it now. "I do know my Nordic hairstyles."

"I'd better make sure she doesn't need help with her costume."

"Yes. Go. I'll wait downstairs. Or maybe I should go. I know you two have a big night ahead of you."

"No. Please stay." He hoped she understood that he meant for her to stay over.

"Overnight?"

"Yes."

"But Delia. I appreciate you asking for my help. I do. But this is the first time I've seen your bedroom, and we've had a whole bunch of sex over the last two weeks. It's clear that you're still not sure about folding me into this part of your life and I understand. I was the one who said we should take it slow. I don't want to intrude."

"You aren't intruding. I want you here. This is long overdue and I'm sorry for that." He pulled her into his arms and kissed her tenderly, hoping he could convey just how much he meant that.

"It's okay, Clay. You don't need to apologize. We're both figuring this out as we go."

* * *

He wanted her to stay. He was letting down the wall.

She reached for his arm and rubbed it gently. The connection between them was familiar and strong. "Check on Delia. I'll be downstairs."

"Perfect."

Clay disappeared through the doorway and Astrid took her time meandering down the upstairs hall, admiring the handful of framed photographs of Clay and Delia. They had the same hair color, but not quite the same features. Astrid wondered if she looked like her mother, if Clay had to see his ex-wife in his sweet daughter.

She continued to the landing, which was open on both sides and overlooked the living room below. Soft strains of late-day sunshine streamed in through tall, skinny windows that looked like matchsticks, artfully arranged on the stairwell wall. Every space Clay created was aesthetically perfect and designed with purpose, a harmonious joining of form and function. Even with the home's seemingly simple modern design, she knew the care and love that had gone into planning it. Warm wood tones, the way the eye was drawn from one space to the next, and the central role of natural light in every room mirrored the true heart and spirit of its creator.

She wandered into his showpiece of a kitchen, just off the living room, and helped herself to a glass of water from the massive double fridge. On the counter was a large bowl of Halloween candy. She couldn't help but smile at the thought of Clay shopping for bags of chocolate bars and peanut butter cups with Delia. Why did everything he did have to be so beguiling?

"Here comes the Snow Princess!" Delia called from upstairs.

Astrid hustled out into the hall in time to see the little girl carefully descending the stairs in her icy-blue-and-silver princess gown. Clay followed behind her, beaming with pride.

"How pretty do I look?" Delia asked, twirling in a circle at the bottom of the stairs.

"You're the prettiest ever. You look exactly like the Snow Princess."

Delia turned to her dad. "Can we go yet?"

"Sure. I just want to talk to Astrid for a minute if that's okay."

"I'll go find my trick-or-treat bag." Delia skittered off.

"Do you want to come with us?" Clay asked.

Astrid did like the idea of being included, but they'd had a breakthrough upstairs and she didn't want to push it. She would have time with Delia. Tonight was all about daddy and daughter. "I would love to, but who's going to hand out the candy?"

"I put the bowl on a chair outside my gate and let the kids grab whatever they want."

Astrid saw the perfect compromise. "Why don't you and Delia trick-or-treat, and I'll take candy duty. I'll be here when you get back."

"Are you sure?"

"This is a special time for you two. She'll only be five once."

He took Astrid's hand, tugging her close, making her light-headed with a kiss that grazed her mouth. "You promise you'll still be here?"

"I'm not going anywhere."

Clay took a few dozen photos of Delia. Then the two marched off down the driveway and through the gate. Astrid decided to bring a chair out to the sidewalk and hand out candy there. She'd get more takers that way. The night air was chilly, but not unbearably so with the light sweater she'd brought. Groups of children streamed past her, dressed as superheroes and witches, princesses and cartoon characters. Astrid loved handing out the candy and speaking to the little ones as their eager faces lit up with excitement at a new treat in their bag. She could often go for days at a time now not thinking about how badly she wanted to become a mom, but on a day like today, that yearning within her had new life.

She worked very hard to stay positive about it. She would become a mother one day, by adoption if necessary. The task before that was finding love. The feelings that were blooming between her and Clay were sure starting to feel like that, but she was in no rush to put a label on anything. They both had their reasons for being wary. Still, she took the phone call about the braid disaster as a good sign. She'd been his first thought. There'd been a time when she wasn't sure she'd even been his last.

An hour and a half later, Clay and Delia returned. They both smiled as Delia held up the enormous bag of loot she'd raked in.

"All done?" Astrid asked.

"I don't think it's possible for her to carry any more candy." Clay glanced at the empty bowl. "Is it seriously all gone?" He sounded more than a little sad.

She showed him the contents of her sweater pocket—

a handful of assorted chocolate bars. "I had a feeling you'd want your own supply."

"You know my sweet tooth better than anyone." He reached for her hand. "Let's go in and put Delia to bed, then open a bottle of wine."

A little thrill wound its way down Astrid's spine. "That sounds wonderful."

The three walked inside. Delia protested when Clay took her bag of candy. "Daddy. That's mine."

"I know. And you can have it tomorrow. You've had more than enough for tonight."

"Don't steal any." To drive her point home, Delia scolded him with her finger.

"I won't. I promise. Why don't you go upstairs and put on your pj's?"

"Can Astrid help me?"

An instant of inner conflict crossed Clay's face, but just as fast, it evaporated. "Sure. I'll be up in a minute to tuck you in."

Astrid felt honored by Delia's request, and went upstairs with her, helping her change into her pajamas and get ready for bed. She tried to ignore the way the littlest of things, like watching as she brushed her teeth, felt so right. Oddly enough, it helped her see why Clay had worried so much about Delia getting attached to her. Astrid was more attached to them both with each passing second. "Do you want me to take out your braids?" Astrid asked.

"No. I want to wear them to school tomorrow." Delia rubbed her tired eyes as Clay appeared in the doorway.

"Good night, Delia," Astrid said from the doorway. She watched Clay tuck his daughter in, admiring him in profile as he leaned down to kiss her on the cheek.

Astrid's heart was practically melting into a puddle on the floor.

He took her hand and they tiptoed back downstairs to the kitchen. Clay opened that promised bottle of wine and poured them each a glass. Astrid traded him a candy bar from her sweater pocket. Amusement flickered in his eyes.

"You totally have my number," he said, then popped it into his mouth.

"Do I?" She still wasn't sure.

He cupped the side of her head with his hand, rubbing his thumb back and forth over her cheek, sending her heart racing. "You do. You were such a lifesaver tonight."

"It was just some braids. I was happy to do it."

"It's more than that. You didn't hesitate to drop everything, jump in your car and get over here."

She leaned into his warmth as he pressed her against the kitchen counter, and she gazed up into his eyes. "I'd do anything for you or Delia. I care about you both deeply." It was liberating to come out with the truth.

"I care about you, too. So much." He kissed her softly, his tongue tracing the contour of her lower lip. "I want you to stay tonight."

She wanted so badly to accept the invitation. His kisses and touch were everything…it would be so easy to say yes and ask him to take her upstairs. But she had to be sure he was thinking about what he was saying. She had to be sure this was real. "But Delia. I don't want you to forget about the things you've tried so hard to protect. Your daughter. And your heart." She smoothed her hand across his chest. "Those are not unimportant things."

He pulled his head back, contemplative and even a bit brooding, showing her shades of the conflicted man he was when they first met. "I know. You're right, they are important." His eyes shifted to an even darker hue. The color had to be reflecting at least some of the struggle inside him.

"So take a minute to think about what tomorrow morning might be like when she wakes up and sees me in the house. Think about what you will say. If we cross that bridge, there's no going back." She sucked in a gulp of air, wondering if her inner conflict came close to matching his. "It's okay if you tell me you're not ready. But it's not okay for you to tell me tomorrow that you want to return to sneaking around the office or meeting up at my place. I don't want to force you into anything, but I do think I deserve that much." She held her breath, not knowing how he was going to take the ultimatum. She'd suggested they take things slow, but she'd never meant for them to go backwards. She needed forward movement in her life now.

"You deserve more than that. So much more."

What was he saying? Was he about to make his old argument about how he couldn't give her what she wanted and needed? "What does that mean, Clay?"

Without warning, he swept her up into his arms. He looked her right in the eye, his eyes full of promises. Astrid's heart was beating so fiercely she could feel it from her head to her toes. "It means that I'm all in."

Twelve

Clay called Miranda on Monday morning as he was driving into work. "How's the best sister in the world?" he asked over speakerphone.

"Excuse me? Who is this?"

"Oh, come on. You know who it is."

Miranda tittered on the other end of the phone. "I know what the caller ID says, but you don't sound at all like yourself."

He sucked in a deep breath, preparing to send this bit of news out into the world. "I'm in love."

Miranda gasped. "No!"

"It's the truth." Having made his confession, he told Miranda all about the weekend with Astrid staying over at the house. He told her how it had put all remaining shreds of worry to rest. Astrid did more than fit perfectly into his life with Delia, she made it better. He loved seeing the two of them together, talking, laughing and having fun. Beyond that, the moments when it was just the two of them were pure magic. Astrid made everyone around her happier, especially him.

"Oh, my God. I am so happy to hear this. What did she say when you told her?"

He hadn't yet admitted his feelings to Astrid, but he'd said it to himself several times over the course of the weekend. It initially came as a surprise, but it had ultimately come naturally, which was exactly what he'd hoped for. He hadn't pushed it. It made sense to both his heart and his logical brain. "I haven't told her. Not yet. I need to find the right time." He also had to decide what went along with those three little words. A ring? An invitation to move in? She'd wanted to take things slow, but right now, he wanted to step on the gas.

"Clay, I have been waiting to hear this for what feels like forever. I'm ridiculously happy."

He pulled his car into the parking garage at Sterling Enterprises. "Well, good. I'm super happy, too."

"I have to go check my email and get into the office, but let's talk later, okay?"

"Sounds like a plan." Clay climbed out of his car. He strode into the building and hopped on the elevator, fighting back an irrational desire to whistle. He was not the sort of guy who did that. The doors slid open when he reached the Sterling offices. "Good morning," he said to Roz, the receptionist, stopping at her desk.

Roz peered up at him, bewildered. "Good morning, Mr. Morgan. Can I help you with something?"

"No. I just realized that I rarely take the time to

thank you for everything you do to make the office run so smoothly."

"Thank you. It's nice to hear you say that."

He started off down the hall, realizing he'd nearly forgotten what it was like to be this happy. For the first time in a very long time, he not only felt as though he had a glimpse of a brighter future, he had a clear view of it. "Good morning," he said to Tara when he spotted her marching out of her office.

"Have you talked to Astrid?" The edge of annoyance in her voice was a jarring contrast to his mood. "I tried to call her, but she's not answering her phone."

Clay cleared his throat. He hadn't merely talked to Astrid that morning. They'd made love, and it had been spectacular. It partly explained his giddiness. "She's not in the office yet, but I'm sure she'll be here very soon." As far as he knew, she was at her apartment getting ready for work.

"We have a problem. That revised deadline she gave us for the Seaport presentation? It doesn't exist. They didn't move the date back. They moved it up. It's Wednesday."

Clay's merriment evaporated. Just like that. "Wait. What? That's in two days. We thought we had *ten*." Clay's thoughts flew to the calendar and his to-do list. There was no way they would catch up and finish everything by Friday. It would require all-nighters, and even then, it might not be enough. How had it happened again that they had a last-minute panic situation on the Seaport project? "That has to be a mistake. Astrid wouldn't get that wrong."

"I got a reminder email from the city, so I called and

asked to speak to Sandy. There is no Sandy working in the city planner's office."

None of this was adding up. At all. From the depths of his pocket, Clay's cell rang. "Maybe this is her. Hold on." He fished it out of his pocket. "It's Miranda. That's weird. I just talked to her." He sent the call to voice mail.

"Take it if you want. I need to update Grant. It's all hands on deck. Let's meet in an hour. And help me find Astrid."

Clay sent Miranda a text. Was that a butt dial? We have a crisis in the office. Talk to you later? His phone rang. It was Miranda. Again. "What's up?"

"I have my own crisis." Her voice was teeming with panic.

"What happened? We were just on the phone ten minutes ago."

"I need to talk to Astrid right now and I can't reach her on her cell phone or her office line."

What in the hell was going on? "Wait. Why do you need to call Astrid? You aren't going to tell her what we talked about, are you?"

"No. That's not why I need to talk to her. I can't tell you. You'll freak out."

Now he was flat-out worried. "Please tell me what's going on."

"No. I need to hear it from her. I need to know if it's true. I just got an email." Her voice cracked. "I don't know how to say this. It says it's from Johnathon."

Clay hadn't been stunned many times in his life, but that was the only word that fit this moment. "That's not possible." Clay didn't want to state the obvious, but it had to be said. His sister must be confused. "He's dead."

"I realize that, Clay. The man was my husband. I was

with him when he died. Hence, my panic at receiving an email from him, especially one that says the things this one does."

"You have to forward it to me right now. If it's making you upset and it has to do with Astrid, you have to share it with me."

"No. Clay. This will hurt you, too, if you read it."

He failed to see how that was possible. "You think I care about that? You are my sister. I am always here for you. Always. Please send me the email. I promise that whatever's in it, I will take it all in stride." *Things today can't get any worse. Or any more strange.*

A heavy sigh came from the other end of the line. "Okay. Sent. It has to be a hoax. Some cruel prank."

The number on Clay's inbox ticked one higher. There was the mysterious message, with the original sender listed as Johnathon Sterling. Even more astounding, it was from his Sterling Enterprises email account. Clay clicked on it and began to read, but when he hit the second sentence, it was like running right into a brick wall.

Dear Miranda,
I need to tell you something that will upset you, but the truth needs to come out. Astrid and I continued our relationship after we were divorced. The last time I made love to her was after you and I were engaged. She has a way of drawing a man in and convincing him she is perfect. Obviously I fell for it more than once. I hope you can forgive me.
Johnathon

Clay had a lot of conflicting thoughts vying for his attention, but the one that came through loudest was that there was no way this could be true. The source, a dead man, certainly called the validity into question. Clay expanded the message header, and the servers all checked out. This had come from a Sterling Enterprises email account. On a very long list of things he needed to do today, he would have to reach out to the company's IT department and see if they could help him solve the mystery.

"Clay? Are you there?" Miranda asked.

"Yeah. Sorry. Let me see what I can figure out about this, okay? This has to be fake. I don't know who would send this, but I'll find out. I'll find Astrid. It will all be fine. I don't want you to worry."

"I feel so helpless and confused right now." Miranda's anguished tone made him want to reach through the phone and hug her. The thought of anyone hurting her put him in an extremely protective frame of mind, but he was sure this bizarre story wouldn't turn out to be true.

"I'll get to the bottom of this. I swear."

"Call me as soon as you know something," Miranda said. "I love you."

"Love you, too."

Clay hung up and took a moment to shut his eyes and breathe. None of this could be real. There had to be a logical explanation. Still, he couldn't keep thoughts of the last few days, weeks, and months with Astrid from shuffling through his mind. He'd fought so hard at first to keep her away, all to protect himself and his daughter. Had he let a beautiful face cloud his judgment again?

That's not it. That can't be it. Everything you feel for her is real. You have to find out the truth.

He tried Astrid's cell, but it went straight to her voice

mail. Clay paced in his office, feeling like a caged animal. He was desperate for Astrid to arrive. All he needed was to see her face and hear her say that this obviously crazy story was a lie.

Luckily, he didn't have to wait long. "You were looking for me?" Astrid appeared in his doorway, holding a bakery bag, fresh-faced and gorgeous. The sight of her smoothed his ragged edges. "I stopped to get you a doughnut."

"That's so sweet." He rushed to her and kissed her cheek. This was no time for sweets, but he was thankful nonetheless. "I've been trying to reach you. Tara has, too."

"What? I didn't get any calls." She dug her phone out of her handbag, her eyes wide with surprise. "I take that back. You did call me. So did Miranda and Tara. I turned the ringer off when I was at your house all weekend and I forgot to turn it back on. What's going on?"

Clay quietly closed the door behind her so they could have some privacy. This could be an awkward conversation and he wanted to protect her from office gossip. "We have two big problems. I think you should sit."

"What in the world? You're scaring me." As he suggested, she perched in one of the chairs opposite his desk.

He took the seat next to her. "The first thing is Seaport. There is no deadline extension. It's this Wednesday."

Astrid reared back her head and her luscious mouth formed a pout. "No. That can't be right. I'll call Sandy and get it straightened out."

"Tara called the city and she doesn't work there, Astrid. They're saying she never did."

"I have her cell number. I can call her directly."

"You should probably do that, but I don't know what good it's going to do. That doesn't change the fact that we had the wrong date, and now we have the right one." Clay was hit with a truly abhorrent thought. What if Astrid was lying? Was she capable? He hated that he was even thinking it—it clawed at his insides—but he couldn't help the way his brain was wired. Skepticism and doubt had long been his default. *Take a breath. She would never lie.*

"I'll call her as soon as you tell me what else is wrong."

This part was going to be treacherous. He didn't relish it at all. The pain of losing Johnathon was still fresh for everyone, but especially the wives. He'd heard it well up in his sister mere minutes ago. "Miranda received an email. As outlandish as this might sound, it not only came from Johnathon's Sterling account, the message itself was written as though it was from him. It says that you and he were romantically involved after your divorce." Every new word out of his mouth made this sound more impossible, but that wasn't as much comfort as he would've liked. He couldn't get past this feeling that something was very, very wrong. "It says that you two slept together after he and Miranda got engaged."

He watched as the color drained from Astrid's face and her expression fell. Her beautiful facade crumbled. More telling, she offered no defense. He felt like the rug had been pulled out from under him. *Oh, my God. Is it really true?*

Astrid was sure she was going to be sick. Her stomach pitched. Her head spun. She wanted to curl into a ball, shut her eyes and make this all go away. But the time had come. The day she'd feared so much was here. She wanted to believe that he would understand, but she was so unsure. Everything between them was still so fragile and new.

Craving the comfort of his touch, she reached for his hand, but he didn't curl his fingers around hers as he normally would. His skin felt cold. In many ways, it felt as if he already knew the truth and had passed judgment. "Let me explain."

His cheeks colored with what she feared might be anger. "Is it true?"

Tell him and get it over with. "It is." The confession brought no relief. He dropped her hand. She could see the toll this was taking on him. She'd known all along that this would happen. That was why she'd tried so hard to shoulder the burden on her own.

"I can't even believe what you're saying. Why did you do that? When he was about to marry someone else?"

"It was an accident."

Impatient and exasperated, he stormed up out of his chair and crossed the room, deepening the sense of divide between them. "You realize how ridiculous that sounds, right?"

"I had no idea he was romantically involved with someone else. I was tucked away at home in Norway. When we divorced, I lost so many friends. I didn't know what he was up to here at home."

"Even if that's true, you kept this from my sister? After you two have gotten so close?" He ran his hands through his hair, his eyes wild with anguish. "Is that why you bought her that stroller? Threw her the party? Out of guilt?"

Astrid knew she was in the wrong here, but that was deeply hurtful. "If it's true? I wouldn't lie about this."

"Oh, but you did. You hid this from Miranda. You hid it from me, the whole time we were together. You had plenty of opportunities to tell me. I'm looking back at every moment we had together and now I have to see it through a lens of lies."

Now she could see how doomed she and Clay had been from the start. She could have told Miranda the day she found out and dealt with the repercussions, but that only would have given him more ammunition for his argument that they didn't work well together. "Please don't look at what we have that way. There were no lies. There was this one thing that I kept to myself."

"And I don't see how you could do that."

"I knew it was just going to hurt everyone. When I arrived at Johnathon's funeral, I knew nothing of Miranda or their marriage. You can ask Tara or Grant. He kept me in the dark. I don't know why he did that." It was yet another mystery of Johnathon that might never be solved.

"The email makes it sound like you seduced him, not the other way around."

"I don't understand that part of what you said. Who would pose as Johnathon and send an email?"

"I don't know, Astrid. None of today makes sense. Why would Sandy appear out of nowhere a few weeks ago and give you the wrong information about Seaport?"

The wheels in Astrid's head were turning…her run-in with Sandy and how all of this might be connected. "That's it. That has to be it. Johnathon's brother. I think there's some connection between Sandy and him." Her mind flew to the first time she met Clay, right in this office. She was not only instantly attracted to him, she was equally intrigued by his quiet intensity.

She walked over to the photo on his credenza, the one of Johnathon and Miranda on their wedding day, flanked by Clay and Delia. She picked it up and showed it to him. "The day I met you, I saw this photo, and that was when it clicked. Remember, I asked when the wedding was? That's why I rushed out into the hall that day. I'm sure you thought I was crazy, but I was in shock." She looked back up at him, realizing this bit of information wasn't convincing him that she was telling the truth. "I told Tara right after that. I think Sandy was out in the hall."

The incredulous look on his face told her all she needed to know. He didn't believe her. "This all feels like you covering your tracks. How am I supposed to trust you now?"

That felt like a dagger aimed straight at her heart. She wanted to defend herself, but even more important, she wanted to say something that would make Clay take a deep breath, step back, and look objectively at what was going on. He was letting his old fears and distrust cloud his judgment. "You can trust me because I love you."

He turned to her and froze, but didn't say a thing. His expression was calculating, his eyes reflecting the complicated processes that went through his head. It was part of parcel of Clay, and such a huge component of what she loved about him. But in that moment, it was the most devastating thing she'd ever endured. Love wasn't a conclusion to arrive at. It was either in your heart or it wasn't. Clearly, he didn't feel the way she did.

She stepped closer to him, aching to be wrapped up in his embrace, but he crossed his arms to keep her out. It was like she was watching him rebuild that old familiar wall around himself, stacking it up, brick by brick. "You really don't believe me, do you?"

"No matter what facts come out, Astrid, there is one set of details that isn't in dispute. You knew I had trust issues. You knew I had very strong reasons to protect myself and Delia and how badly we'd been hurt." His voice was a vessel for his pain, cracked in two. "And you let me let you in, even when you were carrying around a secret that you knew would hurt Miranda. She is the one person who has always been by my side and she's going to be destroyed when she finds out this is true."

"I'm sorry, Clay. I truly am. I will make things right with Miranda. I'll explain it all."

He shook his head emphatically, his jaw tight and his eyes dark. "No. I can't let you do that. It's over, Astrid. There is no more you and me. I can't let you be close to me anymore."

"Just like that? Even when I love you?" Once again, her opening of her heart and soul went unanswered.

There was a knock at the door, which Clay quickly took as his excuse to end their conversation. Tara poked her head in. "Astrid, what happened with the Seaport deadline?"

This was officially the worst day ever. Not only was everyone mad at her, Clay had just ripped her heart out. "Let me try to track down Sandy. Something sketchy is going on."

Tara and Clay exchanged glances. "It doesn't matter at this point," Tara said. "That won't change the deadline. The other firms are going to be ready to present on Wednesday and we have to be, too. Grant is in the conference room. We need to sit down and figure out a strategy. Right now."

Astrid and Clay dutifully followed Tara down the hall, but Astrid felt as though she was about to find her head on the chopping block. She'd stupidly allowed herself to think that she could find new purpose at Sterling. Clearly, she'd managed to ruin what chance she had, and the thought of trying to salvage it was so daunting. All paths at Sterling led to Clay. There was no avoiding him, which had been the trouble all along.

Inside the meeting room, several junior architects and members of the support staff were assembled. Grant stood at the large whiteboard, where he'd written up a flow chart of the things that needed to happen before Wednesday. It was so much work. An absolute mountain of it, and it was all her fault that they had to rush to complete it. Astrid sat at the table, next to Tara. Clay chose to stand on the other side of the room, leaning against the wall.

"Thank you, everyone, for dropping everything to help us save the Seaport project," Grant said. "There was a mistake with the deadline we were working under, and we have an enormous amount of work to finish by Wednesday morning." Grant took a drink of water from a glass on the table. Meanwhile, Astrid felt all eyes on her. If the staff hadn't expressly been told that it was her mistake, the Sterling Enterprises rumor mill had clearly kicked into high gear. "Clay and I will finish the final plans, along with help from the junior architects. Tara and Astrid will work from the administrative side to prepare the presentation and the materials that accompany that."

Tara rose from her seat. "We'll be working late the next two nights, and coming in early the next two mornings. But Grant and I want everyone to know just how much we appreciate your extraordinary effort. The Seaport Promenade project was a passion project for Johnathon Sterling, and it will be an important piece of his legacy if we land it. We have a good chance, but it's going to take all of us to make it happen. Now let's get to work."

The noise level went up as everyone broke into conversation and began to file out of the room. Astrid pulled Tara aside. As terrible as Astrid had felt when she walked into this meeting, it was now worse. If they lost the project, it would be Astrid's fault, and she would have let everyone down when all they were trying to do was honor Johnathon's life and career. "I don't even know what to say other than I'm sorry. I feel like that's so inadequate, though."

"We all make mistakes, Astrid. We'll get through it."

"I know. But it's really important to me to do a good job, and that means helping the team. Right now, I'm hurting us."

"Okay, then. Let's focus on doing the opposite."

Astrid received the message, loud and clear. "Okay. I'll stay overnight the next two nights if I need to."

"Good. Because that might be what we'll need."

Astrid ducked out of the conference room and immediately pulled up the contact information for Sandy on her phone. She called her cell, but it rang and rang. It didn't even go to voice mail. Astrid knew there was something that wasn't right about this, but she had nothing to go on. This phone number was the only piece of information she had about Sandy.

Astrid hurried to her office and gathered her Seaport materials, armfuls of binders and notebooks, and began carting them off to a second meeting room, where she and Tara could collaborate, along with a team of four admins. They worked straight through the day, having lunch and dinner brought in. Astrid made several more attempts at reaching Sandy, but had the same result every time—endless ringing and no answer. Another dead end.

Around 10:00 p.m., Tara sent the admins home and suggested she and Astrid go catch up with Clay and Grant. Astrid was a bundle of nerves walking down the hall, not knowing how Clay would receive her. Tara immediately went to Grant when they arrived, leaving Clay and Astrid to talk.

"Hey," she said. "How's it going for you guys?"

"Slow. Exhausting." Clay's voice was clipped and terse.

Astrid was tired, too, and his attitude toward her wasn't making any of this easier. "I tried to call Sandy. I don't get any answer. I guess she lied to me. I don't really understand it."

"I know you're trying to dig yourself out of this hole, but I think you should probably accept where you are. I spoke to the IT department and they verified the email Miranda got came from Sterling. And since we both know that Sandy has no access to Sterling and hasn't worked here in nearly two months now, it seems to me like those two things are unrelated." He cast a glance at her, but quickly returned his sights to his work. "And it doesn't change anything. It doesn't change anything at all. Let me get back to work so I can get through these next two days, okay?"

Astrid pressed her lips together hard to ward off the tears stinging her eyes. She would not cry. She had to stay positive, even in the face of unimaginable obstacles. Everything she cared about had taken a hit today—her love for Clay, her relationship with Tara and Miranda, and the fate of Sterling Enterprises. These were also the things keeping her in San Diego. The only things.

Maybe the writing was on the wall. She'd wondered if she could build a life here, and she'd made a valiant effort. Perhaps it was time to admit defeat and return to Norway. She'd never last at Sterling beyond Wednesday if this was to be her working relationship with Clay. If she'd thought it had been strained at the beginning, this was so much worse. She loved him and she couldn't undo her feelings. She couldn't wish them away. But she also couldn't do a thing to change everything else that had happened.

She could only find a way to move forward. And it looked as though she would be doing that alone.

Thirteen

Wednesday morning had arrived. Astrid's second all-nighter at Sterling was done. She was exhausted and sad, especially as she wished Tara good luck on the presentation, which was only hours away. She didn't have the chance to say goodbye to Clay, as he was downstairs loading the Sterling Enterprises van, but she'd planned accordingly.

"You two will do great. I know it," Astrid said.

"You're sure about leaving?" Tara asked. "I think we salvaged the presentation, and I know people are giving you the cold shoulder now, but they'll come around. A few sleepless nights will eventually become a distant memory."

Astrid was sure of only one thing, which was that this had been a fun experiment, but she'd become collateral damage. "The thing I loved about working here was being part of the team. That's gone now. For right now, this is the best choice for me."

"Did you tell Clay?"

Astrid held up a note. "I'll leave this on his desk. He can read it when he comes back."

Tara spread her arms wide, and they embraced. "Keep me posted on everything."

"You, too," Astrid said. "Let me know how the presentation goes."

They parted ways and Astrid dropped by Clay's office one last time. She didn't stay long or reminisce as she was apt to do. She couldn't afford to rehash what might have been. After two days of very little sleep, she was too exhausted. She'd done all she could do, and now she had work of a different sort to do. She had to pack.

The clothes she'd brought for Johnathon's funeral went into one of three suitcases, along with everything she'd bought since she arrived. She decided to leave the navy gown she'd worn for the Architect of the Year awards in a garment bag in the closet. That dress had wonderful memories. She hoped that one day she'd be able to look back at it fondly. Right now, it simply hurt too much.

When she was done, she pulled her final suitcase into her foyer. She took one more pass through her beloved apartment, making sure the fridge was empty and lights were turned off. She had someone to come by and water the plants. She would return. She just wasn't quite sure when. Perhaps when the hurt subsided.

Bright light streamed in through the one window that didn't have the shade drawn, California sun dancing on the glossy wood floor. It was hard to believe everything that had happened in the months since Johnathon had died. She'd come to San Diego thinking she was bidding farewell to her ex-husband. She'd never dreamed she was embarking on a whole new life, or that she might find love. She'd never imagined that it would all blow up in such spectacular fashion.

She'd forged a friendship with Tara and Miranda, who were the closest she'd ever come to having sisters. She'd found a new career path, one she believed she was quite good at, despite the missteps she had made. And most important, she'd had a glimpse of true love with Clay. It was still there in her heart, thumping away and reminding her of its presence, but she was resigned to the inevitability of it all. He wasn't able to let her all the way in. She couldn't blame him. She'd pushed his limits.

Astrid's phone beeped with a text. It was from Tara. Presentation went well. Thank you for all you did.

I'm so glad. It was the least I could do.

Leaving soon?

Astrid fought a tear. This was one of the hardest things she'd ever done, but it was the only thing that made sense. She needed time to think. She needed distance to figure out her next step. Yes. Flight departs in a few hours.

Safe travels.

The driver she'd hired arrived at her door and took her bags downstairs to the car.

"I'd like to make one stop before we go to the airport, please," she told him out on the street.

The driver consulted his watch. "Will we have time?"

"Yes. I won't be long." She gave him the address and sat back in the car, trying to remind herself that just like her decision to move to San Diego had been temporary, so could her return to Norway. She didn't have to stay anywhere. She could move to New York. Back to Los Angeles. Or perhaps somewhere else. Wherever it was, she was done with love. There would be no matching what she'd had with Clay. Maybe there would come a day when he could forgive her, if only so she could have some closure.

The driver pulled into Miranda's driveway and opened the door for Astrid.

"I'll just be a few minutes," she said, then marched up to ring the bell.

Miranda answered a minute later, looking surprised. "Astrid. What are you doing here?"

"I know you work from home on Wednesdays." Astrid handed over an envelope. "I wanted to give you this."

Miranda glanced at it, then looked out to the driveway, spotting the driver. "Do you want to come in?"

Astrid shook her head, not wanting to drag this out. "This will be quick. I know that you and I spoke about the Johnathon situation over the phone, but I wanted a chance to apologize in person. I never would have allowed that to happen if I'd known about your engagement. I hope you know me well enough by now to know that's true."

"I know. I do. I'm sorry I was so angry when we spoke about it on Monday. I was in shock."

"And I only kept it a secret because I knew there could never be a resolution. You can't confront Johnathon. You or I will never be able to find out why he did what he did." Astrid's sights fell to Miranda's belly. "More than anything, I didn't want to taint the image you have of the father of your child, especially when you're still grieving."

Miranda smiled. "I understand. I do." She looked down at the envelope. "What's in here?"

"I'd like to give my shares of Sterling to the baby. I don't see any point in me being there anymore. I've finished my work, and Tara and Clay did the presentation this morning. They'll find out before Christmas whether or not they landed the Seaport job."

"Astrid, no. Have you talked to Tara about this?"

Astrid nodded. "I did. She agreed that my presence at Sterling wasn't great for morale right now. But the real truth is that I can't work with Clay." It felt so funny to say that out loud, the very thing he'd always said about her. How things had changed. "There was always this part of him that couldn't let me in."

Miranda looked out at the car again. "Is there somewhere you have to be? I feel like we need to talk about this."

"Actually, I'm headed for the airport. I'm going back to Norway."

"What? No. You can't leave. Don't you want to be here when the baby is born?"

Astrid felt as if her heart was being torn out right now, but she didn't see how she could stay. Miranda and the baby were inextricably tied to Clay. "My parents are expecting me. And they'd like me to be there for Christmas."

"Okay, I understand." Miranda reached for Astrid's shoulder. "But I just want to say one thing. As the person who has been through the worst of the worst with my brother, I can tell you that when he closes himself off, he's protecting something. There have been many times when it was me. There have been many times when it was Delia. That's all it is. His defenses."

Astrid sighed. "I can't fault him for wanting to shield the people he loves." *It's a huge part of why I love him.*

"Maybe you two need to have one last conversation? He'll be here with Delia in a little bit. He decided to take a half day at work so he could spend some time unwinding."

This was why she had to leave San Diego. She couldn't live her life trying to dodge the man she loved, all because it would only dredge up pain. "I'm sorry, Miranda. But I have to go."

Clay left the presentation and headed back to Sterling Enterprises with very little sense of triumph, even when it had gone incredibly well. The problem was Astrid. She'd worked so hard to drag them over the finish line, and she hadn't been there to get any credit or do a victory lap. All of that was on him. He knew how much she struggled to work with him when he was pushing her away. He'd started their working relationship on that course. And he was still having a hard time steering off of it.

The trouble was that every magical memory of Astrid was colored by the pall of her secret. Now that he was a few days removed from the revelation, he was starting to dig down to what was really bothering him.

He was terrified of being blinded by a woman. He was scared of being duped and having his whole life fall apart as a result. It had happened before, and everything had rushed back when he discovered Astrid's secret.

He arrived back at his office and planned to take care of a few minor things before leaving to pick up Delia from school. He'd made plans with Miranda to spend the afternoon relaxing out by the pool. It had been unseasonably warm for early November, and Miranda kept the water at a balmy 82 degrees, all to keep Delia happy. But that was when he spotted an envelope on his desk, with his name scrawled in Astrid's frenetic handwriting.

Dear Clay,

I hope the presentation went well today. If it was half as brilliant as you, it was a home run. I want to let you know that I am going back to Norway. I need to clear my head and think about what my future might hold. I plan to come back eventually, but as to when that will be, I don't know. I also don't know that I will stay.

I don't want you to think of me as a repeat of the hurt in your life. Yes, I'm leaving, but you will never have to guess why. It's not because I don't love you. It's because I do. And I know I've hurt you. I know that by proxy, this will hurt Delia. I'm doing everything I can to minimize the pain so you can heal. I want that for you more than anything.

I will never regret our time together. Even when we were at odds, I had hope that we would find our way through it. I know now that our tim-

ing was all wrong. I arrived when you weren't
ready, and I pushed even though you told me so.
You gave me an opening and I took it, but only
because I was desperate for even a minute with
you. I'm so thankful we had more than that.
With all my love,
Astrid
P.S. Please kiss Delia for me. If she asks where
I went, tell her I've gone looking for the Snow
Princess. I'll bring her back if I track her down.

Perhaps it was the exhaustion, but Clay was struggling to understand what he'd just read. *She's leaving?
She can't do that.* He had to stop her. Right now.

He flung his laptop bag over his shoulder and jogged
down the hall to the lobby. His first instinct was to
take the stairs, but the maintenance people were painting them. *Dammit.* He pressed the elevator button and
stared at the numbers, as if that might possibly make
it go faster. Finally it dinged and the door slid open.

JJ from the tech department appeared out of nowhere. Clay had asked him to dig deeper on the email
that was supposedly from Johnathon. "Mr. Morgan. We
got an answer for you about that message. It wasn't really from a Sterling server."

Clay stuck his arm out to hold the elevator. "Wait.
What?"

"We traced it to a company in Seattle. It's owned by
Mr. Sterling's brother."

Clay felt as though his heart had stopped beating.
Astrid had been right. And this also meant that they
had a serious problem on their hands. For some unknown reason, Johnathon's brother, Andrew, was trying

to sabotage the company. "Wow. Thank you. Can we talk about this tomorrow? I have somewhere I needed to be like five minutes ago." Maybe ten.

"Sure thing, Mr. Morgan."

Clay hopped on board and jabbed the button for the garage, nearly sprinting out to his car when he arrived. The elevator and the parking deck were both notorious dead zones, and he had to call Astrid to keep her from leaving her apartment. He didn't get the chance though. Miranda called him first.

"Miranda," he blurted, pulling out onto the street. "I can't talk right now."

"Have you talked to Astrid? She's leaving. For Norway. Right now."

"I know. I'm on my way to her apartment. I'm hoping to stop her." He shot a look over his shoulder and changed lanes to get around a slow driver.

"She's already on her way to the airport."

"What? No." *Dammit.* He was pointed in the wrong direction, and so much of downtown San Diego was one-way streets. "Are you sure?"

"She was just here. She came by to tell me she was giving her shares of Sterling to the baby."

It was so much worse than he thought. That did not sound like the action of a woman who was planning on coming back. "I have to go to the airport."

"Of course you do. That's why I was calling."

Despite the urgency of the moment, he had to laugh at the absurdity of it, and that his sister was just as invested in this as he was. "You're sure you're okay with Astrid? Did you two have a chance to talk things through?" He impatiently waited for the light to turn green, drumming his thumbs on the steering wheel. "I need to know that right now. Because I have a lot to tell Astrld as soon as I find her."

"I can't believe you would even ask me that. Would you really let my happiness stand in the way of yours?"

What kind of question was that? "Of course I would, Miranda. You are the one person who has always been there for me. I would do anything for you."

"Okay, then. I want you to stop worrying about Delia and me and start worrying about yourself. You can't make Delia happy if you're not happy, and you sure as hell can't make me happy either."

Somewhere in his brain was that same bit of information, but he'd been unable to reach it before. "I hate it when you're right."

"I'm sorry it happens so often."

"Very funny." He was finally headed in the right direction, but he realized he'd forgotten one important detail. "Dammit. I was supposed to pick up Delia from school. Can you do it? I'll come right over to your house when I'm done at the airport."

"If you do it right, you should not be coming to see me after you find Astrid."

"Miranda. Are you seriously trying to talk about sex right now? Because I'm not discussing that with you."

"Don't be an idiot. That's all I ask. Now go."

"Hold on, Miranda. One more thing. I found out the source of the email you got on Monday. It came from Andrew's company up in Seattle."

"I don't understand."

"I don't either, but we're going to need to sort it out. I think he's trying to sabotage Sterling Enterprises. As to why, I do not know, but I think there's a chance he was behind our problems with the Seaport project."

"So Astrid was right all along? All the more reason you need to get to the airport."

"Yeah, I know. I'm on it." He bid goodbye to Miranda and focused on the road. As he ran through yellow lights and made a few risky maneuvers with his car, all he could think about was that he had no idea where to even start with Astrid. There were fifty different things going through his head, all of which started with a long string of apologies.

As he pulled up to the terminal, there were dozens of cars stacked up to drop off passengers. He'd stupidly whizzed right past the valet, and if he tried to circle back around, he could lose at least fifteen minutes. Maybe more.

He was just going to have to make a sacrifice—his car. He zipped around the thick of the traffic jam, then angled between two cars and squeezed into an impossibly tight spot. Not only was the security guard standing on the curb, he was watching him. *Of course.* Clay hopped out and started to run inside.

"Hey! You can't leave your vehicle," the officer said as he jogged past.

"Tow it if you want," Clay shouted back. "I have to find the love of my life." He kept going, not waiting for a response. Consequences were for later. He'd already suffered plenty from his own bullheadedness. Inside, Clay was confronted by the chaos of hundreds of travelers, dragging suitcases behind them and absentmindedly blocking traffic while they stared up at departure boards. He zigged and zagged around people, quickly scanning the baggage check-in lines. There was no sign of Astrid. Hope was evaporating with every second. If she was here, she was getting closer and closer to getting on her plane. And then it occurred to him—he was doing this all wrong.

He pulled out his cell phone and called her number. It rang. And rang. The buzz of the line was about to drive him nuts, when she finally answered. "Clay? What do you want?"

"Where are you?"

"Why do you want to know?"

"Because I love you and I'm an idiot and we have to talk."

"This is horrible timing, Clay. I'm at the airport. I'm about to get on a flight to Norway."

"I know that. I read your letter. I'm at the airport, too."

"I didn't leave that for you so you'd follow me. I was just trying to explain myself. Are you crazy?"

"Probably. Actually, definitely. Just tell me where you are."

"In line for security, about to turn over my passport."

"Don't move an inch. I'll be there in one minute."

Security had taken forever. Astrid was typically able to take the line for first class, but they had closed it today. Something about a shortage of agents. Astrid wasn't about to complain. She was fine waiting as long as everyone else did, but it had dragged on and on forever. Her fellow passengers were all voicing their displeasure at the delay, grumbling under their breaths and standing on tiptoe to see what the problem was ahead. Astrid kept looking in the opposite direction, wondering if Clay was really there. Would he do something so desperate? It didn't seem like him at all. She was next in line when she heard his voice.

"Astrid!" Clay Morgan, the man who was reserved to a fault, was currently shouting her name in the middle of a crowded airport.

She couldn't help but laugh. She thrust her hand up in the air and waved back, only to see him trying to wind his way through the stanchions, past the other passengers, one by one. He was lucky no one was picking a fight with him.

"Don't move." His gaze connected with hers, sending a zip of electricity through her. Damn him for being so irresistible. Damn him for being everything she ever wanted.

Astrid turned to the woman in line behind her. "That's that man I fell in love with."

"He's not going with you on the trip?"

"I think he's trying to prevent it."

"And is that a good thing or a bad thing?" she asked.

"Depends on how good he is at groveling." It was Astrid's turn to present her boarding pass and passport, but Clay had just reached her.

"Please don't get on that flight," he blurted. "We have to talk."

The other passengers griped in near unison.

"Ma'am, I either need your boarding pass or you need to step out of line," the agent said. "But I'm warning you that if you step out, you have to go back to the very end."

Astrid let the woman behind her go ahead, then turned to Clay. "Well?"

"I promise I will make it worth it." Breathless, he grabbed her hand, unhooked the black retractable strap from the stanchion, and pulled her back in the direction where she'd started.

Astrid stumbled ahead, lugging her carry-on. "I can't believe you would try to hunt me down at the airport. What has gotten into you?" This was so unlike anything she'd ever seen Clay do, it was hard to wrap her head around. Still, she found it to be quite thrilling that he would be willing to embarrass himself in public like this. It had to mean something.

They came to a stop once they'd reached the wide concourse between check-in and baggage claim.

Clay turned to her. "I love you, Astrid. I've been falling in love with you since the car ride to Los Angeles, if I'm perfectly honest." He looked up at the ceiling and shook his head. It was like he was processing everything in real time. She'd always loved watching him think. "Or maybe it was the night of the cocktail party at Grant's house. Either way, I'm over the moon for you and I'm begging you to stay. You are everything I have ever wanted and I will be lost without you. Please don't move back to Norway. I'm begging you."

"I told you I wasn't necessarily moving. This trip was to clear my head."

"I think I know another way to clear your head." Before she knew what was happening, Clay pulled her into his arms, pressing his long form against hers and laying the deepest, most passionate kiss on her that she'd ever been on the receiving end of. He cradled the back of her head with his hand, all while she virtually melted into him. When he broke the kiss, he didn't let her go far, holding on to her tight. Their mouths were mere inches apart, his breath warm on her lips. "Well?"

"If anything, that's just you trying to confuse me."

He laughed quietly and pressed another kiss to the

corner of her mouth. "Did it work? Did I buy myself some time?"

Astrid dropped her shoulders. She had no energy to fight him. She only wanted to give in. But they had things to sort out. "I'm going to miss my flight, so yes. You bought yourself some time. The question is what you intend to do with it."

"I'll do whatever you want. I'm serious. I love you, Astrid." He tenderly combed his fingers through her hair. "I should have told you long ago. I was scared. I can admit that now. And when your secret came out, it felt like confirmation of everything I'd feared. It felt like it was all happening again."

"And now? How do you feel now?"

"Like I need to learn to look past what's right in front of my face and try to see what's truly ahead. Try to see the future, not spend all of my time reliving the past."

Astrid swallowed hard, choking back the emotion of the moment. She not only loved hearing him say these things to her, she admired the way he'd put it all together for himself. He'd fought hard to tear off the blinders, rather than clinging to the idea of keeping them on. "I love you so much. I don't really know how to put it into words." She took his hand and pressed it to her chest. "But I hope that you can feel my heart beating. That's all for you. It's all possible because of you. I won't go anywhere if that's what you want."

"That's what I want. Always."

She hadn't prepared herself for that last word, especially on a day like today, when she'd been sure she was leaving and that would be the end of it. To make things even more surreal, it was then that Clay, the proudest man she knew, dropped to his knee, right there in the middle of the airport. He took her hand and peered up at her with his deep and soulful eyes. "I don't have a ring to offer you right now, Astrid, but I can offer you myself. My undivided attention. My heart and everything that goes along with that, good or bad."

"Careful, Clay. You're practically reciting wedding vows." She leaned down and pressed her hand to the cheek of the man who had once held so much mystery. "Your sister told me the quickest way to freak you out is to mention marriage."

He shook his head. "Nope. The only thing that will put me into a panic is the thought of you leaving."

She smiled so wide her cheeks hurt. "Then let's get out of here." He straightened and took her hand, but she stopped before they got to the glass doors. "Oh, shoot. My bags. I've already checked them. They're probably already on the plane."

"Actually, that works out pretty well because I'm pretty sure my car has been towed."

"What?"

He shrugged. "I was in a hurry."

They did stop by the airline baggage desk to let them know of the change in plans. Luckily, her suitcases had not yet been loaded, and they could retrieve them and deliver them for a fee. Clay handed over his credit card. "It's my fault. I'll pay for it."

The clerk nodded and handed over a form for Astrid to fill out. "If you could provide your delivery address, that would be great."

Clay took that and plucked a pen from the holder on the desk, writing down his home address.

"This is moving very fast," Astrid joked.

He lowered his head with no regard for the people around them. Astrid was fine with that. Right now, he was her whole world. He nudged her nose with his before delivering a tender, leg-melting kiss. "I'm not stupid, Astrid. I'm not letting you out of my sight."

* * * * *

COMING SOON!

We really hope you enjoyed reading this book.
If you're looking for more romance, be sure to
head to the shops when new books are
available on

Thursday 15th October

To see which titles are coming soon, please visit
millsandboon.co.uk/nextmonth

LET'S TALK
Romance

For exclusive extracts, competitions
and special offers, find us online:

- facebook.com/millsandboon
- @MillsandBoon
- @MillsandBoonUK

Get in touch on 01413 063232

MILLS & BOON

THE HEART OF ROMANCE

A ROMANCE FOR EVERY KIND OF READER

MODERN
Prepare to be swept off your feet by sophisticated, sexy and seductive heroes, in some of the world's most glamourous and romantic locations, where power and passion collide.
8 stories per month.

HISTORICAL
Escape with historical heroes from time gone by. Whether your passion is for wicked Regency Rakes, muscled Vikings or rugged Highlanders, awaken the romance of the past.
6 stories per month.

MEDICAL
Set your pulse racing with dedicated, delectable doctors in the high-pressure world of medicine, where emotions run high and passion, comfort and love are the best medicine.
6 stories per month.

True Love
Celebrate true love with tender stories of heartfelt romance, from the rush of falling in love to the joy a new baby can bring, and a focus on the emotional heart of a relationship.
8 stories per month.

Desire
Indulge in secrets and scandal, intense drama and plenty of sizzling hot action with powerful and passionate heroes who have it all: wealth, status, good looks…everything but the right woman.
6 stories per month.

HEROES
Experience all the excitement of a gripping thriller, with an intense romance at its heart. Resourceful, true-to-life women and strong, fearless men face danger and desire - a killer combination!
8 stories per month.

DARE
Sensual love stories featuring smart, sassy heroines you'd want as a best friend, and compelling intense heroes who are worthy of them.
4 stories per month.

To see which titles are coming soon, please visit

millsandboon.co.uk/nextmonth

MILLS & BOON

HISTORICAL

Awaken the romance of the past

Escape with historical heroes from time
gone by. Whether your passion is for
wicked Regency Rakes, muscled Viking
warriors or rugged Highlanders, indulge
your fantasies and awaken the
romance of the past.

  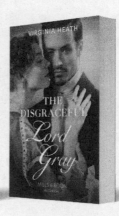

MILLS & BOON
MODERN
Power and Passion

Prepare to be swept off your feet by sophisticated, sexy and seductive heroes, in some of the world's most glamourous and romantic locations, where power and passion collide.

MILLS & BOON

HEROES

At Your Service

Experience all the excitement of a gripping thriller, with an intense romance at its heart. Resourceful, true-to-life women and strong, fearless men face danger and desire - a killer combination!

MILLS & BOON
True Love
Romance from the Heart

Celebrate true love with tender stories of heartfelt romance, from the rush of **falling** in love to the joy a new baby can bring, and a focus on the emotional heart of a relationship.